SERENADE
OF SIRENS

SERENADE OF SIRENS

THE LOST BOYS OF TOSA

K.D. ALLBAUGH

Battle Ridge Rising Sun Press

Published by: Battle Ridge Rising Sun Press

Printed in the United States of America

ISBN paperback: 978-1-7360809-4-8
ISBN eBook: 978-1-7360809-5-5

Book Cover and Interior Design: Creative Publishing Book Design
Cover Art: Bogdan Maksimovic

This book is dedicated to the memory of my mama, Charlotte Bindl. Serenade of Sirens was the first novel I wrote without you listening to excerpts of it, and I missed that time spent with you along with so many other moments.

It was difficult to begin this book without you, but I hope the results would have made you proud. You always told me that you would have loved to write a book of your own, have your name listed within the pages and know that you created it. Your name is here, Mama, and you created the author. Thank you.

CHAPTER 1

JULY 28, 1921 – STONE PLACE, GENEVA LAKE, WISCONSIN

Of all the perilous moments Adelyn St. John had ever endured, this night took precedence.

It had begun as usual, an evening in the St. John family compound, Stone Place, along the shore of Geneva Lake. Adelyn, nicknamed Addy by her friends, had spent a dull hour indoors playing Whist in the game room of the seven-story estate. She had longed to escape from the stuffy room and even stuffier companions. The solitude of the boathouse, with the cool breezes caressing her perspiring skin and the gentle waves easing the emotional turmoil of her soul, called to her.

"Adelyn, Spades were laid. If you can't follow suit, the least you can do is trump his card." Virginia St. John, Addy's mother-in-law, sniffed at her in contempt from across the table. "Honestly, you act as though you have never played the game." She drummed her long fingers on the ornate inlaid oak tabletop in irritation. Her perfectly manicured nails sounded like the report of a gun in the awkward stillness of the room, jangling Addy's fragile nerves even more.

"Now then, Mother, no table talk is allowed." Lucian, Addy's husband, broke the quiet with his attempt at sidestepping his mother's rudeness with his overabundant charm. It seemed to Addy he was continually trying to rescue his wife from the talons of his domineering mother. "Darling, do you have any Spades?" Lucian smiled his encouragement, willing Addy to search the playing cards in her hand for the appropriate suit.

Addy tried to focus on the cards she held in her trembling hand. She blinked her eyes several times, attempting to clear her eyesight, but the hand vacillated in front of her. Bright pinpoints of light like shooting stars crowded her peripheral vision. A familiar wave of nausea began competing for Addy's attention against the sound of her heart beating wildly in her ears. She rose abruptly, toppling her chair backwards as she raced to exit the room while she could still breathe.

"Leave her be." Virginia's command to her son as he stood was absolute. Lucian paused as Addy fled to the hall. He nodded at his mother and resumed his seat with a sigh. It was best for his wife if he did not follow her and thus prompt his mother to do likewise, worsening the situation. Lucian gestured for his friend, Van, to take Addy's vacated place at the card table. The game continued while he stared at the doorway wondering if Addy would make her way to the lake.

Meanwhile Addy had stumbled along the hallway with her hand splayed across the smooth Tennessee marble covering the walls to stabilize herself from falling. She followed the hall to the enormous front doors, reaching for the 14kt gold doorknob. It turned readily in her grasp. Addy had memorized the exact number of steps between her and the path leading down through the wooded lawn to the boathouse. She had retreated to this refuge so many times in the past. She found her way easily in the dark that had descended over the massive estate.

Addy crossed the expanse of the veranda, and the crunch of the pea gravel beneath her slippers caused relief to course through her body. She paused to catch her breath, listening to the sound of the cicadas humming in the trees above her head. Addy leaned her slight frame on one of the immense oaks, her silk dress rasping slightly against the rough bark. Her auburn hair escaped the chignon fashioned for the formal family dinner in tendrils which framed her heart-shaped face.

Addy's heart regained its normal rhythm as she inhaled the night air. From a distance she could smell the water of the lake, a clean scent with undertones of earth and pine. Addy eased out of her tight slippers preferring the feel of the ground on bare feet. She smiled to herself knowing the reaction Virginia would have to her daughter-in-law traipsing through the woods in her current state.

This paragon of the Chicago society elite already regarded Addy as an orphaned, low-class vagabond who had ensnared her precious only son into a hasty marriage abroad. Addy had realized as soon as she crossed the threshold of Stone Place she would never be "good enough" in Virgina's estimation.

Addy's heart began to thump wildly at the briefest thought of her mother-in-law. She left her resting place near the tree and continued down the path towards the boathouse trying to outrun her anxieties. The trail, which was usually well lit, was dark; she made a mental note to tell the groundskeepers about the omission when she returned to the main house.

She sensed the presence of the two men before she heard their footsteps as they stepped out from the trees onto the path in front of her. The tiny hair on the back of her neck stood up as Addy turned to escape back the way she had come. Their shoes hit the gravel with a deafening sound as they ran to catch her from behind.

Rough hands encircled her waist, lifting her off her feet and throwing her to the grass. Addy's head smacked the earth with a sickening thud. She wanted to close her eyes to shut out the pain, but she realized her only option would be to fight for her life.

Her first strike brought her knee to the groin of the burly man who had her pinned to the ground. His scream of agony assured Addy she had hit her mark. He let go of her arms and sagged downwards, bearing most of his weight upon her, crushing her so that she could not breathe.

She mustered her strength to roll, pushing at him with her momentum until she was free of her burden. She sprang to her feet and scrambled up the steep bank leading to the verandah. Blood flowed from her hands, sliced open on the jagged rocks, but she saw the main door a few feet above her head.

A hand entangled itself in the long locks at the back of her head yanking her down the embankment, slamming her body into the rocks covered with her blood. Addy cried out as her hair was pulled from its roots; she fell back down the hillside, landing unconscious in a heap on the path.

She woke a half an hour later bound and gagged at the bottom of a small boat rowed by the slender man who had stopped her escape. There was intense pain when she lifted her head to look at their whereabouts on the lake. A quarter moon emitted enough light for Addy to visualize the Narrows where the shore could be seen from both sides of the water.

They were approaching Lake Geneva to their forward. She felt a glimmer of hope. Perhaps she could attract attention at the dock to gain help from the dock workers. Most people in the small town recognized the members of the St. John family and understood they would be rewarded for giving assistance to one of them in need.

The area was quiet as the boat pulled aside and anchored. Addy saw the lights from Baker House up the hillside. She heard the faint sound of music carried across the hotel to the lake. As people of high society drank and danced the night away, they had no concept one of their own was being abducted from among them.

In the dim light Addy saw a man standing on the dock walking towards the boat. She gasped as she realized she recognized the swagger of his gait and the small stub of a stogie that hung constantly from his mouth. She smelled the Cuban cigar so familiar as Oscar St. John, her father-in-law stormed toward the vessel and the three people in it. Her heart soared at her most unlikely of heroes, and she would even be grateful for Oscar's bullying nature at this moment.

"What in the blazes are you doing here?" Oscar bellowed at her captors. The burly man who was still recovering from Addy's earlier attack slunk farther down into the boat while his comrade glared up at the large man whose face was red with anger. Addy looked from one man to the other with a look of reproach and nodded at Oscar who did not return her gaze.

"I told you not to bring her to the middle of Lake Geneva." Oscar growled the words, spitting in their direction. "She is easily recognized here. You were to take her off in Fontana across the lake where transportation was waiting. When I hired you to do this, you assured me it would be a simple job without incident."

"We are not locals. When you said Geneva Lake and Lake Geneva, I thought it was the same thing. It took a while to find this dock and get the correct coordinates for your landing. Then, this little hellion gave us quite a fight. Fred here, may never be right again." He gestured to the burly man still bent over in the boat.

"I am not interested in lame excuses. Finish the job and do it quietly. The rest of your pay will be waiting at the saloon in Williams Bay once you have dropped her off." Oscar glanced at Addy. If he was affected by the mixture of terrified astonishment on her face, his countenance did not reveal it. "Remember, it is to appear to my son this trollop finally ran off for good. No need for him to be hurt by her actual outcome."

Addy realized not only would her father-in-law not render her assistance, but he was the chief conspirator in her abduction and whatever was to befall her next. Fear bubbled in her stomach like acid. She only understood their destination was Fontana, a small village on the other side of the lake. She did not know once she reached their stop if her life would be spared. She had the time it took to reach Fontana to devise a plan for escape.

"Oscar, are we leaving soon? I am not dressed for outdoor entertainment." A pretty woman grasped Oscar's arm, interrupting Addy's thoughts. The woman wore a thin negligee, and slippers topped with feather boas. One look revealed to Addy, her mother-in-law did not know about this acquaintance.

"Sophie, I told you to wait in the car. You need to listen to what I say or else." Oscar gestured towards his Bentley parked nearby and nodded at the young woman to return to it. Instead, she turned to stare at Addy who sat bound, gagged, and bleeding at the bottom of the boat.

"Is this the lunatic you told me about? I have never seen a crazy person before!" Sophie did not appear fazed by Addy's bloodied and broken physical state, but she was enthralled by the possibility she was beholding a madwoman. She grasped Oscar's arm possessively.

"We are leaving now. Both of you take care of this." Oscar put his arm around his mistress, turning them away from the boat. Addy heard the tinkle of Sophie's laughter as the two of them walked back to the parked car.

The lurch of the vessel as they cast off brought Addy back to reality. She did not have time to ponder her father-in-law and his paramour. She needed to concentrate on escaping her abductors. She shook her head, trying to loosen the gag over her mouth. She tasted the metallic taste of blood and pain shot through her head. Addy knew she could not throw herself overboard in a bound state, because she would drown before she loosened her bonds. Perhaps she might try to get her captors to ease them.

Addy wriggled again, shaking her shoulders and turning her head. Intense discomfort enveloping her told her several ribs were injured along with her clavicle. This news brought another revelation; if she did loosen her bonds and jump into the lake, would she be able to swim in any manner? Geneva Lake was a wide body of water with depths up to 135 feet. Knowing when to attempt her escape was as crucial as knowing how.

There was a little over seven miles to travel from Lake Geneva to Fontana. Soon they would pass back through the Narrows where Addy might be able to swim to shore from either side. Her main concern was Stone Place, which was located right after the Narrows. She did not want to return to the house without being assured of her safety from Oscar. Most of the surrounding neighbors would contact

Stone Place if Addy showed up on their doorsteps. There was only one family Addy trusted to rescue her from her husband's relatives.

Catherine Seipp and her family owned a massive estate known as Die Lorelei until World War I, after which they were compelled to change the very German origin of the name to a Potawatomi word meaning "Black Oaks"; thus, it became Black Pointe. She and her husband, Conrad, had the home built for their family's summer use, bringing their children here from May to October each year.

It was Catherine's viewpoints on women's suffrage and her stands for racial equality that made Lake Geneva high society view her as a pariah, though none were bold enough to tell her to her face. She had befriended Addy almost immediately upon making their acquaintance. It was the time spent with Catherine and her brood which had made Addy feel truly at home.

Addy saw the lights from the houses on both sides of the boat. They were passing through the Narrows and would soon pass Stone Place on the left. Black Pointe's tall look-out tower would then appear through the trees on the hillside. She had to act quickly. She began to squirm vigorously, ignoring the pain shooting through her like an electric current.

"Settle down, Imbecile. I have half a mind to throw you overboard and let you sink to the bottom after what you did to me. No one would ever find you, and only me and Nick here would know. We already know no one would care in the least about what happened to you. What do you say, Nick? Shall we cast her overboard and go collect the money in Williams Bay?" The burly one referred to as Fred glared at Addy and shoved his foot in her side, kicking her injured ribs. Addy gasped in pain.

"Well now, someone has finally started to recover from his near-death injury I see." Nick chuckled as he shifted his weight from his seat at the back of the boat next to the motor. "Come here and take over for me a bit, Freddy. I have done all the work so far and you are going to want half of the pay." He stood as Fred moved to the back seat and took over steering the vessel.

Nick stepped cautiously to the middle where Addy was still huddled in a fetal position on the floor. He knelt and loosened the gag around her mouth leaving the ropes that bound her hands and feet in place.

"It appears Freddy has a gangster ending in mind for you, Girl. I've been told half of the Chicago mob is at the bottom of this lake and the other half put them there." Nick chuckled again.

"I don't know why my father-in-law hired you to do this, but I assure you my husband and I have money too. I can pay you to let me go without further harm. Please help me. I haven't done anything to you." Addy pleaded with her captor, and for the first time tears flooded her eyes as she looked up at him.

"Your father-in-law said you would try to bribe us or seduce us to get your way. He paid us a bonus to ignore you. Shut your face before I finish this right here." Fred shouted from the back of the boat as he abruptly turned towards the shore in anger. The small vessel rocked back and forth vigorously. Addy was certain they would capsize at any moment. She strained at the ropes restraining her hands and feet.

"Fred! What in Sam hill do you think you are doing? You are going to dump all of us. Here, let me steer." Nick left Addy's side and resumed his place beside the motor. He shoved his accomplice out of the seat onto the seat in front of them. Fred doubled over in pain again at the rough treatment. Addy recognized she had only minutes before he recovered and tried to drown her. The look-out tower of Black Pointe appeared on the left.

"The look-out tower is part of Die Lorelei." Addy blurted out the sentence as she formulated her plan. "They named it for the golden-haired siren, Lorelei, who sang to the sailors on the Rhine River. Her songs drew many men and only the ones with good intentions survived. The rest were destroyed because the Siren cannot be fooled. She knows your thoughts and the machinations of your soul. If you listen carefully, you can hear her serenade." Addy repeated the often-told tale from the Seipp family ghost stories. She was rewarded with a brief period of stillness while her captors contemplated the possibility of the legend. The temporary quiet was interrupted by a sudden snort of derision from Fred.

"I am going to put her gag back on. I'm tired of hearing her talk. This time we will wad up a handkerchief and stuff it in her mouth before putting the gag back on. There won't be any more noise out of this one afterwards. I told you to do it the first time." Freddy produced a soiled handkerchief from his pocket and stuffed it in Addy's mouth. He prodded it several times before replacing the strip of cloth that formed her gag. Addy's throat closed as though she was suffocating. He stood over her in triumph.

"I wonder what your Lorelei legend would think of this?" Nick picked up the oar fastened to the side of the boat as he slowed the motor. Freddy chuckled and turned to face Addy, anticipating the violence about to be played out before his eyes.

What he didn't anticipate was the full force of the oar cracking against his own skull, the sound of bone breaking with a sickening thud. Freddy's eyes rolled once and closed as he fell backwards into the dark water. The boat rocked back and forth several times while Addy waited for her own death at the hands of Nick.

"I guess he got what was coming to him, didn't he? Now, lie still and we will be in Fontana right quick. I have an entire paycheck waiting in Williams Bay and no partners to split it with. Come to think of it, maybe your Lorelei saved you after all." Nick brought the motor to life and steered the boat towards the deserted docks in the distance.

Addy lay trembling in the stillness of the night. The end of her life had only been a whisper away. As Nick cut the motor to approach the dock in silence, a distinct sound like a mournful wail from a faraway distance filled the dark air around them. Addy understood in her heart the legend of the siren was not just a story.

CHAPTER 2

JULY 30, 1921 – MILWAUKEE COUNTY ASYLUM FOR THE CHRONICALLY INSANE, WAUWATOSA, WI

The driving rain of a summer afternoon thunderstorm drummed against the windowpane near Addy as she sat on a wood bench outside the doctor's office. A young woman seated next to her startled at the sounds of crashing thunder overhead. She placed her feeble hands over her ears and rocked back and forth. The rickety seat beneath them swayed precariously with each motion until Addy became certain it would split, throwing both women to the ground.

"That's quite the ruckus, isn't it?" Addy slid towards the frightened girl. "I used to tell my little boy the sound of thunder was the angels riding their ponies in heaven above us." Addy wrapped her arm around the trembling shoulders. She could feel every vertebra of the spinal column as it protruded from the young woman's back. She was so emaciated, merely a specimen of flesh upon bone and muscle. Addy could sense the violent tremors weaken as she held the stranger next to her. She glanced at the young face; it was the face of a mere child, fourteen years at the most.

"My mama used to say the same thing. I miss her so bad. I just want to go home with my mama." The piteous whisper pierced Addy's heart as it matched the murmur of her own heart. Addy had arrived at the asylum in the middle of the same night she had been abducted. A private car had been awaiting her arrival in Fontana as her father-in-law had stated. Addy's relief at escaping the fate of her dead abductor, Fred, left her weak and trembling, much like the waif seated next to her now. She tightened her hug as the girl laid her head on Addy's shoulder.

"How long have you been here?" Addy asked the question quietly, trying not to disturb the peaceful cadence of breathing emanating from her new companion. The girl remained quiet with her eyes closed and her lips slightly parted. Addy wondered if slumber were imminent but couldn't fathom how anyone could fall asleep on the roughhewn surface of the bench under the glare of bright lights strung overhead.

"Hmm. Not sure. It all melts together, days and nights. Do you know what date it is?" A soft whisper meant only for Addy's ears indicated the girl was still awake. "My name is Cora by the bye."

"It's the thirtieth of July. I meant how long you had been waiting here for the doctor, Cora. I didn't mean to pry into your life unless you wish to tell me about it." Addy quickly amended her words to give Cora the freedom to answer or ignore her question altogether.

"July thirtieth? What year is it?" Cora opened her eyes and lifted her head to gaze into Addy's. She smiled at the gentleness she saw there. "You are the only person besides Mama Crane who has shown me any kindness at all. What is your name?"

"My name is Addy, and it is 1921." Surely the girl was confused about the year. She couldn't have been held in this place for more than twelve months. Addy smiled back at Cora. "Is your mama here with you somewhere? You mentioned Mama Crane."

"July 30, 1921." Cora wrinkled her brow at the given information. She shook her head. "No, Mama Crane is a nice old lady here in Hall 5 with me and the others. She was the only one to be kind to me at all until you. I guess I haven't seen my own mama for more than a year now if your date is correct. You know this is the insane asylum, right?"

Addy was startled at Cora's answer. How on earth could a girl so young have been kept in this insane asylum for over a year? Cora seemed to have all her mental faculties about her; she certainly didn't appear to be demented. She wanted to ask Cora for more information, but she didn't want to cause the girl any distress in the telling.

Cora seemed to sense Addy's unspoken questions.

"I was taken from my mama and put in this place because my uncle said I was a bad girl. I say it was him who was bad to me, but no one would listen once he put a baby in my belly. He said I had to go far away before I hurt my siblings, but my mama knew better. They sent me here to have the baby and now the baby is missing too. She is so tiny and quiet. All I want is to take her home to my mama so she can see I won't hurt anybody. I am a good mama, really, I am." tears ran down Cora's cheeks as she pleaded with Addy. "Can you help me find my baby?"

Shock reverberated through Addy's body. A rage for the injustices done to this girl ignited in her soul. Her hand touched Cora's head, gently stroking the short crop of matted hair sticking up in every direction. Cora curled up next to her and closed her eyes again as they listened to the rain, now pattering against the window.

It was another fifteen minutes before the door opened across from them suddenly. Doctor Crawford, one of the head doctors of the institution, stood in the doorway. He grimaced in annoyance at Cora while motioning for Addy to rise and follow him into the office. Addy rose, patting Cora's shoulder to comfort her. Cora grasped Addy's hand tightly and resumed her plea,

"Can you help me find my baby? I just want to go home to my mama."

Addy nodded and followed the doctor into the office. It was sparsely furnished with a simple desk and two chairs. A cabinet stood in the corner. The walls in the room were the same brilliant white as the hallways; the smell of antiseptic hung heavily in the air.

She was reassured, at least this place seemed hygienic by most standards. The small room where she had spent the last thirty-six hours had been clean though Addy had not been provided with any water or toiletries. She was dirty and disheveled, a direct contrast to the cleanliness of the space surrounding her.

"Can you hear what I am saying to you?" Dr. Crawford raised his voice in irritation. Addy had allowed herself to become distracted long enough to miss his initial questions. Stress and exhaustion were taking their toll on her faculties.

"I beg your pardon. I didn't hear your question." Addy sank into the straight back chair he indicated with a wave of his hand. "I am extremely tired and very confused as to how I came to be here. I hope you might help me to understand." She utilized her most contrite expression to communicate her repentance.

"You are in Milwaukee County Asylum. You were brought here after suffering from numerous histrionics exhibited by fits of anger, bouts of depression, and a high degree of anxiety. I am told you were a homeless orphan in Europe. Do you know if either of your parents might have had mental defects as well?" Dr. Crawford leaned forward, examining Addy's eyes. He placed his hand under her jaw, pulling her mouth open while tilting her head back at a sharp angle. Addy waited while he looked before responding to his questions.

"I was born in Edinburgh on our family estate. My father served in Parliament and then with distinction in the Leith Battalion of the Royal Scots during the Great War. When he returned to us after serving in West Africa, he insisted I attend school in Switzerland. Though my mother was hesitant, she agreed I should go to Institute Le Rosey in Rolle. While I was there both died in the outbreak of the Spanish Flu. They left the entire estate to me as their only living survivor, so I was not homeless. I can assure you both of my parents were brilliant professors and neither had mental defects as you called them."

"Impressive." Dr. Crawford sneered. "I was told you can spin a rather grand story of your past life before your marriage. Did you meet your husband in Switzerland or in Scotland?" Dr Crawford removed a small notebook from the desk drawer and scribbled a few words on a blank page.

"I met Lucian in Edinburgh as I had left school in Switzerland and returned home to bury my parents and meet with their solicitor about the estate. Lucian had made an offer to purchase some of our city properties, so we met in the solicitor's office to discuss the terms. He offered to help me navigate some of the legal hurdles involved in the inheritance as a young woman is hard put to represent herself in probate. In a matter of a few weeks, we were married by a magistrate in Gretna Green. Can you please tell me if Lucian knows my whereabouts? I can't believe he would be involved in sending me here." Addy glanced at the accumulating dirt under her fingernails and put both hands underneath her on the seat. Humiliation at her current filthy state brought the sting of tears to her eyes.

Dr. Crawford ignored Addy's question. He continued with his line of questioning while scribbling in the notebook.

"Do you often perceive faces on the wall and hear multiple voices? Do these voices encourage you to hurt yourself or others?" Dr. Crawford was blatantly disregarding her answers, relying instead on the report in front of him meant to portray her as a lunatic.

A sudden pounding against the locked door startled both. "Addy! Are you in there? Can you help me find my baby?" Cora's screams grew in intensity as she hammered her fists, rattling the door.

"I hear her voice, Dr. Crawford. What is being done to help this poor child? She has obviously been molested and then cast away by her own uncle." Addy shouted her questions over Cora's wails as Dr. Crawford stood and walked towards the door.

He pushed a button on the wall, attached to a bell, summoning one of the orderlies. He opened the door to find Cora in a sobbing heap on the floor. Addy began to rise from her chair to go to the girl, but she was hindered by the doctor stepping in front of her.

"Take Cora and go find Nurse Fielding. Tell her the baby has been lost once again. We will reschedule the appointment for her appendectomy to next week." Dr. Crawford gave the brusque orders to the orderly who had just run down the hall.

Without another word, the orderly scooped Cora up from the floor and carried her over his shoulder down the hallway. Her pitiful cries persisted until they grew fainter, and silence returned to the office. Dr. Crawford returned to his seat facing Addy and gestured to her to sit down. The scratching of the pen against the paper as he resumed his writing frayed Addy's already battered nerves.

"You are in an asylum, Adelyn. The first lesson you must learn is the other patients are not sane enough to tell you the truth. Cora is, in a word, a hussy. She sold herself to awful men and became so out of control her family could not keep her anymore. But we digress, Cora is not our topic of conversation, though I find your fascination with her and her missing baby intriguing. In fact, that brings me to my next question. Can you tell me about your own child?" Dr. Crawford set down his pen and grasped Addy's forearm. He placed his fingers on her wrist over her pulse point while pulling a pocket watch from his vest with his other hand.

"My little boy's name is Charlie. He is only one year old. I recognized when we set sail from London two months after our marriage that I was already expecting him. By the time we arrived at Lucian's family home in the states, I was extremely ill from the voyage and from morning sickness. I took to my bed for weeks. Lucian's family was not welcoming to me in any way. His mother suspected I had trapped her son into marriage by telling him there was a child before he married me, but it wasn't the case. So, you see, Dr. Crawford, your little report about me is filled with inaccurate information: I was not an orphan, I had more money and land than Lucian did before he married me. I did not trap him into marriage by getting pregnant with Charlie." Addy glared defiantly at the doctor who only glanced in her direction as he placed his watch back inside his vest pocket. He shifted towards the desk to resume his writing.

"Yes, some of your story is written here in 'my little report', but you didn't answer my question about your child, Adelyn. Isn't it true you claim that only two weeks ago, your young son, who can barely walk, went missing while in your care? How does a very small boy suddenly disappear?" Dr. Crawford grabbed both of Addy's arms, pinning them to her sides.

Addy could hear ear-piercing shrieks, and her thoughts immediately turned to poor little Cora who must have returned to her position outside the door. What Addy did not realize was the cries originated from inside the locked room, her own heartbroken wails emanating from the depths of her soul.

CHAPTER 3

JULY 31, 1921 –
HALL 5, WOMEN'S WING

Addy awoke to find herself on a small cot facing a dingy wall. The hot, humid air was filled with the scent of unwashed bodies and excrement. Addy's empty stomach roiled; stinging bile rose to her throat causing her to gag. She looked downwards at her own form.

Her silk dress was gone along with all her undergarments. The replacement was a dirty cotton gown tied a few places in the front; large gaps exposed her skin underneath including her breasts. On the left side of the gown black letters were sewn into the material. It read "H 5 W".

Addy lay still, wracking her brain for any recollection of what had occurred. The last thing she remembered was sitting in Dr. Crawford's office as he questioned her about her past. She tried even harder to remember what happened next. A few more minutes of recalling small glimpses of what had transpired made her cringe.

She recalled screaming out and then the large orderly who had carried Cora away came to get her too. He had carried her outside and down a long path, thrown over his shoulder as though she were a sack of potatoes. Nurses met the orderly and took Addy, punching and slapping her as she cried out for help.

Addy observed bruises already turning dark purple on her wrists and ankles. There was a horrifying memory of the same nurses stripping her naked in front of a room full of people and plunging her into a filled tub. Water burned her lungs as they held her head under for long periods. She had been terrified, she kicked and screamed, which only made them more vicious.

Finally, they lifted her, half-drowned, and threw her onto a table. She was restrained by her wrists and ankles to the table. They cut huge swatches of her hair with dull scissors and cut her fingernails down to the quicks. At this point Addy was begging them to let her die.

Addy stirred enough to raise her hand, touching the remnant of the shorn mess left of her once- crowning beauty. Pain shot through her ribs, and the bile rose to her mouth causing her to choke it back down.

"Mama Crane! I think she's awake!" Cora's voice was close to Addy's back. A hand rubbed on her shoulder, she turned over expecting to see her young friend.

It was not the girl who stared down at Addy but a middle-aged woman with dark hair and touches of gray at her temples. Addy looked into her deep brown eyes and saw genuine compassion in her countenance. She put her weathered hand to Addy's temple then met Addy's hand still entangled in her hair.

"I see they gave you the welcome haircut. Let's see those fingernails. Left those bleeding as usual. Don't worry, Sweetie, I will help with your hair once you have recovered a bit from their ministrations. You are in Hall 5 of the Women's Wing." Ruthie Crane sat beside

Addy on the narrow cot while Cora sat on the cot next to them cradling an old worn doll wrapped in a crocheted blanket.

"Laura and I have been watching over you since Old Burt brought you in last night. Mama Crane usually goes down to the House for the day, but she told them she wouldn't go until you woke up. They were so mad about that, weren't they, Mama Crane?" Cora held the doll in her arms out for Addy to behold.

What had been a beautiful porcelain toy had been reduced to a bald, chipped version of its former glory. Eyes, once opened and shut, now only opened part way or stuck in between, but Cora cradled it as though it were the most precious thing in the world.

"They were mad indeed, but they won't do much on account of the fact if I go bruised or bloody to work at Superintendent Hill's house, Mrs. Hill will make them pay for it. She is about the only one in this place these henchmen fear. Do you think you can sit up if I help you, Addy? You sound like you are choking a bit lying flat." Ruthie placed her hands on Addy's arms and helped her to sit upright while leaning against the wall beside the cot.

A sob escaped Addy as pain raced through her. Her lungs felt as if they were on fire and her head throbbed in agony. She tried to shift her body, pulling her gown to cover her exposed area.

"I've got something to fix this nasty gown too. Don't you worry. Cora and I will have you back in shape in no time. We will need to start repairing you sooner than I would like. Nurse Fielding will expect you to come to the dining hall for supper and I don't want you to go looking like this. Some of the others here pick at the newcomers when they think they can't defend themselves. Do you think we can change your gown?" Ruthie stood and walked over to the cot on the other side of Cora's, pulled an old trunk out from under the bed and opened the lid. She returned with a garment, shoes, and comb in her hands.

"This will be a little large on you, but I think we can make it fit." She held the worn garment out to Addy then turned her back using her body to partially shield Addy from the other women in the room. "If you can slip off the one you have on, and put this one on, we will work on your hair next."

Addy moved slowly as she loosened the ties of the gown she wore and slid her slender shoulders out of it. There were massive bruises on her chest and stomach. She couldn't tell if they were from her abduction or from the nurses or from both altercations.

She slid her head through the neck opening of the dress Ruthie had handed her and put her arms through the short sleeves. It was an older garment that had been somewhat fashionable in its day with even a bit of lace at the collar. Addy was grateful it was clean, and it covered her completely. She detected the same black stitching "H 5 W" was on the left side of the bodice.

"Thank you. This is much better. What does the lettering mean?" Addy smiled as Ruthie turned around again to face her.

"It means you live in Hall 5, Women's Wing. They will check for it wherever you go to make sure you are in the right place. To be found in the wrong one is an excuse for a beating. Now let's see what can be done about your hair. They cut it off unevenly, but I think I can comb it to cover some of it up. It is the most beautiful shade of red I have ever seen in my life." Ruthie combed as she chatted. The five other women in the small dorm room looked at them with curiosity as Ruthie continued to work on her hair.

"I have the same color hair as my mother did and her mother before her. Mum said to be a redhead was to truly be a Scottish lass."

Unbidden tears sprang to her eyes at the thought of her mother. Cora leaned over and wiped Addy's eyes with the edge of the doll blanket while nodding her head.

"I thought I heard some Scottish Gaelic in your speech, but I wasn't sure of it," Ruth replied. "I hail from Belgium myself, came here with my folks as a wee one. They were lace weavers. I learned the family trade as soon as I could hold the bobbins. That is what the Superintendent's wife has me doing at the House most days along with some sewing and such. There, I think we have your hair done. Can you slide over to put the shoes on your feet? Cora and I will help you walk back and forth a few times before they call us for supper."

Ruth returned the comb to the trunk while Addy slid her legs over the side of the bed. Before she could reach for the first shoe next to her, Cora hopped off her cot and grabbed both shoes. She knelt at Addy's feet and lifted her right foot to slip the shoe on.

"This is just like Cinderella putting her slippers on, isn't it? You are much prettier than Cinderella, Addy." Cora slid the left shoe on Addy's foot and hugged both of her legs tightly. "Mama Crane, you should have seen Addy's pretty dress yesterday. It was all shiny and smooth feeling. I want a frock like it someday too." Cora gazed adoringly at Addy from her position on the floor. "Maybe Laura could have a little one for her too?" Cora pulled the doll from her cot onto her lap. One of the doll's eyes stuck open staring blankly in front of her.

"A silk gown sounds really nice, Baby Girl. Both you and Laura should have a lovely dress to wear. Can you go over and ask Ingrid to come and help us get Addy up and walking? I am afraid of you tumbling down if you try to hold Addy up and she falls." Ruthie patted Cora's head as the girl sprang to her feet and laid her doll on

Addy's cot. Cora walked to the other end of the dormitory where the other women were huddled together.

"When she said she was missing her baby yesterday I didn't realize she meant a doll. I thought she meant an actual baby." Addy looked at the doll and back at Ruthie standing next to her cot.

"Well, you see, Addy, nothing here is always as it seems," Ruth's face was grim as she spoke, "but Cora does mean her actual baby. She came here large with child and then had the poor little babe way too early. It didn't have any chance of surviving, but I begged them not to tell her. I asked Mrs. Hill for a cast-off toy bound for the rubbish heap and made a blanket to wrap it in. She has always accepted this as her baby because her heart and mind are so broken she cannot accept the reality."

"The hardest part of this is that child came here as healthy and sane as anyone," Ruth continued. "I tell you this because I know your mind is fine, as mine is and many of the others who surround us. Fight hard against letting them take your mind, my dear girl, because they will fight just as hard to do it." Ruthie glanced back as Cora approached leading a large girl with a blank- looking stare towards them.

"How was she missing her baby if Laura is right here?" Addy whispered.

"The nurses hide Laura as a cruel joke when I am away at the House for the day." Ruthie's quick reply came as Cora and Ingrid arrived beside them to help Addy stand and walk a few steps. Addy continued to stroll back and forth for the next hour until she was walking on her own. She was determined, she would be strong for herself and for her new friends.

The bell rang for supper, and the women began to line up facing the door. Cora picked up her doll and held it close then pressed Laura into Addy's arms.

"I told you she is the sweetest quietest baby. Don't you just love her, Addy?"

"I surely do, sweet girl. I surely do." Addy caught the look of approval from Ruthie as the women filed out of the room into the hallway. They were led to a large open area filled with tables and benches and told to wait in line. The queue began to inch forward as each woman was handed a metal tray with a piece of dried brown bread and a tin cup of broth. Addy followed Cora and Ruthie to a table and sat on the bench next to them.

The meal had been one of Addy's first since her arrival, but her stomach churned at mold growing on the surface of the bread crust and the unidentifiable items floating in the broth. She took small sips of the rancid broth trying to strain the objects with her teeth as the other women ate around her. The silence was deafening inside the cavernous room with only the sounds of tin cups placed on metal trays breaking the gloomy stillness.

A cluster of nurses grouped at the far end of the room. They would gather and point at various patients, then one would break away and go to deliver harsh words and more than one slap across the face. The silent women would not even look up from their own suppers at the punishments being dealt to their peers. No one wished to incur the wrath of the nurses and orderlies. Addy could already sense this was not just a battle for the mind; it was a battle for the will and the soul.

Addy saw Cora pretend to feed a bit of the bread and the broth to the doll beside her as the nurses pointed in their direction. A tall woman with a sharp angular face and hawkish nose walked briskly towards them. Addy had only seconds to act before the woman descended upon poor Cora.

Addy picked up the moldy bread from her tray and threw it at the nurse. "How can I be expected to eat such rubbish? Don't you know who I am? Have you never heard of the St. John Steel Empire? I am *that* St. John, and I won't have this!"

The bread grazed Nurse Fielding's cheek as Addy stood to confront her. "I dined with the likes of the Morgans and the Rockefellers. I assure you, good woman, Mr. St. John shall hear of this!" Addy sat down with a thud on the bench.

Nurse Fielding's face was a mottled red, the precise hue of rage. She grabbed Addy's hair at the back of her head to yank her upwards.

"She is who she says she is. Mrs. Hill told me about her arrival herself and wishes to welcome her in her parlor tomorrow. It won't go well with you if she is covered in even more bruises than she already has. I would be cautious if I were you." Ruthie's calm voice was barely above a whisper, but her words hit their mark as Nurse Fielding suddenly let go of Addy's hair.

"This is why she allowed me to stay with her today, so she would be ready for a visit tomorrow." Ruthie picked up her own piece of bread and dunked it in the broth where it disintegrated into mush in the cup. She resumed sipping the soup as though the conversation had not transpired.

The nurse turned and walked farther down the table where she stopped to deliver a vicious slap to an unwitting elderly woman who sat eating her meal. The dining hall returned to its ominous silence until the bell sounded ending the mealtime.

Addy followed the others to return her tray to the serving line. The only sound was the shuffling of feet as the women left the dining hall to their specified dormitories for the night. Addy breathed a sigh of relief when they reached Hall 5 and shut the door behind them. Cora scrambled onto her cot and stared at Addy in wonder.

"Are you a real princess Addy? You are our Cinderella!" Cora clapped her hands in glee while Ruthie and the others smiled at the joyful girl bouncing on her bed.

Suddenly the door opened, and the orderly known as Old Burt entered the room. Addy braced herself for the beating she contemplated was coming when the guard thrust a basket into her hands muttering,

"Be sure and tell Mrs. Hill and Mr. St. John how good we are to you and the others. No one means any harm." Burt left the room, leaving the women speechless in his wake.

Addy looked in the basket. Apples, raisins, grapes, and pieces of fresh bread filled it to the brim. She glanced at Ruthie while holding the basket out to her.

"It looks like the nurses and orderlies decided to share their supper with you this evening, Addy." Ruthie nodded, encouraging Addy to take the food from the basket.

"Then we shall all have a feast together. Gather around ladies and dine with me." Addy placed the food out on her cot and encouraged all the other women to come and select pieces. Soon they were all seated on the floor in the center of the room consuming the meal with relish while each told Addy her name and her story.

Ingrid, the girl who had helped Addy before supper, was a German immigrant who understood very little English. She had been separated from her family in Milwaukee and could not understand the questions asked of her by the police who found her. They brought her to the asylum because she was supposed to be an imbecile. Ruthie understood German and had tried to convince the doctors Ingrid was not mentally deranged but to no avail.

Mrs. Hall was an elderly woman who had taken ill after her husband passed. She had no children to help her, and the hospital sent her to the asylum to recuperate. She had suffered a small stroke and lost the use of one hand, but she was fully cognizant of who she was and her surroundings. She begged the doctors to release her from the institution and let her return to her apartment in Wauwatosa over the shop she and her husband had owned.

Mary and Ella were sisters who had grown up in an orphanage after their parents died in the Great Chicago Fire. Instead of being released at the age of consent, they were committed to the asylum and had lived all their lives there. They had been deemed unable to survive outside an institution. Neither of them had learned to read or write in the orphanage. Mrs. Hall had tutored them along with Ingrid and Cora in their own little class at night.

Freda was the quietest of the group. She did not speak and often moaned in intervals. She sat by herself and had to be encouraged to eat and drink. Ruthie had learned from the nurses that she had suffered from measles as a child which they claim caused her insanity. Once Ruthie worked with Freda, she surmised the young woman had lost her hearing and most of her vision because of her illness.

Freda's moans were her way of speaking, and each one had a different tone and meaning. The staff could not be bothered and left Freda to waste away by herself but the women in Hall 5 looked out for her. They helped her navigate the hallways and grounds while tapping communication on the palms of her hands.

Addy had already heard Cora's story, and it left only one person to speak. Ruthie chuckled as she set about picking up all the scraps so they would not attract rats in the room.

"My story is one of the most common ones and it is very simple. I married at a young age and worked while my husband attended school and college and built a business from his architectural degree. Once he was famous for building huge fancy buildings and mansions, I was not good enough for him anymore. He needed someone younger, prettier, and more cultured to be his wife. He couldn't divorce me, but he could claim I had lost my senses and have me committed in the asylum."

"It was within his full legal rights to do this to me as my husband," Ruthie admitted, "and it is what he chose. It didn't matter to anyone that I lost all my supposed rights. When the doctor signed the commitment papers his examination consisted of looking in my mouth and asking if I saw faces on the wall." Ruthie sat back down on the floor and immediately Cora curled up beside her and laid her head in Ruthie's lap.

"But as you can see," Ruthie continued, "I am surrounded by a much better family than the husband who cast me away and now you are part of our family too, Addy. And, I can see, you are already a welcome member among us. They will be by soon to shut all the lights off so let's help Freda get in her bed and everyone settled in."

Addy stood with the others and took her turn at the wash basin at the end of the room. She studied each face as they settled onto their cots. Addy St. John understood while she had endured cruelty and hardship during her admission to the Milwaukee County Asylum for the Chronically Insane, she had also been given a new family of greater character and compassion than the St. John family she left behind.

The lights were shut off precisely at 9pm. Addy closed her eyes, her exhaustion coming to claim her, leaving her with a single thought.

Did the asylum protect the people outside of it from the insane inside or did it protect those inside from the insane people outside?

CHAPTER 4

AUGUST 5, 1921 – THE HOME OF SUPERINTENDENT HILL (REFERRED TO AS "THE HOUSE")

Addy sat on the velvet-covered settee in the parlor of Mrs. Hill, the asylum superintendent's wife. She waved a fan in front of her face to combat the intense humidity and heat of the August afternoon. Addy wore a frilly cotton frock that had hastily been altered to fit her slender frame.

The dress Addy usually used in Hall 5 was deemed "not sufficient" by Mrs. Hill's secretary. It seemed while Mrs. Hill was extremely interested in Addy and her European background; her senses were too delicate to encounter the everyday rigors endured by the asylum patients.

Addy had been a frequent visitor to the parlor since her arrival the prior week. The luxuriously furnished room bespoke the lifestyle that surrounded the chief operating officer of the asylum and his family. The gold paisley wallpaper and dark brown velvet furniture balanced with a walnut Chickering upright piano and matching walnut rocking chairs. The large bay window festooned in brown velvet curtains faced Sanctuary Woods, a picturesque forestland set on the outskirts of Wauwatosa.

"Would you care for more lemonade, Addy? I can ring for some more." Mrs. Hill sat across from Addy in a matching velvet chair that reminded her of a small throne. Sophia Hill was resplendent in a bright blue silk floral day dress with a gold fringe. She turned to the table positioned at her right hand and picked up a silver bell, rang it three times and set it back in its place. "You were telling me about your time in Switzerland. Did you meet any members of the Royal Family while you were in school?"

"We were always instructed by school officials not to speak of others in attendance at Le Rosey in order to maintain privacy. I can say there were always a number of Haus Hohenzollern attending until the war. Of course, after the Germans were defeated and the rebellion occurred, that Royal Family was overthrown and placed in exile." Addy held her small glass out for the maid to pour more lemonade. She smiled at the young woman who handed her an additional napkin to wrap around the sweating glass.

"I'm sorry. I don't think you understood me. I meant the Royal Family as in King George V." Sophia Hill nodded her head of blonde curls emphatically. "I am only interested in the Royal Family and not those other countries."

"But you do realize..." Addy paused in her sentence. While she understood most of the European countries had monarchies, she realized her host thought only Great Britain had a Royal Family, a mistake made by many Americans, especially the nouveau riche.

Addy cringed at the thought of what her mother-in-law, Virginia, would say to someone she would consider below her social standings;

vulgar, ostentatious, and lacking any breeding. "You realize the Royal Family was far too good for our little school." The words were like sand in her mouth, but they brought about the desired response in Mrs. Hill.

"Oh, I see. Well, that's too bad because I would love to hear more about them. I want to travel to London someday and visit them myself." Sophia sipped her lemonade. "Did I mention we are hosting a party this evening? Mr. Hill is so excited they are broadcasting the first live baseball game on the radio that he invited a huge group of people to listen with us. It will be the Pittsburgh Pirates versus the Philadelphia Phillies. Can you imagine listening to such a thing on the radio?" Her giggle escaped in a small snort.

Addy nodded politely and drank the cold lemonade. Mrs. Hill had mentioned the baseball game at least three of the four times she had spent in her company without extending an invitation to her. Apparently, she was deemed by Mrs. Hill as an interesting companion for the parlor but not a worthy guest for other social gatherings.

Addy was relieved her attendance would not be required as she had begun to feel like an exhibit in a museum when Mrs. Hill's friends had joined them in the parlor on previous days. The nosy women had even gone as far as poking and prodding her.

One woman trying to feel for lumps on Addy's scalp said, "you can always tell a crazy person by the lumps on their head. "Addy would have quit the parlor more than once if it had not been for Ruthie's gentle reminders that Mrs. Hill's patronage helped make the living conditions in Hall 5 better for all of them. And so, Addy stayed on.

"Would you like to hear some music?" Addy stood at Mrs. Hill's nod of acceptance and walked to the piano, seating herself on the small velvet bench. This instrument had been Addy's oasis for the last week, a place of refuge.

She played several Chopin pieces she knew by heart. Her eyes closed as her hands glided across the ivory keys. The rich sounds of the piano calmed her anxious thoughts and took her far away, back in time, to her parents in Edinburgh and her life there.

Addy opened her eyes to the applause of the house staff standing near the doorway. Ruthie stood among them beaming as she dipped her head in Addy's direction. She left the small group clustered inside the room to stand next to Addy at the piano. Sophia rose from her chair and dismissed the servants with a wave of her hand as she approached Addy and Ruthie.

"Ruthie, I am pleased you joined us as I have some exciting news for our dear Addy." Sophia placed her hand on Addy's shoulder as she continued, "I did not mention this until I had a response to my inquiry, but I contacted Mr. St. John about Addy's presence here and he was exceedingly glad I did. He had been searching everywhere for her and was so relieved to hear she was here and well."

Addy felt an electric current of shock run through her, "Do you mean my husband Lucian and not his father, Mr. St. John?" Addy was not attempting to correct Mrs. Hill's faux pas about addressing the son instead of the father by his surname while the father was still living.

She was trying to determine how much danger Mrs. Hill may have inadvertently placed her in by contacting the person who had her abducted and brought to the asylum in the first place. She exchanged a fearful glance with Ruthie who already understood the gravity of the situation. Addy had spent hours in the middle of the night explaining to Ruthie how Oscar had been the mastermind of the plot against her.

"Yes, of course, your husband, Mr. Lucian St. John. I address my own husband with the proper dignity in the presence of others and assume you did the same." Sophia's reproof was lost on Addy as relief washed over her, and tears sprang to her eyes. Lucian knew where she was! Addy stood up from the piano bench and crossed to the bay window across the room. She observed asylum patients being led in and out of the woods in rows, each one tethered to a long singular rope.

"Anyway, your husband has been searching all over for you and told me he will arrive by tomorrow. He had gone as far as Minnesota to search and is now returning to Wauwatosa in haste. I have decided to host a small party in your honor upon his return. Your reunion will be so heartwarming to my circle of friends." Sophia clapped her hands together in anticipation.

"Ruthie, I will ask you to help Addy wash and dress tomorrow morning. I think one of my dresses would do for the occasion, I have several I don't use anymore." Sophia did not realize how condescending she sounded to the other two women in the room; she was too focused on her own recognition for her supposed altruistic endeavor.

Addy walked back to Hall 5 guided by Ruthie, holding a cast-off silk dress that would be much too large for her. She could not believe Lucian had been searching for her and was arriving tomorrow to take her away from this place. To take her home, to Stone Place, to Geneva Lake, and to what else?

The group of women in Hall 5 were huddled on the far side of the room around Cora's bed as Addy and Ruthie entered. Addy could discern the pool of blood on the floor before she saw the unconscious girl, ashen and still, crumpled in a heap. Ruthie gasped in anguish as she rushed to the cot and knelt beside it.

"They came and took her off this morning soon after you two left us. Old Burt brought her back a few minutes ago and we have been trying to get the bleeding to stop. I didn't know what else to do." Mrs. Hall stood there holding a compress against Cora's abdomen to no avail, blood gushed from a large incision that had not been stitched together properly. Cora grew paler by the moment, her lips turned blue as her life poured from her body in front of them.

"Cora, baby girl, you listen to Mama Crane right now! You are not supposed to leave us this way. You must hang on for Laura. Cora, do you hear me?" Ruthie's wail echoed off the dirty walls as she held the lifeless girl in her arms.

Addy ran to beat forcefully on the door, calling for help for her friend. She stopped at the sound of Ruthie's voice,

"It's too late Addy. It's too late."

Addy turned to watch all the other women circling Ruthie and Cora while joining hands together. She joined the circle as they stood in silence watching Ruthie sit upon the bed and gather Cora, rocking the girl like a babe.

The orderlies opened the door hours later to find the women still gathered around Cora, who had been washed and dressed in the cast-off silk dress with her Laura in her arms. Ingrid had ripped a swatch of the silk from the skirt and wrapped it around the doll as a dress. Both were clothed in silk just as Cora had once imagined.

Nurse Fielding was summoned and came to stare at the dead girl. She glanced at the pool of blood that surrounded the bed and stained the feet of the women who stood guard over Cora. She removed a notebook from her pocket to scribble a note.

"Obviously, the girl died from convulsions as she had fits all of the time. Dr. Crawford performed a routine appendectomy earlier, but she had recovered well and was transferred from the hospital wing to rest in her own bed. Someone has been moving her around and reopened the sutures. The poor thing is in a better place now." Nurse Fielding wrote the death report as she spoke. She did not notice Ruthie pick up the basin of bloody water until it had been thrown on her.

"By appendectomy you mean sterilization, you lying shrew! Your doctor ripped out her uterus!" Ruthie screamed. "And by convulsion you mean bleeding to death! And yet, who will believe any of us against your word? We are crazy!" Loud maniacal laughter erupted from her lips as the orderlies grabbed Ruthie by the arms and proceeded to drag her from the room.

It was nine o'clock the next morning when Addy was led by an orderly into Mrs. Hill's parlor. Lucian was waiting with the bevy of society ladies Mrs. Hill had gathered to witness her good deed. Addy wore the same blood-stained dress from the day before and her hair was matted to the sides of her head with sweat mingled with blood. She held Cora's doll, still swaddled in the scrap of silk dress, tightly against her. Everyone stared until Addy broke the silence that hung in the air as heavily as the humidity of the August morning.

"We must be very quiet, so we don't wake the baby. I was up late into the night trying to comfort her, she was so frightened. The sounds of the sirens from the water call so loudly. It is like my little Charlie; he was frightened at first. When he went to sleep, I put him in the water so he would never be afraid of the sirens. Lorelei doesn't hurt the innocent; she only hurts the guilty."

CHAPTER 5

JULY 24, 1925 – THE SCHUMACHER HOME, 191 ALICE ST., WAUWATOSA

The windows of the modest home on Alice Street were opened wide to catch any whisp of a breeze on the hot and humid July morning. Eight-year-old Buddy Schumacher sat at the kitchen table eating a large bowl of cornflakes doused in fresh milk delivered from the dairy. He peered at the cereal box in front of him until his mother whisked it away and put it back in the pantry.

Florence Schumacher did not usually allow a "cheap breakfast" of cereal to be consumed instead of the usual fare of eggs, bacon, sausages, or oatmeal. She had succumbed to the intense heat and did not wish to add to the temperature in the room by cooking breakfast on the stove.

"Arthur, you know the rules at the breakfast table include not reading a cereal box and ignoring the others present." Florence set a glass of cold orange juice beside her son as she handed one to his older sister, Jean, who sat across the table.

Florence returned to her place at one end of the table and sat as she stared out the kitchen window and drank her tepid coffee.

"Today is supposed to be one of the hottest days this year according to the Milwaukee Sentinel. Your father read it this morning before he left for work."

"Mama, did Papa read it in the newspaper at the breakfast table? Why is the newspaper okay to read at the table but the cereal box isn't?" Buddy's brilliant blue eyes sparkled with mischief as he stuffed another spoonful of cornflakes in his mouth, the milk dripped from his chin.

"Arthur Louis Schumacher, close your mouth when you chew." Florence's tone of voice and no-nonsense look let Buddy know his previous question would not be answered, and a change of topic would be a good idea.

"You know you are in trouble when Mama uses your middle name." ten-year-old Jean giggled, stopping short when she recognized their mother had turned the same look upon her." Mama, could we get ice cream this afternoon? It's been forever since we had one." Jean's brilliant smile caused her mother's hard stare to break and be replaced by a gentle laugh and a nod.

"I believe it has only been a week since we went for ice cream instead of 'forever', but I had already thought of the same idea. Buddy, would you like some ice cream this afternoon?" the hard tone was replaced with her usual tender voice as Florence reached to gently push Buddy's sandy blonde hair from his eyes.

Her youngest was a handful, rough and tumble, but he was also the joy of her heart, reminding her so much of her father who had passed when Buddy was only two. Buddy's good-natured, boisterous personality was the spitting image of the Armstrong family while Jean's quieter and sometimes sensitive personality resembled the Schumacher's. Florence oftentimes could not believe how lucky she and her husband Art were to have this pair.

"Mama, I want ice cream, but could we wait until I come back from the swimming hole? The gang is going this morning, and I thought I might even have a couple of fish or some fresh frog legs to bring back when we are done playing around." Buddy was careful to chew all the cornflakes and swallow them before answering his mother. He wanted to be in her good graces again so she would allow him to walk to the local swimming hole on the Menomonee River with his friends, Arnold and John.

"I suppose this is a perfect morning for it. Will it just be Arnold and John this time? You know I don't like it when you follow some of the older boys around." Florence searched her son's eyes to determine the truth hidden in their depths. She didn't like the influence of some of the older boys in the neighborhood as many of them chewed tobacco and used horrible language. They had even taught Buddy and the other younger boys to hop on and off the moving freight trains that traversed alongside the river.

It did not escape Florence that there had already been an incident earlier in the summer. Some of the older brothers of Buddy's friends thought it would be funny to tie Buddy up and leave him in Sanctuary Woods until Art had finally found him in the middle of the night.

Florence had been outraged and wanted Art to speak with the boys' parents about it, but Buddy had begged his father to spare him humiliation from the other boys. Art, remembering the cruel teasing of his own childhood, had acquiesced. Florence was not about to forget as quickly as Buddy seemed to have forgotten.

"Yup, just me and Arnie and Johnny. I will probably stop by the bent oak in the woods because it is the best way to see the whole town, then join the gang and go to the swimming hole. Sometimes

Mr. Eddy has fresh frog legs already done and he sells them cheap so I will check with him on the way home. I need to get going so they don't leave me behind." Buddy stood and took his bowl, spoon, and glass over to the counter beside the sink. He turned back to look at Florence, his eyes begging for her permission.

"Well, be on your way then. Remember not to talk to the strangers down by the river. Be back by three for ice cream." Florence smiled at the dazzling grin of her son as he rushed over and threw his arms around her neck in a tight hug. He smelled of sweat and dribbled milk and oranges. Her hug tightened for a moment before releasing him. He flew out the front door, banging the screen door loudly, his voice singing in an off- pitch key,

"Oh, a stranger is only a friend you haven't met yet. A stranger could be an angel unaware."

It was half past three when Florence walked down to the end of Alice Street to look towards the river and Sanctuary Woods beyond it. There wasn't any sign of her tardy son, so she decided to walk with Jean to get the ice cream from the drug store. Perhaps missing the treat would teach her errant rascal a little lesson.

She was startled to find Buddy's friends, Arnold and John, in front of the drugstore eating ice cream. She thought she might have missed Buddy who was waiting for her and Jean at home. Florence decided to bring an extra chocolate ice-cream cone home, sure that Buddy would be waiting impatiently on the front stoop.

When Art arrived home at six o'clock, he found melted ice cream and an anxious wife pacing back and forth on the sidewalk in front of the house. He headed down the hill towards the river and walked along until he came to the small bridge leading over into the woods, scanning the ground for any sign of his son. He was sure the older boys were up to their hijinks again and this time he would have strong words for them and their parents.

Art immediately walked the path through the woods to the spot where he had found Buddy previously, but there wasn't a single trace of his son. There was a heaviness in his chest as he walked the rest of the path calling out for Buddy to answer him. The stillness of the forest in the late afternoon seemed to mock him as the long shadows of the day resembled people hiding along the path and in the six-foot swaying reeds lining the riverbanks.

Art retraced his steps back to Alice Street and stopped at the house to gather Florence and Jean. The next stop would be the homes of Buddy's friends Arnold and John. The Youngs lived across the street, so Art knocked on Arnold's door first, bringing the family from their dinner table to the door.

Florence felt an icy fear shoot up her spine when she saw the look on young Arnold's face as they asked where Buddy was. The boy looked guiltily up at his own father and then back down at the ground before uttering a confession that would change the Schumacher's lives,

"Buddy got lost when we jumped on and off the trains and we thought he would come back home. We were afraid he would be mad at us for leaving without him."

Florence did not recall their walk back home nor the call Art placed to the Wauwatosa Police. She didn't hear Jean crying or the many neighbors knocking on the door offering to help search for their son. The only thing Florence could hear was the question she asked herself over and over again,

"Why did I let him go?"

The search lasted through the entire night, the police, the firemen, and most of the Alice Street neighborhood calling for Buddy as they searched. The lanterns dotted the night sky throughout Sanctuary Woods like fireflies as men looked everywhere.

It was after daybreak when the search party convened for a brief period and gathered back in front of the Schumacher house. Art recognized Florence's silhouette in the front room window. He understood she had been stationed there all night, waiting in hopes that Buddy would return by himself and come running up the sidewalk to his mother.

"Mr. Schumacher, I am going back to the station to brief the other officers coming on to the next shift, but I will return in half an hour. All the other officers from the night shift are returning as well. We won't leave you until we find him." Officer John Maloney removed his hat long enough to mop at the sweat dripping down his face with his sleeve. "Please tell Mrs. Schumacher we will be right back. Ask her if she remembers anything else your son said this morning about where he was going on his way to and from the swimming hole. Any small comment might be a huge help to us."

"Buddy said he was stopping at the big bent oak tree," Jean whispered, "and then he would ask Mr. Eddy if he had frog legs for sale. I remember because Buddy has a funny story he tells about the bent oak tree. He insists a pretty lady lives in the tree, and she sings pretty songs you can hear in the woods. I called her a fairy once, but Buddy said she wasn't a fairy, she was a siren." Jean's quiet voice startled Art as she stood at his elbow. "One of Buddy's favorite places in the world is the bent oak tree."

Officer Maloney patted Jean on the head as he nodded his encouragement, "That is very helpful little lady. Why don't you go in and check on your mama and tell her we will find your brother?" He waited as Jean reluctantly left her father's side and walked inside the house. As soon as he saw Jean standing beside her mother, he turned to Art and placed his hand on the sobbing man's shoulder.

"We will have to search all of Sanctuary Woods including the area that sits next to Asylum," John confided. "I believe the tree your daughter referenced is located very close to many of the buildings located on Asylum property. I will gather more officers to go and question some of the patients and staff to see if any of them have seen Buddy today. Possibly one or more of them can help us."

John Maloney realized his task of finding the lost boy had just increased in difficulty one hundred times over.

CHAPTER 6

JULY 25, 1925 – COTTAGE 5 NEAR SANCTUARY WOODS

The predawn light cast a tinge of blue over the small lake in front of the bright yellow cottage built on the edge of Sanctuary Woods. A mist hung over the lake reminding Addy of a soft blanket; her hand touched the downy blue blanket across her lap as she sat in one of the many rocking chairs situated on the porch of her cottage. It had been designed and built specifically for Addy's needs.

She had insisted all her fellow patients in Hall 5 be accommodated in the roomy house which contained four bedrooms, a modern indoor water closet, kitchen, and great room where the ladies gathered throughout the day. The long porch of the cottage faced the new manmade lake and small island complete with a gazebo that had been constructed among the numerous other physical changes created since Addy's arrival four years earlier.

A small line of deep rose sky peeked over the horizon and the stirrings of birds in the trees signaled the world awakened to join Addy in her silent morning musings. So many changes beyond the physical additions to the Asylum property had occurred since Addy had appeared in Mrs. Hill's parlor and shocked everyone with her admission of what had happened to little Charlie.

Mrs. Hill had demanded her husband resign from his position post haste as the deep humiliation Addy had brought upon her with the ladies of Wauwatosa society could not be undone. A new appointment for Superintendent Hill somewhere far away was sought out. Within weeks the Hills had vacated The House and most of their furnishings, as Mrs. Hill had insisted it brought her only sorrow to look upon her own cherished possessions.

Superintendent Hill was replaced with Dr. Moses White, a compassionate physician and psychiatrist. Dr. White sought to change the environment of the asylum to include a focus on physical health as well as mental health. He advocated for the grounds surrounding the buildings to be landscaped to reflect a tranquil setting that helped to heal the mind. His two healing groves for both men and women were planted with lush gardens, cultivated flowers to adorn the rooms, and healthy vegetables for the patients' meals.

He had even gone as far as recommending that many of the current dormitories be demolished and replaced with a new main building that had fireproof roofs and an unlocking safety system. It had been tragically discovered in numerous asylum fires that most of the patients were burned alive before they could be rescued due to the fact they were locked in and could not escape.

Probably the singular most innovative of Dr. White's ideas was the proposal to construct various cottages on the property where several of the patients who were deemed unhazardous to the public could reside in small groups. He strongly endorsed the research that showed that patients who were placed in a group environment with a single personal caretaker rather than in larger dormitories with less individualized staff were far more likely to show progress.

Dr White's proposals were met with interest from the board of directors but also with extreme concern over the cost of the improvements. It initially seemed good economics would overrule good healthcare; the asylum made copious amounts of money from the state for keeping the patients within their walls. tucked away, out of sight from the good people of Wauwatosa. Dr. White was afraid it was a hopeless cause until one person stepped forward to champion the mission.

Lucian had suffered an enormous shock upon learning the fate of his son. His grief shook him to the core as his loss was two-fold. He had lost his son forever and though Addy was present in body; he knew he had lost her forever as well. She could never come back to Lake Geneva; she could never resume her role as his wife. Lucian realized the law dictated that Addy should be thrown into prison for taking her son's life, but he realized no prison could hold Addy stronger than the one already present in her own mind.

Lucian, in turn, shocked his family and friends by responding towards Addy with gentleness and compassion instead of anger and revenge. He contributed large amounts of money to Dr. White's project and encouraged the captains of industry who moved in his social circles to do likewise. While many of them disagreed that exorbitant amounts of money be spent on the feeble and weak-minded they could not deny the persuasive charisma of Lucian St. John.

Lucian took Dr. White's proposals and built strategies to not only improve the institution but to establish new methods of obtaining revenue that would make it able to fund itself in the future. A deluxe sanitarium was built on the other side of Sanctuary Woods.

Wealthy people could come and seek private treatment at exorbitant costs thus providing funds for all aspects of the asylum. Lucian was soon regarded by the entire community as the dearest of benevolent benefactors.

One of the first cottages built during the renovation was for Addy and her friends. The yellow house had many windows that allowed for plenty of natural light and fresh air. Lucian purchased Mrs. Hill's Chickering upright piano and placed it in the great room across from comfortable chairs and rockers so Addy could play at any moment of the day. It was common to hear the melodious notes of Chopin drifting through the Sanctuary Woods and the Menomonee River beyond, day or night.

While happy to leave most of the brutal memories of Hall 5 behind, the ladies decided to name the yellow house Cottage 5, a remembrance of their fellowship amid their suffering. Addy had insisted the home be built near the little cemetery in the woods, the place where Cora had been laid to rest.

It had only been a few months after Cora's passing that Mrs. Hall had suffered another major stroke and had died peacefully in her sleep. Lucian had made certain the dear lady was buried beside her husband in the Wauwatosa Cemetery.

Ingrid had become Freda's eyes and ears, the two forging a deep bond. They shared a large bedroom in the house, Ingrid placing everything in a very specific order so Freda could anticipate where things were located and roam the area freely. Freda had blossomed under Ingrid's care even attempting to vocalize more, one of her first understandable words being "Ingrid".

Mary and Ella had gravitated to the newly established gardens, helping them to grow vegetables and then learning to prepare simple dishes that gradually became increasingly complex. Their culinary skills were noted by the chef hired to cook the meals at the sanitarium who met them daily at the gardens.

Soon the chef offered them positions on the kitchen staff and the ability to be trained by him. Both girls delighted at having an occupation to call their own as well as salaries for their work. They continued to live in the cottage as they were still most at home among their friends, insisting on preparing delicious meals for the others.

The rising sun had made its full arrival; piercing beams of sunlight lit the surface of the lake and chased the mist of night away. Addy leaned over to tuck her blanket closer around Ruthie's legs. She glanced at her friend who sat staring straight ahead, her gray hair braided simply in a single braid down her back.

"It doesn't look like there will be any relief from the heat today. Nary a cloud in the sky. It was a good idea to sit in the coolness of dawn before the sun rose. Should we stay for a while longer or go in and get dressed before breakfast?" Addy patted the weather- worn hand that rested on the arm of the rocker next to her.

There was silence in response, Ruthie had not spoken since the night Cora had died. Dr White had tried to determine if it was the trauma of Cora's death that had so deeply affected her. Addy and the others suspected it was more likely due to "cures" applied after she was dragged away. Ruthie had not returned for a week, when she did, she was covered in sores and bruises and sporting a broken ankle that had not been set properly.

Though countless treatments had been tried to help Ruthie, nothing seemed to breach the wall of stillness that surrounded her. Addy alone continued to treat Ruthie as if she were able to speak and understand. Dr. White told Lucian this was because Addy could not comprehend the reality of Ruthie's condition just as she could not understand the reality of her own.

"I thought I would find the two of you here. The cool air feels good, doesn't it?" Georgia Swenson stepped out onto the porch and faced the lake that now sparkled in the full sunlight of day. Georgia, who had been nicknamed "Georgie" by the women, had been hired as the nurse and caretaker in Cottage 5. She had been interviewed and hired by Lucian to take care of Addy, but she quickly accepted the role of caretaker for Ruthie, Freda, Ingrid, Mary, and Ella as well.

At 25 she had already graduated from nursing school and had left a large Norwegian family behind in Minnesota, so she welcomed the happy company of the group. Georgie was eager to learn from Dr. White how to best help those suffering with mental illnesses and she had been readily accepted for her genuine compassion by Addy and the others.

"Mary and Ella have scrambled some eggs with vegetables and have cut up some fresh fruit for breakfast. Would you like to come in and join them before they leave for work?" Georgie was excellent at guiding those in her care instead of demanding actions. She caressed the top of Ruthie's head with a gentle hand then supported her as Ruthie rose from the chair. Addy stood, starting to follow them, when she paused at the railing and looked towards the woods with a wrinkled brow.

"Georgie, there are people crawling all over Sanctuary Woods like little black ants. What are they doing in our woods? I don't want them bothering Cora."

Georgie paused in the doorway to turn back and look where Addy was pointing in the distance. Sometimes Addy saw things other people didn't, so Georgie was surprised Addy, was indeed, correct.

Dozens of men walked through the woods next to them and some were making their way over the small iron bridge that led across the lake to the island.

One young man, a tall redheaded police officer, emerged from the woods and walked the path that led to Cottage 5. Addy scrambled from her position at the railing to hide behind Georgie who stepped back out onto the porch, in front of both Addy and Ruthie, blocking the officer's view of them.

Officer John Maloney removed the hat from his head and held it respectfully in his hand. Georgie couldn't help but notice the sunlight bouncing off his hair, turning it a bronzed golden color. She blinked as she realized the officer had already begun addressing her.

"Good morning, ladies. I am sorry to disturb you at this early hour, but we are searching for a lost little boy named Buddy."

CHAPTER 7

THAT MORNING, COTTAGE 5

"Do you mean little Buddy Schumacher?" Georgie stepped back out onto the porch, concern knitting her brow as she moved her curly bangs from her eyes. She had no way of knowing someone would be standing on their porch at the crack of dawn.

She had not brushed her unruly but beautiful brown hair into her usual bun that she pinned low at the back of her neck. Georgie had often found in nursing school she was not taken seriously if she did not add an air of severity to her hairstyle. The young doctors assumed a woman could not be a skilled professional and an attractive person at the same time.

"Yes, that's his name. Have you seen Buddy in the last day or so? He didn't return home yesterday, and his parents are very worried about him." Officer Maloney observed the beautiful young woman standing a few feet in front of him as well as the two women located near the door to the house. The older woman was staring straight at him, and the younger one was hiding behind the door frame, peeking out at him.

"Buddy drops by almost daily in the summertime." Georgie replied. "He brings fresh raspberries he has picked or fish he has caught. We always encourage him to fish near our pond instead of the river and he enjoys sharing his bounty with us. Come to think of it, I don't remember seeing Buddy yesterday, but I can ask the other ladies if any of them saw him. Would you care to sit on the porch until I return?" Georgie smiled as she indicated the rocking chairs to her side.

"That's very helpful but I wonder if I might meet the other ladies as well and ask them myself? You understand, as an officer of the law I am trained in which questions to ask and to watch people as they respond." John took the final step to the porch, so he was only a foot from Georgie.

He didn't realize his six-foot frame presented such a menace until he saw her reaction and the reactions of the other women. The older woman stepped forward immediately behind Georgie as if to defend her while the younger woman let out a small shriek and retreated into the house. Meanwhile, Georgie had put her hands on her hips and stood her ground glaring at him, her eyes daring him to cross her and try to enter the house. This interview was not going as he had intended.

"My name is Nurse Georgia Swenson, Officer, and I am telling you that intimidating defenseless women will not get you anywhere." Georgie stood fast, her brown eyes darkening with her mood until they almost seemed black. Ingrid, Ella, and Mary (holding her rolling pin) stepped through the door and formed a wall with Ruthie behind her on the porch.

"Please forgive me ladies," John stammered. "I didn't mean to intimidate you in any way. I have been awake all-night searching for Buddy, and I wasn't thinking straight by approaching you like that. Could I possibly start over again? My name is Officer John Maloney, and I am with the Wauwatosa Police Department. We are looking for anyone who might be able to help us find this little boy and all the information is very important. I just want to take him home to his mama."

John stepped back onto the steps, giving the women more space, and put his hands out, a beseeching gesture meant to ask for their assistance rather than to demand it.

"I accept your apology Officer Maloney, and I want to help you any way I can." Georgie's eyes and face softened as she turned toward the small army behind her. "Ladies, why don't you go in and finish breakfast? I will speak to Officer Maloney and then join you. Ella, will you go and get Addy and tell her to come back to the table? Tell her everything is alright. Ruthie, please go in and eat your meal. I promise you I am fine here." Georgie placed a hand on Ruthie's shoulder, turning her gently towards the door as the others filed back in the house.

Georgie waited until they were inside the house before closing the door and indicating the rockers with her hand. John climbed the steps and chose the rocker farthest from the door while she sat down in the rocker next to him. A sudden blast of loud piano music blared from inside the house. Georgie shook her head slightly before speaking.

"I think it's best if I ask the questions, Officer Maloney, as many of the ladies in the house have suffered abuse at the hands of law enforcement officials and medical professionals, two of the professions that should have protected them instead. They don't trust others easily for good reasons. That being said, I know they will be eager to help find Buddy as he is a favorite here in our home. Would it work if you wrote down your questions for me and allowed me to ask them? I can bring any answers down to the police station right away."

Georgie shook her head in disbelief, "I can't imagine how worried his poor parents are right now."

"That's an excellent idea; I can write them out now." John reached into his coat pocket and produced his notebook and a pen. He jotted down a few questions for Georgie then ripped the page from the book, handing it to her with a grin.

"I hope you can read my chicken scratching," John chuckled. "I'm afraid the nuns at school were never impressed with my handwriting. Before I go, I wonder if you could tell me the location of a certain tree that Buddy's sister mentioned to me? She said he mentioned it yesterday morning before he left the house. He called it 'the bent oak'. He even claimed it houses a beautiful singing siren of some sort in it."

"If you know Sanctuary Woods at all, then you know of the old bent oak," Georgie replied. "The path to the left of the house will take you through the woods and up the hill to the cemetery. Once you have crested the hill, the path will fork, stay to the left several hundred yards and you will enter the women's healing grove. The tree is in the center of the grove. You can't miss it." Georgie glanced back at the door, pausing to listen to the loud music that was still playing from within the house.

"As for the singing siren," Georgie continued, "you will have to meet Addy later. The loudness of the piano indicates she is currently still upset and will be far from cooperative. I encourage your patience because if there is anyone who can help you find Buddy it will be her."

John nodded and stood as Georgie rose from the chair and returned to the house. He followed her directions, taking the path through the woods and up the steep hill. The cemetery was located exactly where she had described it, the small earthen mounds with crude wooden crosses dotting the entire top of the hill. John made a mental note to take a closer look within the cemetery as he understood little boys were often fascinated with graveyards and Buddy might have strayed there.

He stayed to the left at the fork in the path and saw what appeared to be a giant ravine split into two sections. Stairs had been constructed up both the sides of the gully, tall grass and a carpet of fragrant flowers covered the ground. A small waterfall trickled down the rocks on one side into a pond at the bottom. At the top and center on the other side of the ravine was the largest misshapen tree he had ever seen, John realized he had found the bent oak.

The massive tree grew apart from other vegetation, its deep roots slowly choking out anything that had attempted to grow beside it. The base measuring at least four feet in diameter jutted up from roots above ground, resembling the legs of a spider surrounding it. Instead of growing straight up into the sky, the trunk bent at a ninety-degree angle about three feet off the ground, then stretched over a several feet span before angling again and facing upwards.

The lower branches of the upright portion of the trunk were without leaves but provided a perfect ladder on both sides into the leafy branches that spanned out above it. The colossal behemoth stretched far beyond any tree around it in the distance, shading a large portion of the ravine below it. John understood why Buddy loved this tree.

John climbed over the roots until he stood at the base. He craned his head back to try and view the top, but it was almost invisible at this vantage point. He removed his hat, coat, shoes and socks, placing them in a neat pile on the ground. He threw his leg over the side of the trunk where it bent and climbed up. He stood to walk the trunk for several feet (imagining a pirate walking a plank) before reaching the bend that thrust the tree upwards.

John reached for the lowest branch and tugged hard; he wanted to assure himself the old tree would hold considerably more weight than that of an eight-year-old boy. It was immovable so with more confidence he began his ascent, his heart beating faster with the anticipation of reaching the top.

He was only midway when he realized he could look out and see most of the village of Wauwatosa to the right, the Menominee River and the railroad tracks to the front, and the Koepfler farm stretched out to the left. Dozens upon dozens of people dotted the ground below, it was the search party still looking for Buddy.

John noticed at this midway point that numerous branches bent gradually creating a web of forks. Tucked tightly in the forks were several brightly colored objects and an old, bald, porcelain doll with a cracked face.

John had to tug at the doll to pick it up, it was wrapped in a scrap of dirty silk that had been tied around it. He placed the doll back in the fork, wedging it tightly again so it would not dislodge in the wind. The likelihood the doll belonged to a little boy was very small, so he turned his attention to the other objects, a paper bag of smooth rocks, an old tin lunch bucket with a few dried raspberries, and a long stick with fishing line attached. John gathered the objects and turned to make his way back down.

He had only taken a few steps in his descent when he discovered an object lying on top of a branch below. Thousands of leaves had impeded his vision of the object on the ascent, but it appeared directly downward as though someone had been seated where he was and allowed it to drop below.

John scrambled with the other things in his hands and stretched himself out on the branch to grasp the object lying on top of the leaves. It was just within his grasp; he felt the rubber sole before he saw what was in his hand, a red canvas sneaker.

It was an hour later when John stood in front of the Schumacher house watching as Florence Schumacher cradled the red sneaker in her hands, tears running down her face.

"This is Buddy's shoe. Where did you find it? Where is my son?"

Officer John Maloney knew what needed to happen. He would ask Georgie to help him gain Addy's trust so the singing siren could help him to bring Buddy home.

CHAPTER 8

THAT AFTERNOON, WAUWATOSA POLICE DEPARTMENT

The main area of the Wauwatosa Police Department had undergone a sudden transformation in one twenty-four-hour period. What was usually a quiet and orderly room that housed the desks and files of the officers serving there, had become a tumultuous madhouse of newspaper reporters and curious onlookers, all of them wanting to hear the latest update on the missing boy.

John cringed as he entered the melee carrying the bag containing Buddy's shoe and the other objects he had collected from the bent oak in Sanctuary Woods. It had been heart wrenching for him to explain to Art and Florence that the shoe had to come to the station and be held as evidence in the search.

The weary parents had reluctantly agreed after John promised to guard the precious shoe himself, not allowing anyone except the other investigators to see it or hold it. He held the bag tighter to his side as he made eye contact with George Baltes, the Chief of Police, and indicated with a slight nod, a closed-door meeting in the Chief's office down the corridor.

John sank into the chair positioned in front of the Chief's ornate desk. It had been more than twenty-four hours since he had slept or eaten a meal, and the initial adrenaline of the search was quickly wearing off, weariness making his arms and legs feel as if sacks of cement had been chained to them. John removed his hat and wiped at the sweat on his brow with his sleeve, the woolen material of his heavy uniform scraping against the razor stubble on his face. He closed his eyes for what seemed like a moment and was startled awake at the sound of the office door shutting behind him.

"Those newspaper men are circling like buzzards out there. We need to find this boy fast and get this wrapped up. Maloney, tell me you have something." George Baltes, Chief of Police, marched into his office followed by several other officers, Louis Wrasse, William Murphy, and Ernest Hammerschmidt.

Each officer pulled the blinds on the windows and door, shielding them from the pressing mob outside. Baltes, a balding man in his mid-fifties, paused at the corner of his desk to stare at John and the paper bag he placed in front of them.

Bill Murphy took the bag from John's outstretched hand, grabbed a cloth, and withdrew the red tennis shoe, setting it on the desk. The little boy's shoe looked so forlorn, abandoned by its mate and the missing boy. Wrasse took out a notebook from his pocket along with a ruler, measuring the shoe and pausing to jot down the dimensions. Chief Baltes and Hammerschmidt sat in momentary silence, both thinking of their own little boys at home.

"Did you find it near the river?" Officer Wrasse shook his head. "I am thinking it is one of our options here unfortunately. All of us recall looking for little Larry Brennan a few years back, he was seen next to the river and assumed he drowned, but we never recovered his body. The Menomonee can be unforgiving. We have over two hundred people out searching for Buddy, but I think we will have to start dragging the river by tomorrow." Officer Wrasse placed the shoe back in the paper bag and attached an evidence tag to the top.

"I have been with the two other boys most of the morning and they can't seem to decide what happened yesterday. First, they told the parents last night that Buddy was on the train, then, early today, they changed it to a swimming hole, and now they admit one of the older brothers, Gordon Wolf, had been with them, and all the boys were at the quarry instead. I have notified all the railroad stations all the way to St. Paul to be on the lookout for the boy on any incoming train, but it looks like we will have to look in the other spots too. John, did you find the shoe near any of those locations?" Ernest Hammerschmidt leaned against the chair where John sat.

"No," John replied, "it wasn't in or near the river or the swimming hole and I haven't been to the quarry yet. I found it in a huge bent oak in Sanctuary Woods; I followed a lead from several of the residents of the cottages near the woods. One of those residents is supposed to return with more information early this afternoon so I needed to come back here in time to meet her. I think they may be a big help as they recognized the boy, and they know the area well." John watched the other officers trading glances of concern.

"This brings us to the second unfortunate option," Officer Wrasse glanced at the others, "the boy has been taken and is either being held against his will or worse. The vagrants who camp among the reeds along the riverbank would have been my first suspicion, but finding the shoe in Sanctuary Woods brings us to another unsavory type of suspect. Sanctuary Woods is on the asylum grounds."

Louis Wrasse rose from his chair next to John, picked up the bag containing the shoe, and carried it to a large metal filing cabinet in the corner. He opened the bottom drawer and placed the bag inside, shutting the door with a finality that resounded within each officer in the room.

"John, you need to go home and get some sleep before you try to meet with anyone else today. I will wait for this woman with the information if and when she shows up and fill you in later." Bill Murphy patted John's shoulder. "We all want to keep looking as long as it takes, but there is only so much any of us can do."

"No, I need to stay here for when she shows up," John insisted. "I really think she and the ladies that live near the woods are a key part of finding Buddy. I thought I would go upstairs and clean up and borrow one of the beds from the firemen up there. This way I can be on hand, and you can come and get me."

John had already formulated a plan using their joint fire station/ police station as a means of habitation. He felt the minutes taken to return to his home on the outskirts of the village might be minutes Buddy could not afford.

"I will agree to your plan Maloney. Bring me any updates you have as soon as she gets here," Chief Baltes interjected. "Meanwhile, I gave the orders for the bloodhounds to be brought from the prison, and we will continue the searches along the river and at the quarry. Sanctuary Woods and the asylum grounds will be a prime focus of the search as well. I think its best if we don't tell the parents yet about having to search among the vagrants along the river and the insane asylum; this is already bad enough for them to endure. Keep all this quiet, boys. I am told they brought in the radio broadcasters too. Soon the whole state will be looking for Buddy Schumacher." Chief

Baltes stood from his chair and walked to the door. He opened the door to the throng of noisy reporters and flashes of cameras.

Within fifteen minutes John had made his way up the back stairs to the firehouse where he found several of the firemen returning from the search. He borrowed a towel and razor and cleaned himself up using a basin and small mirror. He removed the heavy woolen uniform coat and his dress shirt feeling relief immediately in his undershirt and pants.

One of the firemen handed him a large hot beef sandwich on a plate with cold potato salad and a cold glass of lemonade to wash it down. John was certain he was too exhausted to even eat but he devoured everything within a few minutes. Soon he laid down on one of the many cots the firemen used while on call in the firehouse. Sleep claimed him before his head hit the pillow.

The clock in the village bell tower had chimed three o'clock when John was awakened by Murphy shaking his shoulder. In his sleep deprived state John attempted to roll back and ignore him until he heard him say,

"John, there is a Georgie Swenson downstairs, and she is asking for you. She says she has answers for you."

John sat up straight in bed, almost colliding with Murphy as he slid his legs over the side and felt on the floor for his shoes. He put on his shirt and grabbed his jacket and hat to finish dressing as he ran back down the stairs. The mob of people still covered the main room, so Murphy steered John towards one of the interrogation rooms down the back corridor.

"I will let the Chief know she did arrive, and you are questioning her. No wonder you wanted to stay, Maloney. She is a pretty little thing." Wrasse met them at the door of the interrogation room opening it to allow John and Murphy to pass through. John cringed, hoping Georgie had not heard the comment. It was already bad enough she had to be placed in this room as though she were a suspect without making her more uncomfortable.

If Georgie had heard the comment, she did not reveal her reaction as she turned her deep brown eyes towards him. She smiled slightly in recognition at John and waited for him and Murphy to take their seats opposite her. Murphy brought out his note pad and pen as John made the introductions.

"Miss Swenson, this is Officer Bill Murphy. He has been assigned to assist me. Thank you for coming back down to the station. Do you have any more information for us?"

"Yes," Georgie nodded. "I spoke with Addy after she had calmed down a bit and she told me she had seen Buddy walking yesterday morning. He didn't stop to talk with her as he usually does but rather, he rushed past her as though he were in a hurry. She said he was headed up the path towards the cemetery, but when she arrived at the cemetery a few minutes later, he wasn't there."

"Addy said she didn't see him after that," Georgie continued, "but he often met the other boys in the woods to play 'coppers and robbers' so she assumed he might be hiding in one of the many places the boys have claimed in the woods for their games. It made me wonder if Buddy might have fallen into one of the underground cisterns that have been dug to store rainwater. I am sure Addy, and I can help you look for hiding places if you are willing to approach her in a delicate way?" Georgie looked from John to Murphy to gauge their reactions. Both men nodded.

"We are quite willing. What are your suggestions? "John leaned his arms on the table, ready to take action.

"Well, I know both of you need to act in an official capacity, but I wonder if you might change your clothes. Addy is often frightened by men in uniforms and since she is showing you the robbers' hiding places..." Georgie paused in her sentence.

"We need to not be dressed as coppers." John inserted as Georgie shook her head in agreement, appreciating his understanding of the situation. "This is a brilliant idea, Miss Swenson. I think we can be ready to leave after a matter of minutes. Just give us time to change our clothes and we could drive you back to the cottage if you walked here?" John and Murphy stood in unison to go and put the plan into action.

Soon they were pulling up in front of Cottage 5, John driving his Chevrolet Superior F with the top down. Georgie sat at his side and Murphy rode in the back rumble seat. Both men had changed into short sleeve button up shirts and regular dungarees on loan from the firemen upstairs. John had even borrowed a tan fedora that completed his robber disguise.

Ruthie, Ingrid, and Freda sat in the chairs on the porch shelling snap peas. Georgie climbed the porch steps while the officers stood by the car and waited. John did not want to repeat his earlier mistakes with Addy in his rush to obtain information from her. Ingrid indicated that Addy was inside with a nod to Georgie while she continued to patiently hand snap peas to Freda.

Piano music began as Georgie crossed the threshold, loud ragtime melodies, unlike the tempestuous classical music earlier, but John was unsure what it indicated. He stood as Murphy crossed to the steps and approached Georgie quietly.

"I wonder if I might give this a try, Miss Swenson?" Murphy inquired. "My sister, Helen has mongolism. The doctors wanted to put her in an institution from birth, but my mother wouldn't allow them to, she brought her home. Helen has become the joy of our lives. We just have to understand that we enter her world instead of expecting her to live in ours. I know not all of the situations are the same." Murphy took off his cap and looked towards Addy playing at the piano.

"I think you understand perfectly." Georgie nodded her encouragement as Murphy made his way across the room to the piano. He sat next to Addy on the piano bench and listened as she played the syncopated rhythm with accents on the offbeats perfectly.

Addy continued to play the Joplin piece, ignoring Murphy's presence next to her entirely. She paused for a moment before transitioning to the next song playing in her mind when suddenly there was a perfect duet being played with her own, a tremendous feat considering the fact she played without the aid of sheet music.

Addy glanced to notice Murphy playing seamlessly with her, the notes a complete compliment to her own. She increased the tempo, a challenge of sorts and found he matched the tempo without missing a beat. They played the rest of the song in reckless abandon, drawing everyone else to the great room to witness the near miracle.

Ingrid brought Freda forward, placing Freda's hands on the back of the upright so she could listen by feeling the vibrations of the notes. Addy laughed aloud to see the rapture on Freda's face at the cacophony of music. The song came to a crescendo and then ended suddenly. Addy clapped her hands in glee and stood from her place on the bench.

"Georgie says you two want to look for places to hide as robbers. So, as long as you aren't coppers, let's get going. We are losing daylight." Addy marched out the door past Georgie and John and headed down the path towards the woods.

Addy led the way up the hill with Georgie, John, and Murphy following at a respectful distance. She paused at the iron gate of the cemetery. A brief look of sorrow passed over her dainty face. Addy lifted the latch and walked to the back center of the large graveyard.

She took a direct path to a grave with a humble wooden cross embossed with smooth stones. More of the smooth stones surrounded the boundary of the grave creating a simple but beautiful border. Addy knelt beside the grave, waiting for Georgie and the officers to approach.

"Visiting Cora is always first each day. She is the queen of Sanctuary Woods, and we pay tribute by finding stones to place near her. Buddy finds the very best ones and leaves them here for me to use. He hasn't left any today and that is strange." Addy glanced around her, taking in the woods surrounding the cemetery. "If he hasn't brought Cora some stones then perhaps Laura will know more about it." Addy sprang to her feet and sprinted towards the gate, turning to her right and following the path that led to the Women's Grove.

Georgie, John, and Murphy ran to keep up with Addy as she sped along the trail. They picked their way over tree roots and deep ruts. Addy did not even glance towards her feet, the path was so well known to her. Presently, Addy stood beneath the massive bent oak, removing her shoes and stockings before scampering onto the tree trunk and climbing the path John had taken up the tree like a sprite.

"Do we follow her to keep her from harm?" John asked as he started to remove his shoes and Murphy bent over to take his off as well. Georgie stayed them both with a motion of her hand.

"We don't go up the tree unless we have been invited and few are summoned," Georgie confided. "There is a doll placed in the safety of the limbs that belonged to the girl in the grave. Buddy is one of the very few Addy has given permission to use the bent oak. I have been up there myself, but I don't relish the height, so I usually wait for Addy to return." Georgie peered at the leaves above them. She frowned as she spotted Addy's rapid descent from her perch onto the lateral portion of the trunk where Addy plopped down dejectedly.

Georgie crossed the distance to Addy perched above her in record time, forgetting she did not like the distance downwards in her concern for her. She knelt beside her on the massive trunk as Addy burst into tears, taking the young woman into her arms and rocking her gently. Murphy and John scanned the tree to try and find what was causing Addy such distress, both hoping she had not just found the remains of the missing boy.

"Laura is missing. She is not in the tree, Georgie! Now who will tell us where Buddy has gone?"

The sun was setting as the small party made their way out of Sanctuary Woods towards the cottage. Although Addy had led them on an exhausting hike through the woods with over a dozen hiding places to check, they had not found any trace of Buddy. Georgie held Addy's hand, leading her home.

Bloodhounds baying in the near distance told John the search along the river had not produced a lead yet, and everyone would continue to search into the night. He knew the stones in the bag he had found near the doll now had more significance, but he needed to find out who had taken the doll he had left in the tree.

He and Murphy had searched all around the tree to make certain the doll had not dropped from the perch even though John remembered he had tightly wedged it into its spot. Who had removed the doll, and did they have Buddy?

John was so deep in thought he did not notice the vehicle parked next to his own. A new Rolls Royce Silver Ghost Picadilly Roadster blocked his car in the driveway, and an irate looking man approached from the porch. Murphy stopped suddenly, reaching for the small pistol stored in his boot, but Georgie stepped between him and the rapidly approaching Lucian St. John.

"Where have you been and what have you done to my wife?" Lucian's face was red with anger as he shouted the question. Ruthie and the others inside the cottage ran out to the porch. Georgie stretched her hands towards Lucian and continued to walk in his direction. Addy stood beside John, transfixed on the pair, and yet seemingly unconcerned.

John was stunned into momentary silence. He had mistakenly thought Georgie was unmarried; she had not corrected him when he called her "Miss Swenson". Perhaps it was more likely John had wished for Georgie to be single and therefore he had assumed it. Now he had stumbled into a domestic conflict without even realizing it.

"Lucian, I didn't realize you were returning today," Georgie pleaded. "We wouldn't have left if we had known. Addy and I have been trying to help search for a little boy who went missing yesterday. Certainly, Ingrid or Mary told you where we were?" Georgie stepped next to where Lucian stood in the middle of the walk leading to the porch. He wore a white cotton shirt open at the neck without his usual tie and jacket.

"They only mentioned you had gone to look for hiding places for coppers and robbers. It sounded ridiculous then and looks even more ridiculous now. Who are these gentlemen?" Lucian ran his hand through his black hair in frustration as he looked at Georgie for an answer.

"We are Wauwatosa policemen. My name is Officer John Maloney, and this is Detective Bill Murphy. We are searching for Buddy

Schumacher. Mrs. Swenson and Addy helped us by showing us the places the boy is known to hide. I am sorry you were alarmed, Mr. Swenson." John found his voice again after recovering from his initial shock. He wasn't about to let poor Georgie defend him to her angry husband.

Lucian's brow furrowed in confusion and Georgie turned back to look at John with her mouth hanging partly open. A small gasp escaped her as she blinked several times and looked back at Lucian again. It was Addy who laughed.

"That's a good one, Copper," Addy chuckled. "He's not married to her; he's married to me!" Addy's laughter grew louder at the astonished look on John's face. Addy walked past Georgie and Lucian and headed for the porch. She hugged Ruthie and led her towards the cottage door, entering the domicile with the others following her and shutting the door behind them. Soon, the piano music began. It was loud and classical.

"There have been multiple misunderstandings occurring simultaneously." Georgie smiled at John and Murphy who appeared frozen in place. "Mr. St. John is married to Addy; he hired me to take care of her several years ago. He visits her often to make certain she has everything she needs."

Georgie turned to face Lucian while she continued her explanation," These officers needed Addy to help them search for places the missing boy might be hiding. They aren't dressed in their uniforms because it frightens Addy to see them. I went with them to make certain Addy would be fine."

Lucian nodded his understanding at the explanation. He approached John and Murphy with his hand outstretched, shaking their hands in turn. He turned to stare at the cottage and listened to the loud piano music emanating from it.

"Is there anything I can do to help in your search, Officers? I would be willing to postpone my business trip to New York if I could be of assistance. I know how it feels to be a parent whose child is missing, and I will do whatever needed to help someone else." Lucian's face mirrored the pain John had seen in the faces of Art and Florence Schumacher. It was possible he could be an immense comfort to them.

"I think you may be a big help to the Schumachers, Mr. St. John. If you wish, you can meet us at the police station tomorrow morning and we can iron out the details." John motioned to Murphy and headed for his car. "Thank you for your help. Is it Miss Swenson or Mrs.?" He paused next to Georgie while Lucian hopped in his roadster and moved it out of the way so they could proceed down the driveway.

"It's Miss Swenson but you can both call me Georgie. I think it might be a little less confusing." Georgie waved at John and Murphy as they entered the car to leave. Lucian returned to stand next to her as the car drove away.

"Do they know about what Addy did with Charlie?" Lucian whispered the one question Georgie had been trying to avoid asking herself all day. The two of them stood in silence as the piano music dwindled and the quiet settled over the cottage in the twilight.

CHAPTER 9

JULY 26, 1925 – WAUWATOSA POLICE DEPARTMENT

The din of over fifty police officers working in the same room mixed with the commotion of dozens of newspaper reporters and community members who held vigil inside the work area of the Wauwatosa Police Department. The previous days' search with the bloodhounds had produced one scent trail of the boy leading straight to the river and the railroad tracks.

Chief Baltes had ordered the dragging of the Menomonee River at daylight and another search of the quarry west of Hawley Road. A local handyman had come forward claiming he had seen a boy of Buddy's age and description playing among the rocks in the quarry near the water on the day Buddy went missing.

John returned to the station after collapsing in his own bed at home for several hours and taking a long bath. He picked his way through the throng of assembled citizenry towards his desk in the back corner of the room. Murphy waited for him, freshly shaved and holding two mugs of black coffee.

"The Chief has called for a briefing in an hour. Mr. Schumacher is supposed to arrive soon though I don't know how he will make it through this bunch," Murphy scowled at the reporters who seemed to cover every surface of the room.

"Do you think the St. John fellow will actually show up today? I have seen a lot of his ilk, and they play a good game but rarely follow through with it." Murphy handed John a steaming cup of coffee. The rich aroma made John's mouth water as he waited for it to cool a bit before attempting a sip. Murphy took a huge gulp of his own scalding brew without even wincing.

"He seemed convincing to me," John replied, "but I have more than one question about him including his story of his own missing child. It feels like there is something they are not telling us about their situation and if it's something that will help us in this search, then I aim to find out what it is. I heard they started to drag the river early this morning. I was so sure we might find him in one of those hiding places yesterday, alive and unharmed. "John didn't finish his thought as Murphy already understood the longer the boy was missing the less likely it was, he might still be alive.

It was 10:30 a.m. on the dot when the noise in the room increased to a considerable degree, an indication Art Schumacher had arrived and was attempting to gain entry through the mass of people surrounding him. Officer Hammerschmidt, a burly bear of a man cut through the crowd, leading the slightly built Art Schumacher towards the Chief's office. John and Murphy left their place at the desk and used the back hallway to circumvent most of the crowd gathered.

The fishing pole, dinner pail, and Buddy's red shoe sat on the Chief's desk. John noted that the paper bag containing the rocks had been left sitting on top of the filing cabinet, the Chief deciding it was not as critical evidence as the other items.

Art Schumacher sat in the chair next to the desk surrounded by at least twenty other officers crowding into the room. The District Attorney, Eugene Wengert, sat in a chair next to Art. He was flanked on both sides by two police officers whom John did not recognize.

"Mr. Schumacher, we hoped to have more news for you this morning, but our search for the past day hasn't yielded much yet." Chief Baltes began. "I assure you we are increasing the number of officers on the case around the clock and DA Wengert has asked two detectives from the Milwaukee Police Department to join our search as well. Detective Kraemer has investigated several missing people over the past twenty years, and Detective Zellmer has assisted him in a number of those cases. I am letting our officers know that while we continue in our own areas, all of you will answer and work with Kraemer and Zellmer from this point forward." Chief Baltes looked around the room, until his gaze landed on John and Murphy standing in the corner next to the filing cabinet.

"Maloney and Murphy will lead from our department since they have been on the case from the first call. Hammerschmidt and Wrasse will continue to follow up with the boys who were with Buddy that morning. Do I understand you have rounded up a few of the vagrants from the riverbank to see if the boys recognize any of them?" Chief Baltes directed the last question to Hammerschmidt who nodded affirmatively.

"Yah, we have one of the hobos they call Mr. Eddy in the back. He has been known to hang around the river area and the swimming hole. He's also been spotted in Sanctuary Woods prior to this. I asked Mr. Young to bring his son Arnold down this morning to see if he recognizes Mr. Eddy and if he was the man they now insist chased them from the train. We gathered up quite a few vagrants down there, but we have been weeding through them, and we are down to three or four." Hammerschmidt looked up from his notes in front of him.

"Is Mr. Eddy a suspect because he was in the area or because he is a vagrant?" John asked. "There are a lot of individuals who reside around the area that should be questioned then just like he was." John shifted from his position nearest to the filing cabinet and placed the paper bag of rocks on the desk next to the other objects.

"For that matter, Mr. Schumacher, is there anyone else we should be questioning? Can you think of anyone who might want to take your son?" John said the words most of the officers in the room were thinking; Buddy was not lost, he had been abducted.

Art Schumacher looked downwards at his hands in his lap. "Yes, Officer Maloney, I think there might be. Last year I received a threatening note. The man was upset about something he believed Florence's father had done and threatened to get revenge against me and mine. I didn't give any credence to it because he is a hothead, and I thought it was just a rant and nothing else. Florence reminded me of the letter last night because she was worried it might mean something more. I am not sure it does, but I thought you should know."

"That makes a huge difference in this investigation, Mr. Schumacher. We must consider all the aspects and someone seeking revenge against you is a strong motive. Is the person you mentioned still in this area, and have you mended the broken ties with them?" Detective Adolph Kraemer walked through the group until he stood beside John.

"I have found in dozens of cases that the solutions lie in the smallest of clues. Can you come with Detective Zellmer and myself to an interview room and give us more details about the letter? This is a lead we must follow. Good work, Maloney." The older, more experienced detective nodded to the young officer beside him.

There was a knock at the door as Sergeant Bates stuck his head in the room.

"Chief, there is a Lucian St. John here and he is insistent Maloney asked him to come and meet with Mr. Schumacher this morning." Bates looked sheepish as he continued, "He seems to be the kind of gent you don't keep waiting if you know what I mean?"

Chief Baltes looked to John for acknowledgment, and upon John's nod he dismissed the group. "Hammerschmidt, let me know when the Young boy arrives for the identification. Detectives Kraemer and Zellmer, we will get an interview room set up for you and send Mr. Schumacher your way. Wrasse, take everyone else and go out and organize this morning's search party."

"I am told they are sending a huge troop of boy scouts because the lad is one of their number," Chief Baltes continued, "so we will have to set them up, probably on Koepfler's farmland to keep the boys away from the river. Have them span across and sweep from one end to the other and tell everyone to leave no stone unturned. Bates, send Mr. St. John in after the rest are cleared." Baltes sat in his chair, already perspiring from the heat of the day and the closeness of so many officers in the room.

Lucian St. John was ushered into the room which had been emptied except for Mr. Schumacher, Chief Baltes, Murphy, and John. He appeared vastly different from his first meeting with John and Murphy. He was impeccably dressed in a light tan suit complete with a crisp, white cotton shirt, a silk blue tie, and an expensive tan straw boater hat with a blue silk band. He paused at the door while Chief Baltes rose from his chair and came to shake his hand.

"Mr. St. John! I didn't realize they meant Lucian St. John of St. John Steel when they announced your arrival. I am honored by your visit to our precinct. How can we be of assistance to you?" Baltes spoke hurriedly as he showed Lucian towards his own chair behind his desk. Lucian paused and put out his hand to Art Schumacher sitting in the chair in front of the desk.

"Thank you, Chief Baltes but it is I who has come to try to be of assistance to you in the search for this little boy. Your officers told me some of the details when I met them unexpectedly last night at my wife's home." Lucian bobbed his head in greeting to John and Murphy.

"Mr. Schumacher, I have known the agony of wondering where my missing son was, and I came to offer you and Mrs. Schumacher all of my support. Might I ask if there has been a reward offered for information regarding Buddy?" Lucian sat in the chair next to Art, declining the offer of the Chief's more auspicious place behind the desk.

"Thank you, Mr. St. John," Art Schumacher replied. "My wife and I have already put forward a $250 reward and this morning the Wauwatosa Business Chamber doubled it in hopes of someone would come forward with more information. We have been surrounded with offers of help and comfort from the entire village; your generous offer of assistance is also greatly appreciated."

The softspoken man picked up his son's red tennis shoe from the desk in front of them. "The greatest help has come from all of the police department, especially Officer Maloney and Detective Murphy."

"Yes, indeed," Lucian agreed. "Both are good men. I hope you will allow me to double the $500 amount in hopes more information will surface quickly. It is important things are done very rapidly; time is of the essence as I am sure they have told you. I will have my office in Chicago forward the money to the police department this morning if you agree?"

Lucian reached into his jacket pocket, extracting a pen and paper, jotting down a note and replacing the paper in his pocket while laying the pen aside on the desk. His eyes glanced over the items on the desk and landed on the shoe Art still held. John noticed the look of sympathy in Lucian's eyes.

"Was that your son's shoe? It's important to keep his things close to comfort you. I have every hope these officers will see him home to you and your wife." Lucian's voice was barely above a whisper; he leaned closer and touched Art's shoulder.

"Yes, this is the shoe he had on that morning. Officer Maloney found it in Sanctuary Woods. I feel sure he and Detective Murphy will find him soon." Art placed the shoe next to the other items on the desk. He stood with Chief Baltes and made his way out the door towards the interview room where Kraemer and Zellmer were waiting. Lucian watched him exit before he turned back to John.

"I hope this will help in some way. If there is anything else, I can do please reach out to my office. I left the number with the Sergeant at the desk. I have been delayed in my business trip so I will be on my way." Lucian stood and moved to the exit when John spoke up.

"Mr. St. John, you have mentioned your own son was missing at one time. Would you mind telling us what happened?" John voiced what was on Murphy's mind as the two men waited for Lucian's response.

"Yes, of course. It is probably a necessary detail though I am hoping it isn't related to this search in any way. My son Charlie was taken from our home in Lake Geneva almost four years ago. We searched everywhere for him, expecting he was abducted and would be held for a large ransom. It was an excruciating wait." Lucian turned the fancy straw boater in his hands as he spoke.

"Was that what affected your wife? The grief of your missing son?" Murphy looked to John with more understanding of Addy's affliction.

"No, I am afraid Addy was 'affected' first as she later admitted to drowning our son in the lake because mysterious sirens called to her. I am hoping Charlie's abduction and Buddy's are not related.

CHAPTER 10

WAUWATOSA
POLICE DEPARTMENT

John's stomach felt as if he had swallowed molten lead. Addy was responsible for the abduction and murder of her own son and now another little boy who had been in her company was missing. He looked at Murphy for his reaction. His partner's ashen face told him everything he needed to know. John walked past Lucian and shut the door Lucian had opened.

"How in the world could you think these two things might not be related Mr. St. John? This little boy is in danger, and you need to tell us everything that could be remotely related whether or not it reflects poorly on your wife. Why isn't Addy in prison if she committed murder?" John walked back to the desk and leaned against it. He was struggling to accept that the sweet young woman he had seen yesterday was a cold-blooded killer.

All his prior training taught him not to allow emotions or sentiment to bias an investigation, but his intuition as an officer who had dealt with criminals for years and understood most of the typical proclivities could not fathom how he had missed that this seemingly angelic sprite had a dark evil soul.

"Addy had been committed to the asylum by my father, and I came to bring her home, thinking he was incorrect in his action. She stood in the asylum Superintendent's parlor and declared before Wauwatosa society she had 'put Charlie in the water to calm him because the sirens were so loud.' She was convinced in some nonsense from our neighbors about the name of their estate, Die Lorelei, which was titled after a legend about a siren on the cliffs over the Rhine River in Germany. She thinks Lorelei is real." Lucian crossed back to the desk and stood by the chair he had vacated.

"Addy was deemed not guilty by reason of insanity in a closed court to protect our family's reputation," continued Lucian. "She is monitored all the time by Georgie and by the large staff from the asylum, whom she thinks are groundskeepers. There isn't any time of the day she isn't being observed so the little boy would have been safer in her company than just about anyone else's."

"I checked with all the staff, and no one saw Addy with him the day he disappeared. I understand if you would like to speak with them as well. You will need to check at the main building and ask for Nurse Fielding. She can direct you to them. I wasn't trying to misdirect you or hamper the search; I was only trying to protect Addy from more public scrutiny and the circus of newspaper men out there." Lucian glanced towards the windows with shades pulled against the prying eyes on the other side.

"All of this information is pertinent," said Murphy, "and it was a mistake for you to assume we didn't need to be informed. We will check with the asylum staff as you suggested because they might have seen something else that didn't involve Addy so it will actually protect her. You made the mistake that as police officers we only look for suspects rather than looking for the actual perpetrators. We are not interested in finding someone to fit the crime if they are not the person who committed it. The only ones who need to fear the law are the ones who break it."

Murphy sat in a chair he pulled out and picked up Buddy's shoe from the desk. "Only the person who took this little boy needs to be afraid right now because we will find him. Please make certain we can contact you while on your business trip because I am sure we will have more questions."

Lucian nodded and turned back to exit through the office door. They could hear the pop of flashbulbs as Lucian entered the main room to exit the building. John took the items related to the search from the desk and placed them back in the bottom drawer of the filing cabinet. He removed a few of the stones from the paper bag and grasped them in his hand. Murphy rose from his chair, bringing the shoe to the cabinet and setting it with the other objects.

"Well," said Murphy, "this changes a few things, doesn't it? I am not convinced Addy did anything, but we need to include her on our list for now. It's a shame Georgie didn't mention any of this before so we would have known. I can see why she would protect Addy, but she's also very concerned about Buddy, going out of her way to help us find him. It still doesn't all add up in my way of thinking." Murphy glanced at his friend who stared at the stones in his palm.

Sergeant Bates popped his head inside the door, "The Young boy is here with his father, and the Chief wants you two down in the basement to witness this." The door shut again leaving the two officers heading for the jail downstairs.

Arnold Young, one of Buddy's friends, sat at a table in an ante-room outside the cellblock. His dark hair curled over his ears causing him to scratch at his right ear repeatedly. He was dressed in a red T-shirt and blue Dungarees with blue tennis shoes much like the red tennis shoe that sat in the filing cabinet upstairs. Arnold fidgeted in his chair and looked nervously at his father as John and Murphy entered the room already inhabited by Chief Baltes, Detectives Kraemer and Zellmer, and DA Wengert.

"Now, Arnold, we just wanted to know if you can tell us again what happened the morning Buddy disappeared? These officers have been looking everywhere for him, and you can be a big help to them." DA Wengert spoke gently to the boy who looked from one officer to the next.

"Well, we was going to the swimming hole, you know, Blackridge, not the other one and we always jump onto a train 'cause they go real slow down by the depot. We had all jumped on and rode and we was about to jump off when this man in a blue suit yelled at us. We all jumped off and ran but Buddy jumped off and he didn't run; he stayed near the tracks. The man jumped off too and chased after us but then he stopped after a bit. We thought Buddy would be right behind us but then we didn't see him again. We went on home and thought Buddy went a different way like through Sanctuary Woods 'cause he likes it up there next to the crazy house." Arnold spewed the story out so quickly, the officers writing it down in their notes had to scramble to get all of it.

"I understand. Do you think you would be able to recognize the man who chased you if you saw him again?" DA Wengert was an expert in leading a witness exactly where he wanted them to go. To his satisfaction, the young boy nodded vigorously.

The door opened and Hammerschmidt entered, leading a gaunt man with an obvious limp. His shirt and pants were filthy, and his dark brown hair was matted to one side of his head. The stench of unwashed body assailed the inhabitants of the room causing the DA to remove a handkerchief from his pocket and press it to his nose.

The man was manacled at the wrists; his eyes were downcast as he hobbled alongside Hammerschmidt. His bare feet were covered in open sores. He looked the part of the homeless vagrant, the caste of society that everyone else wished to ignore until they needed someone to blame.

John bristled at the sight of the spectacle before him. All the other men in the room were aware that proper procedure indicated placing this man in a lineup where the boy could pick him out from the rest. They understood this was a violation of the homeless man's legal rights. He moved towards the DA to put a stop to this egregious breach when Arnold spoke up to the amazement of them all, saying,

"This ain't the man who chased us. I don't know who this guy is."

The disappointment was evident on the faces of the Chief and the DA. Hammerschmidt tugged on the man's arm nearly toppling him in the process. Murphy put out his hand to steady him as they passed. The man lifted his head to look Murphy in the eye while placing his hand on Murphy's arm.

"Come on with me Eddy. We will get you something to eat now." Hammerschmidt led Eddy from the room as the others sat staring at Arnold.

"We will be going now if there isn't anything else?" Mr. Young, a thickset man with a heavy German accent spoke for the first time since John had entered the room. "I had to take time off from work at the lumberyard to bring the boy in here and it did nothing." He huffed as he stood and grabbed his son's arm. "Folks are saying you boys don't know yourselves from the backside of a donkey and I think that might be about right." Mr. Young left the room towing Arnold behind him.

"When Wrasse brought this guy in, I was so sure we had our man." Chief Baltes broke the silence in the room. "I want a roundup of anyone else down in the area who has no good reason for being there and I want them all brought in before the day is through. One of those hobos or tramps is our suspect so we won't miss a single one. Tell Hammerschmidt to take Eddy over to the poor farm as they can hold him for two weeks. We know where to find him if we get more evidence against him." Baltes led DA Wengert from the room.

"Can anyone explain how the man we just saw could honestly run after those kids and chase them?" Murphy was the first to speak after the Chief's hasty orders and exit. "I don't think we are helping this boy by finding people we can blame rather than finding who has taken him."

"It's a typical mistake but one we can't afford to make," Detective Kraemer admitted. "In our private interview, Arthur Schumacher admitted the person who sent the threatening letter to him is a distant associate of his wife's family. Florence Schumacher was an Armstrong before she married. Her father, John Armstrong, was one of the highest-ranking officials in the city of Milwaukee."

"It is well known that the feuds among the beer barons are still going strong," Kraemer continued, "they have been known to burn the bridges surrounding the city to prevent the competition from transporting their beer. It is also widely understood that most of the city officials are in the deep pockets of the beer barons. If one of the officials crossed these backers, the results could be this or worse. Mr. Armstrong was famous for opposing these oligarchies. I think the Schumachers felt that since Florence's father has passed, any threat has passed, but these vendettas are rarely ever forgotten." Detective Kraemer looked from Maloney to Murphy. "If this is the case, it will be difficult to get the boy back and to determine just which one of them is involved."

"So, we have the definite possibility of a cabal plot against the family," said John. "I can see why this is being kept from the public but why are we chasing after other far less likely possibilities? Our manpower is diminished for the search that needs to continue and then the investigation that is also ongoing. Aren't we better served by limiting the investigation to more precise areas?" John joined the detectives who sat at the table sorting through stacks of paper.

"Ideally, yes," said Deective Zellmer. "But your Chief of Police and DA are interested in the public's opinion because they have elected positions. They must make it appear that the police have a suspect close at hand and the general public is safe in their homes even though it might not be the case. While Kraemer was looking into the Armstrong connections I was studying Milwaukee County public records for the past eight years. Did you know there are numerous missing and murdered boys in this county and none of their cases have been solved? Many of them have never been recovered?"

Detective Bruno Zellmer was a quiet man with a studious appearance. He seemed more suited to teaching in a university than the raucous work of law enforcement, but it was that intellectual giftedness applied to the psychology of criminal behavior which caused him to excel in his chosen field.

"Five years ago, we investigated the disappearance of Homer Lemay from Milwaukee," Kraemer recalled. "He was taken from his home near West Allis at the age of six. I went all the way to Argentina to follow up on possible leads, but we never found him. The next year, there was an unidentified boy found close to Waukesha, who had been badly beaten and molested. He was dressed in expensive clothing, so he was nicknamed Little Lord Fauntleroy. He was only seven or so. He was found in the deep water of a quarry." Kraemer shook his head at the memory. John realized why the investigators were focusing close attention on the nearby quarry at State and Hawley Streets, only a few blocks from Buddy's home.

"Two years ago," continued Zellmer, "they found fourteen-year-old Gottfried Dionizi wrapped up in a woman's petticoat and hidden in a culvert. That was within two miles of where we sit but outside the Wauwatosa jurisdiction so your precinct would not have been notified. The saddest part of the case is that because he had just immigrated here from Slovenia with his parents, it was decided he had gotten into 'mischief' and it wasn't pursued any longer. What 'mischief' does a fourteen-year-old boy get into that gets him molested, murdered and degraded? "Zellmer's voice broke at the question he put forth to the others who sat in silence.

"It has been kept secret from the press and from most of the department, but we were called into your case because two boys about a mile away in West Allis went missing two days before Buddy disappeared. The officials are worried about the appearance of a series of abductions. I am saying it is more than just the 'appearance' of it," Zellmer added.

"What you are telling us is that we have a huge mess on our hands, and we are running out of time to rescue Buddy while our superiors try to keep up the facade that 'all is well' by chasing after the homeless people." Murphy had an incredible ability to cut to the heart of the matter.

"Pretty much," said Kraemer. "When we take what we have and join it with the fact that several of these abductions also happened near the local insane asylum we have a nightmare of a case. I was told you two followed up with a search on the asylum grounds and found the boy's shoe there, so we wanted to compare notes with you. I think we should each concentrate on a specific area and cover more ground that way." Kraemer's direct approach impressed John.

"Yes, we have looked in numerous places that the boy hid in the woods," said John, "and we have at least one person of interest in an asylum patient, a woman who killed her own son. Those around her insist she is monitored all the time, but we are still going to investigate it further. We were planning to return to question the staff at the main hospital on the grounds." John gave an account for Addy to the best of his ability.

The door burst open, an agitated Chief Baltes entering. His red face revealed the level of his exasperation. He slammed a paper down on the table, scattering the piles of papers that had just been sorted.

"Kraemer and Zellmer, we need you to get to Grant Park in South Milwaukee as soon as possible. Leave by the back exit and don't say anything to the press outside. Make certain they don't follow you. We have to get this nipped in the bud right now." Baltes slammed the door as Zellmer picked up a police report and read aloud.

"Grant Park, South Milwaukee, Period made: 7/26/1925. 0800 hours. Officer reports a young female, eleven years of age, was taken from the park area near the water. She had short, cropped sandy blonde hair and wore a boy's shirt and overalls at the time. She was found near Carrollville on Highway 32 at 0900 hours alive and relatively unharmed. The girl stated she was taken by two men and bound and gagged with a handkerchief stuffed inside her mouth.

One man pulled her overalls off while the other man drove. Upon finding she was a female, the man swore and slapped her hard in the face. The car slowed and the girl pushed out the door of the moving car. Another motorist found the girl and called the police. Immediate assistance from Milwaukee detectives in charge of Buddy Schumacher case is requested."

CHAPTER 11

COTTAGE 5
NEAR SANCTUARY WOODS

Georgie stood at the sink drying small glass jars as Ingrid washed and rinsed them. The wood counters and large table were covered with small pint vessels, ready to be filled with raspberry jam bubbling on the stove in multiple large pots. A large water canner sat on the back burner, the initial sterilization of each jar being paramount to the preservation process.

Mary stirred the three steaming pots full of raspberries and sugar, watching, lest one start to burn and ruin the molten scarlet mixture within it. Ella sterilized the jars after they were washed by placing them in the water canner for ten minutes then placing them upside down to cool just enough to touch.

Freda, Ruthie, and Addy were seated at the table readying the lids and rings. They would wait for the jam to be poured into the jars then place the lids and rings on each jar. Afterwards, Ella would process the jars in the canner for five minutes then remove them and allow them to cool.

The heavy fruity scent of raspberries filled the cottage. Mary stuck a large metal spoon into one of the pots, lifting it to test the thickness of the mixture. The jam was ready when the fruity drops thickened into a continuous stream that ran from the spoon to the surface below it. She nodded as a scarlet ribbon flowed from the spoon, and lifted the heavy pot, carrying it to the table. Georgie helped ladle the jam into the still warm jars while Mary returned to the other two pots still on the stove.

"Smells like summer." Freda smiled at her own sentence as Addy patted her hand in encouragement. Addy guarded Freda as Georgie filled each jar, making sure the blind woman did not touch the scalding hot jam by accident. Georgie noted Addy's care and concern for her friend. Her instinctual actions were not those of a person who would hurt anyone, especially a child. In fact, of all the women who lived under the roof of Cottage 5 it was Addy who exhibited the sincerest attentiveness towards everyone around her. It confused Georgie that Addy could be the one considered a danger to anyone.

All the women had spent the early morning hours of the day in the healing grove in Sanctuary Woods. The raspberry thickets were located beyond the bent oak. The brambles that had sported a small cluster here and there only a week previous now burgeoned, weighing the canes down with the overabundant weight of fruit.

They had picked silently, enjoying the coolness of the morning and the trills of the birds watching them just beyond their reach. The ground surrounding the thicket had been trampled, one of the many physical signs the search for Buddy continued over the entire landscape that encompassed them. Dew still clung to the grass below and to the berry laden bushes at hand, dampening their shoes and aprons.

The sun soon brought its sultry heat. The noise from the dragging of the river down below them drowned out the music of the birds.

Georgie hurried to finish the task and remove her charges from their exposure to the intensity of the sun and to the censure of the citizens wandering the grounds. Many of the men stopped and stared at them, recognizing the women as patients at the asylum. A few had uttered derogatory comments loud enough for them to hear.

"They should be keeping all of the morons indoors. It's bad enough to have a missing kid out here without mixing their lot in." The hurtful words were hurled like rocks at their heads.

"This grove is part of the asylum gardens. We have every right to be here. You are the ones trespassing right now but since you are looking for the little boy we will overlook it at this time." Georgie could not help but respond to the insults. She gathered up the pails and baskets overflowing with berries and collected her group to retreat to the sanctuary of their cottage.

As Georgie lifted one of the heavy pails off the ground, she discovered a small heap of smooth stones stacked neatly next to the end of the row of brambles. It was too deliberate to be a random pile, and the stones were the only ones of their kind on the ground. Georgie put the pail back down and knelt next to the stones for a closer look. She had to move some of the prickly long tendrils of the brambles out of the way to reveal the stack. Georgie's heart started to beat rapidly. Could this be a clue related to Buddy?

"Those are Buddy's stones. He gets them from the quarry and brings them to Cora. They are so smooth from the blasting and the mineral water in the quarry. See? This one is an agate." Addy stood next to Georgie looking down at the arrangement, pointing at a translucent brown stone with white lines in concentric circles.

Addy had confirmed Georgie's hunch. This was something they needed to show to Officer Maloney and Detective Murphy. Georgie pushed the long-tangled brambles back over it, covering it until she could show it to the police.

The jam making was nearing completion as the sun cast long shadows through the open windows on the western wall. Ella made a quick supper of fresh jam on thick slices of a warm loaf of bread and placed it in the middle of the table for everyone to enjoy the fruits of their labor. Georgie heard a car engine coming up the driveway followed by the sounds of two car doors opening and shutting.

Georgie hurried towards the porch expecting to see Maloney and Murphy ascending the steps. She was surprised to see Lucian consulting with his driver, Gregson, near the car Lucian used to travel; an unassuming black Model T Ford, far less ostentatious than the Rolls Royce he normally drove when visiting.

Gregson looked up from their conversation to note Georgie's presence on the stairs of the porch. He tipped his hat at her before turning to open the driver's side car door. Soon he sped back down the driveway while Lucian approached Georgie.

"Where is the Rolls? Are you leaving us?" Georgie spoke lightly, ignoring the slight disappointment she experienced at not seeing John Maloney in front of her.

"I parked the Rolls in a rented garage so Gregson could take me to the train station in Chicago. I needed to be in New York two days ago but decided it was important to help in the search for the little boy before I left. Have the police been back today?" Lucian looked around the yard as if mentioning the officers could summon them before him. "I have more to discuss with you before I leave but I wanted to visit Addy first." Lucian stepped through the door Georgie held open for him and greeted everyone sitting at the dining table.

"Is that fresh raspberry jam I smell? You have all been busy today I see." He smiled graciously at the plate Ella offered to him and sat down at the table next to his wife helping himself to a slice of bread and jam. "This is absolute heaven on earth."

Georgie brought a tall glass of iced tea garnished with a few of the extra raspberries and handed it to Lucian. He took several large swallows before setting the glass on the table. "Now I wish I could stay here with all of you instead of enduring a long hot train ride to New York. Is there any more bread?" Lucian looked towards Mary who glanced at him shyly from where she stood at the kitchen sink.

Mary nodded and sliced a huge chunk, slathering it with jam and carrying it to Lucian herself, blushing furiously at his dazzling smile of thanks. Georgie noted Lucian had an innate charm that could not be denied by any of the ladies in the room except for the one whose attention he most coveted.

"Bye then." Addy spoke the two words as she stood and walked towards the piano. Lucian's face fell, his broken heart showing in every feature. He hid his head in his hands and closed his eyes as Addy sat at the piano and began to play a Joplin tune. He paused a moment before standing and gathering his plate and glass, carrying them to the still blushing Mary. Georgie saw him pause at the door and watch Addy play before he exited onto the porch.

"I will be back in a few minutes." Georgie hurried towards the door expecting Lucian to hurry off down the driveway without saying goodbye. Instead, he was waiting at the end of the walk, watching the swans in the pond in front of him.

"Walk with me." Lucian took Georgie's arm and led her towards the small bridge over the pond. They walked in silence until they reached the gazebo and sat on the bench inside.

"Sometimes I hope the things we do for her will make a difference, other times I don't think anything we do will reach her." Lucian spoke quietly, the pain in his voice causing a slight tremor.

"I think you make an incredible difference. She is happy and surrounded by people she loves." Georgie touched Lucian's hand lightly with her own.

"People she loves, except for me." Lucian looked straight forward as he spoke. "I wanted to tell you that I told the police officers all about Addy and Charlie this morning. They had valid questions and deserved my honesty about the situation. They are going to question all the staff about Addy so I guess we will soon find out if she has slipped away from anyone. We both know she has managed it a couple of times but without any repercussions we knew of at the time."

"Lucian, Addy did not hurt Buddy. I know it. She wouldn't do that." Georgie tugged his hand causing him to look at her. She had no idea how beautiful she was with her soft brown curls blowing slightly across her eyes in the breeze.

"I want to believe it too Georgie, just as much as I wanted to believe she couldn't..." Lucian paused. "We have to face the reality of what Addy has done before and make certain she can't be a danger to anyone. I hate it, but I am going to New York to meet with a specialist who treats insane people with violent pasts. They have been secretly trying a surgery on several patients in Europe. He may be willing to help with Addy if it is needed." Lucian turned back towards the pond, his face a mask of stone.

"No, not that, Lucian. Please." Georgie was aware of the trials involving removing part of a patient's brain. It did not cure the patient, but it made several of them calm, without emotion or violent outbursts; the other patients had died from the surgery. Tears ran down Georgie's face as she stood from the bench and walked to the gazebo railing.

"It will be the absolute last resort I promise you." Lucian followed her and turned her to face him. "Do you know what it feels like to think she may have hurt that little boy, and I am responsible? Do you know what it feels like to pour my love into her and receive only coldness back? Do you know this will be my reality for the rest of our lives?" Lucian shook Georgie's shoulders slightly as he asked the questions near his heart.

It was in the moment of feeling his grief and wanting to comfort him Georgie threw her arms around Lucian's neck and drew him close to her. His forehead touched hers in one second and their lips met in the next. His lips were warm and wonderful as he kissed her and drew her even tighter in an embrace. Georgie couldn't think or breathe but she didn't want him to stop.

"I can't. We can't. I have a wife. She doesn't acknowledge me, but I have a wife." Lucian stepped back leaving Georgie bereft. The momentary emotion which crowded Georgie's brain fled, leaving the realization of what had happened and a deep guilt in her heart. She was here to take care of Addy. Addy needed to be her focus.

"I will let you know the information from my meeting with the specialist when I return. Don't let Addy out of your sight and let me know if there are any updates about the boy." Lucian moved past Georgie, walking back the way they had come. They crossed the bridge again and took the path back to the house.

Georgie was so caught up in her own thoughts and emotions she failed to notice the men standing on the porch watching her and Lucian walk back to the cottage together. Her breath caught in her throat as she saw the face of John Maloney, his eyes stormy and brow furrowed. Murphy stood beside him holding a small object in a towel.

"We came as soon as this was found in the river," said John, "because I thought you would want to know. It is obvious Addy is not as well monitored as Mr. St John indicated this morning as we have been waiting here for the two of you for over twenty minutes. This leads our part of the investigation into a new direction." John motioned for Murphy to open the towel.

Detective Murphy unwound the towel from the soaked object as water dripped from it onto the porch. Even in the dimming light of early evening Georgie could see the tattered silk and the chipped porcelain face of the bald doll. She unwittingly grasped Lucian's hand to keep herself from falling to the ground.

Addy loved Laura and they had found the beloved doll in the river.

CHAPTER 12

JULY 27, 1925 – WAUWATOSA ASYLUM FOR THE CHRONICALLY INSANE

The intense July heat was already insufferable as John and Murphy climbed the steps leading into the main building of the asylum hospital. Sweat gathered in beads on John's brow as he stood waiting for the orderly to escort them to the office of the head nurse. His irritation had only increased since visiting the cottage last night and finding Georgie in what appeared to be a romantic tryst with Lucian St. John.

Sleep had evaded him even though the search for Buddy lasted long into the wee hours of the morning; he was exhausted from his efforts and from the mental weariness that had pervaded his thinking. John lay in his bed tossing and turning before finally rising and sitting on the front stoop of the modest house he shared with his sister and her family on Stickney Avenue.

He tried to push any thoughts of Georgie from his head, focusing instead on the objects he had found in the bent oak and how each one might relate to the missing boy. After an hour, John returned to his bed and slept fitfully until dawn.

Murphy had remained unusually quiet this morning, he seemed to understand John needed space to clear his head. The two had checked in with Chief Baltes before heading to the asylum to interview some of the staff members. Both the Chief and DA Wengert were following a lead from La Crosse, Wisconsin. A man had been arrested by a railroad detective there and the description sent by telegraph matched "the man in the blue suit" described by the boys who were with Buddy on the morning of his disappearance.

Baltes was headed for the opposite side of the state to bring the arrested man back, in hopes the boys could identify him as the man who had chased them and taken Buddy. It seemed to John the police chief would go to the ends of the earth to prove that the perpetrator was not local and had been arrested when the entire focus should be on where the little boy was being held.

"Nurse Fielding is ready to see you now, if you follow me this way." The young orderly approached the officers who stood waiting in the main hall. The heavy scent of antiseptic assailed John's nose as he followed Murphy and the young man through the pristine white hallways that combined back and forth to form a sort of labyrinth. They ascended several staircases until they reached the top floor of the building.

The metamorphosis from the unadorned hospital below to this ornately decorated garret was astonishing. A stylish brocade wallpaper met with dark wood wainscotting adorned the walls and a large area rug covered in fleur-de-lis was placed over the hardwood floor. Large bay windows on the other side of the room allowed natural light to flood the room. A roll top desk had been placed on the far wall, but the central figure of the room was a large wooden rocking chair placed in front of the windows facing them and away from the entrance.

The orderly cleared his throat to gain the attention of the woman sitting in the rocking chair. He motioned for John and Murphy to approach her.

"Nurse Fielding, this is Officer John Maloney and Detective William Murphy of the Wauwatosa Police Department. Will there be anything else Ma'am?"

The woman raised her hand in a dismissive gesture, and the orderly fled the room in haste. John noted there weren't any other chairs gathered for visitors as he approached the windows and turned to face the woman. She was at least sixty-five years of age, her graying hair pulled back into a severe bun at the nape of her neck, and her black dress with its high collar making her seem unusually pale. She did not look in John and Murphy's direction at first, she continued to rock in the chair as she gazed out onto the asylum grounds.

"Mr. St. John informed me you had some questions for me regarding his wife." Nurse Fielding had not asked a question; she merely stated a fact.

"Yes, we wanted to ask some questions about Addy's activities on the morning of July 24th. Mr. St. John indicated that the asylum has staff members on the grounds who keep track of her whereabouts." Murphy took his notebook and pen from his pocket.

"The asylum itself does not employ those men; Mr. St. John does in order that Adelyn can make use of the grounds surrounding her cottage. He has put a great deal of money into building up the entire property and employing staff to keep her comfortable including the pretty young nurse he hired to live there. Although at times I can't tell if the nurse is present for Mrs. St. John or Mr. St. John but that is neither here nor there." Nurse Fielding cackled to herself as she touched her palms together, her hands resembling those of a nun in prayer.

"Might we ask you where you were on that morning and if you saw anything of the little boy or Addy?" John's gut recoiled at the woman's mention of the relationship between Georgie and St. John. It was another indication his assumptions about more than just an employer/employee association were correct.

"I live here on this floor," replied Nurse Fielding. "Mr. St. John had this remodeled for my personal use. I didn't see the little Schumacher boy that day although he was known to roam throughout the asylum grounds frequently. He has always appeared to be a well-behaved young man, so no one stopped him from visiting, unlike some of his cohorts who were known to be troublemakers."

"Those other boys often set fires in the reeds near the river and stole baked goods from the asylum kitchen's bakery," Nurse Fielding continued. They were especially brutal to the vagrants who camp along the river. I wouldn't put it past them to have hidden the boy themselves and now they are afraid of the repercussions since the searches began."

Nurse Fielding folded her hands across her lap and continued rocking. "The older Wolf boy is a miscreant, and he picks on the younger boys." Nurse Fielding was referring to the older brother of Buddy's friend, John Wolf, who had admitted to being present that day.

"And did you see Addy that morning? Did she go into the woods?" John asked part of his original question again. The woman had supplied a lot of detailed information but none of it pertained to what he had asked of her, a sign she was attempting to control the narrative to fit her own. The fact she was a loyal recipient of Lucian St. John's philanthropy was not lost on him.

"Yes, I did see Adelyn that morning, right here from this chair as you can see the cottage plainly." She pointed to Cottage 5 on her left and the path to the woods beyond it. "She went up the path towards the cemetery as she does almost every day. An unfortunate wayward girl died right after Adelyn arrived here and she visits the grave daily. She returned in less than fifteen minutes and made her way back into the cottage. I remember thinking how odd it was, as she often spends half the day in the woods, but I assumed it was due to the heat of the day. I also remember Adelyn was not by herself as she walked to the cemetery, but she came back alone." There was a long pause as Nurse Fielding returned her gaze to the windows.

"Who accompanied Addy into the woods that morning?" Murphy paused his notetaking to look up and exchange glances with John.

"Ruth Crane went into the woods with Adelyn and did not return with her. If I were you, I would investigate her instead of Adelyn St. John. She is known to be violent and unpredictable." Nurse Fielding stopped the rocker suddenly, rose from her chair and walked to her rolltop desk on the far wall. She unlocked a drawer and rummaged through it until she found her desired object and withdrew it from the drawer.

"Ruth Crane, the woman who doesn't speak and sits in a chair should be considered as a dangerous suspect. How so?" Murphy shook his head in disagreement with the nurse's assessment of the elderly woman in the cottage.

"The quietest conspirator is the most dangerous," Nurse Fielding cautioned. "The woman was sent here after several children in her care had been mysteriously harmed though she tried to claim her husband was just trying to be rid of her. She violently attacked the young, deceased girl I spoke of earlier then tried to blame her demise on a surgeon who had done a routine procedure successfully. We found the child still in Mrs. Crane's clutches, bleeding to death, her sutures ripped back open."

"I have tried to convince Mr. St. John she is a menace and should be imprisoned, but he insists she is Adelyn's favorite pet. I hope she has not claimed another victim in the meantime." Nurse Fielding held out her hand to them and John and Murphy walked over to observe the object she held. A small daguerreotype in a gold frame showed a younger Ruth Crane surrounded by three little boys.

"All of these boys were in her care, two are missing and one is known to be dead." Nurse Fielding closed her hand around the picture, carrying it back to her desk drawer, locking it away again. "That is all I know, Officers. I will ring for the orderly and he can show you where to find the men who guard Adelyn." Nurse Fielding walked to a rope near the door and pulled it, ringing a bell.

Murphy and John followed the orderly from the garret and down through the hospital towards the entrance.

"If you follow the road to your left, it will take you down past the cottages and towards the woods. Take the path through the woods and after the women's grove there is a garden and then some buildings where the root cellar is located. The men are in one of the buildings there. Mr. St John redid it so they would be on hand all times of the day. They are expecting you." The orderly saw John and Murphy outside the main door before he turned back towards the building.

"It's just as easy to leave the car here by the main building and walk there as to park next to the cottages." John's suggestion brought the first grin of the day from Murphy.

"And no one in the cottage is likely to realize we are present if **she** doesn't see your car." Murphy interjected as the two walked towards the cottages. "What did you make of all of the new evidence? I think the nurse has a few too many conspiracies for my taste."

"I guess so. The only person she didn't accuse of high crimes against humanity is the beloved Mr. St. John, the patron saint of asylums." John glanced around the outside of the cottage as they drew near. He could hear the music from the piano even from a distance. He wondered if they could bypass the cottage and find another path up to the woods.

"Well, he does already have Saint in his name so that is handy." Murphy chuckled at his own pun." I suppose we need to at least note her observations about the Wolf boy and about Mrs. Crane and take them to Kraemer and Zellmer. I am hoping these men St. John hired can account for both Addy and Mrs. Crane's whereabouts that day so we can remove both from the suspect list. It feels like we just keep adding more suspects rather than ruling any out."

"At least we add them to the list and don't try to find one to fit our list. I think the Chief is really searching for someone to fit his bill to go after the man in La Crosse. To blame a tramp or a vagabond will make him feel better. I felt for Mr. Eddy the other day too; I was surprised he didn't end up on the old nurse's whodunit list. Every time we enter these grounds, I hope against hope we will find Buddy alive and well." John lowered his voice as they walked past Cottage 5 towards the path to the woods.

"Officer Maloney and Detective Murphy! I was just heading for the police station to see you. I was remiss in not telling you something last night when you were here." A familiar voice came from the cottage porch making John's blood boil. Georgie stood on the steps. She was pale and there were dark circles under her eyes. She looked as weary as John felt but he was immune to feeling any sympathy towards her.

"It seems you are remiss in telling us quite a few things, Miss Swenson. What is it this time?" The strident tone of John's voice made Georgie wince. Murphy looked from one person to the other and quickly overtook the conversation.

"Did you have something else Georgie? I understand this has not been an easy time for any of us. Maloney here has gone without enough sleep for days and it makes him an old bear at times." Murphy's firm but gentle voice brought tears to Georgie's eyes.

"Yes, when we were in the raspberry patch yesterday morning, I found a small pile of stones arranged and hidden under one of the bushes. Addy was convinced they are part of the stones Buddy collected from the quarry. I covered it back up and left it there so you could see it for yourselves. I meant to say something but when I saw the doll..." Georgie's voice trailed off; tears trickled down her cheeks.

"That is important. We are supposed to meet with the men who were hired to watch over Addy, and I understand their building is located past the raspberry patch. Are you willing to walk with us that far?" Murphy observed John's face closely. His partner was angry but interested in the information.

"Yes, Ingrid is here to watch over... everyone else. She will alert me if they leave the cottage." Georgie stepped off the porch and walked to where Murphy stood. The two of them began walking up the hill with John following them. They made the climb up the hill in an awkward silence, the sounds of the blasting in the quarry bouncing off the bluffs and echoing around them.

"They are using blasts in the deep water of the quarry. The water can get over thirty feet in certain parts, so dynamite blasts are necessary to bring anything from the bottom to the top." Murphy left off in his explanation that they were searching for a body. Georgie nodded.

Soon they reached the raspberry patch past the women's grove. Georgie led them to the stones she had covered under the brambles.

John knelt on the ground and used his handkerchief to gather the stones without touching them. He placed them in a small bag Murphy had for collected evidence.

"These are exactly like the other stones we found and associated with Buddy. Thank you for showing us." John looked at Georgie's face and saw the tears still pooling there. He felt a mixture of anger at her and compassion for her. "If you find anything else, please let us know right away. We are here to find Buddy first but also to find the person who has taken him. I hope in the midst of that we can prove Addy had nothing to do with it, but we must remain unbiased as we collect the evidence. I hope you can understand our position."

"I do understand, and I want to help you. Everything in me wants to believe Addy would never hurt anyone, but I can't stand by if she has hurt a child." Georgie wiped at a tear that had wandered down her cheek. John fished his fresh handkerchief from his vest pocket and handed it to her.

"Thank you. I will walk back while you continue." Georgie smiled tremulously as she dabbed at her eyes then handed the handkerchief back to him. He took it from her and tucked it back in his pants pocket where the few stones from the paper bag were tucked away. He stood for a few moments as Georgie walked away back towards the woods.

John and Murphy took the path to the buildings the orderly had described and found one of the men, Adam Carr, sitting outside the building whittling a piece of wood with a pocketknife. He stood as they approached. He laid the pocketknife on the steps and stuck the piece of wood in his pocket.

"Hot one, isn't it? I am waiting for a good thunderstorm to break this heat. Are you the cops Mr. St. John mentioned? He said you wanted to know about where Miss Addy was on the day the boy disappeared." Adam Carr seemed like an open book, friendly and helpful.

"That's right. Can you tell us who had the watch that morning?" Murphy shook Adam's outstretched hand while looking him in the eye. Adam did not look away from him, which was a good sign.

"Yes, sir. It was me. I had the morning watch. Miss Addy and Miss Ruthie came up to the cemetery that morning and I stood just down the hill at a respectful distance. Miss Addy went back down to the cottage in a short while and Miss Ruthie stayed there in the cemetery for maybe an hour or so before she went back down too." Adam walked back to a bench and picked up an apple from a basket and sliced it with the pocketknife he retrieved from the steps.

He offered apples to Maloney and Murphy who accepted them. He also offered the pocketknife to them. John declined, but Murphy accepted it to cut his apple in half. The crunch of biting into crispy apples pierced the quiet around them. No one was in a hurry to speak.

"So, both women only went as far as the cemetery and then returned home? You are saying you could see both the whole time?" John asked the questions carefully, eliciting some necessary information about both women.

"Yup. I could see both ladies and I saw the little boy too. He ran past them and past me straight up the hill like a scared rabbit. I didn't see him again after that." Adam pointed towards the river below them. "I thought he might be running towards the river, but I can't be sure of it."

Murphy looked at John in amazement. This could have been the last sighting of Buddy before he was abducted. They thanked Adam and walked back down the path through Sanctuary Woods. The piano music still drifted from the cottage as they passed it.

It was early afternoon by the time they reached their desks at the precinct. Kraemer and Zellmer were not present in the general room. When Murphy asked if any of the other officers had seen them, one of the officers replied,

"They both lit out of here an hour ago. A waitress in Columbus swears she saw Buddy with two men, and he was crying and asking for help before they drove away."

CHAPTER 13

AUGUST 10, 1925 – THE SCHUMACHER HOME, 191 ALICE ST., WAUWATOSA

The knock on the front door resounded throughout the Schumacher home on Alice Street. Florence's sister, Gertrude, hurried to answer the door, stopping at the hall mirror to straighten her apron and smooth her hair on the way.

It had been over two weeks since Florence had collapsed from nervous exhaustion after searching for their son for nearly forty-eight hours straight. She had kept to the house under doctor's orders, not appearing for the masses of newspaper reporters who still grouped outside on the lawn.

Gertrude opened the door for Drew Pearson, a reporter from the Milwaukee Sentinel. Drew stood in a blue suit and gray fedora waiting patiently among a throng of other reporters on the doorstep. He had brought a camera with him as instructed by his editor to try and catch an image for the afternoon edition. The other reporters jostled each other to get near him as he made his way up the porch steps.

"Does Mrs. Schumacher have a moment to speak with the rest of us too? We have been waiting a long time to hear from her." Gus Brenner, the reporter from the Wauwatosa News, stepped over the flower bushes to the side of the porch railing to be seen by Gertrude. His publisher, Cornelius Benoy, lived down the street and had been dropping by with various "gifts" for the family in an attempt to gain access to the elusive Mrs. Schumacher, but to no avail.

"I'm sorry. Mrs. Schumacher said she would only speak with Mr. Pearson today. She was very touched to hear he has been donating so much of his spare time helping to search for our boy. He was one of the few who stayed out all night to accompany Mr. Schumacher in his latest search of Koepfler's farmland. Please observe the quiet rule Chief Baltes posted to give the family some peace and quiet." Gertrude pointed to the police order, ushering Drew inside the porch door as she spoke to the other reporters, then firmly shutting the door behind her.

"If you follow me to the dining room, my sister will be down momentarily." Gertrude led the way through the modest and immaculate house to the family dining room where she indicated a chair at the dining table for Drew. "I am sure I don't have to remind you that Florence's health is very delicate right now and you will need to be brief. Would you care for a cold glass of lemonade while you wait?"

"Yes, Mrs. Brown, lemonade would be very welcome. I wonder if you might be able to answer a few of my questions so I don't overtax Mrs. Schumacher? I don't wish to upset her." Drew sat in the chair that had been indicated, setting his notepad and the camera on the table in front of him.

"I suppose I can try although there are some subjects the police have asked us not to discuss. What was it you wanted to know?"

Gertrude paused next to the table while Drew picked the notebook up and took a pen from his suit pocket.

"Can you tell me the family's reactions to the various possible sightings of Buddy over the last two weeks? Do you still hope to find him?" Drew paused, realizing the insensitivity of the rest of the question he was trying to ask. "I'm sorry, Mrs. Brown, you don't have to answer that."

"Well, every time we heard someone saw Buddy in Columbus, in Portage, in Sheboygan, in Packwaukee, and then Oshkosh we felt a modicum of relief followed by intense disappointment when they did not find him. Florence and Art have not given up any hope whatsoever that Buddy will still come home to them alive and well; parents can never give up those hopes, you understand, but the rest of us are preparing ourselves for a different outcome with the passage of time. My greatest hope is he isn't out there suffering alone somewhere." Gertrude lifted the edge of her apron to her eyes as she turned to exit through the kitchen door.

Drew scribbled her answer down on his notepad. A soft rustling sound to his right, near the entrance to the parlor, caused him to look up. A little blonde girl in a bright blue sundress stood staring at him from the arched doorway. She held a teddy bear in her arms which she shifted to hide behind her back as she continued to observe Drew warily.

"Hello! My name is Drew. You must be Jean. How are you today?" Drew smiled his encouragement to the little girl.

"Mama said not to talk to any stranger ever. A stranger took Buddy away. You are a stranger." The little girl's voice was flat and emotionless. She furrowed her brow at Drew, "Did you take my brother? If you did, will you please bring him back now? It makes

Mama cry all the time." Her voice took on a pleading tone that broke Drew's heart.

"Jean, honey, what are you doing in here? Aunt Gertie has some lemonade and cookies in the kitchen for you, why don't you go sit in there and eat them." Gertrude reappeared holding two glasses of lemonade. She set one on a coaster in front of Drew and the other on a coaster at the place opposite him. "She has been in the house way too much but there is really nothing to do about it. The poor little thing is terrified to go outside and play and even has someone sleeping in her room at night because she is afraid someone will come to take her too. I can't blame her, though. I have been trying to convince Florence to let me take her to my home, but my sister won't let Jean out of her sight. Also, understandable. I guess that is more of an answer to your question of how we are all handling this."

Florence Schumacher, a dark-haired beauty, entered the room looking wan and bleary-eyed. She wore a light blue dress, and her hair had been combed and fashioned into an ornate braid that wound over the crown of her head. She held a baby shoe in her hands which she carried to the dining table. laying it in the center of the table between herself and Drew. She sat in the chair that had been pulled out and lifted a handkerchief to her eyes already pooled with tears.

"Good morning, Mrs. Schumacher. Thank you for asking me to visit you. I want to tell our readers your story, but I also want to assure you I don't wish to intrude into your home with numerous questions for you to answer. I wonder if you might like to tell me what you would like for our readers to know." Drew sat quietly hoping Florence would feel free to speak when she was ready.

"Mr. Pearson, thank you for looking for our son. So many reporters have been in our yard day and night, climbing over our fences and trampling our flower beds, but very few reporters have assisted the police in trying to find him. I haven't been well, or I would have gone back out to search myself. My husband suggested if I gave you an interview it might cause someone who knows something about Buddy's disappearance to come forward. I am willing to give a million interviews if it would do that so here, we sit." Florence sat with her hands folded in front of her on the table. She gave a faint smile to Drew before she continued,

"What do I want your readers to know? I want them to know that our son, Arthur Schumacher, Jr is four feet eight inches tall, weighs sixty-five pounds, with sandy brown hair and the most beautiful blue eyes. He is only eight years old. He was wearing blue denim overalls and red canvas shoes that morning. He left to go to Blackridge Island on the Menomonee River, and he didn't return home. I know someone out there may have information about him they might think isn't important or they might think they will be in trouble, but I assure them we only want our son to come home. I would give all I have and more for his return."

A soft sob escaped Florence as she lifted the handkerchief to her lips and closed her eyes. Drew saw the anguish that flowed through her as if the wind had suddenly burst into the room in a gale. He found his hand shook as he wrote her words down in the notebook.

"I don't know what I would do if not for my faith in God," continued Florence. "There isn't any way to make it through this without constant prayer. It's prayer that gives us the courage to go on each day. The members of my church, Mount Olive Lutheran, have prayed around the clock for Buddy's safe recovery. I think there are many others of all kinds of faiths praying for him too. I would ask everyone to lay aside differences in beliefs and just pray because

God is listening." Florence picked up the baby shoe and ran her fingers over it.

"We need to continue our searches every day," continued Florence. "There are objects that have been found which help the police figure out where to look next. The officers and all the people of our beloved 'Tosa' have been tireless in their efforts. I want Buddy to know we are looking for you, darling boy, and Mama and Papa want you to be strong and hold on." Florence closed her eyes and leaned her forehead in her hand while holding her son's baby shoe in her other hand.

Drew realized she had given all she had for the moment in an effort to save her son. He would write his best article so her endeavor would not be in vain.

"Thank you for your time, Mrs. Schumacher. I will see myself out." Drew stood and nodded at Gertrude, who stood in the kitchen doorway, tears streaming down her face. He didn't want any of them to be exposed to the mass of reporters camping outside waiting like vultures for the sight of their tears. Drew walked back the way Gertrude had brought him. As Drew found the foyer, the front door opened, and Art Schumacher entered the house, shutting the front door quickly behind him.

Art's brows rose momentarily at the sight of the reporter standing in his house, but he quickly recognized Drew and shook his hand. He motioned for Drew to follow him to the small study set off the living room, closing the door behind them for privacy.

"I take it, Florence spoke to you. I am glad about it. She needs to feel as if she is doing something, but the truth is there is so little for us to do. I have checked with the police and am considering dressing up as one of the tramps who rides the rails. I will take a few trains to see if the other men who ride the rails will speak to someone of their own set. None of them have been too helpful to the police, I think it's a matter of distrust between the two groups. I have pored over what feels like every inch of this entire village with no results. I will let you know personally anything I am allowed to tell you. Thank you for coming today." Art shook Drew's hand again and led him to the front door.

"Let me know if you need someone to come with you for backup. I would happily help. We will bring your little boy home." Drew paused at the door to watch the expression of the weary man in front of him.

"Mr. Pearson, it's my fear our son is either dead or too far away for me to be of any help, but I am his father, and I will continue on." Art opened the front door for Drew, forgetting in his wearied state, the large group of newspaper reporters gathered who had overheard his every word.

CHAPTER 14

AUGUST 22, 1925 – ALHAMBRA THEATER, WISCONSIN AVE, MILWAUKEE

Georgie stared in awe at the opulent marquee glowing in the Milwaukee twilight; the seventy-five-foot vertical sign could be seen for several miles when lit. She stood waiting with Addy, Mary, and Ella on the sidewalk in front of the massive theater as Lucian and Adam Carr parked the cars further down Wisconsin Avenue. The Alhambra had been built by the Uihlein family of the Schlitz brewery fame and converted from a vaudeville stage to a motion picture movie theater with three thousand seats.

"It looks like a palace from a picture book." Mary whispered to the group describing the Moorish style domes mixed with Roman architecture. "I am a little afraid of being lost in the shuffle." She glanced at the large crowds lining up at the box office to purchase tickets.

"We will all stay together. Don't worry, Mary, we won't get lost." Addy hugged Mary and took Ella's hand in her own. "It reminds me a little of the Taj Mahal in India. My parents took me there when I was a small girl. That mausoleum was built by an emperor who wanted to enshrine the tomb of his wife, he did not wish to be separated from her even in death." Addy's smile of remembrance for her parents gave her an ethereal glow.

"I understand the emperor's wishes. Some people should never be separated. "Lucian's quiet voice interrupted Addy's recollection as he approached from behind. "It's a good thing I already had tickets set aside for a box. It affords us some privacy, and we will walk past this mob waiting to get in." Lucian took Addy's hand and tucked it through his arm, leading the group to the head usher stationed at the entrance.

"I have seats reserved for St. John." Lucian paused before proceeding through the door held open for them. The usher led them through the main lobby, resplendent in cream and gold with tiled floors in a mosaic star pattern. A small elevator took the party to the Mezzanine where the luxury boxes were located. Lucian handed the usher a large gratuity as they took their seats inside their box. Deep red velour draperies hung from the sides of the one-hundred-foot stage displaying an enormous movie screen under the curved proscenium arch.

"Look at the orchestra and the fountain! This is so beautiful it wouldn't matter if there was a picture movie or not." Addy sat between Lucian and Georgie with Mary and Ella on Georgie's other side. Adam had entered the theater with them but then left when they had reached their box. It was well known most of the movie houses had an illegal bar built into the basement area; the Alhambra being no exception.

"Well, there had better be a movie as I have been waiting to take you to this one. Charlie Chaplin is one of the best thespians there is." Lucian chuckled to see the delight in Addy's eyes. "Be prepared to be entertained ladies. I have heard 'The Gold Rush' is his finest work so far. And, as far as the theater goes, it's a dandy. It was the largest in the world for a while."

"I read the architects who built this theater also built the Palace Theater in New York City. Did you see it while you were there?" Georgie looked at Lucian who only had eyes for his stunning wife beside him. Georgie tried to ignore the small pang of guilt she felt over her last meeting with Lucian that had ended in a passionate embrace. Lucian seemed to have forgotten about it entirely, treating her like his employee since returning last week from his trip.

"Hmm? No. I didn't have time for entertainment while I was there, only serious business dealings to address. St. John Steel doesn't run itself." Lucian was polite but distant in his reply. Georgie wondered if consulting with the psychiatric specialists had also been a large part of the serious business. She was hoping Lucian had changed his mind about the drastic treatment for Addy. The last few weeks had been nerve-racking for Georgie, wondering where Buddy was and wondering about what would happen to Addy.

The next ninety-two minutes were filled with the comical fantasy about the Klondike Gold Rush in Alaska. They booed the villain, Black Larsen, and cheered for the hero, Big Jim. The heroine, a beauty named Georgia had Georgie blushing when Addy yelled out, "Our Georgie is prettier than her!"

Georgie was so enthralled by the action and the music; she did not notice Adam sneak into his seat beside Lucian halfway through the film. They all joined in the thunderous applause given at the end of the movie before leaving their box and exiting the building.

The setting of the sun had not lessened the humidity in the air as they strolled down Wisconsin Avenue towards the cars. Spacious, extravagant houses lined both sides of the busy street. Many of the beer barons had built their mansions in this part of the city trying to escape the unfavorable disease-ridden air of Lake Michigan.

They walked along admiring the different architectural styles until they reached Lucian's Rolls Royce parked on their side of the busy street. A Model T was parked a few spaces away with Gregson waiting outside the door. Georgie looked in confusion at Lucian and Adam; Gregson had not accompanied them on their trip to the theater but now he was waiting for them to return.

"Adam will be escorting Ella and Mary back home and Georgie, you are to ride with us." Lucian directed a nervous Ella and Mary towards the other car while Georgie followed them.

"Lucian," said Georgie, "I think Ella and Mary might feel more comfortable if I ride with them as I did on the way here. I don't mind riding in the back." Georgie continued to walk towards the Model T when Gregson stepped in between her and the car.

"I am sorry, Georgie," said Lucian. "There isn't enough room in the back. You will have to ride with us. I am sure the ladies will be fine with these two gents." Lucian turned his dazzling smile on Ella and Mary, who both nodded and followed Adam to the middle seat of the Model T. Georgie stood there staring at the car when Lucian grasped her arm and pulled her towards the Rolls where Addy was waiting in the front seat.

"It's a good idea to always do what I tell you when I tell you, Georgie. Don't forget that." Lucian kept his voice low with a hint of a threat. "We are going to make some changes regarding Addy and it's important for you to remember who is in charge."

Georgie was quiet on the ride home. Addy, as soon as she had noticed Georgie entered the back seat of the Rolls, quickly changed her position from the front passenger seat to the back seat beside her friend. Addy chattered as they drove along Wisconsin Avenue towards Wauwatosa.

"Look Georgie! There is the Central Library, I love that place. All those wonderful books on display and the public museum inside it. And there is Marquette University on the left. They were the first Catholic university to enroll female scholars; my parents were both so impressed with their avant-garde philosophies. In the distance you can see the Pabst Mansion on Grand Avenue. It contains priceless art and sculptures. When I first arrived from Europe, I thought I had left the culture and history behind me, but I love Milwaukee for its old-world atmosphere." Addy pointed at the various landmarks excitedly, her green eyes shimmering with delight.

Normally Georgie would have enjoyed Addy's excitement, but she had sensed a sudden and portentous shift in her relationship with Lucian that left her with suspicion about their trip to the theater tonight. Lucian was obviously hiding something in the Model T, something so important he was willing to threaten Georgie over it.

Georgie now wondered where Adam had been during the movie and how Gregson had shown up out of nowhere. Could Adam have left and met Gregson to obtain whatever was hidden in the back of the Model T? Her mind was whirring with possibilities when it came to a screeching halt as Lucian replied to Addy.

"I think you have missed so many of the things you were used to in Europe my darling. I have been thinking about suggesting a trip abroad for us. What would you think of that, Addy? We would have to leave from New York, but I did some checking while I was there, and passage could still be booked before winter."

"Did you hear that, Georgie? We might go to Europe! I can't wait for you to see Paris and London and especially Edinburgh." Addy hugged Georgie as she squealed with delight, then suddenly turned sober again, "What about Ruthie and Ingrid? We can't leave Freda behind, and Mary and Ella have their work now. How will we ever get all of them ready to go with us?"

"Not everyone will be able to go with us, Addy. I would make sure the others are well cared for in our absence. As for Georgie, I guess the decision is up to her." Lucian glanced behind at Georgie's pale face making direct eye contact with her.

The message was clear. Cooperate with him or he would take Addy far away where Georgie might never see her again. He had the ability to stop helping the other women financially, leaving them destitute and helpless within a system of abuse. The amount of money Lucian had given to the asylum was equal to the power he had to control it and all of them.

The rest of the car ride was silent as Georgie contemplated the almost negligible options left to her. Her one reoccurring thought was of a young Wauwatosa police officer and his gentle partner who had made a large impression on everyone in Cottage 5. She might have to be brave enough to discover whatever Lucian was hiding in the car and then ask for their assistance. Until then she would have to play Lucian's game.

"A trip to Europe sounds perfect, but I think Lucian knows what is best." Georgie's sudden declaration had Addy squealing and Lucian nodding his approval at her seeming acquiescence.

CHAPTER 15

AUGUST 23, 1925 – WAUWATOSA POLICE DEPARTMENT

The small interview room that had been transformed into a central search headquarters was quieter than usual; the large crowds of reporters and citizens having been shown to the lawn outside so the police officers could resume their regular beats.

John and Murphy had moved most of their belongings and files from their regular desks to this room as they spent most of their time on the Schumacher boy's case, leaving their regular calls to the other remaining officers. They sat at the central table with Zellmer and Kraemer who had just returned from another failed attempt to find Buddy.

"I thought for sure this one was it." Kraemer sat with a report from Cudahy in his hand. "A drugstore clerk in the southern suburbs of Milwaukee had sworn he saw Buddy with two men in a touring car with Illinois license plates. The boy was even dressed in clothes that matched the description of what Buddy was wearing when he disappeared. When the men espied the clerk watching them, they sped away but not before the boy cried out for help. I thought we had them and the boy, but they disappeared without a trace."

"It was very helpful that the witnesses in Columbus had written down the license plate number for us when they saw a car with Buddy inside. It was not helpful to find that the same car belonged to an old farmer who said it had not been out of his garage for over a month. The waitress in Columbus who had spotted him was so eager to help find Buddy she volunteered to come with us to Sheboygan and look at the car, but she said it wasn't the same car she had seen even though it was the correct license number. Apparently, it was another dead end." Zellmer related the details of the most recent searches to John and Murphy as he sat at the table and whittled on a stick with his pocketknife.

"We followed the lead to Lake Beulah where more than one witness heard sounds of a child screaming from one of the resort cottages; ended up searching nearly every cottage all around the lake but no one had seen Buddy. How does a child just keep vanishing from sight?" John picked up the stones he had taken from the brown paper bag he had found in the bent oak. He had a strong feeling Buddy might have left those stones there for a reason, but he could not figure out what the reason was and if it related to the disappearance.

"Now, Chief Baltes is pushing the theory that Buddy stayed on the train and fell into one of the ice cars. If it were so, wouldn't someone further down the line have located him as they have been searching all the railroad cars that passed through Wauwatosa? It feels like we are grasping at straws to assume he had an accident when we haven't located him after nearly a month of searching all the ground area, blasting the quarry, and dragging the river three times. That little boy isn't here." Murphy paced the length of the room. "But it begs the question then, of 'where in the world is he?'"

"It's been my experience," said Zellmer, "that an abduction of this nature was perpetrated by more than one individual which would fit with the witness descriptions, but they must have the capability of changing vehicles quickly whenever they need. I think it is a good sign we still have eyewitness sightings which means that Buddy is alive. The news of the seven-year-old boy missing from his home in Chicago last week didn't end as favorably. They found his body in Lake Michigan yesterday and confirmed that he had been molested and murdered only a few hours before they found him."

Zellmer put the stick and his knife down on the table in front of him as he recounted the tragic news. "I think it will be important to consider working all of these missing boys' cases together as though they are related instead of hoping for simple accidents as individual causes. It would be a terrible truth for this area to consider, but it is a necessary one if we want to stop it."

"I agree with you, Zell, but it will be an uphill battle to get the upper ranking officials and the politicians to admit there is a clear and present danger to the public that has not been apprehended. We shouldn't have to battle them along with the bad guys, but it sure feels like we do." Kraemer rose from his seat at the table and went to the chair where he had placed his hat and suit jacket. "Meanwhile, I have a wife and three kids I have not seen for the better part of the week, so I am heading out and spending part of the afternoon with them. Call me at home if anything comes in."

Sergeant Bates appeared in the doorway with a wrapped parcel in his hand. He entered the room, shutting the door behind him. Bates handed the parcel to Kraemer who stood near the door ready to exit.

"Five boys just found this floating in the water near a vacant lot in South Milwaukee. The precinct down there sent it to you boys right away. The Chief said to hide it from everyone else." Bates relayed the message as Kraemer unwrapped the parcel to reveal a piece of wood that had been smoothed with a pocketknife and written on with pencil. Kraemer read the note aloud for the others.

"I killed the Schumacher boy for revenge. I tied a stone around his neck and threw him off a government pier near a quarry. You will never find me, but you might find him if you look. Signed, Tommy Sutton."

Kraemer held out the scrap of wood to Zellmer then turned back to Bates. "Call my wife at home and tell her not today." Kraemer rejoined the group at the table.

"Blackridge, the original swimming hole, might fit this description but we have searched up and down along the Menomonee River. The only government pier I recall is the one up near Port Washington. The Belgium area nearby has a quarry with deep water. It will pay to make the trip up today and call for blasting that quarry if the information warrants it. We have to follow every lead, but I can't help feeling that someone keeps leading us on these wild goose chases for a reason." Zellmer stood, placing his pocketknife back in his pants pocket and grabbing his coat and hat.

"Zellmer and I will head to Port Washington and call if we need more help in the search," said Kraemer. "You and Murphy can head back towards Blackridge with the description from the note in hand to see if it fits the details too. This is a strong clue because we purposely withheld the information about the revenge note to Art Schumacher from the newspapers and now someone is admitting it is revenge.

Very few people knew about that." Kraemer led Zellmer from the room while John copied the note into his notebook. Murphy gathered the rest of the evidence to secure it in the Chief's office before they left the building.

John's car pulled off Watertown Plank Road onto the driveway of the asylum. The ornate granite pillars lined the entrance as they made their way up the curved parkway towards the entrance to Sanctuary Woods near Cottage 5. They had decided it was easier to access Blackridge through the woods rather than drive through the rough path fashioned for the future Menomonee River Parkway.

As they rounded the curve leading to the cottage, Georgie appeared, walking along the lane towards them. She looked startled to see them, but she waved to hail them as they approached. John pulled the car over into the grass, allowing room for other possible cars to pass by them. Murphy noticed Georgie was trembling even though she kept a smile on her face as she opened the passenger side door and climbed in beside him.

"I was just coming to find you two. How did you know I needed your help?" Georgie looked around them as she spoke. Murphy glanced at John quickly, noting her nervous behavior before he responded.

"Well, we seem to have a sixth sense when it pertains to the ladies of Cottage 5. What help did you need?" Murphy smiled at Georgie, encouraging her to continue.

"I might be overreacting, but I have been very apprehensive since we returned from an outing in downtown Milwaukee last night. I rode with Mary and Ella with Mr. Carr driving the Model T to the theater, but Lucian wouldn't allow me to return with them. He insisted I ride with him instead." Georgie wrung a white handkerchief in her hands as she spoke.

"Might he enjoy your company? Was there something else that caused your concern?" Murphy tried to remain unbiased as he asked the questions, but John was more direct.

"Did he attempt to make advances towards you? Has he harmed you in any way?" John's voice rose as he asked the questions until he noted tears forming in Georgie's eyes. "I'm sorry. I didn't mean to upset you, Georgie. I am only trying to protect you."

"Can you tell us what happened Georgie?" Murphy interrupted John trying to put the young woman at ease.

"No, Lucian didn't try anything. Addy was right there. I started to ignore him and go to the other car, and he grabbed my arm and forced me to follow him. I have never seen him like that. It made me think he might be hiding something in the back of the Model T he didn't want me to see. Mr. Carr and Gregson, the usual driver, also acted suspicious. Gregson had not accompanied us to the theater but then he suddenly appeared out of nowhere for our return. It could be my sensitivity to being treated in such a way, but I wanted to know what was in the car. I had decided to look once we returned home."

"You didn't go out there and look for yourself, did you? Georgie that could have been dangerous!" John interjected his concern.

"I planned to go and look but I was too frightened of what I might find so I decided to come and find you." Georgie admitted. "Lucian had them park the Model T in front of the cottage last night and it has been there ever since. He left a little while ago to meet with the Police Chief; he intends to raise the reward for finding Buddy by another $500. It won't be long until he returns or until they move the car, so we don't have much time."

"Well, let's go take a look then." Murphy nodded at John to pull the car back onto the driveway. It only took a few minutes to get to the cottage where they could see the Model T parked off to the side under a tree. John parked his car on the other side of the cottage obscuring it from view and the three of them walked towards the front of the cottage. They paused at the porch railing to look up the path leading to the woods; no one appeared to be in sight of the cottage.

"We do have a problem with opening the back of the car if we don't have a warrant to search it. Anything we find could be thrown out as evidence if we found it in an illegal manner." Murphy stood facing the woods, scanning the trees carefully as he spoke to the other two standing behind him.

"I think I might have an idea," said Georgie. "Would it be illegal if one of us opened it and you were able to look over our shoulder? I was willing to open it by myself; I should be willing to open it with two policemen standing here with me." Georgie's suggestion made John wince. He didn't want her to be involved at all.

"What are you looking for?" Addy appeared in the doorway of the cottage with Ruthie beside her. Georgie glanced at John before answering her.

"I remembered I left my light blue sweater somewhere last night and I wondered if I might have left it in the back of the Model T." Georgie's answer had Addy nodding her head in agreement. Addy marched over to the parked car without hesitation and tugged on the rumble seat to open it. John and Murphy positioned themselves so they could have a full view of the back seat.

Addy tugged harder on her second attempt and the seat popped open. Her melodious laughter filled the air as she pointed to the rumble seat and the crates stacked neatly inside it.

"No sweater here, Georgie. Just tons of apples. Did you check in the hallway for it? I will go and look for you." Addy left the back of the car open and skipped towards the house to find the missing sweater.

"I'm sorry to have bothered you with this. Obviously, I over-reacted to the situation last night and then let my imagination run wild. I feel bad for taking you away from more important matters." Georgie walked over next to the rumble seat and picked up one of the apples from the crates.

"Most likely Lucian brought these back for Mary and Ella to preserve with the other fruits we have been making. He is very considerate towards them." Georgie carried the apple to Ruthie who stood watching all of them on the porch.

Murphy stepped closer to the car, examining the crates and the content within them. Piles of ripe apples filled the crates giving off a strong fruity aroma. Murphy shrugged as he closed the latch to the back seat again.

"I guess we will add this to our list of standstill leads for the week. I hope Kraemer and Zellmer are getting better results." Murphy muttered to himself before he walked back to where Georgie stood on the porch. "We need to get to Blackridge while there is still enough daylight. If you are concerned about anything else Georgie, let us know and don't go investigating on your own. It was the right idea to bring this to us."

"I thought there would be something more substantial in the car. Why would he be so concerned about a bunch of apples?" John voiced his thoughts as the two walked through Sanctuary Woods. The path was shaded and provided momentary relief from the heat of the day as they walked through the Women's Grove and past the bent oak towards the river.

"I don't know what Mr. St. John thinks, but I can pretty much tell you what you think." Murphy led John to the area on the riverbank that had been trampled by the masses of people searching. They read the description from the note and looked around the area to find any similarities. The tall reeds along the river rustled as an unkempt man emerged onto the path in front of them. Upon seeing the two officers the man pointed back towards the reeds angrily.

"Come and see what someone did to my home. Why would they wreck it? I didn't do nothing to nobody." The man gestured for John and Murphy to follow him through the reeds where a small fort had been constructed as a dwelling.

Small objects were scattered around littering the ground and crude furniture had been broken down into pieces and strewn along the riverbank. John was irate at the carelessness of those who had ransacked the poor man's humble dwelling. He reached into his vest pocket and produced several coins, handing them to the man while Murphy tried to collect the scattered things on the ground, piling them in a semblance of order. All the broken furniture was beyond repair, so they stacked it to make a pile of firewood for the man in a cleared area just beyond the reeds.

"What is it I think?" John had suddenly recalled Murphy's earlier statement as the two worked together to reconstruct a makeshift dwelling using new sticks dragged from the nearby trees and strong reeds cut out of the riverbank.

"You think it isn't noticeable to me that you are falling for Georgie Swenson, and you would be wrong about that." Murphy chuckled at the incredulous look on his partner's face. "I don't blame you at all for feeling that way, she is a remarkable young woman. I want to remind you we need to get this case solved first and find that little boy, so you aren't accidentally compromising your part of the investigation. If it's a real thing it will wait and if it's not, you're better off not jumping in too quickly." Murphy moved another pile of debris aside to set the pole he held into the ground.

"Maloney, come here and look at this." Murphy knelt next to the spot he had just cleared, pointing at what he had found.

A small pile of smooth quarry stones matching the ones from the raspberry patch and the ones John found in the bag in the bent oak stood in the cleared-out area in front of them.

"Do you know anything about these stones?" Murphy asked the hobo who came to stand beside him. He shook his head.

"I ain't seen those before and a couple of the other things left behind too. I think someone was staying here while I was visiting down the line a bit for the last month. That's a common thing among our folk but it ain't common to tear the place apart after using it. No one would do that to another guy's house in the jungle." The hobo indicated the reeds that grew thick around them by the term the vagrants of the area used for them. "It's a good hiding place when a fella needs to lay low awhile, but you treat other's houses with respect."

John scooped up the stones into his handkerchief, placing them into his pocket while Murphy fished out some more spare change and handed it to the man in front of them.

"You let us know right away if you see anything else out of sorts and we will make sure no one bothers you down here." Murphy shook the hobo's hand before both officers turned towards the path leading back to Sanctuary Woods.

As they approached the bent oak the sound of a woman singing floated along the breeze in the twilight. John paused at the base of the tree peering upwards into the branches that spanned the skyline above them. The voice had almost an ethereal quality; the Scottish lilt matched the call of the mourning doves perched in the lower branches.

'Hie thee home, bonny boy. Hie thee home.
The day grows long waiting for thy return.
Hie thee home.'

"She climbs the bent oak every day at twilight and sings. Buddy has always loved to sit and listen to her sing, so she is sure it will bring him home. I pray she is right." Georgie sat on a log nearby looking at Addy in the tree above them.

Ruthie sat next to Georgie fashioning a daisy chain from numerous flowers gathered in her lap. She placed the finished crown of yellow and white flowers on Georgie's head then leaned her head against Georgie's shoulder as they sat and listened to Addy's song.

'Hie thee home bonny boy. Hie thee home.
Answer the call of the Siren's song.
Hie thee home.'

CHAPTER 16

AUGUST 24, 1925 – SUCKER BROOK, PORT WASHINGTON

Adolph Kraemer stood at the shore as numerous boats laden with men dragged the small lake near Sucker Brook. Grappling hooks with ropes attached were plunged into the depths until the hooks hit the bottom of the lake where they were dragged by the motion of the boats.

An occasional shout would go up among the assembled searchers, one of the hooks would snag a heavier object and all would wait in silence while the object was brought to the surface. Each time, Kraemer had a mental war within himself about what outcome he wished for; his first inclination was they would not find the little boy this way and the second inclination was they would find him and put an end to his family's suffering and his own overwork as well.

Kraemer looked down at the hastily written note from his wife, Betsy. The missive had been delivered when they brought the equipment and the board with the message scribbled upon it from the precinct to him and Zellmer in this desolate area slightly north of Port Washington. Both officers had spent the night in the car in a nearby quarry after speaking to numerous local witnesses.

All the witnesses had confirmed they had seen two suspicious men with a little boy around the pier nearly four weeks previous. This had been the strongest lead since the sighting in Columbus, but Kraemer knew he had to remain impartial and dispassionate that this would be the conclusion of their month-long search for Buddy. Each failure to find the boy became more excruciating than the last.

Zellmer sat on a knoll above the lake watching the men who dragged the river and the crowds of curious onlookers who lined the lakeshore. He sat on a small camp chair holding a newspaper in his hands. His dark sunglasses covering his eyes and the small Kentucky cheroot hanging from his mouth gave him an air of disinterest in the proceedings; most people looking at him would presume Zellmer was a lazy slacker, but Kraemer understood his partner better than most.

Kraemer knew Zellmer had separated from the crowd in a slightly elevated position so he could carefully survey all the people present without their knowledge. More than once in their investigations the astute officer had observed the small idiosyncrasies of behavior that led to finding suspects in the gathering crowds. Many times, the suspect would return to assist the authorities in a search.

"We have something!" A yell went up from one of the boats hushing the buzzing crowds into an eerie silence. The man pulled at the rope he was holding with the assistance of two other men. The object in the murky water below was heavy.

Kramer turned to glance at Zellmer who was scanning the crowds watching for anyone who showed an unusual interest or anyone who might be devoid of emotion or those who showed too much emotion.

Kraemer did not have Zellmer's ability to detect criminals in this manner, but he respected his partner's expertise.

Kraemer looked at the crowd gathered on the shore, most of them every day working folks with morbid senses of curiosity. Word had traveled through the small town like lightning and by daybreak that morning a huge group had gathered along with the newspaper reporters who seemed to circle Kraemer and Zellmer like vultures wherever they went. Kraemer recognized one of the reporters from the Milwaukee Sentinel, Drew Pearson, as the reporter approached him on the pier.

"Chief Baltes said this was a wild goose chase but from the looks of the board you received, it most likely came from this very pier." Drew kicked at the old footings holding the pier in place. There were several loose boards that could be easily removed, a fact Kraemer had already noted in his investigation of the area yesterday.

"Mr. Schumacher wanted to come out here with me but I talked him out of it. No one should find their child like this and have this memory ingrained in their head. He finally relented and stayed at the house with Mrs. Schumacher for the morning. He insists he will go out searching near Koepfler's farm again this afternoon. I think every blade of grass has been searched there and throughout Sanctuary Woods and Blackridge, but I can't say I would do anything different if I were Buddy's father." Drew stuck both of his hands in his pockets as he observed the process out on the lake. His face showed his concern for the family.

"A father would do anything he could to find his child." Kraemer agreed with the statement without giving any additional information. While this reporter appeared to have more compassion than the rest, he was still the press and should be considered off limits for investigating officers. "How did you happen to see the board you mentioned?" A small trigger of suspicion prompted Kraemer's question. It had been a well-known tactic for the newspaper reporters to invent clues for the police to find and thereby produce more stories that sold more newspapers.

"Chief Baltes showed the board at the precinct yesterday. He said it was a hoax and while you and Detective Zellmer were insistent on investigating it, he was aiding in the investigation by distributing over two thousand flyers all over the country. Lucian St. John was there with the Chief and the District Attorney; he has offered another five hundred dollars to the reward money and pledged more help be brought in from private investigators." Drew turned to face Kraemer momentarily,

"Mr. Schumacher doesn't want to accept the extra money. He and his wife feel you and Detective Zellmer along with Officer Maloney and Detective Murphy are the only ones who have Buddy's best interest at heart. Most of the rest of this has brought publicity they did not ask for or desire and has only detracted from finding their son. I am sure this is taking a toll on all of you, but I wanted you to know their thoughts about your efforts."

Kraemer felt the tightening of emotion in his throat. He continued to look out at the lake as he cleared his throat and gave a slight nod in the reporter's direction. The two stood in silence waiting for a signal from the boat. The object, at least three feet long and dark in color, had just come to the surface.

"It's just another tree log. Everybody get back to it." The shout reached the shore causing a buzz of conversation among the crowd and a wave of relief for Kraemer. He found in the honesty of that moment of discovery that he wanted to keep searching until they could bring Buddy home alive and well, no matter what the odds against that conclusion and no matter how great his own personal sacrifices were.

"Tell the Schumacher's we won't ever give up." Kraemer said quietly as he walked away from the reporter and off the pier. He noticed Zellmer had risen from his chair and seemed to be staring straight down in front of him into the crowd below. Kraemer walked up the knoll until he reached his partner at the top.

"I saw the reporter speaking to you," said Zellmer. "He seems genuine enough unlike a few of the others, but I have been watching him, nonetheless." Zellmer pointed to the far shore of the small lake, an inlet of land which stood between the smaller body of water they were searching and Lake Michigan beyond it. "This reminds me of the 'rum coves' they have discovered near Racine. Captain Olander of the Racine Police Department has found evidence that bootleggers are using the coves to smuggle whiskey into Wisconsin from Michigan and they are taking some of the moonshine distilled here in the state and sending it out. This place is hidden just like those, and few people venture out here except the occasional fisherman."

"I suppose this type of spot could be used for various kinds of criminal activity," said Zellmer. "As curious as the townspeople are I would wonder if they didn't see anything. Everyone seems to know everyone else's business around here. Maybe we need to ask about different types of suspicious behavior instead of a specific sighting of a little boy. It could lead us back around to the boy."

Kraemer could see the wisdom in Zellmer's opinion. One criminal activity often spawned another. "Chief Baltes just dealt another blow," said Kraemer. "He showed the board with the message to the press so there isn't any way for us to keep the information confidential now. We still have it as evidence, but it has been compromised."

At the news, Zellmer threw the folded newspaper he had been holding in a rare show of temper. He turned to face the lake again, his mouth set in a determined straight line.

"We realized we couldn't trust most of them with this and he appears to want to prove it daily. I am going to drive into town and try to call Murphy and Maloney at the precinct. I think they are the only ones we keep in our information circle from here on in. These political antics could be the death of that little boy." Zellmer turned to walk down the knoll towards the car parked near the pier.

"Tell them to send the dive team from the Port of Milwaukee tomorrow morning. We need to exhaust this lead, and the dragging of the lake is getting us nowhere again." Kraemer tried to keep the frustration he was feeling from his voice. He walked to Zellmer's camp chair and seated himself while removing Betsy's note from his coat pocket to reread.

The words written across the page were written by an angry wife who felt neglected,

"You were missed this afternoon as you are every day by your family Bobby hit a home run in the baseball game you were supposed to attend. Instead of feeling happy your son feels sad because once again you were not there to see it. It makes me wonder that while you are looking for a lost son if you will ultimately lose your own."

Kraemer understood his wife's pain and agreed with her wholeheartedly. His family made greater sacrifices than most people would ever recognize or understand in order for him to be able to bring home the lost and protect the public from those who wished to harm them. Someone had taken Buddy Schumacher and possibly other boys, and he meant what he had told the reporter earlier.

"We won't ever give up."

CHAPTER 17

SEPTEMBER 2, 1925 –
THE SCHUMACHER HOME,
191 ALICE ST., WAUWATOSA

The long rays of the afternoon sun illuminated the Schumacher dining room with brilliant beams of light. Dust motes danced in the beams, a testament to the negligence of the daily housekeeping that had once been Florence's utmost priority. She sat at the dining room table, set in the customary service for four, holding Buddy's slingshot in her trembling hands.

How many times had she reprimanded her son for carrying the slingshot to the table and laying it on the crisp white tablecloth next to her second-best China, the blue willow pattern with the exotic pagodas and gold rims? Now she would give anything for him to skip through the door in his jaunty little boy way, his blond hair mussed and lay this very slingshot on her precious white cloth.

Florence stood and walked to the large windows that overlooked their front lawn. It was quiet. The huge crowds of reporters had left over a week ago leaving her flower beds trampled and ornate shrubs broken down in their wake.

The street had returned to a remnant of what it had been before Buddy disappeared over five weeks before, an orderly tree-lined avenue with children running up and down the sidewalks and the sounds of screen doors opening and slamming shut as little boys arrived home for dinner.

Did those mothers know what a blessed sound that irritating screen door was? The herald of their sons returning home to them safe and sound. Florence touched the windowpane where a shaft of sunlight pierced it. She imagined touching a little face often smudged with dirt. The memory made her smile momentarily.

Her sister Gertrude had returned to her family in North Prairie taking Jean with her. At first, Florence had been opposed to the idea of Jean leaving, the thought of her little girl being out of sight caused her to panic. Gertrude had patiently explained that Jean needed the respite from the daily vigil of searching for her brother.

The once bubbling, expressive child had become shy and fearful of the world outside their door. School would soon begin again, and Jean had been cloistered inside the house since that fateful day in late July. She needed fresh air and sunshine and the chance to play with other children again.

Gertrude had given Florence her solemn vow that Jean would be under her protective watch the entire time. Finally, Florence's mother, the formidable Alice Armstrong, had intervened on Jean's behalf, sending the child off with her older daughter after taking Jean out to the local Wauwatosa shops to purchase new clothing for the school year.

Jean had returned from the shopping trip with Granny Armstrong laden with packages containing new dresses, underclothing, a new coat, and three pairs of shoes, her face beaming for the first time in weeks. Florence had realized in that moment Jean needed the "normal things" of her life to return and at this point in time she and Art would not be able to give Jean those things. She had helped pack the little blue suitcase that had also been purchased by Granny Armstrong for the visit to North Prairie.

Jean had asked to take one of Buddy's stuffed bears with her, an old worn-out one he had named Fred. Florence's first thought was to keep all her son's toys together just as he had left them in his room, knowing the last person to touch each precious plaything had been him, but then she caught the look of sadness in Jean's eyes and realized her daughter needed the comfort more.

Jean had left the house with Fred in her arms waving to Florence and Art as she hopped in the back seat of Uncle Charles's car. Florence had fought the thought she might never see Jean again and waved to her, a smile masking her overwhelming fears.

The house was too quiet at times, Art had left early each morning to continue his search, always checking at the police station for an update on his way home to her. Florence made simple meals and did the routine tasks of washing dishes, washing clothes, and making beds, her constant anxiety sapping her strength for other work. She no longer cared what her neighbors might think if they saw her house as anything but perfect. There were far more important cares in her world.

Even her usual impeccable grooming- a meticulous hairstyle, elegant makeup, and manicured hands had reverted to neatly combed hair pulled back from her face and a washed face without other adornment. Dark circles had appeared under her eyes seemingly overnight giving her large eyes a forlorn look. She had lost at least twenty pounds; her fashionable dresses hung on her gaunt frame like a child wearing their sibling's hand me downs that were still too large.

The most noticeable change in her appearance was the gray hair now framing her careworn face in streaks. Stress had altered her appearance to such a degree that her own mother was taken aback after witnessing the transformation in just a few weeks' absence from her.

Florence noticed a car pulling into their driveway, Officer Maloney and Detective Murphy stepped from it and approached her front door. Her heart hammered so hard in her chest that the sound of it in her ears almost drowned out the sound of the doorbell. Florence walked to the door, she had to force herself to move, dreading the possible news the officers might be bringing while she was here all alone.

She was vulnerable, susceptible to all forms of physical and emotional attacks, terrified, her heart longing for the caring arms of her husband to protect her at this moment. A realization jolted her as she reached for the doorknob; was this what Buddy had felt at the moment he was taken? Hot tears sprang into her eyes. She needed to be brave just as she needed him to be brave until they could find him.

"Good afternoon, Mrs. Schumacher. We are sorry to disturb you at home." John paused in his greeting to take in the terrified visage of the woman standing before him. He reached out to steady her, the trembling of her limbs causing her to sway and grasp the doorway for support. "Mr. Schumacher asked us to stop by with an update of the search near Port Washington after we had not found anything else last week. Could I help you inside where we can find a seat for you? We haven't brought any tragic news Ma'am." John understood her slight nod as permission; he held her arm and saw her back to the dining room where they had received the officers several times already.

"Thank you, Officer Maloney. I'm afraid I don't know when Mr. Schumacher will return this afternoon. Sometimes he is home by now but other days he is gone until late in the day. We used to be able to tell the time by his nightly arrival at six o'clock, but nothing is as it used to be as I am sure you understand." Florence sat at the table staring at the slingshot still lying where she had left it.

"We could say we understand, but in truth, we can't even imagine what you are enduring." Detective Murphy's quiet voice came from the chair to Florence's right, the chair that belonged to Buddy. "As Officer Maloney mentioned, we brought an update on our search near Port Washington. After a thorough search by Detectives Kraemer and Zellmer no further evidence was located in the area. It is yet another failed attempt to locate your son," Murphy paused to gather the best choice of words.

"You didn't find our son's body." Art Schumacher stood in the doorway leading into the dining room from the kitchen. He had entered the house from the back door unnoticed. "We don't view that as a failure on your part. Lord knows the four of you have searched without ceasing and we appreciate your willingness to continue even though everyone else has moved on to other things."

Art moved into the dining room, stopping behind Florence's chair and putting his hands gently upon his wife's shoulders. "We have to believe that the lack of finding his remains means there is still a chance our son is alive."

"There is still a chance, and we will not stop searching with that in mind." John nodded his reassurance as he looked into the teary eyes of the lost boy's mother. "Detective Zellmer left for Fort Wayne, Indiana yesterday. He and Detective Kraemer have been sending notices to Salvation Army kitchens all over and volunteers in Indiana insist a boy matching Buddy's description was seen riding on the back of a truck with Illinois license plates two days ago. Detective Kraemer sends his greetings to you; he took an afternoon off today to attend his son's last baseball game of the season. He felt bad for giving up some time for the search today."

"Tell him never to feel regret over spending time with his boy. There are so many things I wish I had done differently with our son and if I get a second chance, I will not be hesitant to forget about the small things that seemed so important and are not a priority at all in comparison now. God only loans us our children for a very short time in life before they are grown. Things like slingshots at the dinner table are now a welcome sight instead of a rule infraction." Florence picked up the slingshot and handed it to Murphy.

"This is a fine example of a slingshot. Did Buddy use a particular type of rock with it? Some boys have favorite things like that." Murphy's question caught John's attention immediately.

"Oh my, yes," said Florence. "His favorite rocks come from the local quarry. Small, round, smooth stones of a certain weight. There was hardly a washday that I wasn't picking stones from his pockets as he carries them all the time. He is a good boy; he doesn't shoot at birds or animals like some of the neighbor boys, but he loves shooting at targets of bad guys he makes. Now I wish he hadn't forgotten it at home that day." Florence took the slingshot back and held it in her hands as she spoke.

"Thank you, Mrs. Schumacher. You have just helped us more than you know. As Detective Kraemer keeps reminding us; all the information we receive is important because the small pieces make up the whole part. It looks like you are planning a dinner so we will leave you to it." John stood and shook Art's hand.

"We weren't necessarily planning dinner. I set the table as I have always done it, for the four of us. I would like to ask if you might like to stay for some cake. I know it's nearly dinner time but today is

Buddy's ninth birthday and I had the bakery bring his cake just as we have always done it. It would help me to share it with both of you." Florence lifted her eyes to John where he stood and then to Murphy who still sat beside her. Art's eyes filled with tears as he tried to smile in agreement with his wife's request.

"Nothing would give us more honor. Thank you for sharing it. I think cake for dinner is a great idea for all of us." John took the seat to the left of Florence as Art headed to the kitchen. He returned with a double layer chocolate cake with chocolate frosting and set it next to Florence. She cut the generous slices and handed them to each person around the table. Florence then spoke to her missing son.

"Happy Birthday, Buddy. Mama, Papa, Jean, and everyone else loves you so so much."

CHAPTER 18

SEPTEMBER 7, 1925 – SANCTUARY WOODS

Addy sat in her perch atop of the bent oak watching the golden leaves swirling in the breeze. She loved autumn in Wisconsin best of any season she had endured since leaving her beloved Scotland. It had already been six years of her life in the United States, the land of "opportunity", the nation that welcomed 'the tired, the poor, the huddled masses yearning to breathe free.'

She had witnessed immense beauty like the showering of leaves in a myriad of colors before her eyes, but she had also witnessed the ugliness of hatred, bigotry, and privilege that tried to rear its head against the bastion of democracy in this new country.

She believed that, just like her ancestral homeland of Highlanders, American citizens would need to keep constant vigil against the enemy within who would lure them into surrendering their own rights and responsibilities to the divine right of kings that was anything but divine.

She realized few people stood in the gap against authoritarian tyranny but those who did stood with such ferocity of heart and courage it made the oligarchies tremble. There must always be those who stand for the right even when everyone else stands against them. Addy knew she was one of those people.

Addy relished her few rare moments of complete solitude. She loved the group of women who lived in Cottage 5, but there were times when she needed to be alone with her thoughts. She pulled a copy of the New York Times from her bag, having had to hide the newspaper to read it.

Lucian brought copies with him to the cottage but assumed that as women their only use for his leftovers was to repurpose them for lining shelves and cleaning windows. In Lucian's world women weren't supposed to think independently or form their own opinions separate from those of a man. Addy couldn't truly live in Lucian's world.

Addy had been fascinated by the newspaper articles describing the development of Albert Einstein's Theory of Relativity and the description of the finding of the burial place of Tutankhamun in the Valley of the Kings. In a more notorious vein, she had read that a man named Adolf Hitler who had led a failed coup in Germany, wrote his first volume of *Mein Kampf* which extolled the Aryan race as superior to others, a gangster named Al Capone had moved his criminal syndicate operations from New York to nearby Chicago, and in Italy, Benito Mussolini had declared himself a dictator.

Her heart had soared over the articles on the Great Serum Run, the brave journey which took a diphtheria antitoxin by dogsled over the wilds of Alaska to rescue people from an epidemic of the deadly disease. Addy understood from these articles that the world was a much larger place outside Cottage 5, but many of those far-reaching events would personally affect her. She had learned from her parents to think and act as a citizen of the world rather than a citizen of a small place in one country.

Addy folded the newspaper after reading it entirely. She placed it back in her bag to be tucked away under her bed with the others. She saved the newspapers to help ground herself in the reality around her when so many things tried to pull her from reality. Georgie had discovered the hidden cache during a spring-cleaning last year and had nicely left it alone, attributing the collection to Addy's mental dysfunction.

Addy's thoughts turned to recent events in Cottage 5. Lucian had mentioned returning home to Scotland again the previous night. He seemed more inclined than ever to travel with her and Georgie. Addy had been elated at the initial idea, but now huge reservations loomed before her. She had wanted to return home knowing Scotland could never be a real home to her without her parents there.

The beauty of the landscape and the richness of traditions would only sustain her for a short while before she realized her true home was with the women who surrounded her daily in their little cottage. Lucian had put large amounts of money in a trust to provide for the cottage and its inhabitants while Addy resided there but what might happen to them if she didn't? Lucian's benevolence only extended as far as his equity in any project. Addy recognized her responsibilities for her friends who had become her family.

It was during her reflection that Addy discovered a small kitten scaling the huge bent oak towards the perch where she sat. The kitten's soft gray fur had black diluted tortoiseshell swirls that were remarkable even from a distance. The tiny animal's trek along the steep trunk up to the higher branches fascinated Addy, the kitten's tenaciousness overcoming its fear of falling from the lofty height.

It continued the perilous climb though its slight body was trembling from exhaustion and fright. Addy knew better than to climb down and attempt to rescue the kitten, it would certainly fall from struggling to free itself of her unsolicited assistance. Her good intentions would only result in its tragic end.

"Keep climbing, Cat. You can do it." Addy called down to the creature from her perch just above it. "Don't look down at the ground and where you have been, focus on the sky above and keep going." Addy spoke the words of encouragement to her own heart as well as to the shaking feline still climbing slowly towards her. She was rewarded with the sound of a soft purr from the cat as it recognized her as a friend instead of a foe. It continued its climb, gaining speed, as it looked straight at Addy and her outstretched hands.

"Well, look at what you have done all by yourself. Quite a feat for a tiny creature." Addy welcomed the kitten as it scrambled from the branch onto her lap, burrowing its fluffy gray head into the folds of her apron. It began to turn around several times, finding a comfortable place to lie down and was soon curled up, fast asleep.

Addy stroked its soft fur and looked at the gorgeous swirls on its side up close; it reminded her of a work of art that would hang in the Louvre. Small snores emitted from the creature making Addy chuckle out loud, her heart was already completely smitten.

"I wonder where you came from. You don't seem very old, maybe just recently separated from your mama and your littermates." Addy spoke in a low tone to the sleeping kitten not wishing to frighten it. "Not to worry little one, I will keep you safe until someone comes to claim you." Addy stroked the kitten again receiving a sleepy purr and a stretch of the little legs out in front of it. She untied her apron strings and wrapped the kitten snugly in the apron then placed it in her bag which she wore slung across her chest.

The kitten started for a moment then returned to its slumber while Addy gathered her things to depart. She glanced briefly at the farmland across from the woods and espied a young couple partaking in a late day picnic by the path that wound through Koepfler's farm.

Many of the members of the various search parties had returned to their normal everyday tasks including the school children who had begun a new school year leaving Sanctuary Woods and the riverbanks in an eerie quietness.

Addy climbed down from her perch with a steadfastness that exhibited her years of practice. The kitten slept through their entire descent and continued sleeping as Addy followed the path back to the cottage. Each step towards home filled her with the resolve to stay with her family in the only safe place she knew. If Lucian was determined to travel to Europe, he would have to do so without her.

Addy and the kitten received a joyous welcome upon their return. Each woman took a turn holding and petting the newcomer to their household. Ingrid found a small crate and a fleecy blanket to create a bed while Mary poured a small saucer of milk and chopped a bit of leftover fish for a meal. The kitten ate hungrily then jumped to Ruthie's lap and settled down for a nap while she stroked its fuzzy head. Even Georgie agreed the kitten was a wonderful addition to their household.

"Cats are always good to have to chase away the rodents although this guy might have to grow a little bit first." Georgie grew up on a large farm in Minnesota where barn cats were a necessity. She could also clearly see all the others loved the little beast who had already made their house his own.

"In Scotland a gray tortoiseshell cat is considered a harbinger of good luck as well as the black cats. I was surprised when coming to America how many people shunned the black cats, thinking they were bad luck omens. To have such a cat here is certainly a sign of the hope for good things." Addy smiled as the kitten jumped from Ruthie's lap onto Freda's, rubbing its body against the blind woman's hands eliciting a delighted giggle from her.

"We welcome the hope for good things. What will you call him Addy?" Georgie watched as Ella dangled a piece of yarn in front of the kitten causing a wild chase around the room as everyone laughed at the sight.

"I think his name is Little Buddy," Addy declared decidedly, "because we hope for only good things."

CHAPTER 19

SEPTEMBER 13, 1925 – THE SCHUMACHER HOME, 191 ALICE ST., WAUWATOSA

The sun was just above the horizon in the west as Art Schumacher turned the corner onto Alice Street. Florence sat beside him in the passenger seat and Jean had already curled up fast asleep in the back seat. It had been difficult for Art to convince his wife to take a much-needed Sunday outing to visit her family in North Prairie, but the look of joyful anticipation on Jean's face had sealed the deal.

The weather had been perfect for autumn in Wisconsin, sunny with the slight breeze holding a tinge of crispness. The farmstead about thirty miles away in Waukesha County sat near the border of a vast forest. Art recalled Florence loved to walk among the pines and drink in their spicy scent. He had taken her for a long walk that afternoon and watched as she closed her eyes and breathed in deeply. He had also observed the silent tears streaming down her cheeks as she walked along the path with him.

Florence's mother, Alice, had been good medicine for all of them, especially Jean. She had prepared a Sunday lunch which included many of Florence's favorites: fried chicken, potato salad, and a rhubarb dessert. Alice had noted Florence's gaunt frame and had decided to take the matter into her own maternal hands. Florence smiled appreciatively at the efforts but ate small portions of each; she continued having a hard time swallowing past the enormous lump of grief in her throat. Alice had packed the remainder of the meal in a large picnic basket that was now nestled between them in the front seat.

It had been late afternoon when Florence declared they needed to leave for home. Previously they had stayed for a simple dinner, but Art knew Florence was at her limits of forbearance. She needed to be at home in case, after seven weeks, their son suddenly came skipping up the sidewalk into her arms. Even now, as they approached their street, her body portrayed her anxiety, she leaned forward in the seat while biting the fingernail of her left pointer finger. Art took one hand off the steering wheel, reaching for her hand in her mouth and gently holding it in his own.

They had pulled into the driveway before Art noticed the two police cars parked just beyond their house. His eyes went immediately to his wife who had already seen them and turned to look at him, her eyes filled with abject fear. He could hear the gentle snores from his daughter and prayed Jean would stay asleep.

Florence gasped when she saw Detectives Kraemer, Zellmer, and Murphy along with Officer Maloney step from the vehicles. Her grip on Art's hand became viselike as he sat there forgetting to shift the gear and turn off the engine. The grind of the motor reminded him; he pulled his hand from Florence's grip and shifted the gear while turning off the vehicle. He hopped out of the driver's side door and made his way to the passenger door to open it for Florence. His glance at the back seat told him Jean was still curled up asleep.

Art's heart plummeted into his stomach when he saw their pastor, Reverend Dallman step from their porch where he had been awaiting their return. Florence stumbled slightly beside him, her legs starting to give way. He put his right arm around her waist as he held her firmly by the arm with his left. Detective Murphy stepped forward offering his arm for support on her other side. Florence gratefully took ahold of Murphy's arm.

"May we help Mrs. Schumacher into the house while you get Jean? We don't want to wake her up and have her terrified of us." John stood in front of Art and Florence with his hands outstretched offering his assistance. Art looked at Florence who nodded and transferred her arm over to the officer's. Art could see the grief in John's eyes as he gently took Florence's arm, and he and Murphy helped her towards the house. Art returned to the car in the driveway and opened the passenger's side door, releasing the lever that folded the seat forward.

"We are home sleepyhead. Papa will carry you up to bed Jean." Art tried to keep his voice light and cheery. He was glad the drowsiness prevented Jean from seeing his visibly shaking hands as he reached in and scooped her up. Reverend Dallman grabbed the picnic basket then closed the car door following Art and Jean into the house.

It was slow and robotic motions that led Art up the stairs carrying his child to the safety of her bed. His mind screamed frantically within him, but his body continued to move almost of its own volition. He removed Jean's shoes and placed her in the bed, kissing her forehead and tucking the blanket around her. At the door he paused for a moment.

"Papa, leave the light on please." Jean's sleepy voice registered in his brain. Art nodded and walked out the door, closing it behind him. He walked back down the stairs, each step thudding on the stair beneath his foot. Gravity had tripled its pull upon his body. He grasped the banister, the broad rail where Buddy had slid to a landing below hundreds of times.

Florence was seated in the dining room surrounded by the officers and Reverend Dallman. Mrs. Dallman stood at the doorway to the kitchen ready to bring anything they might need. There was only one thing Art needed, his son.

"Mr. and Mrs. Schumacher we are sorry to bring this news to you. Your son was found this afternoon. He is deceased." Detective Kraemer's gruff voice broke slightly as he delivered the news Art had anticipated but dreaded. "We came as soon as he was located but you were gone for the day. Mrs. Schumacher's brothers were here at the house and offered to come and identify him as is required by law. His remains have been turned over to the coroner for investigation."

Art sank into the chair next to Florence. He heard her cries, but almost couldn't fathom they came from her, they were deep guttural sounds, the keening of a grieving mother. He felt the need to cry, to shout, to swear, but nothing would come forth. His emotions were paralyzed, his soul an empty void.

Detective Murphy knelt beside him, placing his hand on Art's shoulder. The detective understood there were no words under heaven which could make this better at that moment.

"Come with me. I need to know." Art pushed himself up into a standing position. He staggered down the hallway towards his study, all four officers following. Reverend and Mrs. Dallman sat down on each side of Florence embracing her as she continued to wail.

"I need to hear the details of how he was found and where. My wife will not be able to handle any of that for a long while, but I will not be able to wait with her." Art sat down in his chair while the officers took the other seats in the room. "Forgive me if I seem cold to you. I find I am unable to feel anything in the moment of my greatest loss."

"Mr. Schumacher you don't have to explain anything to us. Everyone handles their grief differently. I understand your need for information as it is how I process my emotions as well." Detective Zellmer was the first to speak. He removed his notebook from his vest pocket. "I could read the report as we have recorded it, and you can ask questions of us if that would suffice." At Art's nod, Zellmer opened the notebook to read.

"At 1300 hours on September 13, 1925, Joseph Vozar, (Milwaukee) accompanied by his son and a neighbor reported finding a body near Underwood Creek on C.A. Koepfler's farm (Wauwatosa). Mr. Vozar stated he had been mushroom hunting on the property at 1100 hours when he located a deceased boy in a brush pile near the path that leads to the farmhouse. He was uncertain at that time who the boy might be and returned home to Milwaukee to bring his son and neighbor back to the place. They brought a picture of the missing boy, Arthur (Buddy) Schumacher from the local papers and determined the picture matched the boy they had discovered. They came to the police station to file a report and to lead Detectives Kraemer and Zellmer to the location of the discovery. The young boy had denim overalls and one red canvas shoe; his overall description matched that of the missing boy. He was found lying face down, with arms outstretched and clothing torn. He was covered in numerous

bruises and lacerations but nothing which would indicate a fall from a train that was located over a half mile away. The remains were identified by Fred Armstrong, brother of the boy's mother, Florence Armstrong Schumacher. Deputy Coroner Walter Krueger was contacted to begin his investigation into the cause of death. Foul play is strongly suspected."

"How in the world could he have been located in a place that has been searched dozens of times? Are you telling me we all just walked right past him?" Art's incredulity made his voice harsh. "Do you think someone took him and killed him? Did you see signs of foul play?"

"From the position of his body and the initial wounds we observed, it appears he was restrained at the wrists and ankles at one point. It's our opinion he may have been killed somewhere else and moved to this location very recently. It also did not appear he had been deceased for the period that he had been missing. The coroner will be able to tell us more tomorrow morning as he is working on the autopsy even as we speak. Obviously, we all hoped for a very different outcome, and kept the hope that we might find him still alive. We can't tell you how sorry we are, Mr. Schumacher." Detective Kraemer cleared his throat and looked up at the ceiling to regain his composure before continuing," We will find out what happened to him and who did this if it's the last thing I ever do."

"You have done everything that was in your power to do. When can I see him myself?" Art felt emotion starting to clog his throat. The pain in his heart intensified by the minute like a white-hot branding iron stabbing him repeatedly.

"The coroner asked me to tell you he will take good care of your boy for the night. Let him do his job and he will make certain Buddy is cleaned up in case his mother wishes to view him as well. He asked for some of the boy's clothing to be sent with us as the other clothing is now evidence in the investigation. I can check with Mrs. Dallman before I leave." John knew his words of assurance were as futile as his efforts to find Buddy had been. Never had he been so devastated and furious at the same time.

"Yes, she can help you. Try not to wake Jean please. Let her sleep, the poor girl's whole life will change when she wakes up tomorrow morning. If you will excuse me, I feel the need to be alone." Small sobs had begun to escape Art with each breath he took. He understood a tidal wave of grief was coming, it was imminent, it would be unrelenting.

The four officers took their leave of the grieving father, returning briefly to consult with Reverend Dallman and Mrs. Dallman who retrieved the clothing from the little boy's bedroom. They opened the front door to find Alice Armstrong and Gertrude Brown entering the house in search of their daughter and sister. The lawn was already filled with people, neighbors and newspaper reporters who waited in a silent vigil. Drew Pearson stood near the back of the crowd. He approached Murphy and John as they made their way to the car.

"I thought you guys would want to know Chief Baltes already gave the press an interview about an hour ago. He sent an officer out to the Koepfler farm with Gus Brenner of the Wauwatosa News to take pictures of the exact spot. I would hate to see the Schumacher's view that in the headlines tomorrow morning." Drew shook his head in disgust as he described what he called yellow journalism. "No one should have to endure what this family is enduring right now."

"We will wait for the actual coroner results before releasing more information tomorrow morning," said Kraemer. "Meanwhile, please advise Mr. Brenner I will be mad as hops if he messes up our crime scene by trouncing through it. We may have found that little boy today, but now we will hunt down his killer." Kraemer raised his voice so Brenner and all the other pressmen present could hear him. "To whomever hurt that boy, understand I will find you and I will make you pay."

CHAPTER 20

SEPTEMBER 14, 1925 – WAUWATOSA POLICE DEPARTMENT

The steady hum of activity for the previous seven weeks had suddenly halted, replaced with a hush that blanketed the entire precinct with its spectral silence. The occasional scrape of a chair on the floor or the tap-tap of the typewriter resounded in the heavy quietness, sounds usually masked by the bustling din echoed throughout the main office. The officers gathered in small groups or sat in solitude, the grief of finding the little boy's remains having left a palpable sense of loss among the seasoned lawmen.

Deputy Coroner Krueger entered the building through the main door and suddenly the noise of the newspaper reporters flocked outside vanquished the stillness. The officers rose from their various chairs and lined the hallway as the Deputy Coroner made his way down the hallway towards Chief Baltes' office where Kraemer, Zellmer, Murphy and John waited with the district attorney and the chief of police. Sergeant Bates knocked on the door, opened it for the Deputy Coroner, and guided the young man into the crowded office.

"Thank you for coming as soon as you were able this morning. I know you had a very long night." District Attorney Wengert greeted Krueger and ushered him into a chair next to the Chief's desk. The young man took the offered seat and set a briefcase on the desk in front of him. He removed a pair of spectacles from his vest pocket and put them on before opening the briefcase.

"Yes, this was a difficult autopsy as it was for someone so young. The death of a child is the hardest to comprehend, especially when the young life was taken at the hand of another person. I brought the official report and part of the evidence with me. The coroner's office will send the rest of the evidence after some more tests have been conducted. I felt there is a key piece of evidence as it is the 'murder weapon' so to speak, so I brought it with me, but we have a pathologist on his way from Chicago to do more testing on it." Krueger removed a small envelope from the briefcase, opened it and after placing a rubber glove on his hand pulled a handkerchief from the envelope. The handkerchief was dirty, yellowed with wear, and hemmed with blue thread.

"Upon thorough investigation of the deceased boy's mouth we found this lodged in the back of the throat. It had been wadded up and jammed in there hard, probably with another object as an adult hand would be too large to force it into the boy's pharynx. Most likely this was done to quiet the boy's screams, and a gag would have been placed over the mouth as well so the boy could not remove it. The wadded folds sealed his windpipe causing asphyxiation. The marks on his body indicated he had been restrained by the wrists and ankles for long periods of time, and he had been beaten repeatedly as there are varying degrees of bruises that were inflicted at different times. "Krueger cleared his throat and adjusted his spectacles with his free hand, trying to remain unemotional while delivering his report to the much more experienced law officers gathered around him.

He understood that professionally he had to remain detached to do his job in the best way possible, but describing the torture the eight-year-old had endured was heartrending. Krueger cleared his throat a second time.

"I would like to take a closer look at the handkerchief if I might." Kraemer spoke up, rescuing the young deputy coroner from his struggle with the emotion they all felt. He donned a pair of rubber gloves and carefully removed the handkerchief from the trembling hand. It was at least sixteen inches square, hemmed with a light blue thread, and bore the initial '*A*' in one corner. The inexpensive cotton material had several stains which prevented them from seeing any other distinguishable evidence.

"You said a pathologist is enroute to conduct more testing on some of the evidence. I assume the handkerchief is one of those pieces of evidence?" Zellmer stood beside Kraemer examining the cloth his partner held. "What tests did you have in mind? It will be imperative to take numerous pictures of the handkerchief as it is now. Even the stains may hold clues to where it was. Has anyone asked if Buddy had a handkerchief on him when he left home? The initial might stand for his first name, Arthur."

Zellmer walked to the filing cabinet and removed a camera with a large flash bulb attached. He brought it back to where Kraemer stood and the only sound in the room for the next few moments was the snapping and whir of the flashbulb as pictures were taken from every angle. The others gathered around, each examining the small piece of cloth without touching it. To understand this seemingly innocent token had been the instrument of death for an even more innocent little boy was disquieting to say the least.

"Dr. Miloslavich, the pathologist, said he intends to put the handkerchief in a solution to try and whiten it without ruining it. If there are any other marks hidden by the dirt and stains, he should be able to identify them with high powered lenses. This has been effective with numerous other cases. Coroner Grudemann is at the morgue now waiting for the pathologist to arrive. He sent for Mr. Raasch from the funeral home before I left this morning hoping more could be done about the boy's appearance before the parents arrive by midmorning. I am told both Mr. and Mrs. Schumacher requested Detectives Kraemer, Zellmer, Murphy, and Officer Maloney be present with them when they see their son. Other than that, they asked for some privacy from the department and the press, which I am sure everyone understands." Krueger removed another small bag from his briefcase and placed it on the desk. "These were found in his overall pockets, unusual for an adult, but probably customary for a small boy."

Murphy picked up the small bag Krueger had placed on the desk, opened it and handed it to John who was standing next to him. John looked inside the small bag, blinked, and looked again to make sure his eyes had not deceived him. It contained four small smooth stones exactly like the others they had found in various locations since Buddy's disappearance. John handed the bag to Zellmer who peered inside then closed the bag and placed it back on the desk.

The other men were still engrossed in the examination of the handkerchief and missed the quiet interchange between the three officers who understood the importance of finding these stones in several locations. It was now more than apparent that Buddy, even in the face of tremendous fear and pain, had left them a trail to follow to find him and to find the monster who had done this to him. They had missed their opportunity to find the boy before he lost his life, but they would follow every lead until they found his killer and bring him to justice.

"And a little child shall lead them." Zellmer spoke for all of them as he picked up the bag of stones and carried them to the filing cabinet to store with the others. He closed the filing cabinet and turned to face Murphy and John.

"And where he leads us, we will follow."

CHAPTER 21

SEPTEMBER 15, 1925 – SANCTUARY WOODS

Addy had sought the solace of her refuge in the bent oak tree as soon as the heavens had turned a peachy pink hue in the eastern sky that morning. The tragic news of finding the little boy discarded in the brush on the farm next door had crushed the hearts of all the inhabitants of Cottage 5, each woman grieving in her own way since receiving the news the previous day via the morning newspaper.

Mary and Ella had started baking bars and cookies to send for the funeral wake which would follow in a few days' time. Ingrid and Freda had sat together at the table, the seeing girl guiding the hands of the blind girl while they shaped yards of black tulle into garland to take to the little home on Alice Street for the grieving family.

Ruthie had sat next to Cora's grave for hours, hot tears running down her weathered cheeks for both children who had been taken from this world far too soon. Georgie had remained unusually silent, stationed in a rocker on the front porch facing the path that led to the woods, recalling again the last day she had seen Buddy skip along that path and asking herself repeatedly how she could have prevented this from happening to him.

Little Buddy, the gray kitten, was sleeping peacefully curled in the knapsack Addy wore across her chest. His soft sighs broke the stillness of the woods around them where even the wildlife seemed to understand the utter desolation, the unspeakable grief of the tragedy that had taken place within the area.

Addy had refused to look towards the Koepfler farm since scaling the oak in the early morning light. She knew numerous police officers had remained at the spot where Buddy had been found, and the newspaper men had trampled the grass surrounding the brush until a small crater had formed.

Cars lined the roadway leading to the farm with curious onlookers flocking to see the infamous site until an unofficial line had formed for viewing. Addy shuddered at the thought of anyone being nosy enough to intrude on what should be the private grief of the Schumacher family for their own snoopiness.

A sudden motion to her left drew Addy's attention towards the tall reeds that lined the Menomonee River. Mr. Eddy, one of the local vagrants, stepped from his dwelling in the reeds referred to as a "yunkle", the German pronunciation of "jungle".

At the same moment, Little Buddy awoke from his extended nap expressing an urgent need to make water. Addy knew she had only a minute or two to transfer the kitten to the safety of the ground. She lithely descended from her lofty perch placing her charge in a mound of soft dirt at the base of the tree to do his business.

"Miss Addy, what creature do you have there?" Mr. Eddy approached her on the path as he pointed to the cat beside her. "He has the most unusual markings I have ever seen." The gaunt man looked exhausted and ill. His limp, the result of being kicked by a horse several years before, was more pronounced than usual. He smiled at the antics of the kitten scratching dramatically in the dirt with its front and back paws simultaneously.

"Isn't he a remarkable cat, Mr. Eddy? He found me here in the woods and hasn't left my side since. He is the darling of all my friends in Cottage 5." Addy leaned over to scoop up the kitten who had finished his business and was now rubbing himself vigorously on her ankles. She held the kitten out to him, and he eagerly accepted it into his arms. He stroked the soft gray fur until Little Buddy let out a full-fledged purr of appreciation and rubbed his face against Mr. Eddy's hand.

"This little mite is beyond remarkable as you say. He has a very intelligent look about him; he will make an excellent mouser as he grows. Just don't dote on him to the point that his natural instincts don't kick in and you will have one fine cat indeed." Mr. Eddy held the kitten up to examine him and then carefully handed him back to Addy who nodded in agreement with his assessment.

"I haven't seen you around for a few weeks, have you been feeling poorly again? Ingrid has a receipt for a tonic that might help. I am sure she would mix it up for you. It tastes awful, but she insists that's how you know the tonic works." Addy made a face at the thought of the revolting taste while she noted the pallor of her friend.

"No," replied Mr. Eddy, "it isn't anything to do with my ailments although at times my head feels as if it might burst, but that is the result of being kicked straight in the noggin by the horse I was trying to rein in. No, instead, the fine officers of the Wauwatosa Police Department felt it best to pen me up in the House of Corrections for the last seven weeks. I was kept from the sunshine that is my life's blood and made to work long hours in the laundry rooms. I'm not sure Hades itself is as hot as that sweltering place, but I don't wish to find out."

"After all that time," he continued, "I was suddenly released in the middle of the night and brought back here to the woods where my yunkle has been destroyed in the meantime. I won't complain, however, as I am grateful to be released and outside once again. I was momentarily upset when I found someone took my old, tattered bible, but then I realized some poor soul might need it more than I do." Mr. Eddy pointed towards his dwelling in the reeds as he explained his circumstances without a hint of self-pity.

"We have missed you and all of your fish and frog legs you brought by the cottage. Stop by when you have a minute and pick up some of the baked goods that Ella and Mary have been stockpiling. They will be as happy as I am to see you again." Addy understood the humble man would not go and ask for food, but he would be happy to share his own catches of fish and be reimbursed for them as had been the custom between them for several years.

She still marveled that this man had been a successful farmer before he attempted to stop a stampeding horse from trampling a group of children Instead of being hailed as a hero, he had been labeled as "odd" and ostracized from the small community in which he had resided all his life. He had taken to riding the rails and living as a vagrant because he was such an outcast.

"I will go and fashion a fishing pole and see how the fish are biting," said Mr. Eddy, "then stop by later on with a fresh catch for them. My fishing pole was taken in my absence too, probably one of those rascally town boys who like to play pranks on me now and again."

"Speaking of boys," Eddy whispered, "do you know if they found the little guy that got lost? They hauled me to the downtown precinct to ask about him when I would have gladly helped in the search. Such a nice little fellow. He is never involved in the dirty pranks of the others."

Mr. Eddy looked expectantly at Addy for an answer about Buddy. Grief felt like a stone in her stomach as she shook her head in response. Mr. Eddy tilted his head slightly, trying to comprehend her meaning, his brow knit in consternation.

Their conversation was interrupted by the arrival of several Wauwatosa police officers, Officer Edward Siepman leading the others up the path from Koepfler's farm towards them. Little Buddy hissed and scratched Addy in his attempt to flee the men who descended upon them. Addy placed the cat on the massive trunk of the tree that ran parallel to the ground so he could scramble part of the way up the tree and out of their reach. The kitten glared from his perch while Addy turned back to see the officers forcefully taking hold of Mr. Eddy, throwing him to the ground in the process.

"What is the meaning of this?" Addy screamed her question into the face of the nearest officer. She watched as the policemen all knelt on the frail man's back. She was certain they would crush him beneath their weight.

She heard the muffled sound of Mr. Eddy's attempt to draw breaths with his face in the dirt. He would soon be smothered. Addy started towards her friend when she was grabbed by the officer nearest to her. Pain shot through her upper arm at his vicelike grip. Addy's scream of pain and fear rent the former silence of the surrounding woods.

"Not her. Leave her be if you know what's good for you. She has friends in high places all over this town." Siepman spoke curtly to the officer who held Addy's arm. The chastised officer released her as suddenly as he had grabbed her, leaving her bruised and terrified for Mr. Eddy.

"Just go on home Mrs. St. John. We don't want to see you hurt by this moronic degenerate. His days of preying on the innocent have come to an end." Siepman and the others rose from their positions on top of Mr. Eddy, pulling him to a standing position while shackling his hands behind him.

Addy stared in horror at Mr. Eddy. He was bleeding from his nose while large clots of dirt clung to the corners of his mouth. He gasped for breath, his legs buckling beneath him. The officers allowed him to hit the ground headfirst with his hands shackled behind him, the sound of his landing making a sickening thud. They pulled him to his feet again while holding him in place between them. Mr. Eddy sagged by his arms; his head lolled to one side unconsciously. Tears sprang to Addy's eyes; a hot fury rose in her chest.

"I demand that you tell me what you are doing! I want to speak with Officer Mahoney and Detective Murphy!" Addy tried to advocate for the helpless man before her as the two officers began to drag Mr. Eddy back down the path. Siepman paused before following the others towards the waiting police cars.

"What are we doing? We are capturing the murderer of Buddy Schumacher, that's what we are doing. Go and talk to Murphy and Maloney. They had nothing to do with this arrest, ineffective as they are. We will see how important they are now. I would suggest you stay clear of these woods little miss, you aren't safe out here." Siepman chuckled as he walked away, leaving Addy with his very real threat ringing in her ears.

Addy clambered onto the tree trunk and called for Little Buddy who came scrambling down into her waiting arms. Addy didn't know what to do next, but she knew she needed to do something to help

Mr. Eddy, and she needed to do it quickly. She ran for home and for Georgie and the rest of her family. She had not been able to rescue the little boy from his tormentors, but she would do everything in her power to help rescue the outcast from his.

CHAPTER 22

SAME DAY, WAUWATOSA POLICE DEPARTMENT

John sat in the small room the four officers had used for the last seven weeks staring at the collected evidence from the Schumacher case displayed on the table before him. Kraemer and Zellmer had left earlier that morning to revisit the area where the young girl had been abducted near Grant Park in South Milwaukee. The police report had indicated the abductors had used a handkerchief as part of the gag before they threw the child out of the car near Carrollville back in late July.

Zellmer wanted to examine the handkerchief that had been used, but the South Milwaukee police indicated it must have been left near the scene by the flustered witnesses who had found the little girl. Zellmer was fairly certain the two cases were linked, and the handkerchiefs were key pieces of evidence, so locating the missing handkerchief along the road in Carrollville was crucial.

Murphy opened the door and stepped into the room bearing two steaming cups of black coffee. He set one of the cups next to John and went to sit in a chair across the table while he sipped from his own cup. He removed his notebook from his coat pocket that had been slung over the back of the chair. Next, he donned the rubber gloves located in a box at the end of the table.

Each piece of evidence had been tagged and was covered with the fine white granular powder used to take fingerprints from several of the objects. Murphy was particularly intrigued by the use of dactyloscopy, the science of studying the loops, whorls, and arches individual to each human finger. He had attended the 1904 World's Fair in St Louis as a young teenager to see the detectives from Scotland Yard demonstrate their ability to identify a possible suspect by the newfound practice.

"I feel there is still something hidden among these objects that is a crucial clue. It will lead us to apprehending the monster who did this." John lifted the bag of stones from the table with his gloved hand. The FBI fingerprint specialist from Chicago had come to perform the testing, painstakingly removing fingerprints from the stones and identifying them as belonging to Buddy Schumacher whose prints had been obtained from his personal belongings in his bedroom. Many of the other objects bore Buddy's fingerprints as well as those of unidentified individuals.

The specialist had even gone to Alice Street and obtained the fingerprints of most of the extended family members so those prints could be ruled out on the objects due to casual contact in the same household. There were still unidentified fingerprints that remained. Most likely those unidentified prints were from Buddy's murderer.

"As Kraemer keeps reiterating, there are no small clues and one of these could be a key to breaking this wide open." Murphy picked up the fishing pole fashioned from a smooth wooden rod and line. This was the only item that didn't bear Buddy's fingerprints although it had more of the unidentified prints from the other objects. They had mistakenly assumed the fishing pole belonged to the little boy and had been stashed in the bent oak with his other belongings, but now it was a new mystery where the pole had originated and who hid it there.

A commotion down the hallway drew both officers to the door of the room. Upon opening the door, they found a large group of reporters and police officers surrounding the vagrant who had been brought into the precinct days after Buddy disappeared. Both John and Murphy left their makeshift office and joined the throng gathered in the main room.

Gus Breinin, one of the more notorious local newspapermen stood at the center of the group taking pictures of two of the boys who had been with Buddy on the day he disappeared. Arnold Young and John Wolf sat on a bench opposite of the vagrant, Mr. Eddy, pointing at the man while the cameras whizzed and popped around them. Chief Baltes and Officer Siepman stood to one side watching the events unfold before them like a circus with multiple rings.

"These two brave boys have come forward to positively identify this man as the one who chased them on the railroad tracks the morning the young boy disappeared. He has been arrested for the abduction and murder of Buddy Schumacher. The citizens of Wauwatosa and Milwaukee County can now rest easily that the violent degenerate has been taken off the streets." Chief Baltes' voice raised above the din of reporters while he pointed at the injured man on the bench beside him. The two boys on the opposite looked sheepish, their downward stares at the floor indicating their level of discomfort.

Murphy was the first to step into the circle and in front of the camera that was still flashing every other second. He put himself in front of Mr. Eddy who was slumped over on the bench, severely injured with blood still dripping from his nose and mouth. A large bump protruded on his forehead already turning nasty shades of blue and purple and both eyes were blackened from a blunt force trauma to his head.

"Who took this man into custody and under whose direction? Detectives Kramer and Zellmer are leading this investigation and there were no indications an arrest was about to be made today." John stepped up beside Gus Breinin, grabbed the camera from his hands and turned towards the office he shared with the others. The reporter followed at a distance while keeping his camera in sight.

"I arrested him under the direction of the Chief of Police. I guess he didn't think it was important to inform you fellows of it." Siepman stepped forward trying to block John's way back through the crowd. "A lot of us think it's high time you boys stop playing cops and robbers and get something done. All of these newfangled contraptions don't make good policework. A good intuition and a few good clues are all you really need." Siepman oozed arrogance inches from John's face, his breath stinking of old cigars.

"In all your 'intuition' did you think to get this man medical help, or have you been too busy putting on a show?" Murphy rebuked Siepman while kneeling next to Mr. Eddy to further assess his injuries. "He has been beaten to a pulp." Murphy pulled keys from his pocket and unlocked the handcuffs that restrained the injured man's hands.

"He was resisting arrest, and we had to subdue him. I would think you would be more concerned about his innocent victim than you are him." Siepman turned to face Murphy. He took several steps towards Murphy to stop him from releasing Mr. Eddy when Chief Baltes stopped his progress.

"Let's take this into my office. Officer Hammerschmidt, you take the prisoner down to the cells and Maloney, Murphy, and Siepman you follow me. DA Wengert and Mr. St. John are waiting for me in my office." Chief Baltes barked his orders, expecting immediate compliance.

Hammerschmidt stepped forward to help Mr. Eddy to his feet while Murphy and John followed the chief towards his office. John hoped Kramer and Zellmer would return soon and help him return the precinct to a less chaotic state.

When John entered the chief's office, he observed that the district attorney and Lucian were seated in chairs in the far corner of the room. They had been speaking in hushed tones and ceased as soon as the others stepped into the room.

John exchanged a hurried glance with Murphy as the two seated themselves on the opposite side of the room. All the evidence from the case had been moved to the Chief's desk in the period of time they had been in the main room. It was heaped in a pile on the desk as though someone had scooped it up and carried it all together.

"It has been brought to my attention by more than one concerned citizen that the current investigation has been going way too slow," Baltes barked. "The need to find this boy's murderer and arrest them is foremost and all the investigation methods that have been introduced along the way have hampered it from happening. Those modern things might be all the rage in Chicago or New York, but here in Wauwatosa we prefer good old-fashioned policework."

"Mr. St. John had offered the help from some of the private investigators employed by his company," Baltes continued, "and it wasn't long until they found leads indicating our original suspect was probably our only suspect. Officer Siepman was acting on the authority of my office and the District Attorney's in his arrest. He even found Mr. Eddy a short distance from where the body had been discovered only two days ago."

"We questioned Arnold Young and John Wolf yesterday and they were able to verify it was indeed our suspect who had chased them and went after Buddy Schumacher. All these things together are the basis for the arrest. I don't think I need to explain to any of you that as the Chief of Police, I have the full authority to act upon this without the permission of anyone else." Baltes' tone was direct and authoritative. DA Wengert nodded his agreement with the Chief's assessment.

John could hear his heart beating so hard that it thundered in his ears until it almost drowned out everything around him. Their careful investigation and tireless work for almost two months had been upended by the whim of the political machinations of those in power. How could he ever explain this to Buddy's parents? How could they protect the children of Wauwatosa from the real murderer when their parents believed the false narrative that had been craftily designed to lull them into a sense of security?

John rose from his seat to speak out when Murphy stayed him with a quick gesture and a shake of his head. There was a time and a place to respond, and this was neither though it would take all their combined restraint to keep from doing so.

Buddy's funeral was scheduled for that afternoon, and the family had asked John, Murphy, Kraemer, and Zellmer to attend. They had less than an hour to be at Mount Olive Lutheran Church and they would not be late because they had tied themselves to an argument that needed much more time to resolve.

"We will inform Kraemer and Zellmer their assistance is no longer required. Murphy and Maloney you will be assigned to other work as well. I will lead this investigation from here on in." Chief Baltes mistakenly took John and Murphy's silence as agreement and turned to Lucian who sat watching the two officers from across the room.

"Mr. St. John mentioned that Mr. Vozer should be brought back in and given the reward money in front of the reporters, and I agree with his plan. Siepman, you will help conduct some of the interviews with witnesses and try to find any other witnesses who can corroborate the accusations against Mr. Eddy," Chief Baltes concluded.

Twenty minutes later John and Murphy met Kraemer and Zellmer in the parking lot of the Lutheran church. The crowd was already overflowing into the lawn, the doors of the church left open so people outside could hear. The four officers stood on the lawn and listened to the minister's eulogy, the songs of the choir, and the soft sobs among the crowd of onlookers.

At the end of the funeral, a small white coffin was carried out of the church as four of Buddy's playmates, acting as honorary pallbearers, followed close behind. The streets between the church and the cemetery were closed for the procession, the quiet respect for the family filling the space around the Schumachers as they made their way to the top of the hill and their son's final resting place. Carloads of flowers were placed around the grave as Art, Florence, and Jean huddled together next to the minister.

The officers waited their turn in line to offer condolences after the final prayer. Kraemer paused as he shook the hand of Buddy's father and looked into the grief-stricken eyes that had run out of tears to shed.

"No matter what you hear, Mr. and Mrs. Schumacher know that the four of us will not give up just as we have already told you. You can rest now and let the burden fall on our shoulders. We will carry it for you from here. We will carry it for your son so he can be at peace." Kraemer's voice trembled with emotion as he took the hand of the grieving mother in his own. He knew it would be a long and heavy burden to bear, but one absolutely necessary to give the family peace and to have that same peace for himself and the officers surrounding him.

The four officers walked down the hill, Zellmer keeping apart from the others as he meticulously scanned the massive crowd around them. He suddenly stopped and turned to look back up the hill towards the hearse and hundreds of mourners descending the hill behind them. Kraemer waited for him, knowing his partner had ascertained something of importance. John and Murphy paused, also waiting for Zellmer, who finally acknowledged what they had all been feeling.

"We may have to investigate this on our own time," said Zellmer, "but we will get it done. The Wauwatosa Police Department does not have the murderer in custody. In fact, I think he is here today. Hopefully, he will grow complacent when he thinks we are no longer pursuing him and that is when we will catch him in a mistake. This is going to take all the patience we can muster and the ability to act as though we agree with the egregious path of the current investigation. He must think he is safe, but he will never be safe from us."

CHAPTER 23

SEPTEMBER 16, 1925 – COTTAGE 5 NEAR SANCTUARY WOODS

The crisp morning air held the scent of autumn as Georgie sat in the front porch rocker holding a skein of yarn for Ruthie beside her. The older woman's nimble hands made the knitting needles flick back and forth as they watched the birds flutter near the bird feeder hanging from the tree next to them. The smaller birds seemed willing to flock together, sharing the repast, each getting their own share, but a large blue jay in a nearby tree seemed bent on taking everyone's share.

The jay screamed and flew at the smaller birds trying to scare them from the feeder while taking large portions for himself. Each time he left with his large portion, the smaller birds would gather again trying to gather the leftovers strewn about the bottom of the feeder and the ground. The jay would then return to steal even the smaller portions that the other birds had gleaned.

Georgie felt indignation at the raucous jeers of the greedy large bird with the brilliant blue crest. It needed far less than what it took from the other birds and yet was not satisfied until it took everything, leaving the others with nothing.

She watched the jay fly off into the distance, bearing the lion's share towards its own nest. She laid the skein of yarn aside and stood stretching her legs. Georgie walked to the barrel which held the birdseed, lifted the lid and removed a filled scoop. She carried the scoop to the feeder, refilled it and returned the scoop to the barrel. Georgie laughed at the flurried activity of the smaller birds gathered for the refilled feeder.

Suddenly, the blue jay returned with an ear-splitting scream, scattering the smaller birds again. Georgie stood and yelled at the nasty bird, waving her hands above her head to give it a taste of its own medicine. The bully startled at her actions then realized that the feeder was above Georgie's head and resumed its thievery.

Georgie sensed Ruthie step up beside her and place a gentle hand on her shoulder. Ruthie nudged Georgie out of the way and wound up, throwing a large ball of yarn at the feeder. It hit the mark with amazing accuracy, missing the bird, but striking the feeder with enough force to terrify the thug from his perch and away from the feeder altogether. There was a small pause before the other birds returned to the feeder, each taking their portion and flying off to their nests.

"I read tyranny only succeeds when good men or women do nothing. I guess it applies to the birds as well, Ruthie." Georgie returned to the rocker and picked up the skein of yarn again. "It looks as though you are already half-way finished with the blanket you started for Mr. Eddy only yesterday. It still amazes me how quickly you can accomplish it. This is a beautiful color too." Georgie fingered the slate blue yarn in her hands.

Since Addy had returned with the news of Mr. Eddy's arrest yesterday afternoon, the women had been working on a basket of items to take to their friend. They had gathered jars of canned fruit and baked goods along with a pair of slippers, magazines, and the blanket Ruthie was working on currently.

Addy had found a large bible in one of the storage chests and a small pocket bible from her own dresser, placing both in the basket for Mr. Eddy's use. Georgie wished to speak with Lucian about retaining an attorney to help the homeless man who had so little of his own, but she had not seen Lucian since he had left the house two days prior.

Addy appeared on the path from the woods in the company of John and Murphy. Georgie could hear Addy's pleas for their friend as she walked with the two officers towards the porch. Ruthie's gaze turned from the bird feeder she had been guarding to the beautiful auburn-haired young woman for whom she had appointed herself as a guardian. Ruthie smiled slightly as Murphy bent over to pick up the ball of yarn lying at the base of the tree. He carried it towards the porch as he respectfully listened to Addy's plea.

"Everyone who knows Mr. Eddy at all understands he would never hurt anyone, most of all, a child. Did you know that Mr. Eddy was badly hurt by a stampeding horse while trying to protect some children? That's the reason for his limp. There are people who would judge him for his awkwardness, but it too was caused by the same incident that injured his head." Addy's voice rose as she climbed the porch steps and walked to the rocker on the opposite side of Ruthie. She plopped down into the rocker and sighed.

"We believe what you say, Miss Addy," said Murphy. "But it isn't in our power to release Mr. Eddy. The Chief of Police and the District Attorney have taken over the case. They are hard at work gathering evidence against him. I was told this morning they brought an evangelist from a local mission to speak to him and 'probe his soul for the real truth'. Detective Kraemer was livid when he found out and broke up the interview but not before Mr. Eddy had said a few condemning things about himself. I am sorry to say it will take an excellent attorney to take this case and keep him out of the trouble he is already in after that interview." Murphy leaned against the porch railing opposite where the ladies sat and placed the ball of yarn in a basket near Georgie's feet.

"Mr. Eddy has deeply religious convictions," said Georgie. "It's unfair for anyone to take advantage of that and convince him he's guilty when he's not. I am planning to take up the matter of retaining an attorney with Mr. St. John when he returns. I feel he will help once he understands the situation. He is very fair about such things and extremely generous." Georgie looked up to see the blue jay circling the feeder once again. She grimaced at the bird before noticing that Ruthie had scooped up the ball of yarn once again.

John climbed the porch steps and came to stand beside Murphy. They exchanged a quick look between them and Murphy shook his head slightly. John stared down at his feet while he shuffled them then looked up to see Georgie and Addy watching him intently.

The blue jay screamed again; the loud call rent the air over their heads as it circled the feeder diving at the other birds. John clenched his fist at his side. If there was anything he detested in life it was a bully who preyed on those it determined it could force into submission by means of manipulation.

"I would be interested to know if Mr. Eddy has ever mentioned any of his family members and where they might be located. I think it would be very helpful to contact them and explain the direness of his current situation. They might be able to provide assistance the rest of us cannot because we are not directly related. I know he should have had a medical exam yesterday and a family member would be within their rights to demand that he be taken to a doctor." John's suggestion was brilliant. A relative of the suspect could request the charges be formally read and hire the much-needed attorney to represent him.

"Come to think of it, Mr. Eddy did leave a book with us that contained the name and address of his brother a few years back. I think it is still in the top drawer of the desk. I will go and get it for you right now." Georgie rose from her seat. She stomped her foot in the direction of the bird feeder which was being overrun by the mercenary jay before turning towards the door and entering the house. She returned a few minutes later holding a worn book with a broken spine. She handed the book to John who flipped open the front cover.

Shaky handwriting, scrawled in pencil revealed the name of Charles Vreeland and an address in Davenport, Iowa. A note written beside it designated the name as *"my dear brother"*. John handed the book to Murphy who glanced at the name while taking the notebook and pen out of his coat pocket to copy it down.

After writing down the information, Murphy closed the book to read the cover. The faint print was still visible, it read, *The Phantom of the Opera by Gaston Leroux*. It was the tale of an outcast who only wished for the love and kindness of others. Murphy handed the book back to Georgie who placed it in the yarn basket at her feet.

"We will contact his brother today and ask if he can come to visit Mr. Eddy. Officer Maloney and I have been assigned to other work, but we are going to continue to investigate on our own time along with Detectives Kraemer and Zellmer. I can take what you want to send to him back to the jail for you. They are not allowing him to have any visitors at this time." Murphy looked towards the tree to his left and the blue jay that continued to scream threats at the other birds. "I call those dirty birds because they take food from the other birds and even eat their eggs from the nests. This one appears determined to take over your feeder, doesn't he? Someone should teach the dirty bird a lesson."

Murphy watched in amazement as Ruthie stood from her rocker, walked to the porch rail and threw the large yarn ball with astounding accuracy. The yarn smacked into the feeder, and the jay flew away in fright, blue feathers fluttering. Ruthie demurely walked back to her rocker and took her seat, picking up her knitting project and continuing to work without looking at the others.

What came next surprised everyone as a quiet, shaky, gravelly voice came from the woman who almost never spoke.

"That's what you do to a bully. Take that, dirty bird." Ruthie nodded at all of them before she resumed her work in her trembling hands.

CHAPTER 24

SEPTEMBER 18,1925 – C. A. KOEPFLER FARM NEAR WAUWATOSA

The mid-September wind blustered, moving the tall reeds near the Menomonee River in a synchronized sway. District Attorney Eugene Wengert stepped from the front passenger side of the police car and motioned for Officer Siepman to remove Mr. Eddy from the back door on the other side of the car.

Siepman opened the door and grabbed the haggard man who was shackled at the wrists and ankles. Eddy stumbled as he tried to stand, hitting the car door with significant force. Siepman continued to pull on his prisoner until he stood upright on the side of the road.

Mr. Eddy squinted in the glare of the sun but lifted his head towards the light and closed his eyes for a moment. It had been many days since he had been allowed to get a breath of fresh air outside. He shuffled along as Siepman pulled him down the lane towards the small bridge that connected the main lane of the farmhouse to the fields beyond it.

The reeds along the Menomonee River in the distance seemed to beckon to their former inhabitant as Eddy was pulled towards the area where they had found the little boy's body only five days prior.

Carl Koepfler, the owner of the farm, stood on a path just ahead of the group as they made their way towards the tangled brush which marked the spot. The older, balding man stared at Eddy who looked straight at the ground to prevent himself from stumbling. Koepfler pointed at the site while he spit a large globule of chewing tobacco on the ground at Eddy's feet.

"This is right where the man found Buddy. It seems hard to figure as the wife, and I had brought the family out to this very point just two days before he was found. There couldn't have been more than fifteen feet from where we sat to here. I don't reckon the boy was here at that time because we would have seen him for certain. The wife hasn't been able to sleep for days, crying over that poor little guy." Carl spat brown tobacco juice again as he shook his head at the memory.

"Thank you, Mr. Koepfler. Have you seen anything else unusual in that time period? Have you witnessed people in the area?" D.A. Wengert gestured towards Eddy who stood silently at the front of the group with his head still down and his eyes closed.

"No more people than usual. It's a nice area for picnicking, close to the river and such. Some of the migrants from the trains pass through but most don't stay very long. We don't mind their being around if they clean up after themselves and most do. Of course, there had been a lot of searchers passing through in the last few weeks, but we never imagined with as many people as searched this whole property that anyone would ever locate the boy here."

"Mr. St. John stopped up at the house yesterday," Carl continued, "and said part of the reward money should be given to our family for all the inconveniences we have suffered. It's nice and all, but we don't really think we should gain anything from someone else's loss so we told him we would pass on it. "Carl stuck his hands in his trousers and sniffed while trying to clear his throat.

"That's very kind to say. I am afraid I don't have any say in who gets the reward money. I was wondering if you have ever seen this man on your property and if so, when?" Wengert pointed again at Eddy who opened his eyes and looked straight into Carl's face.

"Well, sure. Mr. Eddy is a regular in these parts. Most of the people who live in the area know him. I can't say as to when I saw him last because it has been quite a few weeks which was unusual for him. He's always just walked along the paths and cleans up his messes and sometimes the messes of some of the others that got left behind. The wife bought lots of fish and frog legs from him and says he is an honest soul. We haven't had one single problem with him." Carl stood his ground against the perturbed countenance of the district attorney at the failure to identify Eddy as the chief suspect.

"There are some of the other tramps who ride the rails that could be considered dangerous," Carl lowered his voice. "It's why I always keep a loaded shotgun inside the entrance to the house and trained the wife and kids to use it. There's one fellow they call 'The Dane' who is a nasty sort. He would be far more likely of a suspect to hurt an innocent little boy. As far as I am concerned, you guys are barking up the wrong tree if you think Mr. Eddy hurt that child or anyone else."

"Thank you for your time, Mr. Koepfler. I am sure you are a busy man so we will continue our questioning while you return to your labors." Wengert turned from the bewildered farmer to summon Siepman to bring Eddy closer.

"If you can see this spot, Eddy, try to remember what happened here," Wengert pressed. "You have told us that you often have times where you have lost your memory and I think if you can look at this place again and hear the description, it might trigger your memory. I don't have to tell you how important the truth is to the Almighty himself."

Wengert walked a few paces ahead of where Eddy stood looking at the ground in front of them. "The boy was found lying on his stomach. His head was right here, and his feet were positioned this way. It appears someone had carried him and dropped him off this way. Is that what it looks like to you? Is that how it could have happened?" Wengert indicated the exact locations of Buddy's head and feet positions while Eddy winced at the blunt descriptions.

"I don't know what happened to him. Before God, I am innocent." Eddy reached with his hands to remove his hat as tears streamed down his face. "Buddy was a sweet little boy. My heart is broken, someone hurt him, and I was not here to stop them. All of you know I was in the House of Corrections until a few days ago because you were the ones who put me there in the first place. I will do anything I can to help you find the person who did this, but I won't say I did it when I didn't. Meanwhile, aren't you concerned the real person may try to hurt another child?"

"Leave the theories to the officials who are qualified to investigate," said Wengert. "You were in the area when the boy went missing, you admit you knew him, you admit you have periods of time that you can't remember, and we have other children coming forward to say you have tried to hurt them in the past. All of this looks very bad for you. It would be better to be truthful if you are the good Christian you claim to be."

"Imagine the pain of this poor little boy's mother," Wengert shook his head, "how she wants to know who killed her only son. I was hoping you would be honest and admit what we know you have done, but I can see the true heart of a degenerate in you." Wengert stormed away from the group, leaving the officers to follow him while dragging Mr. Eddy with them.

The ride back to the Wauwatosa precinct was made in stony silence. Siepman dragged Eddy alongside as they entered the main room of the building. Newspaper men waited and the lightbulbs of the cameras were flashing everywhere as Eddy walked dejectedly between the officers. His hopes of being quickly cleared and released were fading fast.

Officer Hammerschmidt met Siepman in the middle of the room. He pointed at a small woman who sat in one of the straight back chairs to the side of the large group. "That is Mrs. Emma Abel. She lives over towards North Avenue. She came in to tell us about running across Mr. Eddy here a few months ago. He had a handkerchief that was dirty, so she got him some soap to clean it. She claims she can identify the handkerchief if she sees it again. I went to get the Chief and found out that Wengert had taken a trip out to Koepfler's farm. We have been waiting for all of you to return."

Siepman chuckled as he pushed Eddy towards the hallway and the stairs to the cells. "Looks like we have even more damning evidence against you, old man. It would have been better for you to just confess out there and get it over with."

Detective Murphy stepped forward from his desk with an outstretched hand. "I will take him back to the cells while you check in with the Chief and Wengert." He took Mr. Eddy's arm from Siepman and guided him through the throng of reporters gathered around them.

Siepman was mildly surprised at Murphy's change in demeanor towards him, but he was so anxious to get to the Chief's office and claim some of the credit, that he relinquished his prisoner's arm. He made a beeline to the woman who was seated looking nervously at the cameras being pointed in her face.

"Come with me, Mrs. Abel. The handkerchief you can identify as belonging to the suspect is located this way." Siepman enjoyed the simultaneous gasps of the reporters who had heard every word he had just loudly pronounced to the room. The woman rose from her chair and followed Siepman across the room towards the Chief's office.

Murphy had traveled part of the way down the stairs, leading Mr. Eddy beside him when he paused and looked over the banister. The stairway was empty and quiet.

"I was given the address of your brother in Iowa." Murphy whispered. "I contacted him, and he is on his way to help you. Don't answer any more of their questions until he hires an attorney to represent you. Miss Addy sent another bible, and Miss Ruthie made a blanket for you. I hid them under the cot in your cell as they seemed to take from you everything else that we brought in a few days ago."

Murphy led the man down the rest of the stairs to his cell and unlocked the shackles binding his wrists and feet. Deep red sores covered his wrists where the handcuffs had been left for too long. "I will bring in an ointment for those sores too."

"I know what Job meant when he said, 'He has redeemed my soul from going to the pit, and my life shall see the light.' Thank you." Eddy whispered his comment as he sat on his cot. He reached immediately for the bible Murphy had stashed below and held it reverently in his hands. The worn leather cover opened to gold gilded pages that were whisper thin.

Murphy left the man to study and meditate and returned upstairs to find John watching the display of seating Mrs. Abel in front of numerous reporters and bringing the handkerchief from the Chief's office for her to identify in front of everyone. Siepman looked like a cat who had just eaten a canary as he crooned to the audience staged before him.

"It is the good citizens of Wauwatosa like Mrs. George Abel who will assist us in bringing the murderer of Buddy Schumacher to justice. Mrs. Abel came forward to testify she had seen the handkerchief that was on the person of our main suspect only weeks prior to the abduction and murder. She will be able to confirm the same handkerchief she saw that day is the one pulled from the throat of the murdered boy." Siepman crowed to the group of reporters like the ringmaster of a three-ring circus. John had difficulty hiding his disgust for the showmanship.

Chief Baltes and DA Wengert appeared from the hallway, both men visibly upset. Baltes, who was well known for his temperamental outbursts, brought the reason for their discomfiture to light. He shouted into the room, his voice echoing off the walls.

"When we checked on the evidence, several of the items were missing including the clothing and most specifically, the handkerchief. They are nowhere to be found."

CHAPTER 25

SEPTEMBER 21, 1925 – WAUWATOSA POLICE DEPARTMENT

John sat with his back to the wall. He felt the irony of his physical state being aligned with his current moral stance. The immense pressure he was experiencing was due to standing by while the chief of police and the district attorney railroaded an innocent man into confessing to the murder of a child.

Kraemer and Zellmer had been summarily dismissed from the case by the chief of police, but the hierarchy of Milwaukee County had persisted in keeping the two seasoned detectives in the investigation.

Yesterday, Under Sheriff Herman Kroening reinstated Kraemer and Zellmer and called for an additional investigation into the disappearance of vital pieces of evidence from the Wauwatosa Police Department. He likened the actions of the Police Department, and especially those of the District Attorney's office, to the bumbling antics of the Keystone Cops of movie fame.

Chief Baltes had responded to the Milwaukee County Sheriff's interference by assigning Kramer and Zellmer to mundane tasks involving the coroner's office. Kraemer had dealt with petty officials before in his long tenure of police work, so it did not deter him from his focus on finding Buddy's killer. He and Zellmer had left that morning to meet with the coroner and chief medical officer in the offices downtown after planning to meet John and Murphy near Sanctuary Woods in the afternoon.

John had been reassigned to a patrol near the newly built golf course on North Avenue which bordered the Koepfler farm to the north. He chafed at the idea of guarding butterflies and landscaped lawns while there was serious policework to accomplish, but Murphy continued to remind him of their united front of supposed compliance in the current investigation.

Murphy had been left on the investigation after Chief Baltes had been assured of his cooperation with their methods of interrogation and evidence gathering. Outwardly Murphy helped Siepman, and the other more "loyal" officers assigned by the chief gathered testimonies from the local citizens.

He was certain the new rash of testimonies cropping up against Mr. Eddy was prompted by a concerted effort from within the police department and quite possibly the offer of more rewards for information.

The amount of money that had been given out in the last week for testimonies corroborating the guilt of their lone suspect surpassed the initial amount given to Mr. Vozer for locating the boy's body. It seemed an open market for anyone who had a story to tell defaming Mr. Eddy.

Murphy sat across from John interviewing a young fifteen-year-old boy and his mother. The boy sat twisting his cap between his hands, his eyes cast down on the floor beneath his bare feet. The mother wore what looked like her best dress and hat, her scarlet red lipstick perfectly applied as she smiled at Murphy and John across from her.

"You told Officer Siepman you had encountered Mr. Eddy in the woods recently. Can you tell me exactly what happened?" Murphy sat at the small table with his notebook and pen before him. "It's very important you are exact with your descriptions."

"Yeah, I was going through Sanctuary Woods on my way towards the train for Blackridge just like the little boy did that got taken. This guy stepped out from the reeds near the river and called me over to see his little pup he said he had in the reeds. I like pups a lot and don't have one of my own, so I went over there by him to see it. I thought maybe he would offer to give me the pup to keep." The boy looked at his mother who nodded her head at him, encouraging him to continue his story.

"Did you see a puppy when you went towards him? Usually, a puppy will be running around or barking." Murphy looked up from writing his notes. The boy shifted in the chair and tapped one foot on the ground as he shook his head.

"No, I didn't see no pups, but I didn't have any reason to think it wasn't sleeping or something. Anyways, I went towards him like I said, and he grabbed ahold of my arm and started dragging me towards the reeds where he hides. I told him to let go of me, but he wouldn't do it. He kept on dragging me and telling me to keep quiet. I was pretty scared by then." The boy looked up from the floor and shook his head vehemently at Murphy. "He didn't have no pup in there and then he did something really bad to me."

"Can you be more descriptive of what he did? I am sorry if it is upsetting to describe, but it's very important to the testimony against him." Murphy exchanged glances with John who sighed loudly.

"Well, he tried to pull on my pants and then he took out a handkerchief and tried to stuff it in my mouth. I yelled and kicked at him and was able to stand up and run off. He followed me for a while, but I was too quick for him and got away. He was trying to molest me just like he done to other boys around here." The boy's words quickened as he told the story, he blurted them out as though he had rehearsed them more than once.

"Did you see the handkerchief up close? What color was it?"

"It was a dingy white and had a little 'A' in the corner of it." The mother inserted the answer for her son who looked at her in confusion and then back at Murphy. "We was told by the other officer there is still reward money to be had for people who can help with evidence. My boy has some pretty big evidence so I would assume the reward is just as big?"

"I am not in charge of the reward money. Can you tell me when this happened to you?" Murphy directed the question back at the boy who sat staring at him with his mouth wide open.

"It was only two weeks ago, on the 13th or 14th, I think. Ma says we can get a pup and some other stuff with our part in the reward," the boy looked hopefully at Murphy. "Are we done here?"

"Yes, I think we are done. You can check with Officer Siepman as he is the one offering rewards. I have written down your testimony as you gave it to me. You may be called to testify in a court of law. You both understand that if any of this testimony is false then you are guilty of a crime? It is a very serious offense." Murphy spoke calmly as he looked at the son and then the mother. Both nodded in agreement and stood, already searching for Officer Siepman and their reward money.

John spoke to Murphy, "You realize none of that is true right? Mr. Eddy was still in the house of corrections on those dates. She gave a description of the handkerchief from the newspaper and that boy is way too large for Mr. Eddy to be able to manhandle him in any way. The boy could have overpowered him in a second. They are here to collect money like all of the other ones ahead of them."

John stood from his chair and leaned next to where Murphy sat writing in his notebook. "How long do we have to put up with this farce? This isn't even remotely a legal or due process."

"I do realize that. I also realize if I don't keep taking these testimonies, they will replace me with someone willing to add more 'facts' to them. This testimony is so blatantly false that any defense attorney could pick it apart in a second. Mr. Eddy's brother is due to arrive any time now and hopefully he will bring a good attorney with him." Murphy looked up at John while gesturing toward the far corner of the room. The boy and his mother were beaming as Siepman counted out bills and placed them in the mother's hands. John shoved his chair in anger and picked up his hat and coat.

"I am going to go and watch the grass grow at the Blue Mound Country Club. I will meet you, Kraemer, and Zellmer at two o'clock near the bent oak." John made his way towards the door, passing the still smiling mother and son.

Murphy rose from his seat and made his way towards the stairs that led to the cells below. He had checked on Mr. Eddy earlier in the morning and thought he would look in on him again before leaving the station. Loud voices emanated from the cells below. Murphy quickened his pace on the stairs.

Chief Baltes was in the cell with Mr. Eddy as Murphy approached. "We understand you seem to have a hard time remembering a lot of what happened during the time the boy went missing, and I think it's not your fault. We have a medicine we can put into this tea, and it will probably help you to remember more of what occurred. You need to be willing to take the tea with the medicine, but I am sure you want to know what happened just as much as we do."

Siepman entered the cell carrying a mug of steaming liquid on a tray. Mr. Eddy looked from one officer to another trying to decide what to do. Murphy stepped into the cell and stood beside Siepman who set the tray on the cot.

"What medication is this?" Murphy looked at Siepman then at the chief who stood beside Mr. Eddy across the cell.

"It's called Scopolamine. The tea is called Devil's breath but don't tell him that. He is already over religious." Siepman chuckled as he whispered to Murphy. "They use it as a truth serum, and I guess it works pretty good. Mr. St. John says they use it frequently in the bigger cities."

Murphy had heard of the Devil's breath, a hallucinogenic from the Borrachero tree which made its victims into zombies, easily manipulated. It had been introduced only a few years earlier and still had plenty of controversy surrounding it. He knew poor Mr. Eddy would be helpless, agreeing to all the accusations against him, once he ingested the strong drug.

"I don't think my client will be taking your 'medication' at this time. In fact, I will need time to consult with him and his brother in private." Louis Koenig, the attorney, stepped into the small cell followed by Eddy's brother Charles. "Do you have an interview room available for our use?"

Chief Baltes looked startled and then furious as he exited the cell with Siepman on his heels. Murphy was left with the attorney and the two brothers. He reached out to shake Charles' hand.

"You arrived in the nick of time. We have an interview room upstairs that was used for the investigation until recently. I can help

Mr. Eddy upstairs and get you settled in." Murphy led the men up the stairs and towards the small room he had used with the other officers. Mr. Eddy leaned hard on him, his legs trembling with weakness. Murphy noted the sadness and concern written all over Charles' face as he surveyed his brother's feeble condition.

Murphy helped Eddy into a chair and brought other chairs forward for the others. He noticed that Charles took the chair offered to him and placed it right next to his brother, seating himself in proximity and offering physical support. Attorney Koenig placed his leather briefcase on the table and opened it.

"Eddy, I am here to defend you not only against the charges but also against the obvious mistreatment you have received as a prisoner of Milwaukee County. I have contacted a physician who is on the way to evaluate your injuries and current medical condition. I plan to submit a writ of habeas corpus for cruel treatment. The police officers are no longer allowed to question you without my presence."

"Like I told Detective Murphy here, I am brought up from the pit." Eddy leaned against the arms of his brother who sat weeping beside him. Murphy left the room and walked back to his desk knowing Mr. Eddy was finally in good hands.

The four officers met at the bent oak at the appointed time. Murphy shared the good news that legal representation for Mr. Eddy had finally arrived and was already shaking up the chief and district attorney's offices. The fact that Milwaukee County was now pursuing action against Wengert for losing key evidence would distract both Wengert and Baltes for a long time.

"I find it absurd Baltes would claim fingerprinting and criminal profiling are considered ridiculous but giving a prisoner truth serum is not," said Zellman. "I wonder where he is getting these ideas for interrogation. All of my research has shown that scopolamine is used to subdue people and manipulate them into doing anything that is requested."

Zellman leaned against the massive base of the bent oak as he watched the river in the distance. "I suppose it is ideal if you want the person to validate your version of the 'truth' but it is useless in memory recall. In fact, most people who have been given the drug have no memory of anything that occurred while under its influence."

"I am fairly certain we are the only ones searching for the actual truth in this case." growled Kraemer. "Zellmer and I spent the morning filling out more paperwork for the coroner and the medical examiner. They think that if they keep us overloaded with busy work, we won't have time to investigate and find out what actually happened."

"I will remind the defense attorney to reexamine all the witnesses' testimonies and find which ones have been rewarded with the never-ending money that seems to have no limits. Most of those people need to be made aware that the penalties for perjury are severe." Kraemer paced back and forth along the path as he talked, the pent-up frustration taking a physical toll on his body.

"I think I might have stumbled across interesting information as I talked with the construction crew at the new golf course this morning." John said, climbing to the parallel trunk of the tree and sitting down, his legs dangling beneath him.

"One of the men who helped put in the new greens mentioned that some of their work was treacherous because there were so many underground caverns in the area," John continued. "They would dig and suddenly drop through until they found old plat maps that showed many of the surrounding farms had the same caverns. The Swan farm and the Gilbert farm were purchased to extend the greens, and they sit almost adjacent to the Koepfler farm, and the land used to build the asylum. I wonder how many hidden underground areas there are and if anyone else knew they existed."

"That is an excellent lead, Maloney! Can you get ahold of those plat maps for us?" Kraemer slapped his thigh with determination. "It makes me want to go searching right now!"

He hiked away as the others stood to follow him. They worked their way up the rest of the hill and down to the left; away from Koepfler's farm and towards the older portions of the asylum. After five minutes of walking, they found the shed where John and Murphy had met the asylum employee, Adam Carr, in the early days of their investigation. They passed by the shed and continued to walk the faint path when suddenly Kraemer let out a shout to the rest.

"I am standing on an old wooden trap door that was covered up with some brush." Kraemer bounced lightly on the door as he bent over to push the debris away from the opening. He and Murphy opened the door to reveal a wood ladder leading into what appeared to be a root cellar. The officers descended the ladder, feeling the excitement of their discovery mount. An old kerosene lantern stood on a bench; John took a match from his coat pocket and lit the lantern carefully.

The orange-yellow glow of the lantern light cast eerie shadows on the earthen walls around them. Old herbs and a few jars were scattered about but nothing else seemed to indicate that this was anything but a run of the mill root cellar. They looked carefully and turned back towards the ladder to exit. Murphy felt a chill run up his spine as John inhaled loudly in astonishment.

The light cast on the exit revealed a small stack of smooth stones piled immediately behind the ladder just out of sight.

CHAPTER 26

SEPTEMBER 23, 1925 – COTTAGE 5

The faint strains of Chopin drifted out to Georgie as she sat in the gazebo surrounded by the tranquil water of the pond. The surface was as smooth as glass as it sparkled in the afternoon sun. Birds called to each other from the surrounding trees and the faint buzz of the occasional bumble bee added to the concert Addy played on the piano from the cottage.

Georgie watched a pair of swans gather their cygnets, the downy gray of their young in sharp contrast to the brilliant white of the parents. The birds seemed to glide across the smooth surface as they hunted for small insects and aquatic foliage.

While other birds often kicked their young from the nests by the fall, the swans were noted for staying together through the winter and into the next spring. The cygnets had a much better chance of surviving the hazards by sticking together.

Georgie felt a sense of kinship with the swans' concord; she shared the same harmony with the eclectic group of women who communed together in Cottage 5. To the outside world they were outcasts, forgotten and discarded, but to each other, understanding the real internal value of the individual person and their combined strengths protected them from the harshness that surrounded their little refuge.

Lucian had returned from another business trip the day before, bringing back his idea of taking Addy and Georgie with him to Europe. He had suggested that several of his employees could stay and watch over the other ladies while they made their way to Scotland, but Georgie was left with a strange sense of foreboding about the prospect.

She didn't know how well Addy might handle the rigors of the trip in her delicate mental condition. She thought it was better for her to stay here among the comforts of their home and allow Addy to maintain her progress. The safety of the others was also a concern; Georgie knew, that like the swans, they had a much better chance of surviving the hazards by sticking together.

Lucian seemed very determined to take Addy with him despite Addy voicing her own reservations about leaving. It had resulted in a shouting match between the two of them and Lucian exiting as suddenly as he had appeared.

Addy had taken the departure to mean she had won the argument, but Georgie knew Lucian did not give way so easily. He had retreated momentarily to come back again at a later unknown date. Georgie was unsettled at what Lucian might do next and had sought the refuge of the gazebo to gather her thoughts and formulate her own plan.

"A penny for your thoughts. You seem very lost in them." The sound of John's voice a few feet away startled Georgie from her musings. He stood next to the bench where she sat, his hat in his hands as he gazed out at the swans she had been watching. "They are the most beautiful creatures, aren't they? One would never guess what ferocious animals they can be if they are threatened. I heard of a male swan drowning a man because the man tried to take one of the cygnets."

"Sometimes even the gentlest of creatures have the capacity to harm if they or their loved ones are threatened." murmured Georgie glancing at John as he sat on the end of the bench a couple of feet away. She could smell the fresh scent of the soap he used, a spicy, manly aroma.

"Did you come to visit me or the swans? If it's the swans, I can leave you alone with them provided you don't get too close." Georgie smiled at the slight dimple in his chin as he grinned at her comment.

"I came to ask Addy a few questions," John explained. "We have discovered there are several underground caverns in the area, and I wondered if Addy knew any of the locations. She is a resident expert on the asylum grounds. I saw you sitting out here so I decided to check with you before asking her any questions. Murphy is much better with her than I am, but he is busy at the precinct this afternoon. Do you think she might be willing to talk with me?"

John tilted his head as he turned his head towards Georgie. He was usually taken aback by her beauty, but she was exceptionally stunning in this setting, the light from the sun bouncing off the water and reflecting in her eyes, a gentle brown color.

"I think Addy will try to help you, John. You have proven yourself to be a good friend to all of us. She was upset last night but she seems to be doing better this morning and from the sound of the music she is currently playing she seems to have calmed down. I will walk back to the cottage with you to try and help you with her." Georgie rose from the bench and waited for John to stand and follow her across the bridge and up the path to the cottage.

As they approached the porch, the piano music from within suddenly stopped. John heard the hinges of the screen door squeak as Addy pushed it open and stood before him holding a small gray kitten. The kitten yawned, having been snatched up while sleeping, revealing its tiny but sharp teeth. It eyed John cautiously as he reached forward to gently pet the top of its head. After a few moments the telltale purr of contentment let John know, he had gained a new friend and ally.

"This is Little Buddy. He is the sweetest little man if he likes you, but he seems to approve of you already Officer Maloney. Have you come to tell us that they have let poor Mr. Eddy go? I was there when they took him away. They beat him half to death for no reason. I thought the police motto was, 'To protect and to serve' or is that just for the citizens who have been deemed acceptable of such treatment? Either we are all protected under the law or none of us really are." Addy gestured at John several times, inadvertently shaking the small cat. He rescued the kitten as he nodded in agreement with Addy's words.

"I strongly disagree with how Mr. Eddy has been treated. I hope he will be released very soon. I came to ask for your help with our investigation. If there is anything you can tell us it may help us to get him released even faster. Would you be willing to answer a few questions for me?" John stroked the kitten in his hands before handing it back to Addy. The kitten's loud purr made her smile.

"Well, since you have charmed Little Buddy so completely, I guess I have no choice but to cooperate with you. He knows intuitively who the good people are and who the bad ones are as well. You should have heard him hiss and growl at those awful officers who abused Mr. Eddy. How can I help you, Officer Maloney?" Addy led John and Georgie to the rockers and sat in the first one while John took the one next to her. Georgie sat on the third rocker on his other side.

"Thank you, Miss Addy. I became aware of the fact there are underground caverns in this area, and I wondered if you have ever come across any of them while you were walking on the grounds. We found a root cellar past the women's grove the other day and feel it may be an important part of our investigation." John took his notebook and pencil from his pocket.

"I knew about the root cellar as I found it in my wanderings," Addy recalled. "I don't know about any other cellars or caverns on the grounds, but I do know there was a massive tunnel built underneath the original asylum. It was used for heating the asylum buildings by producing steam through it, but it was abandoned when the new hospital was built. The caretaker of the old asylum told me all about it when I first arrived, but he has passed away since then. I don't know how one would gain access to it, but I am sure at least one person around here still knows all about it."

Addy placed Little Buddy on the porch floor as the kitten attempted to jump from her lap. She smiled as he marched to John's leg and began to rub his head and body against it, the mark of true love and devotion.

"I would assume the one person you referred to would be none other than Nurse Fielding." John remembered his eerie visit with the asylum's head nurse early in the search for Buddy. She had not been overly helpful nor friendly, but he was willing to revisit her if it meant insight on the underground steam tunnels.

John observed the strange look on Addy's face when he mentioned the head nurse's name. Her eyes clouded over, and a shadow of anger tinged her countenance. She rocked back and forth swiftly, scaring Little Buddy who ran and hid behind Georgie's chair.

"Be careful in your dealings with that one Officer Maloney," Addy warned. "She has been the cause of much trouble and grief in the lives of people I hold dear. She reminds me of the spider who waits for its prey to come to its web and become entangled. Surely you understand some of the biggest criminals are not the ones in jails and asylums; they are the ones in positions of power and authority."

Addy stood from her chair and marched back into the cottage leaving Little Buddy to mewl piteously about being left behind. John knelt beside Georgie's rocker and coaxed the kitten out from behind the chair. He patted its head gently and handed it to Georgie who snuggled it against her face.

In the matter of thirty minutes John found himself in the turret apartment of Nurse Fielding. She was just as reticent and unfriendly as she had been on his previous visit. John asked his question about the underground steam tunnels without mentioning Addy's input on the matter. Obviously, the two women were not amicable by any measure.

He cringed inwardly as he remembered Addy's depiction of the gray-haired woman as a spider waiting in her web. Her pure black garb did nothing to dispel the notion, but it was the shrewd look in her piercing eyes that caused him the most discomfort.

"I can't imagine why you would need information regarding the original asylum structures," Nurse Fielding glowered, "when your Chief of Police personally assured me the murderer has been arrested and will soon be standing trial. When he told me one of the degenerates from the trains had done this I was not at all surprised. In fact, I had warned city officials about the dangers of these hobos and tramps years ago but being a mere woman, they did not heed my warnings."

"It is tragic," she sighed as she continued. "It took the murder of a child to take the problem seriously. District Attorney Wengert has assured me new city ordinances regarding vagrants have already been drafted." Nurse Fielding sniffed with disapproval.

She sat in her lone rocking chair while John stood in front of her by the large window. He felt like a schoolboy who had been called into the principal's office for disobedience.

"Not all of the investigation has been accomplished, and we still need the information about the steam tunnels. Do you know where we can access them? The existence of the tunnels would have been extremely helpful information to have while we were still searching for the boy." John could not resist the last sentence; he hoped she could see he was not afraid of her bullying tactics. He could see the flame of ire igniting in her eyes.

"Of course, I have the information about the access points but since this is not public property you cannot simply come in here and begin searching without my permission or a search warrant. I do not give you my permission as this is an exercise in futility and a waste of taxpayer's money. I don't doubt when your Chief hears of this (and he shall) you will receive not permission to obtain your search warrant, but a firm rebuke instead. Now, if that is all, Officer Maloney, I am quite busy. See yourself out." Nurse Fielding waved her hand dismissively at him and turned her eyes toward the window.

"I will be back with the search warrant, and it will be noted you were uncooperative, a surprising reaction since you claim to have the community's best interests in mind, Nurse Fielding." John started for the door when he heard her low cackle of laughter following him out of the room. John knew he needed to get back to the precinct as quickly as possible and try to convince Chief Baltes that a search warrant was needed before the courtroom adjourned for the day.

Murphy met John in the main office amid a room filled with noise and confusion. Chief Baltes and District Attorney Wengert were not present but most of the rest of the precinct had gathered as well as a bevy of angry citizens and noisy reporters. John was focused on finding the Chief of Police until Murphy took his elbow and guided him into the small office they had shared with Kraemer and Zellmer. Mr. Eddy's attorney, Louis Koenig, waited for them there.

"You have missed some of the afternoon's excitement, Officer Maloney," Koenig greeted him. "Several of the witnesses who had come forward to claim Eddy had harmed other boys suddenly changed their minds today. It didn't hurt that I had published a small editorial piece in the Milwaukee Sentinel about the penalties of giving false testimonies with the help of Drew Pearson. Then, the two boys, Arnold Young and John Wolfe, recanted their testimony that Eddy had been the man who chased them from the train. This removes Eddy from the scene as we all know he was not present in the first place." Louis Koenig stood and opened his briefcase on the table in front of him.

"If that weren't enough," Murphy interjected, "they brought Mrs. Abel back in because Wengert claimed to have found the missing handkerchief. It looked similar but I am not even sure it was the original handkerchief. Mrs. Abel looked at it and said she didn't recognize it, so she refused to identify it as the one belonging to Mr. Eddy. Baltes was furious and stormed out of the precinct. He has been missing ever since. Koenig here, filed a motion and got all the charges against Mr. Eddy dropped. He was released to his brother an hour ago. I told his brother to get him out of town on the next train." Murphy clapped John on the back as he chuckled to himself.

John's mind was reeling at all the day's developments, but even in the middle of his excitement over the news he knew he needed to get a search warrant for the asylum as soon as possible.

"Where did Baltes and Wengert go? I need them to talk to the judge about a search warrant right away. We need to search the grounds of the asylum." John looked from Murphy to the shocked face of Koenig as they stared at him in bewilderment.

"How in the blazes did you know it was someone from the asylum who called and caused them to run out of here?" Koenig asked the question that nailed the certainty already taking over John's heart and mind.

CHAPTER 27

SEPTEMBER 24, 1925 – THE OLD ASYLUM

John looked in exasperation at the underground tunnel that surrounded the group of officers. The barren walls and floor seemed to mock him as their footsteps echoed throughout the cavernous area. John had not been able to speak with the Chief of Police or the District Attorney since returning to the precinct yesterday afternoon. He had gone before the judge at the earliest appointed time this morning to obtain a search warrant, but any evidence he had hoped to discover had already been removed.

Nurse Fielding's face had been a mask of composure when she received the warrant and directed John along with Murphy, Kraemer, and Zellmer to the building that began as an entrance to the underground steam tunnels beneath the old asylum.

The building had a small sign on the door indicating it was a bath house, but John suspected something much more sinister as he surveyed the long metal troughs that lined the room. Murphy had found a trap door on the far side of the large room that led to the tunnel below.

John had still held out hope they would find evidence linking Buddy's disappearance to the tunnel, but it seemed every trace of indications a crime had been committed had been swept clean in the wee small hours of the previous night. He walked the long tunnel in its entirety hoping to find even one stone but found only emptiness.

"All of it is gone. I should have known Nurse Fielding would alert whoever was involved and allow them to get ahead of us. This is my fault. I should have handled it differently. This wouldn't have happened if you boys had been in charge." John shook his head in despair as he acknowledged the superior skills of Detectives Kraemer and Zellmer.

"I disagree," Kraemer declared. "It seems someone has been at least one step ahead of all of us during this entire investigation, John. Both Zellmer and I have felt the same as you do now, as though we were a day late and a dollar short."

"The only thing we have is that they know we are in pursuit and sooner or later they will make a mistake. We will get them when they make that one mistake, John. I have seen it happen dozens of times before this, and it will happen again." Kraemer patted John's shoulder as he spoke, a rare show of emotion from the matter-of- fact police veteran.

"I think there is more evidence than we realize here." Zellmer knelt on the ground and swiped his fingers against the rough wooden floor. "This abandoned space is too clean. It has been swept and scrubbed clean recently. There should be cobwebs and piles of dust collecting everywhere like the building above it but there is nothing. Obviously, someone has been using this abandoned space few people knew was even in existence."

"I will go back and interview Nurse Fielding myself," Zellmer continued. "In fact, I may insist that she accompany me to the precinct for questioning to take her out of her domain. If she thinks she can be charged as an accessory for withholding information, it may make her much more cooperative. You made an excellent call, John. Don't doubt your skills of investigation just because we have been at this a lot longer than you."

John paused again as they climbed the steep staircase up to the deserted bathhouse above. Whatever had taken place here someone had gone to extraordinary measures to hide it from public view for a reason. Kraemer was right. They would catch this murderer, hopefully before he could hurt anyone else.

John found Zellmer at the top of the stairs examining the floor near the trap door. Most of the dirt and debris had been swept away from the front of the entrance and the opening, but there was still significant dust collected behind the door obscured from sight if the door was in an open/upright position.

"Gentlemen, we have a mistake." Zellmer closed the trap door and knelt on top of it to examine a shoeprint left in the dust. "Someone was standing here with their foot behind the door to open the trap door and while they cleaned away the other prints, they left this one in their hurry to get away." Zellmer pointed to a perfect shoeprint made by a man's pointed- toe dress shoe.

"This is a more expensive shoe, definitely not the work boot of a common person. You can see it is a wingtip from the narrow expanse. "Zellmer took out the camera from the large bag next to him and began to take several pictures of the shoeprint from various angles. "This is such a complete print we may even be able to determine a shoe size from measuring."

"John, you and Murphy can head back to the precinct as it will take Zellmer quite a while to gather all of his evidence. I will go with him to bring Nurse Fielding back to the police station, and we will meet you back there." Kraemer stood in the doorway of the bath house and lit a cigar anticipating a long wait for his meticulous partner. He batted at the cobwebs in the doorway that hung slightly over his head as he leaned against the doorframe.

"I think we should stop by the cottage and thank Miss Addy on our way to the car. It was her information that led me to the discovery of the tunnel." John started down the path towards Cottage 5 as Murphy followed him quietly.

They were within a few feet of the back of the cottage when they heard male voices coming from somewhere in the front. John experienced a moment of alarm as he hastened his steps towards the front. Could someone have figured out Miss Addy had revealed the information regarding the tunnel and now they were there to silence her?

Addy was sitting in her regular rocking chair with Little Buddy curled in her lap. The other rockers were occupied by Mr. Eddy and his brother Charles. Charles stood in alarm upon seeing the uniforms of the police officers; he stepped in front of his brother ready to defend him. He immediately relaxed when he recognized Officers Murphy and Maloney and stepped forward to shake their hands in greeting.

"My brother and I are scheduled to leave on the afternoon train for Iowa. He insisted on saying goodbye to Miss Addy before we departed. I am happy to see both of you as I wanted a chance to tell you how grateful we are that you contacted me to come and help him." Charles's hand trembled slightly with emotion in Murphy's grip.

John noticed the grin on Mr. Eddy's face as he announced, "Charles insists I go home to Iowa with him. He says it is my home too. Our mother is still there and is eager to see me again. I will miss many of my friends here, but it is time to go."

Eddy stood to join his brother near the stairs. "Thank you for returning my book to me, Miss Addy. I will read your letter in it later when I have my reading glasses. Reading is one of the things that makes my head hurt something terrible since my accident."

Georgie appeared in the doorway with a basket filled with sandwiches and cookies. Ruthie followed close behind her and stood next to Addy's rocking chair. Georgie handed the basket to Charles and gave Mr. Eddy a hug before they stepped down the porch stairs. John and Murphy joined the ladies on the porch to watch as the brothers walked away towards the train depot. Mr. Eddy turned back with one final wave before they were gone from sight.

"We came to thank Miss Addy for the information regarding the steam tunnel. It appears it was very useful for our investigation." John smiled at Addy and watched as the small gray kitten woke to the sound of his voice and attempted to jump from Addy's lap to find his newest friend.

Addy laughed and handed the kitten to John who nestled the tiny creature in the crook of his arm while petting the top of his head. Loud purrs emanated from the kitten which made everyone laugh including the usually stoic Ruthie.

"Where did you find the entrance? Did the old battleaxe tell you where it was hidden?" Addy leaned forward almost whispering the last words to John who stood across from her. Murphy noticed Ruthie gripped the rocking chair at the reference to Nurse Fielding. Her pale face glistened with sweat even though the late September weather had started to cool.

"She was obligated to tell us when we presented a search warrant. The entrance is in an old building listed as a bath house originally." John noted the shaking of Ruthie's legs before she started to fall.

Murphy was nearest and caught the older woman before she hit the porch floor, easing her into a sitting position while Georgie came to assist. Ruthie's head lolled to one side; her unconscious form held gently in place by Murphy and Georgie.

John gave the kitten back to Addy and came to stand in front of the trio on the floor. He carefully scooped up the slight woman and motioned for Georgie to open the porch door for him. The two of them disappeared into the house while Murphy stood and took the rocker next to Addy. He noted her hard stare directed at the pond in front of them. He waited in calm silence for Addy to speak when she was ready.

"Ruthie was taken to that bath house the night our dear friend died from a botched surgery. She has never been able to tell us what happened there, but I will tell you many of the worst criminals are the ones in charge of the most vulnerable members of society. Who will protect us from them while they accuse us of being the criminals?" Addy stood from her rocker and entered the cottage leaving Murphy to ponder her question.

John and Georgie reappeared, Georgie bearing another basket of sandwiches and cookies. She handed the basket to Murphy.

"I need to get back to Ruthie. Thank you both for looking after us." Georgie left them on the porch, and they exited towards their car parked across the field. Murphy was quiet as he continued to ponder what Addy had told him.

Soon they were back at the police station carrying the basket of lunch towards the main room. They would enjoy the picnic Georgie packed for them while they waited for Kraemer and Zellmer to return.

"Where have you two been? They have called out another search party and everyone is supposed to report." Officer Hammerschmidt stood from his desk and approached John and Murphy. "An eight-year-old boy named Mike Lecher is missing from the west side of Milwaukee. His home is only two miles from where the Schumacher boy disappeared. Chief Baltes and the DA are looking for the two of you and Kraemer and Zellmer. Everyone wants to know where Mr. Eddy is as he had been released by then. This is what happens when you let a criminal go free."

Murphy was again reminded of Addy's words to him earlier. "No, this is what happens when you let a criminal hide in plain sight."

CHAPTER 28

SEPTEMBER 25, 1925 – WAUWATOSA POLICE DEPARTMENT

The dim light of pre-dawn morning cast a pink hue through the large windows of the police station. Concerned citizens had gathered in groups across the sidewalk while exhausted police officers arrived and departed with local businessmen in small posses. John and Murphy had led an expedition along the banks of the Menomonee River near the asylum.

Once again, the flashlights and lanterns dotted the dark night like a mass of fireflies as the men searched for the missing eight-year-old boy. Detective Kraemer had taken several officers along with local farmers to the Koepfler farm where Buddy had been found. Detective Zellmer had stayed behind in one of the examination rooms with the incensed Nurse Fielding who had been taken from her office at the asylum straight to the police precinct.

"You have no right to hold me here. I have done nothing but serve the community and this is the treatment I receive for it. Believe me, when your bosses hear about this, heads will roll." Nurse Fielding's small black eyes blazed with rage as she slammed her fist on the wood table in front of her.

"I am one of the few people who stand between the innocent citizens and the deranged psychopaths that live less than a mile from their doors. You have no idea who you are dealing with young man." Her empty threats were thrown one after the other at Zellmer's head, but the officer did not flinch in the onslaught.

"You are not being held at this point, Nurse Fielding," Zellmer replied. "You are simply being questioned about the tunnels underneath the old asylum and who might have been using them. It is obvious someone has been there and a discerning matron as yourself would know the comings and goings of everyone around her. As you say, it is for the safety of the public, which seems to be your highest priority."

"If you refuse to answer the questions, then we will have to proceed with an obstruction charge. You will most definitely be held in one of the cells below. If there has not been any illegal activity in the tunnels, then you should be able to explain the situation quite easily and be on your way in a short time. The choice is all yours, madam." Zellmer sat calmly across the table with a notepad and pen at the ready.

"I don't have to answer any more of your questions. I want to speak to District Attorney Wengert and I want a lawyer right now." The shrewish woman cocked her tiny head to one side reminding Zellmer of a crow. "Your illustrious career here in Wauwatosa is about to end."

"I will note you have requested legal counsel." Zellmer replied. "This does end our questioning for the moment. You will wait here until counsel can be sought out and at this time it will be a long wait. As for my personal career in Wauwatosa, I am a veteran Milwaukee police detective who was called in to consult with this department, so I have no 'bosses to make my head roll' here as you so eloquently stated in your multitude of threats. I will ask one of the other officers to attend to you as we are quite busy tonight."

Zellmer rose from his chair and started for the door, glad to be rid of the spiteful woman. The thought reminded him of Ruthie's reaction to this woman's name and the mention of the bath house; he wondered what the poor woman had endured at the hands of this "pillar of the community".

Zellmer met John and Murphy in the main room as they returned from their search. Hot coffee was poured into tall mugs and passed around to the men who sat in a circle of chairs at the far end of the large room. Zellmer could tell from the countenances of his fellow officers that the boy had not been located yet. It seemed surreal the same scene played out only a few months before was now being replayed.

John looked up to see Art Schumacher enter the front door. Buddy's father looked as though he had aged ten years in only a few months; his thin, haggard face and graying hair told a story of his grief and frustration. Art removed his hat. Looking around the room, his gaze fell on John and Murphy as he made his way through the crowd of people towards them.

"I heard that a boy is missing. I came to help you search." His simple words spoke volumes to the officers who had searched so long for his son and continued to search for his son's killer. "I can't do anything more to help my boy, but maybe I can do something to help this one. Where should I go to look?"

"Thank you, Mr. Schumacher. We have been sending people out in shifts, and I will tell Officer Hammerschmidt to add you to the next shift. Please come and have some coffee with us while you wait." John motioned to the circle of men while Murphy went to fetch another mug of coffee.

He handed the steaming mug to Art while motioning to a chair among the others. All the men nodded to the bereaved father in a show of respect as he took his place among them. John returned from adding Art's name to the search list and sat down between him and Murphy.

"The long hours of the night are absolutely the worst. It's then you replay in your mind all the things you might have done to keep your child safe and the guilt that you didn't is a heavy burden. 'If only I had' is one of the most despairing trains of thought because there is nothing one can do to fix it after the fact." Art's quiet voice carried throughout the room, stilling the other conversations as he spoke.

"Other people mean well, they expect you to move on with life, but I have found my heart and soul are stuck in time to the night that I came home and found my son was missing. I am not sure there is such a thing as moving on." The stillness in the room was deafening; the sheer emotion of Art's thoughts put into words affecting even the most stoic of them.

Kraemer entered the front door followed by his group of volunteers. Zellmer could tell immediately something was amiss, something had gone terribly wrong by the look of outrage on his partner's face. He steeled himself to hear that young Mike Lecher had been found deceased on the same farm where Buddy Schumacher had been located. He was not prepared for Kraemer's announcement to the entire room.

"We were returning from the Koepfler farm when we were flagged down by an officer from Milwaukee's west side. Another boy, eight-year-old Roy Tolzmann, has just been reported missing by his parents. He failed to return home after a routine trip to a local store, and the parents couldn't find him anywhere. They fear that along with the Lecher boy, he has also been taken."

The soul-wrenching sobs that came from Art Schumacher echoed against the walls and permeated the hearts of every man in the room.

CHAPTER 29

LATER THAT DAY, SANCTUARY WOODS

A strong breeze rustled the vibrant leaves covering the trees over Georgie's head as she sat at the base of the old bent oak. Dappled sunlight transformed the tree trunk surrounding her into a mosaic of color and shade. Georgie closed her eyes and listened to the sounds of the woods, the gentle call of a mourning dove, the swish of the reeds at the bank of the river, and the faint trickle of water as the Menomonee River flowed past in the distance. Georgie sensed the peace, which the solitary woods proffered, warming her senses.

She was glad she had accepted Addy's offer of a walk through the woods, their customary stop at young Cora's grave to leave a bouquet of wildflowers, then the trek up the hillside and through the women's grove along the stone stairs and to the enormous tree that was Addy's refuge.

Georgie glanced upwards. She could not see Addy in her hiding place above, but she knew long periods of time in quiet solitude were spent there. Sometimes Georgie wished she too had a hiding place from the grim realities that seemed to surround them.

The police officers had stopped by Cottage 5 last evening to ask if they had seen a small boy who had gone missing from a nearby location in Milwaukee. Georgie had not recognized any of the police officers and wondered if John and Murphy were also out searching for the little boy. It seemed it was the exact situation which had brought John to their doorstep only a few months prior.

Georgie realized with a start that while she still grieved the loss of Buddy, she was thankful John had been introduced into her life. So many things had changed in her since his arrival, and she knew he was a part of those changes. She had come from a small town to the big city looking for excitement and a debonair young man to sweep her off her feet, but she now realized it was in the humble, kind, police officer that her interests and love grew.

"I have just returned from business in New York city. I stopped at the cottage, but the old mute woman wouldn't say where you had gone. I swear she grows crazier by the day. I decided to walk the path to see if you had come this way." Lucian's voice from the top of the knoll broke the peace of the surrounding woods.

"I see you are by yourself so perhaps it is as good a time as any to talk about our plans for Europe." Lucian approached the trunk Georgie sat on and leaned against it, his shoulder touching her leg in a way that would have thrilled her at one time. Georgie noted it only made her want to edge away from him which she did by shifting her weight.

Georgie glanced up at the tree above her while Lucian busied himself lighting a cigar. She had not corrected him about being alone but the silence from above seemed to beg her not to reveal Addy's hidden presence. Maybe Addy needed to hear what Lucian had to say about her when he thought she was not present. Oftentimes it was the truest mark of a person's character, how they speak of other people in their absence. Georgie made the decision not to correct him.

"I thought Addy's opposition to the trip would bring an end to the matter. I am concerned that if she is pressed into leaving the only place she feels safe, the results might bring a relapse of illness for her." Georgie attempted to argue Addy's opposition to the trip without causing an argument with Lucian.

Georgie knew she did not want to accompany Lucian either, another change wrought by the introduction of a young Wauwatosa police officer. Suddenly the possibility of world travel with a wealthy man like Lucian did not excite the same feelings for her.

Lucian snorted in derision. "What Addy will or will not like is not a primary consideration. My business dealings have concluded in Wisconsin, and it has become an urgent matter to travel abroad for at least the next year. My parents are meeting us in Edinburgh. Both the house in Lake Geneva and the house in Chicago will be shut up for the interim."

"Even most of my assets will be moved to Switzerland. There won't be an easy way to continue to send funds to the asylum for the cottage and Addy's care. You are still welcome to travel with us at my expense as it will comfort Addy to have you there. All of this has been decided already, Georgie. It isn't up for debate." Lucian shifted, leaning hard against Georgie, pinning her leg to the tree trunk beneath her.

"What about the other ladies Lucian? You promised Addy nothing would change at Cottage 5. What on earth will happen to them?" Georgie felt icy fear beginning to creep along her spine as she looked into Lucian's eyes and beheld a blank darkness there.

"They will go back to the main asylum," Lucian's tone was cold. "They aren't my problem, and they aren't yours. Remember you were hired to take care of Addy and the attachment you allowed yourself for these others is far from professional. This trip will benefit you as well. You are a beautiful woman, if you allow my attention to you knowing that I will remain married to Addy it will enrich you in numerous ways."

"I can introduce you to the very elite of Europe and who knows where you can go from there. Many times, the mistress is far better off than the wife." Lucian continued to lean hard on her leg as he turned his body towards her, resting his free hand on her upper thigh.

"I will not travel anywhere with you, Lucian," Georgie declared. "I will never be your mistress or anything else for that matter. When I see how you have broken your word to Addy it can only make me think you would do the same to me once you tire of me. You treat both of us as though we are simply objects for you to acquire and then dispose of as you see fit."

"If I don't agree to go with you then Addy will never agree to go either. It would be better off for you to leave her here with me and leave by yourself because she will fight you over this." Georgie wrenched herself from his grip and jumped to the ground below.

"I anticipated your opposition, Georgie. I would never leave Addy behind with you. I have already scheduled the surgical procedure for histrionics in New York suggested by the specialists there. A few simple taps into the brain and Addy won't mind anything else ever again. She will follow me about like a lamb with or without you. So, by all means, leave us. In fact, make sure you are gone by the end of the week. Addy will be leaving soon and your job here is at an end." Lucian extinguished his cigar, stomping it into the ground next to Georgie's feet. He turned and walked away, back up the path, until he was out of sight.

Georgie let out a breath she hadn't realized she was holding. Rage burned within her and her lungs burned as though they were filling with water. She gulped and gasped trying to take a breath while her arms and legs shook uncontrollably. What was she going to do to save Addy from her own husband, the man who had all legal rights over her?

She felt a hand placed on her shoulder, a calm and gentle grip as Georgie turned to face Addy who had silently descended her tree. Instead of being beside herself with emotion, Addy appeared undisturbed by what she had just heard.

Surely, she didn't understand what Lucian intended to do to her, the procedure that would remove all of Addy's emotions and all her memories and personality as well. Georgie gasped again, trying to take a breath against the elephant that seemed to perch upon her chest.

"There now, just lean against me and close your eyes. Try to take a breath when you feel me taking one." Addy turned Georgie until she faced away from her and pulled Georgie close, Georgie's back resting against Addy's chest. Addy took a deep breath.

Georgie could feel the air against her back and her lungs suddenly released as she took a small breath with Addy. The immense pressure on her chest lessened as Georgie concentrated on the slow breathing. She realized this was something she had done for Addy numerous times before in times of anxiety and now her friend was returning the favor.

After a few minutes Georgie felt better. She turned to look into Addy's face expecting to see fear registered there. Instead, Addy's eyes held a steely gaze of determination, her face clear from alarm. Addy stooped to pick up her bag and took Georgie's hand, leading her along the path towards the cottage. Georgie followed in mute surprise, the transformation in Addy almost inconceivable to comprehend. Addy broke the silence as she marched along.

"We have to formulate a plan, Georgie, and we don't have very much time to do it. We need to gather everyone together before Lucian tries to return for me. It will take all of us women working together, but we have managed it before, and we shall again."

LATER THAT EVENING, WAUWATOSA POLICE DEPARTMENT

Detective Zellmer sat at the table in the small examination room facing Nurse Fielding and her counsel, Carl Levy. The attorney had made his appearance only twenty minutes before, asking to speak with his new client before sitting down with the detectives.

Zellmer knew Levy was not from a local law firm. He had traveled from a prestigious firm in Chicago, thus delaying his arrival and leaving Nurse Fielding to spend much of her day in a holding cell. The meeting between client and attorney was very brief. Zellmer surmised that whoever had engaged her legal counsel had already briefed the attorney on the matter at hand.

"Surely you understand that you can't hold my client here indefinitely unless you have a charge against her. Nurse Fielding is a valuable part of the administration of the asylum and is needed at her post for the daily operations to continue. I have contacted District Attorney Wengert, and he is agreeable to allowing her to leave without further delay." Levy's smirk rankled Zellmer as was intended. He had gone above the detective's head to get his client released and wanted to rub it in Zellmer's face.

"I had only a few simple questions for your client regarding the abandoned tunnels on the asylum property. She refused to answer them without legal counsel, and we have simply been waiting for you to arrive. If she took a moment or two to answer my questions, she can be on her way." Zellmer wanted to make certain Nurse Fielding understood her undesirable hours spent in the holding cell were her own doing.

"Well, after conferring with my client, she is invoking her fifth amendment rights not to testify or answer questions at this time. If you don't have any charges, we will be leaving now. I should warn you moving forward you are not to contact her again without the presence of her legal counsel." Levy stood, staring at Zellmer with open contempt. He motioned for Nurse Fielding to stand with him. Zellmer knew this was an important piece in this puzzle, and that, yet again, the murderer would continue to evade the police.

"You do realize there are two more little boys missing? Little boys like Buddy Schumacher whom you told us was a nice young man. What kind of person hurts little kids? For that matter, what kind of person protects someone who hurts little kids? Those tunnels were very likely used during Buddy's abduction. Knowing more about it might help us find these other boys before the same thing that happened to him happens to them." Zellmer's calm voice followed Nurse Fielding as she stood and walked towards the door. She paused for a moment before exiting. Then, she straightened her back and shoulders with a sigh and left without glancing back at the detective.

"I can see from your expression how well that went." Kraemer stuck his head inside the open door. "She is obviously hiding something for someone, but she isn't the only one. How many people are willing to cover up what is going on here and why would they cover it up? It reminds me a lot of the cases involving the upper levels of the mob in Chicago when I was a young police officer there. People were either involved themselves or they were too scared of the repercussions to help the police solve one murder after another. When powerful people are involved in crimes, justice becomes a victim."

"I think you just provided a connection, Kraemer." Zellmer stood and walked to a small chalkboard on the wall. He picked up the chalk and wrote *Milwaukee* and *Chicago* at the top. "I recalled that Carl Levy was a high-priced attorney from Chicago, much too expensive for the likes of Nurse Fielding, so I knew he had been hired by someone else." Zellmer wrote the name *Levy* under *Chicago*.

"It was when you mentioned the crime bosses in Chicago that I remembered Levy represented Johnny Torrio last year along with Frankie Yale in the hit on Big Jim Colosimo. The District Attorney determined there wasn't enough evidence to charge either with contracting the hit." Zellmer jotted down the names *Torrio* and *Yale* under *Chicago*.

"You do realize Torrio's number one guy has been seen here in Wisconsin as well as in Chicago. Al Capone reportedly has homes somewhere in Brookfield and Elkhorn, but he is as elusive as they come." Kramer walked to stand beside Zellmer and stared at the chalkboard in front of them.

"Capone and Torrio are best known for bootlegging, but I don't think either has ever been linked to child abductions. In fact, along with John Dillinger, they have almost a folk hero reputation among the local citizens." Kraemer watched as Zellmer added *Capone* under both *Chicago* and *Milwaukee*.

"I don't think they are directly related to Buddy's murder, but could there be a possible link between their bootlegging operations and whoever murdered Buddy? Those tunnels would be perfect." Zellmer paused. He drew a line down from Capone's name under *Milwaukee* and left a blank space. Kraemer nodded his head emphatically in agreement.

"The tunnels are perfect for moonshine stills! Remember the spot we checked out near Port Washington and the rum coves near Racine? They could use those places to transport liquor in and out of the area let alone Wauwatosa's close proximity to Chicago." Kraemer slugged Zellmer in the arm. "You may have just discovered a strong link in our crime scenes. Do you think the hierarchy of Wauwatosa is involved including the matron of the asylum?"

"No," Zellmer replied. "I see Baltes and Wengert as more political chess pieces that someone with a lot of power is influencing. Somehow, Nurse Fielding has knowledge of who was in the tunnels, but not necessarily of what they were doing."

"I saw her take a pause when I said that if she helped this person, she would help them to harm children. She did not want to be included in that number. I say we watch her from a distance and allow her conscience to settle in on her. I think she will lead us to the person who is in charge." Zellmer put the chalk back on the small tray and continued to study the board.

Murphy knocked on the door and entered the small room. He carried several articles he had retrieved from the Schumacher evidence box: the fishing pole, the dinner pail, the bag of stones, and Buddy's red tennis shoe. He placed them on the small table and glanced at the chalkboard, reading the names and showing his surprise at what was listed. He came to stand beside the other two and studied the chalkboard closer.

"You must be thinking of a link between the disappearances and bootlegging?" asked Murphy. "I admit I have had the same thought several times. This has such complex organization to it and almost a flaunting of the activity in front of law enforcement. The little girl who was thrown from the car was near Carrollville which is enroute to Racine. The other seven-year-old boy from Chicago was also found in Lake Michigan near what would be the same route."

"Even several of the locations where Buddy was reported to have been seen in the early days all seem to have a circular pattern around Milwaukee and Chicago routes." Murphy picked up the chalk and added *Racine, Carrollville,* and *Port Washington* around the other two cities. "If someone traversed those routes as a bootlegger, they would have the opportunity to be in all of the locations of the disappearances and sightings at various times."

"From what we know about the major names listed none of them have been involved in child abductions but someone else associated with them might be." As he spoke, Kraemer turned towards the table. "I see you brought some of the Schumacher evidence in with you. Did you find anything else concerning them?"

"I signed these out of the evidence locker a while back," replied Murphy, "and took them back to the FBI specialist from Chicago who had tested them for fingerprints originally. If you remember, he said there was one set of fingerprints that remained the same on most of the items. These fingerprints did not belong to Buddy or any of his family members. This was a crucial piece of evidence because someone associated with Buddy's abduction and murder is likely the owner of those prints. I took more pieces of evidence to him when I picked these up today and he is testing the items right now. I am hoping for a match of prints from those items to the prints on the evidence."

"I did this on my own so no one else in the department would have to answer Chief Baltes about it, and that's why I kept it to myself." Murphy turned back to the evidence strewn across the table. "I am to the point of taking high risks as far as my career is concerned so we can solve this once and for all."

"We are in agreement about that, Murphy. Zellmer and I are willing to crack a few eggs or egos too. Has there been any more news on either search for the Lecher or Tolzmann boys? I know they moved some of the search areas into West Allis and Brookfield, but we still have search parties out there as well?" Kraemer sat at the table and sipped from a mug of tepid coffee.

"I haven't heard anything," Murphy replied, "but I know Maloney has been out there almost nonstop since yesterday. They covered all the places we searched for the Schumacher boy, and nothing has surfaced yet. Meanwhile we have two more distraught sets of parents and a terrified community."

"They talked about closing the school for a period because they are afraid to send the children, but several community members have started walking groups of kids to school. They surmised they are safer gathered at school all day than having kids isolated and sneaking off places by themselves. The Tolzmann boy didn't make it two blocks from his own home before he went missing and, like the Schumacher boy, it was in broad daylight." Murphy joined Kraemer at the table.

"This has to be someone other people don't notice as standing out," Zellmer mused, "certainly not a Mr. Eddy type or a vagrant as they keep trying to portray. I am glad Mr. Eddy was cleared by the time stamp on his departing train ticket and his brother as a witness. He couldn't have been here to abduct either boy just like he couldn't have been there the first time."

Murphy looked up to see John approaching the examination room at a rapid pace. Officer Wrasse was with him and several of the firefighters from next door. John had obviously rushed to find them as he was out of breath. Murphy stood and came closer to his partner. He discerned the heavy scent of smoke and saw the soot on John's face and hands.

"I was returning from the search party by the river and saw the fire department had been dispatched nearby," John explained. "A barn on the Hartung property near 63rd Street above the quarry had been set on fire. It looked very suspicious, so the firefighters from our search party came to find me. They put the blaze out quickly but found Roy Tolzmann inside. He had been dismembered by a nearby hay knife."

"I need all of you to return to the barn with me as the firefighters are guarding the scene until we can examine it ourselves. Someone will have to be dispatched to the Tolzmann home soon as word seems to spread quickly and it was difficult to keep the reporters out of the way." John leaned his weary head against the door frame. He answered the unspoken question in the room.

"We did not find Mike Lecher, but I fear his time is running out.

CHAPTER 31

SEPTEMBER 26, 1925 – COTTAGE 5

Addy looked around the large table at the women gathered for what might be their final time. She and Georgie had left the spot by the old bent oak the day before and immediately assembled their rag-tag group including Freda, Ingrid, Mary, Ella, and themselves. Georgie explained in detail Lucian's plans to take Addy and depart for Europe indefinitely, leaving all the rest of them without home and board due to lack of financial support.

They had listened in silent terror as the images of their former lives at the main asylum invaded their collective memories. None of them were willing to return to the direct jurisdiction of Nurse Fielding and her henchmen.

They were hard put to know where else they could go and find the refuge that Cottage 5 had afforded them. Their chief concern, however, was Addy's unwilling departure without her consent and the possibility of a terrifying medical procedure that would leave her insensible forever.

The hours of the late night melted into the hours of the early morning as they discussed possible options. Georgie had suggested an initial stay at her parents' farm near Dresbach, Minnesota. She felt she had few options that did not include returning to her parents for at least a brief interim and she knew her large family, including numerous older brothers and sisters who lived all around her parents, would welcome her friends with open arms and warm hearts.

She would be able to sign the other women out of the asylum on a temporary release for travel and then they would face more permanent decisions in the coming months. All of them agreed they wanted to remain together, so this seemed a viable option for everyone except Addy who refused to leave with the group. She knew Lucian would only use his extensive network to search for her, find her, and take her back with him by force if necessary.

"Leaving with all of you would only put the rest of you at risk," Addy explained. "Lucian could use the threat of harm to the rest of you to coerce me into doing whatever he wants. Once he has his mind set, heaven help the unfortunate souls who might get in his path. I need to stay here. I have formulated a plan to evade him without running away so that he can't follow me."

"You will all need to promise me you will leave on this afternoon's train and not look back. I promise I will try to join you again in the near future." Addy smiled her reassurance to the others as she held the sleeping Little Buddy in her arms. The kitten's loud purring was accentuated in the stillness of the early morning. "I would ask you to take this little fellow with you. He will enjoy the farm life in Minnesota, I am sure."

"Addy," said Georgie, "I think we should send everyone else out ahead, but I should stay behind with you. Who will be there to help you if your plan doesn't go as you intended? One of my brothers lives in Prairie du Chien which is part of the way there. I know he would be willing to meet the train and make sure everyone gets to the other train to Dresbach safely."

Georgie took Addy's hand in her own in a gentle appeal. "If Lucian overpowers you or drugs you it might be too late for me to try and rescue you from the medical procedure he has planned in New York City. I would never forgive myself if something happened to you."

"I will be perfectly safe." Addy assured them. "I am worried your presence might accidentally have an adverse effect which could cause my plan to fail. This isn't something I planned at the last minute, Georgie. I have had one form or another of this plan for years, and I have saved it for a time of extreme circumstances. I think you will agree it is warranted now."

"My parents always taught me to have a means of escape from any situation as they had witnessed some of the eugenics studies happening in Europe and the passing of the Mental Deficiency Act in 1913 which caused them great alarm. They understood that anyone can be declared to have mental deficiencies and be taken away without a diagnosis or the conviction of a crime. They warned anyone who would listen at the university that a time may come when entire ethnic groups might be deemed unfit and be taken away without equity. I pray we never see such a time, but we should be ready in any case. All of the others around this table can assure you that this does happen." Addy looked at the beloved faces surrounding her, knowing each story like her own bore witness to the truth of her premise.

Georgie marveled at Addy's seeming tranquility amid this perilous situation. She knew Addy's mental illness might prevent her from realizing the "normal" feelings of fear, but she was struck by the thought Addy appeared far more in her right senses than Georgie felt herself currently. She finally nodded her head in agreement with Addy's proposal. Addy nodded back, handed the sleeping kitten to Ruthie, and stood to exit the kitchen for her bedroom. She reappeared carrying a small wooden box she unlocked with a key.

"Lucian brought several of my personal items from Stone Place including my keepsake box. He never checked inside it because he knew it was filled with sentimental trinkets including our son's lock of hair and his little bootie from his christening. I kept a few small tokens from my parents as well and the intense emotionalism they provoked in me made him uncomfortable. I was always glad of it because he never suspected that I kept anything else along with the trinkets." Addy laid the precious tokens aside and lifted a false bottom of the box. The others gasped as she poured a huge pile of money into various denominations of bills onto the table in front of them.

"There is plenty here for train tickets and living expenses until new arrangements are made. I have even saved enough from my parents' trust to possibly purchase our own cottage so we might return here if we wish. All of it is safely hidden away in bank accounts as part of that escape plan, I mentioned. We are not without means."

The group set about packing bags for their impromptu trip. Addy packed a small bag of her own necessities while Georgie called her parents in Dresbach and her brother in Prairie du Chien. It was decided they would travel to Georgie's brother's home and rest there before resuming the journey to the small town in Minnesota.

Ella and Mary packed a large hamper with a multitude of sandwiches and other food for their trip. Ingrid packed an extra bag of the items that Freda used to assist her with her lack of sight. It was early afternoon when they decided everything was in order and they should be underway.

Georgie purchased the train tickets and returned to the group waiting on the platform. Addy had lined a basket with a soft cloth, providing a soft bed for the gray kitten who slept peacefully, unaware of his surroundings. Addy held her face close to the fuzzy figure, nuzzling his soft ears against her cheek. A small niggle of regret crowded Addy's throat, but she cleared it quickly and handed the basket to Ella while she turned to hug Ruthie tightly. She then made her way towards each woman with an embrace ending with Georgie.

"Try not to worry, it's only borrowing against trouble that hasn't yet happened. I will call you. Take good care of everyone and we will be back together soon." Addy whispered into Georgie's ear as Georgie tried to keep herself from crying.

The tears collected in Georgie's throat as she nodded her head and placed her hand on Addy's cheek. The wind blew Addy's auburn curls. Georgie moved one curl from the center of her face, smoothing it back into her bobby pin at the side of her head.

Addy watched the others board the train as the second whistle sounded. She gave a quick cheerful wave and turned quickly down the street away from the depot and towards the center of Wauwatosa. She knew her destination was only a few blocks from the depot, but she walked quickly, hoping she would not see the familiar Rolls Royce before she reached it.

"Well, I fancy meeting you here. It has been a long while, but I would recognize that crazy red hair anywhere." A familiar voice close behind Addy made her heart sink into her stomach. It had been over four years, but Addy recognized the voice of her captor, Nick. Addy did not turn but quickened her steps towards her goal.

She felt the crush of Nick's grip as he grabbed her upper arm and spun her to face him on the sidewalk. His malevolent grin enraged her, and she attempted to yank her arm from his grasp.

"Now, you don't want to fight against me. We have already taken all your friends from your little cottage, and their lives depend on your cooperation. Come quietly with me and they might live through this." Nick's boldfaced lie made Addy even angrier.

Her friends were safe away from here, but Addy would not reveal that to him for anything. Addy glared at him while continuing to attempt to back away. She heard a car's engine slowing beside them on the street. Addy quickly turned her head, her body flooded with relief to see Adam Carr, one of the asylum employees, at the wheel of a Model T.

"Mr. Carr. It's so good to see you. I am afraid this man is bothering me and won't stop. Can you give me a ride?" Addy wrenched herself free from Nick's grip and started towards the car. She noticed the strange look on Adam's face before his words registered in her brain.

"Just be quiet and get in the car, Addy. No one else has to get hurt. It would be a shame to hurt those gals especially the mute one and the blind one, but they will get hurt and it will be all your fault." Adam put the engine into park and began to open the car door as Nick followed Addy from behind. "It is a mistake to scream or try to run. It just means more torture for them and you."

Addy stopped in her tracks for a second. She couldn't believe the words coming from the mouth of the man she considered their friend. She felt Nick's iron grip on both of her arms as he leaned close to her ear.

"It's a shame my brother here never told you about our kinship, but I reckon he thought you might not like him so much after our last encounter. I wonder how good old Fred is doing at the bottom of Geneva Lake. Didn't you blame that on a mermaid or something like it? Poor Fred was getting spooked by your ghost story before he fell into the lake." Nick chuckled, a low gravely sound that grated against her ear as he pushed her towards the car.

Once again Addy had only a few moments to decide what to do. She knew Nick was likely to finish the job he had begun at their first meeting and this time she would not survive it. None of this had been part of her plan.

"It wasn't a mermaid. It was a siren, and I hope she comes for you next." Addy shouted her answer, trying to attract attention to herself being abducted in broad daylight in the middle of Wauwatosa. She planted the sharp heel of her shoe in the middle of Nick's foot while shoving her elbow back into his stomach. She heard the air swoosh out of him as Nick groaned and released his hold on her.

Addy ran screaming down the sidewalk towards her destination, the Wauwatosa Police Department. She begged God to allow her to live long enough to reach John and Murphy within the building.

Addy ran another block and could see the police station in front of her. She heard the roar of the car engine behind her as Adam chased her down in the Model T. She could not afford to look back as she raced for the steps of the building. Suddenly she was tackled from behind, her body crashing to the ground. She could hear her bones breaking from the force of hitting the sidewalk. Pain shot through her body as she cried out.

"Gentlemen, step away from this woman. Ma'am, are you hurt? Let me help you." John's voice floated through the waves of pain that threatened to overtake Addy and send her into the blackness of unconsciousness at any moment.

"Miss Addy? What on earth has happened here? John gently turned Addy over and looked at her face in shock and recognition.

He turned to see the Carr brothers flee the scene while he held her in his arms and called for help.

"Officer Maloney, I came to find you and Officer Murphy. I have to tell you something important." Addy sputtered the words as John picked her up from the ground and carried her into the precinct. She was frightened she would sink into unconsciousness before she had a chance to do what she had come to do. She took a deep breath that caused the intense pain to branch out through her limbs as though she were set on fire. She had to tell him now.

"I came here to tell you that I took little Buddy Schumacher. I did it. I came to turn myself in." Addy's words were blurted out before a room of shocked police officers before she passed out into oblivion.

CHAPTER 32

LATER THAT EVENING, WAUWATOSA POLICE DEPARTMENT

Addy awoke in a small examination room right off the main area. Darkness surrounded her and the room was quiet with only the occasional muffled noises from the larger room outside. She shifted herself in the cot that she lay in, intense pain shooting up and down her left arm into her shoulder blade. She kept her eyes closed trying to recall what had happened since she had arrived at the police station in the arms of Officer Maloney.

Small snippets of memory, like snapshots in a photo album buzzed about in her mind; there was a doctor who had given her a foul-tasting brown liquid and went about inflicting great bodily pain until she had passed out again, there were the concerned faces of Officer Maloney and Detectives Kraemer and Zellmer floating above her face at times like heads without bodies attached to them, and there was the sensation her own body floated above the cot making Addy believe she was dying.

The clearest memory from the long afternoon was of a gentle hand placed on her cheek and forehead whenever she cried out in agony. It reminded Addy of her mother: loving and comforting and protective. As she lay on the cot now, trying to adjust her eyes to the low level of light, Addy tried to recall more about the person who had comforted her as she cried. She realized it could not be her mother; she lay in a grave in Edinburgh. A small sigh escaped her lips as Addy batted her eyes a few more times trying to remove the cobwebs from her brain.

"Now, don't move around too much. You have only just fallen asleep for a short while without crying and movement will aggravate the pain even more. Close your eyes and rest now." The hand stroked the side of Addy's face; it was cool to the touch bringing relief. Addy focused on the sound of the voice. It was familiar, but it sounded as though it traveled to her through waves of water which distorted the tones.

Addy opened her eyes again attempting to bring her mind from the cloud bank of fog that surrounded it. Suddenly, a lucidity sparked realization in Addy's muddled brain.

"Ruthie? Is that you? What are you doing here?" Addy turned her head to the side and peered in the dimness to seek out the face of her dearest friend. "Why aren't you on the train with Georgie and the others?"

"I boarded the train, but I explained to Georgie that I had made the worst mistake of my life the day I left Cora alone in Hall 5," Ruthie whispered. "I would never forgive myself if something happened to you because I was not here to help you in your time of need. Georgie made the quick decision to help me find the nearest porter from the train station and have him escort me to where I thought you would be."

"I had no doubt you felt safe to face Lucian because you were going to be in the company of Officer Maloney and Detective

Murphy, so I knew exactly where to go. I arrived only minutes after Officer Maloney carried you in here and they called for a doctor. Be assured that whatever your plan I will not interfere. No one will notice an old woman who does not even speak. In fact, I hear and see all kinds of things because people don't think I can reason just because I have not spoken very much." Ruthie took a cold cloth and placed it on Addy's head while she spoke softly.

"But you have not been able to speak since...." Addy's voice trailed off as the memory of Cora's horrifying death due to a botched hysterectomy assailed her thoughts. She could almost smell the metallic scent of the profuse blood which covered the small dying girl and all of those who surrounded her, especially Ruthie. "Since we saw you again after they brought you back to Hall 5. Ruthie, why can you speak now when you couldn't then?"

"It was not so much a matter of not having the ability to speak, it was a matter of having nothing else under the sun to say," Ruthie admitted. "I felt I had seen some of the worst that humanity had ever done to other humans and all the rest of the words were a waste of time. My heart and my mind had given up, but you never gave up on me, Addy. You kept me with you when so many others would have cast me aside."

"My own husband cast me aside but not you and the others in Cottage 5. I am speaking now because I will speak in your defense until I have no more breath in my body." Ruthie leaned down and kissed Addy's forehead as she removed the cloth from it. A tear trickled down Ruthie's cheek and splashed against Addy's chin as Ruthie sat up again.

Suddenly, Addy felt the same love and security she had always felt in the presence of her mother. Mama Crane, the name young

Cora had lovingly given to Ruthie, was here with her, and Addy knew whatever she faced next she would not be alone. After so many years of shutting the world out and not allowing anyone close enough to see all her pain, Addy had someone to walk this solitary path with her.

"Ruthie, I told something to Officer Maloney, and I need you to know it too." Addy felt the lead weight of fear edge its way into her heart. After realizing Ruthie's commitment to her she feared above all else that Ruthie would reject her once she told her story. Addy wanted to hide this again along with all of the other things she had hidden deep inside. But she knew Ruthie deserved to know everything no matter what it was.

"Officer Maloney has already told me what you said. Don't worry, we will find a way through this together. I don't judge you, Addy, just as you have never judged me or any of the others. We can speak more about this when you are feeling more alert. I know Officer Maloney has been waiting to ask more questions, but he wanted to give the doctor plenty of time to set your broken arm before he started." Ruthie stood and moved towards the door, opening it slightly and whispering to someone stationed outside.

"They brought a cot to one of their rooms and they have been guarding you since you arrived." Ruthie returned with a cold cup of water and gently lifted Addy's head enough to give her a sip.

"I am sure they do have guards for me, to prevent me from escaping, but I promise I won't try to run away, Ruthie. I came here of my own free will when I could have gone anywhere else in the world to escape Lucian and all of this." Addy shifted her weight on the bed and tried to sit upright. Ruthie rushed back to her side and helped her to sit while carefully guarding her broken arm.

"My dear girl," Ruthie whispered, "Officer Maloney isn't guarding you because he thinks you will escape. He is guarding you because he is convinced those men were trying to abduct you and harm you. He was relieved when I told him the others were on their way to a safe place. He is bent on keeping you safe as well."

"There are at least three officers positioned outside while he and Detectives Kraemer and Zellmer continue to search for the other little missing boy. Addy, it is very important you tell me one thing. Did you have anything to do with the other missing boys, and do you know where the Lecher boy is?" Ruthie braced herself for Addy's answer.

"I didn't even know there were other boys missing. You mean they are searching for another boy? I don't understand." Addy's voice rose slightly as the thought of what might have happened agitated her. Ruthie nodded her head in understanding of Addy's response.

"Just what I thought. You had nothing to do with them. Are you ready to speak with Officer Maloney and the others?" Ruthie moved towards the door again at Addy's nod in the affirmative.

John Maloney entered the room, allowing a small stream of light from the room behind him to light his way. Addy saw the other two detectives, Kraemer and Zellmer, who had been working with Officer Maloney since early August. She didn't see her favorite Detective Murphy anywhere and was afraid he might be refusing to see her after learning of her admission of guilt.

"I can see you are looking around for Detective Murphy, Miss Addy. He left for Chicago early this morning, but he is supposed to return today. I am certain he will want to visit with you as soon as he returns. "John pulled a chair from the side of the room where the furniture had been pushed to make room for the cot that sat on the opposite wall. Detectives Kraemer and Zellmer sat in chairs on the other side of the room while John sat next to Addy's cot.

"Miss Ruthie, I am going to send you with Officer Wrasse to one of the other rooms." John inclined his head towards the waiting officer. "He will get you some supper and find a place for you to rest for a bit. I know you would like to remain with Miss Addy right now, but as part of our investigation we are required to question both of you separately. I will send for you as soon as we have finished so you won't be concerned about Miss Addy." John motioned for Officer Wrasse to step forward and show the reluctant Ruthie the way towards the second examination room.

"I will be right back, Addy. Just tell them the truth and we will deal with all of it together." Ruthie nodded at John as she passed through the door and followed Officer Wrasse down the hall. All three police officers looked surprised upon hearing Ruthie speak to Addy, having never heard her utter a word.

"I can see this is to be a day of revelations. Miss Addy," John began. "We have quite a few questions for you, but I want to address what happened to you in front of the station first. I had a difficult time seeing who was driving the car as I was trying to rescue you and I haven't seen the other man who tackled you to the ground before, so I was wondering if you can tell us who they are. I am very concerned about your safety."

Addy's response was interrupted by a commotion in the outer room. The door was flung wide open, and Lucian stormed in with Sergeant Bates following close behind. Lucian paused when he saw his wife lying on the cot with her left arm in a sling.

Detective Kraemer stood from his chair to face him as he took several more steps towards Addy and the cot. Zellmer noted how Addy seemed to shrink away and avert her eyes while Lucian attempted to tower over her and John, who was still seated at her side.

"Does someone want to explain what in the world happened here? Why is my wife being held against her will?" Lucian shouted. "I was looking for her at the cottage and ran across Mr. Carr who explained that she had been taken by the police."

"I have come to take her with me as we have very little time before we leave for New York. Addy was supposed to be packing her things for the trip, but instead I find this mess." Lucian removed his black fedora in frustration and held it in his hand while he ran his other hand through his hair. He glared at Kraemer and John who both stood between him and Addy.

"Mr. St. John, we are not holding your wife against her will. Officer Maloney rescued her from an attack out in front of the precinct. He brought her in here and called for a doctor to attend her right away. We have been trying to protect her from whomever meant to harm her." Kraemer stood toe to toe with Lucian without flinching. He realized this man liked his own power, and he liked to display his power over others.

"What kind of police station is this if people get attacked right outside? I have had my doubts about your ability to protect the public before, but this confirms all of my concerns." Lucian swung the conversation over to accusations, intending to put the officers on the defensive, but Kraemer and John were not taking the bait.

"If we are finished here, I will collect Addy, and we will be on our way to the train station." Lucian tried to step forward, but he was blocked by the burly Kraemer who planted himself squarely in front of Addy, blocking Lucian's access to her.

"I am afraid you are mistaken, Mr. St. John. We are far from being finished." Zellmer's quiet voice in the corner caused Lucian to turn to look at him. "Unfortunately, Mrs. St. John has admitted to abducting Buddy Schumacher this last July. We have only begun our questioning and investigation into this matter. As you can understand, we will be holding her for questioning and continuing to guard her from further attacks. I wouldn't be surprised if the two matters are related to each other." Zellmer assessed Lucian as he spoke to the enraged man in a slow and precise manner.

Lucian's expression had changed from one of rage to one more of trepidation. Within a few moments the mask of rage was back in full force as Lucian took a step in Zellmer's direction with the intention of intimidating him. Zellmer sat calmly in his chair and continued to watch Lucian closely.

"You will not ask her anything." Lucian growled. "She has been committed to an insane asylum, so she has no realization of the things she says. The next moment she may tell you she is the bloody Queen of England! She was found not guilty because of insanity, so you need to release her to my care and let us be on our way." Lucian's voice raised so that it echoed off the walls surrounding them. Work outside in the main room ceased as everyone looked to see what the commotion was in the examination room.

"Mrs. St John's verdict in the first case does not extend to this case, Sir." Zellmer explained patiently. "This crime will be considered a separate incident from the first one, and she will have to answer for any commission of crimes. Otherwise, an insane person would have a free license under the law to continue committing heinous crimes of all sorts without being held responsible for them."

"Of course, we will have to question you as well as you are her guardian along with Miss Swenson as her caregiver. I am afraid your trip will have to be postponed for the foreseeable future." Zellmer picked up the red shoe Murphy had left on the table the night before. "Buddy Schumacher and his family deserve justice."

"You will not question her until I obtain a lawyer for her. She has fifth amendment rights." Lucian spat the words at Zellmer. He was now beside himself with anger and what looked to be a measure of fear.

"I am leaving right now to get a lawyer, and I will return shortly. Do not think your poor handling of this entire investigation will be forgotten. I will have your badges before I'm done." Lucian spun on his heel and strode from the room slamming the door behind him.

"It looks like our questioning will have to wait a while, Miss Addy. I hope we didn't upset you with this discussion. You only need to tell us the truth as Miss Ruthie suggested. I will go and see if we can find Miss Ruthie so she can come back and sit with you now." John rose from his chair and followed Kraemer and Zellmer, who both gathered the evidence from the table, and exited the room. The three continued down the hallway until they reached John's desk where they carefully placed the evidence in a locked drawer until Murphy returned.

"I wonder who he will bring back as the lawyer?" John asked his question aloud to the other two officers. "We need to prepare for a gigantic legal battle."

"*If* he comes back with a lawyer. There was fear in his eyes, and it appeared after he read the names we listed on the chalkboard beside me. I would say we get someone to follow Mr. St. John, as he knows much more than he is telling us." Zellmer walked away from John and Kraemer to look for Ruthie in the examination room nearest to the room that held Addy. He led Ruthie back towards Addy's room and paused before he opened the door for the elderly woman.

"We both know Addy did not abduct Buddy Schumacher," Zellmer appealed to Ruthie, "and I think you can tell me why she claimed she did. Please think about it for a little bit and then come to find me down the hall so we can talk."

Ruthie looked Zellmer in the eye and nodded her head slowly in agreement before entering Addy's room and closing the door behind her.

CHAPTER 33

SEPTEMBER 27, WAUWATOSA POLICE DEPARTMENT

The morning sun had not yet appeared on the horizon but the level of activity in the Wauwatosa Police Department reminded Murphy of an active beehive. Murphy had returned from his short trip to Chicago to find an injured Miss Addy along with Miss Ruthie. Miss Addy had made a stunning confession to John, and Lucian St. John tried to take his wife from the station before storming out himself.

Murphy had not returned until after Miss Addy had fallen into a deep sleep with the help of the laudanum left by the doctor who had attended her. John had placed another cot in the room and tried to convince Miss Ruthie to rest along with her friend, the older woman looking exhausted and worried. John had left to grab a few hours of rest before he led the search for the Lecher boy who was still missing and presumed dead by many.

Kraemer went home for a few hours as was his custom so he could see his children before they left for school in the morning. Zellmer had remained and slept in a corner propped up in a chair.

Murphy realized all of them had spent far too much time at the station and not enough time in their homes with families and friends, but when children were missing and harmed there were sacrifices that must be made. His hope was that the sacrifices would be enough to apprehend the guilty and protect the innocent.

Zellmer had explained that they had removed the Schumacher evidence from the examination room and had placed it in the locked drawer of John's desk until Murphy could return. Murphy took a small paper bag from his suit coat pocket and unlocked the desk drawer that held the other evidence.

The bag had the seal of the FBI specialist on it and Murphy placed it in the drawer with the other items. He hoped this was one more piece of the puzzle that would lead them to cracking the case wide open. The specialist would have the results for him within two days.

Murphy heard the door across the room open and saw Miss Ruthie standing in the doorway. She looked tousled from sleep and pensive as she surveyed the room around her. Murphy approached her thinking she might have need of the facilities at this early hour of the morning. She looked frightened when she saw him but then recognition dawned as he approached, and she relaxed visibly upon seeing Murphy's familiar face smiling at her.

"Hello Miss Ruthie. If you are in need of freshening up, I can guide you to the facilities." Murphy saw the gentle nod of her head and led her towards the back hallway and down a short flight of stairs to the lavatory.

Upon his return to the main room, he noted Zellmer had moved from his chair and stood next to a woman garbed entirely in black who sat dejectedly near John's desk. The look on Zellmer's face caused Murphy to cross the room towards them as the woman kept her back to the room and to Murphy.

"I have come to tell you what I know before I leave Wauwatosa this morning. I have left a written notice of resignation at the asylum though I intend to be gone before the director finds it. I don't need to tell you that time is of the essence because when they find I have revealed what I know they will come for me too." Nurse Fielding sat in the chair, her eyes red and swollen from crying. She started when she heard Murphy's footsteps approaching. He put his hands up with his palms facing her in a gesture of showing that he meant no harm to her.

"I am very grateful you have returned to speak with us before your departure." Zellmer replied. "You could have left without a word. Detective Murphy and I can take you into one of the smaller rooms if that makes you feel more secure." Zellmer motioned towards the examination room next to the room where Addy slept. Nurse Fielding stood from her chair on trembling legs and began to follow Zellmer to the room he indicated.

They were at the doorway when Ruthie entered the main room on her return from the lavatory. She stopped dead in her tracks; a frozen grimace etched across her face as she stared at Nurse Fielding. Small gurgles came from Ruthie's throat as if she was trying to vocalize, but nothing would come forth.

"You need to hide her away." Nurse Fielding pointed at Ruthie. "They are out looking for her and the rest of them. The Carr brothers came to the main hospital and tore apart several areas in their search, thinking we had hidden them, but I was able to say truthfully, I had no idea where they were. They practically destroyed the cottage trying to find anything that would lead them to Georgie Swenson and the rest of them." Nurse Fielding looked from Murphy to Zellmer and then back to Ruthie who still stood transfixed before her. "She isn't safe. None of us are safe."

Murphy reached out and gently grabbed Ruthie's arm, leading her past Nurse Fielding and towards the door where Addy was. He opened the door and saw Addy still sleeping on her cot. He motioned for Ruthie to enter the room and followed her inside.

"I can see you are very upset by what she said. I assure you we will protect you and Addy. I will send an officer here with a hot cup of coffee for you and he will station himself right outside for your protection. Is there anything else you need in the meantime, Miss Ruthie?" Murphy whispered so as not to disturb Addy who still slept soundly on the cot across the room.

"Thank you. Georgie and the others took the train and are in Prairie du Chien by now. They are traveling to Minnesota. Addy said they needed to leave for their protection. I am telling you because if you think they need police protection as well, you are the one I trust to help them." Ruthie sat down on her cot and hugged herself tightly while watching Addy across from her.

"I will check on that right now, Miss Ruthie. Thank you for telling me. I need to return to the other room now." Murphy left the room and instructed a young officer seated nearby to get a cup of coffee and bring it to the elderly woman and then stay outside the door until he returned. He rejoined Zellmer and Nurse Fielding who sat across the table from each other in the exam room next door.

"Nurse Fielding, would you repeat what you have told me for Detective Murphy? I will write notes as you do." Zellmer had his notebook and pen on the table. He picked up the pen and began to write as she spoke.

"I came back after being let go the other day because I could not resolve being involved with the harm to the Schumacher boy or to any other children for that matter. At first, I thought it was only a coincidence that all of the activity in the tunnels below the asylum occurred at the same time, but after Detective Zellmer pointed out that more children have been taken and possibly hurt, I knew I needed to do whatever I could to help them." Nurse Fielding removed a handkerchief from a small bag at her feet and dabbed her eyes before resuming.

"When the asylum hospital was rebuilt," she explained, "there were few people who knew about the tunnels built under the old hospital. Many of the old asylum staff had left taking that information and the knowledge of the things that had occurred in the old hospital with them. The new director wanted to change how the patients were treated and housed. It took a lot of money to make those changes, so he welcomed several benefactors who made generous donations."

"The newer addition of a sanitarium began to help subsidize the overall asylum project after the first couple of years," Nurse Fielding continued, "but a couple of the benefactors continued to give money. One benefactor in particular came and built some of the new additions with crews of his own workers from Chicago. He had access to all the original architectural plans including the old tunnels. It wasn't long before he began to make use of a few of the sections of the tunnels."

"I was given extra money to look the other way as he moved some of his operations in and took over that part of the asylum grounds. He assured me his operation was not necessarily of a criminal nature. I thought it was a good way to set aside money for my retirement, and I simply kept quiet." Nurse Fielding paused as she slowly shook her head and dabbed her eyes with the handkerchief again.

"I was not alone in receiving payments from this benefactor, but it is up to the others who did to take responsibility for it. He is a powerful man with even more powerful connections. He often came in and out of Wauwatosa, bringing some questionable acquaintances with him. Once I asked about some of these acquaintances, but he firmly told me to forget anyone I had seen with him for my own safety. He explained he was here to protect me, but these other people would not hesitate to harm anyone who got in their way," she closed her eyes at the memory.

"From then on, I found I counted on him as a source of revenue and as a protector. He was very good at making people dependent upon him and making them unable to break the association with him easily. When you questioned me the other day, my only option as I saw it was to protect him and his associates because he was my only protection. I can now see the error in my thinking," there was a slight pause before she continued.

"I went back to the asylum and the thought of the little Schumacher boy being brought to those tunnels and tortured would not leave my thoughts. I don't think my benefactor himself was involved with the children, but his associates are criminals and murderers, with any number of evil proclivities. I realized there was a strong possibility they could have been involved with Buddy Schumacher's murder and the abductions of the other boys as well. I will admit I tried to just leave and abandon my post without coming here; I am terrified they will find me, but I could not leave knowing there are more children out there who may need help." Nurse Fielding put her head down on her hands that were spread across the table. "God help me. I couldn't leave knowing those boys were still missing."

"Nurse Fielding, I suspect I already know what operations were being conducted in those tunnels, but can you confirm what it was and who your benefactor is for us?" Zellmer gently touched her shoulder as he looked at Murphy who sat in complete amazement. She continued to sob into her hands for a few moments while they waited for her to continue.

"It was the manufacturing and distribution of alcohol," she admitted. "They set up a series of stills in the tunnels and distilled the alcohol there. Then they waited for the cover of night to transport it towards Chicago and various points up and down Lake Michigan. Not everyone agrees with the eighteenth amendment, so it felt as though it was more of a civil disobedience rather than a crime."

"I can see now it attracted a criminal element to the area that harmed our community irreparably. I have no knowledge of anyone harming children because I would have never agreed to remain silent if I had, but if this information leads you to whomever has been harming these children, then I will not regret what I have risked giving it to you." Nurse Fielding straightened her back in the chair and put her hand to her hair, smoothing it back in place.

"We had suspected bootlegging after viewing the tunnels ourselves so that confirms it. I know it's difficult, but please tell us who is the leader of this operation." Murphy steeled himself for the answer he anticipated.

"Lucian St. John," her voice was clear. "He brought everything here and set it up under the guise of having his wife kept here for criminal insanity. Apparently, he and his father Oscar had been drugging Addy St. John for over a year in order to have her committed here. This would allow them to set up their operations. What he didn't anticipate was Mrs. St John would drown their son in her drug-induced state before he sent her to Wauwatosa."

"I was to continue in administering the hallucinogen to her once I received her as a patient," Nurse Fielding shook her head, "but she had a complete breakdown after the unfortunate death of a young woman named Cora. I didn't administer the drug to her because it was not warranted, but I regret what happened to her to this day. While a husband has the full right under the law to have his wife committed for any reason, she was not deserving of what happened to her in order to set up the bootlegging operation."

Zellmer dropped the pen he held in shock as he listened to Nurse Fielding's admission. He had suspected the wealthy St. John family of being involved with this aspect of organized crime, but he had not had the direct connection he needed, nor did he suspect how much Addy St. John had suffered at their hands. He picked the pen back up and continued to record Nurse Fielding's words.

"Was the drug you were supposed to give her called Scopolamine or the common term, Dragon's breath?" Murphy suddenly realized another connection; it had been Lucian who had suggested the same drug be given to Mr. Eddy so he would admit to killing Buddy under its influence. Most likely Lucian was covering for someone else who had committed the crime, someone closely associated to illegal alcohol. Suddenly, so many pieces of the puzzle were falling into place.

"Yes, that was it. He had given her tea initially and then switched to small doses of liquid when it didn't bring on the mental state in her he desired." Nurse Fielding confirmed yet another portion for Murphy.

"Nurse Fielding, you have mentioned you are in danger. I know the attorney who came to represent you the other day has defended some members of the powerful crime families in Chicago. Are they the ones who will harm you if they find out you were here with us?" Zellmer wanted to identify if the risk to Addy was the same one as Nurse Fielding was facing. The Chicago syndicate was well known for their responses to anyone who "snitched"; hardly anyone survived the response. He felt a sudden alarm for Addy and Ruthie as well as the lady in front of him.

"No." Nurse Fielding shook her head. "While I suspected a few of the more famous names in Chicago were involved with this, I don't have any direct proof. Mr. Levy made certain I didn't know about any of the more prominent clients before he left me the other day. He was not present to defend me. He was here to prevent me from revealing anyone he felt was of worth to them."

"He was as surprised as I was when you revealed the investigation into the missing children," she admitted. "He seemed very upset about it and even commented he would have to take the information back to his clients in Chicago. It seems it will not be safe for those people if the Chicago family finds they are involved in harming Buddy or the others. It is both Carr brothers who are the most present danger to me and to the other ladies from the cottage. We alone can connect them to the criminal activities here and possibly to the abductions that took place at the same time." Nurse Fielding looked at the door nervously as the doorknob started to turn.

Officer Hammerschmidt entered, knocking as he opened the door in his rush to enter the room. Murphy stood and reached for his pistol in his side holster before recognizing the officer entering.

"Hammerschmidt! Knock before you enter an examination room! That is a good way to get shot." Murphy holstered his weapon while looking at the shaking Hammerschmidt who realized his error and the tragedy he might have caused. Nurse Fielding put her head back on her hands in sheer relief on seeing the other officer when she had anticipated Nick or Adam Carr brandishing a tommy gun.

"Sorry, Murphy." Hammerschmidt replied shakily. "I was trying to hurry and come get you for Wrasse. He was one of the officers following Mr. St. John. He said they followed him towards the river, and the car made a sudden turn off the road. When they tried to catch up, St. John and both Carr brothers were nowhere to be found. They disappeared virtually into the air! They can't find them anywhere. They are gone, Sir." Hammerschmidt shook his head and looked from Murphy to Zellmer to the sobbing nurse who understood the danger of their escape.

"It looks like you are staying here with us for the time being, Nurse Fielding. It is not safe for you to be anywhere out there by yourself." Murphy stood to exit the room.

He needed to summon John and Kraemer and bring them back to the station right away. He also needed to alert the police in Prairie du Chien with the news Georgie, and the rest of the ladies might be in imminent danger. Lucian and the Carr brothers were at large.

All the sacrifices had been made over the last few months, and the pieces seemed to be falling into place. Now, if they could only find Mike Lecher before it was too late.

CHAPTER 34

LATER THAT MORNING

Addy awoke feeling stiff and sore. She turned her head to see Ruthie sitting on a cot across from her. The older woman was in a fetal position with her knees against her chest and her arms wrapped around her legs as she leaned against the wall. Her forehead rested on her knees, and her eyes were closed. Addy heard a soft sniffing sound emanating from a woman whom she had never seen cry in the years she had known her. Addy steeled herself against the pain throbbing in her arm and attempted to sit up so she could go to Ruthie and comfort her.

Ruthie lifted her head when she heard Addy stirring. Addy noticed her red eyes and flushed face. Addy swung her feet from the bed to the floor and stood. Wobbling slightly, she made the few steps to Ruthie's cot and sat down beside her friend.

"Ruthie, what is it? If you are still concerned about me, I assure you I will be fine. We both know I have been through worse than this and survived. In fact, we both have been through worse things, haven't we? We have perfected the art of survival against the odds."

Addy touched Ruthie's shoulder tenderly and felt the silent sobs shaking her frail body.

Addy slid her right arm around Ruthie's shoulders and leaned her face against Ruthie's hair. A torrent of sobbing broke from the usually stoic woman, threatening to overtake her completely. Addy waited patiently while Ruthie cried. Sometimes there were no words for the deepest griefs of the heart.

They sat together for several minutes until Ruthie eventually picked up her head to look at her dearest friend. Her eyes held a look of utter despair as she held Addy's gaze. She accepted the handkerchief Addy handed her from her pocket and wiped her wet cheeks and eyes. Ruthie's body shuddered occasionally as the torrent of sobs subsided, reminding Addy of her little boy, Charlie, who would hiccup and shudder after crying his heart out. Addy remembered that all she had wanted to do was make Charlie's world better for him. She felt the same for Ruthie.

"I guess that was a long time in coming but I'm sorry I couldn't contain myself any longer. You have enough concerns right now without me adding to them." Ruthie turned to face Addy on the cot. "I stayed behind to help you but I'm afraid I have already made a mess of things." Ruthie took Addy's hand in her own before she continued.

"I told Detective Murphy where Georgie and the others were earlier, and now I realize he might be working with Lucian. What if he has already sent someone to take them from the train? If something happens, it is entirely my fault." Tears sprang into Ruthie's eyes again.

"Ruthie! Why would you think Detective Murphy is working with Lucian? He and Officer Maloney have done nothing to harm us and everything to protect us. I think it's good you told him where the others are. I had considered doing it myself." Addy's eyes grew round with shock as she looked at her friend in amazement. "Officer Maloney saved me from Adam Carr and his brother yesterday. They would have killed me if they had taken me. Detective Zellmer refused to allow Lucian to take me from the police station as well. We have enemies, but they are not these police officers."

"We do have enemies, Addy. One of them is sitting next door, probably plotting with Detective Murphy as we speak. I saw Nurse Fielding come in here with my own eyes. You know, as well as I do, she is one of our worst enemies. She helped kill Cora and she let them try to kill me. I have been convinced for a long time she was working for Lucian, and now she is here plotting with them!" Ruthie's face contorted in anger. She would never forget the torture she had endured for standing up to the head nurse of the asylum after watching Cora die.

"Nurse Fielding is here. Why would she come here, Ruthie? She can't force us to go back to the asylum, can she? I won't go back there." Addy turned towards the door, terror casting a shadow over her face. "They think I took the Schumacher boy, so now I will have to convince them of it; I will go to prison before I let Nurse Fielding take me anywhere. You should run right now, Ruthie. Take the train to Prairie du Chien and find Georgie. I will create a distraction, and you can escape. Just don't let Nurse Fielding see you or she will come after you. This was definitely not part of my plan."

Both women looked up as the door opened and John walked through it. He was followed by Detective Murphy and Detective Zellmer. They closed the door and walked to the far end of the room next to the table and chalkboard. It was the first time Addy had read the chalkboard in the room and the names and locations written on it.

Addy's forehead wrinkled as she read the names to herself. Capone? Torrio? Yale? These were all names she had read in the newspapers she collected under her bed. Then she saw the blank left open under Capone's name in Milwaukee and a sudden chill went up her spine.

"How are you feeling this morning, Miss Addy and Miss Ruthie? I will have one of the officers bring some breakfast for you and please let us know if you need anything else. We don't customarily have people stay in the offices on the main floor. Most of our visitors are in the jail below." John studied the wary looks on both faces as he pulled out a chair and sat in it. "Miss Addy, we are wondering if you can tell us who attacked you. We have another eyewitness, and we are wondering if you can confirm their testimony."

"Why are you keeping me in here? Don't I belong in jail? I told you I took that little boy and you are treating me like a guest at a hotel. Please allow Ruthie to leave as she has nothing to do with any of this or with any of the names you have listed over there." Addy lifted her good hand and pointed at the chalkboard beside Zellmer. Ruthie shifted her weight, putting her feet on the floor as she glanced at Detective Zellmer.

"I have a conjecture about your confession, Miss Addy." Zellmer replied. "My thought is you needed refuge from being removed from Wauwatosa and you sought it out at our police station. You realized your husband would have a full legal right to take you with him unless you were being held for questioning, so you decided to confess to something that would make us hold you until the matter was cleared up. It's quite brilliant really."

"One of the downsides, however, is it would make us stop looking for who actually took Buddy Schumacher if we had believed what you said. I know you would not want that to happen because you cared deeply about him. We are also still searching for another boy his age who may not have very much time left before he suffers the same fate. Are you telling us you also took him and the boy we found dead in the barn the other day? Is that what you are trying to tell us?" Zellmer's voice was calm as he spelled out Addy's plan to the letter. She slowly shook her head no.

"I didn't think so. Please tell Officer Maloney who tried to abduct you because it is much more likely those men have a tie to what has been happening. I know you would have done anything to help find Buddy and we need you to do the same to help us find this other little boy. I want to assure you that you and Miss Ruthie have been placed in protective custody, which means you are under our protection but not under arrest." Zellmer turned to the chalkboard, picked up the chalk and wrote *Lucian St John* in the blank space. He drew a line down and created another blank space beneath.

"I had seen the first man the night I was taken from the house in Lake Geneva and brought to the asylum." Addy admitted. "He murdered his partner right in front of me. I only knew him as Nick at the time. I saw him again yesterday and I knew he had come to take me and probably kill me. I was coming to turn myself in as you suggested, and so I ran towards the police station. Adam Carr pulled a car out in front of me, and I thought I was rescued. It turned out he and Nick are brothers and have both been working for Oscar and Lucian the whole time. I managed to pull free and run, but Nick caught up and threw me to the ground."

"It was then Officer Maloney arrived and saved me from them. They tried to convince me they had already taken Georgie and the others from the cottage and that they would kill them if I didn't cooperate, but I knew they were lying as I had watched the others board the train and leave." Addy gave a weak smile to John. "Georgie is safe and on her way to her family. Ruthie told Detective Murphy earlier. I know you would want to make sure she and the others are safe."

Murphy chuckled out loud as John nodded quickly at Addy and looked at his feet. "I sent word to the Prairie du Chien police early this morning. They are sending an officer to escort them on the train to their destination. It was a good idea for Miss Ruthie to share the information with me as Lucian and the Carr brothers have escaped. All of you are in danger until they are apprehended. Miss Ruthie likely prevented further catastrophes from occurring."

Murphy nodded towards Zellmer who had started taking notes in his notebook. "Did you hear how they threatened to hurt her loved ones? It would be a viable way to remove anyone from a busy street even in broad daylight."

"The victim would go quietly thinking they were saving their family. It would probably work on little boys too." Zellmer followed Murphy's reasoning; the Carr brothers could have used the same tactic to remove Buddy and the others without a scene.

Only Addy provided the necessary loud reaction that caused others to pay attention and come to assist her. Zellmer made a mental note. Law enforcement and parents needed to start teaching children to make a scene: cry, scream, have a tantrum, when necessary to save their own lives.

"Detective Murphy, if we aren't under arrest can you please tell me why you are meeting with Nurse Fielding? Ruthie said she was here. If we need protection from Lucian and the Carr brothers, we certainly need protection from her as well. I refuse to go anywhere with her." Addy stood from the cot and straightened her back in resolution. She glanced at Ruthie who sat beside her staring at the floor.

"Nurse Fielding is not here to take you anywhere. She came to bring important testimony that helped us immensely. She is in as much danger as you are if not more. You have nothing to fear from her." Detective Murphy noticed Ruthie's reaction as Nurse Fielding's name was mentioned.

She pulled her legs back up into the fetal position and hugged them to her chest. He had seen similar reactions from other survivors of abuse and trauma. "She mentioned that terrible things had been done in the past at the asylum," Murphy explained. "She regrets her part in them and came to try and help us find the little boy who is still missing. I think she understands while we can't change our past, we can choose to alter our future."

"There are also things we do and say that can never be undone. We can be sorry for them later on, but we can't erase the damage." Ruthie lifted her head and stared straight at Murphy while she spoke. "This act might prove she has a conscience regarding hurting children, but she has never exhibited a conscience about hurting anyone else. I hope she can live with all she has done and all she has allowed others to do, because the rest of us have to live with the aftermath." Ruthie put her legs down, her feelings of needing their protection having lessened.

"We asked her to think of any place that the Carr brothers might have hidden things including the boys. I would ask the same question of both of you. Did you notice anyone bringing things in or out of the tunnels? Did they have places in Wauwatosa or the area where they spent time?" Zellmer paused in his notetaking and glanced at Ruthie who had resumed her position of sitting up with her feet on the floor.

"They had used the 'jungles' in the reeds by the river before, because Adam bragged about throwing out the men who built them. He said the poor and destitute are only there to build things for those who are better. Everyone else liked Adam because he was charming, but I didn't because he spoke in front of me like I didn't exist." Ruthie surprised the officers by speaking out.

"Most likely, I didn't exist to him." Ruthie continued. "I know he once mentioned throwing some of the men from the abandoned railroad cars hidden back behind the depot. He called it the 'boneyard' to Mr. Lucian. Things were apparently moved in and out of it frequently because Mr. Lucian became very angry that Adam had used it."

Murphy sprang to his feet along with John and Zellmer. "They moved things in and out and could have rotated use with the tunnels and the vehicles. We searched them early on but didn't double back and they counted on that once they knew it had been searched thoroughly." Murphy ran from the room to gather his hat and coat. He called for several officers to follow him, John, Zellmer, and Kraemer to the boneyard.

An abandoned passenger train, with boarded up windows and doors, was the last one on the tracks. Kraemer pulled at the board covering the door farthest from the view of the street and it gave way easily. They scrambled up into the railroad car, their eyes adjusting to the darkness within. A stench of human filth and rotten food made their eyes water as they made their way along the passenger seats towards the back of the car.

John made it to the last seat first and found eight-year-old Mike Lecher sprawled out on some hay. He was unclothed except for his filthy underwear, his face bloody and bruised almost beyond recognition. There was a gag stuffed in his mouth, and he was hog tied at the wrists and ankles. John's voice caught in his throat as he knelt beside him and called out to the others.

"I found him. He's still alive."

CHAPTER 35

SEPTEMBER 28, 1925 – LAKE GENEVA, WISCONSIN

The black Model T ford wheezed down the old farming road near Rochester, Wisconsin as Adam Carr guided it towards Lake Geneva. He glanced at Lucian who nodded in and out of sleep while Nick snored loudly from the back seat. They had driven during the cover of night from a small cabin near Lake Beulah that had been used as a hideout more than once in the past two years.

Adam recalled with amusement watching from a short distance away as two of the Milwaukee police detectives had stormed the individual cabins near them in search of the little Schumacher boy. If it hadn't been for a sudden warning, they had received from one of the many ladies who chased after Lucian, those coppers might have caught up with them all the way back in late August and found the little boy still alive. Adam had been amused to read all the stories about the missing boy in the newspapers; it gave him a sense of power over the police and the Wauwatosa community.

Taking that little boy had been very different from the others he and Nick had abducted over the years. It had been prompted by Lucian as a way to repay a debt he owed to a Milwaukee County official who had a huge vendetta against the boy's Grandpa Armstrong. The old man Armstrong had caused a huge loss to beer barons and thus to the bootleggers by refusing to turn a blind eye to their businesses.

Bribes that usually kept the traps shut of other little peons in the Milwaukee County political cogs did not work against Mr. Armstrong. Lucian had warned the Carr brothers that it was only supposed to be an abduction and hopefully a large ransom set forth by the family and the community, but they had not anticipated the arrival of Detectives Kraemer and Zellmer from outside the Wauwatosa police department.

Adam recalled Detective Kraemer chasing him and his brother all over the country and finally out of the country to Argentina to try and find little Homer Lemay a few years prior to the Schumacher abduction. The man was relentless in his pursuit and had nearly nabbed Adam and Nick several times. They had escaped once or twice by a matter of minutes. Other people might have felt shaken by the nearness of their capture, but to Adam it was all part of the thrill.

He tried not to think of his brother's fetish for kidnapping, torturing, and killing little boys as anything but an oddness about him that had been present since Nick was only a young boy himself. Nick had begun by taking pets from people, torturing and killing them, the process growing increasingly sinister as Nick matured.

Even their own mother, regarded as the sweetest little church lady in Akins, Oklahoma, had washed her hands of both her boys. She regarded Nick as the devil incarnate and Adam as his henchman. She threw them out at the tender ages of twelve and fourteen declaring herself to be done as their mother.

Their only memories of their father were of the severe beatings he inflicted on them from the time they could walk until the time he died of heart failure in the middle of a hayfield when the boys were only eight and ten.

A massive bump in the dark road shook the entire vehicle and brought Adam back from his recollections to their present situation. Lucian grunted as he fell forward and hit the dashboard in front of him. The Model T shuddered, the engine making an additional whining sound to the wheezing already occurring. Adam slowed the car while trying to prod it forward to their destination of Stone Place.

The usual and quickest route to Lake Geneva from Lake Beulah had been disregarded as it took them too close to Elkhorn and possibly into the hands of the very angry members of the Chicago Outfit who had a large home in the woods near there.

Attorney Carl Levy returned to Chicago after appearing in Wauwatosa. His information about Adam and Nick's abductions infuriated the crime family since they had close ties with Lucian's bootlegging activities and did not condone harming children. Now they were fleeing from police capture and the notorious crime family.

"Where are we now?" Lucian groaned as he rubbed his forehead and looked at the predawn landscape surrounding them. Dark trees loomed overhead with nothing but the small trail of a road winding in front of them into the deserted woods. The sounds of a screech owl nested somewhere nearby jangled Lucian's nerves. He had wanted to take the belongings he had with him and flee the country, but his parents had left important documents at Stone Place when they had fled.

Lucian had not heard from his father since they had reached New York City. He assumed his parents were booking a passage to London and would sail at the earliest embarkation. Oscar had been insistent that Lucian retrieve the documents. claiming their financial ruin was in the balance if Lucian failed to procure them.

"I know we passed Browns Lake and Bohners Lake a while ago. I think we are coming up on Slades Corners where we can turn west towards Lake Geneva. This is a roundabout route, and we have stuck to small roads staying away from the major towns along the way. We will need more fuel sooner rather than later and I am hoping to pick up something to eat. We left without eating supper last night." Adam explained the lengthy car trip to reach their destination.

He studied Lucian's face in the dim morning light. He resembled a statue, chiseled to perfection even with the hard grimace that had settled across his face. Lucian had hired Adam and Nick to run his bootlegging operation while he remained under the guise of an outstanding and benevolent benefactor of the community.

All of it had gone well until Nick had accidentally killed the Schumacher boy while they were transferring him from one location to another. He had stuffed a handkerchief in the boy's mouth before putting a gag back on, and the extra wadded material had suffocated him. Lucian had been upset, but he regarded the young boy's death as a small deterrent to their large-scale operations. Lucian had gone out of his way to frame the crazy feeble-minded guy from the trains, paying people to testify against him and offering rewards.

They might have gotten away with it if it hadn't been for those detectives chasing them again and the fact the boy's death had reawakened the old familiar fetish that caused Nick to go and take more kids right in the middle of the day, one right after the other.

Adam had tried to keep the other two boys' abductions hidden from Lucian, but Detective Zellmer had shown up and questioned the old battle axe from the asylum about the tunnels they had been using for both purposes. She went screaming to the lawyer about the fact that little kids had been hurt. Adam would like to have a few moments alone with Nurse Fielding. She would shut up forever afterwards.

"We need to reach the house before it gets too light out," Lucian was thinking aloud. "You will take food from the larder while Nick siphons off gasoline from one of the vehicles for the car. We can't afford anyone but the house servants seeing us in the area. The nosy people in downtown Lake Geneva are likely to tell the police or, even worse, our associates from Chicago."

"We can lay low near the house until tonight and then leave for St Louis. I have people there who will take us on the trains heading east to New York. All of this would be much simpler if we could just make the trip into Chicago but that would be signing our death warrants. They will be looking for us to go east right away instead of west." Lucian had a clear plan for his escape.

"What's going to happen to little Mrs. St John? Wasn't she the reason we stayed so long in one place? I thought she was going with us." Nick had awakened in the back seat and had been listening to the exchange between his brother and the boss. "I can't help but like her, she sure is a spitfire. You should have seen her spook good old Fred with her stories about a vengeful ghost lady who kills people on that lake." Nick guffawed at the memory of the night they had abducted Addy.

"She would probably have been with us if you hadn't decided to try and take her down right in front of the police department, you stupid idgit." Lucian growled his answer through clenched teeth. It was possible Nick might have to join good old Fred at the bottom of Geneva Lake before he and Adam left in the morning. He had kept the bumbling oaf around for Adam's sake, but now he was too much of a liability to keep. Lucian would make sure Nick did the jobs needed of him before disposing of him.

Adam glanced at Lucian's expression as the boss glared at his brother. He had an uneasy feeling Lucian would try to rid himself of Nick. He was Nick's big brother, and he couldn't let that happen. He had always protected Nick, and this rich by-blow might be able to dictate everyone else's lives, but he wasn't going to hurt his brother.

Perhaps it was time for Mr. St. John to have an unfortunate accident. They could take the money and valuables from the house to sell, go back to Argentina, and hide for a few years just like last time. There was an uneasy silence as two of the three men in the car silently plotted the murder of one of the others.

Pink rays of light dotted the horizon as Adam pulled the car into a space near the dock of a hidden cove on Buttons Bay. The St. John family steamer was kept in this out- of- the way water inlet for their private use. Adam opened the car door and went to the back trunk. He removed the two pistols that had been stashed there before they tried to abduct Addy, tucking them into his belt at the back and covering them with his coat.

He moved the front seat forward to allow Nick to scramble from the back seat. He watched as Lucian walked to the boat, holding his valise, and waited for them to join him on the dock. Adam had no doubt there was another gun inside the valise. He made the decision that he needed to bring Lucian down before he attempted to kill Nick.

Adam tried to step in front of Nick as the two walked towards Lucian on the dock. It was a flash of seconds while he watched Lucian drop the valise and crouch beside it, pulling a handgun from within its depths. He reached for the pistols at his waist while Nick attempted to push him out of the path of gunfire and into the lake.

The serene lake with the morning fog surrounding it muffled the crackle of the repeated gun shots ringing out in the hidden cove. Then, as suddenly as it had begun, all was silent again.

CHAPTER 36

SEPTEMBER 29, 1925 – SUNNYHILL HOME, WAUWATOSA

The morning sun warmed Addy's face as she sat in the breakfast room with Ruthie. They had been brought along with Nurse Fielding to this ornate mansion located on West Milwaukee Avenue after the decision had been made to relocate them and guard the three women around the clock.

Several locations had been discussed by John and the other detectives. They chose Sunnyhill for its closeness to the precinct, its spacious accommodation, and its high cupola tower which stretched above the Wauwatosa skyline allowing a security detail to watch for intruders from any direction.

Addy had seen the cupola from her bent oak tree and had always imagined the stately mansion being the residence of royalty. It had been built for a local physician as a display for his multitude of collections. Display cases lined several rooms and housed the most interesting fossils Addy had ever seen. Along with the cupola, which was accessed by a ladder, there were several gables adorned in Gothic style with ornate bargeboard trim.

The interior had two spiral staircases. One wound to the upper-level bedrooms and another wound down to the kitchens below. The family who had purchased Sunnyhill from the physician after his wife died turned the huge house into rooms for boarding. This made it a perfect place for Addy and the others to hide.

Addy took a small bite of the hot buttered toast in front of her. Food had tasted like sawdust in her mouth since the doctor had begun administering the laudanum to relieve the pain in her arm. Addy was aware of the side effects of different medicines, and she had weaned herself from the potent opiate since her arrival at Sunnyhill Home. She did not know what her future might hold, but she realized she needed clarity of mind to deal with whatever fate dealt to her next.

Finally, she could taste the creamy fresh butter and the rich nutty whole grains of the warm wheat bread again after going days without any sense of taste. She glanced at Ruthie, who was tapping the shell of a poached egg held in a tiny porcelain cup made for that specific purpose. Addy felt sudden hunger pangs, her mouth watering at the thought of the poached egg beside her own plate. She picked up the egg spoon and began tapping the egg, joining Ruthie in her endeavor.

"We sound like two chicks about to hatch." Addy giggled as she opened the shell of the egg and spooned out some of the egg white. "This reminds me of Sunday mornings at home with my parents. There were always poached eggs and hot scones with clotted cream and marmalade. Of course, we drank tea instead of this incredibly strong coffee these Americans seem to prefer." Addy added cream to the steaming mug of coffee in front of her and stirred it with a spoon.

"I miss some of the European customs but there are many of the American practices that are far more to my liking." Ruthie reflected. "I was proud to become a citizen of this country and believed the freedoms belonging to each citizen were also afforded to me. I simply thought if you worked hard and lived an honest life you would be a free citizen as promised. I didn't comprehend that for women, especially for women deemed to have mental illnesses, the word freedom meant something vastly different than it did for others. It's particularly difficult when I realize one of the main people who withheld so many of my freedoms is now sleeping just down the hallway from us and under the same protection we are."

Ruthie finished her poached egg and picked up the cup of black steaming coffee that sat next to her plate. "At least she has had the decency not to show herself to us since we arrived here. I would not hold myself responsible for what I said if I had to carry on conversations with our former captor."

"I think she has been hiding away in the small room down the corridor and having a tray for her meals." Addy whispered. "I saw one of the servants heading up the backstairs with a breakfast tray this morning. It is bad enough to be cooped up inside the house because we can't be seen outside. It would be especially bad to be cooped up in one room instead of this entire mansion."

Addy put her coffee cup down and glanced out the window to see John, Detectives Murphy, Kraemer, and Zellmer all approaching on the walk at the side of the house. Her heart skipped a beat at the looks on their faces, they did not come bearing good news. She would have to be clear about handling whatever she was dealt.

The men were allowed entrance by the sentry posted at the side door. John saw the two women at breakfast and headed towards them with a purposeful step. He removed his hat and nodded a greeting towards Addy and Ruthie who both sat transfixed and stared at the officers. A servant entered the breakfast room bearing a large tray with coffee and fresh biscuits for the men. They took places around the table with Addy and Ruthie and waited for the servant to exit the room.

"Miss Addy, Miss Ruthie, we came to tell you several things but the most impactful is indeed, difficult, to say the least." John began the conversation in his usual refreshingly straightforward manner that Addy revered and had come to trust. "We received news from the Lake Geneva police department last night. We regret to inform you your husband, Lucian, was found deceased along with both Adam and Nicholas Carr just outside the city in a hidden cove in Buttons Bay. Their deaths were attributed to foul play as all three died of numerous gunshot wounds. The police are still trying to piece together what exactly happened; they each had a handgun on them or nearby but most of the gunshot wounds were caused by tommy guns that have not been recovered. It would appear from the footprints that there were at least two more assailants armed with the tommy guns. I am sorry for your loss, Miss Addy."

Addy blinked several times. She was certain she hadn't heard Officer Maloney correctly. Lucian was dead. He had left her, and he was never coming back. Shock absorbed her in waves as she sat staring at Officer Maloney and the others. She could not find any words to utter, so she sat in silence.

"I wish Georgie were here to help you at this moment. I promise we will give you any assistance that we can. Unfortunately, that is not all the news we have. Should I wait for a while before I continue?" John gently put his hand over Addy's. He continued at the shake of her head.

"We also received news from New York City this morning. Oscar and Virginia St. John were instantly killed in a car explosion on their way to their ship on the 26th. This makes you the sole survivor in the St. John family." John's voice trailed off when he detected the sudden pallor of Addy's face. He poured a glass of water from a pitcher in the center of the table and encouraged Addy to take a sip.

Ruthie left her seat across from Addy and came to stand behind her, enveloping the young woman in her arms. Everyone else held their silence for a few minutes while the two women embraced.

Addy finally rose from her chair and crossed to the large picture window, leaning her head against the pane warmed by the rays of the sun. Brilliant light danced around her silhouette giving her an almost ethereal quality, her auburn hair glistening as it cascaded down her back.

"What happens next?" Addy's words were few and simple and yet held multitudes of possibilities. She straightened her shoulders and turned to face the policemen gathered around her. "Are we still in any danger? What about Georgie and the others? What about..." Addy's voice faded as she pointed to the room above them indicating the woman who sat in imposed solitude there.

"I brought news of our most recent evidence." Detective Murphy spoke softly while he stood to cross the room and stand beside Addy at the window. "I had taken several items to the FBI specialist in Chicago to have fingerprints taken from them to see if we could match any of them to the unknown fingerprints he found on Buddy's possessions at the time of his abduction. One of the items was a pen Lucian brought with him to sign a check; he left it in the police station, and I wrapped it up right away for future testing. As Detective Kraemer is always saying, it is the smallest thing that provides the biggest clues. The test came back to confirm the fingerprints from his pen were not a match to the fingerprints on the items."

"I then submitted a pocketknife Adam Carr had used and handed to me to slice an apple." Murphy continued. "I admit I kept the pocketknife and wrapped it up as well. The testing of the fingerprints on it matched the unknown fingerprints on the Schumacher boy's items. While it isn't completely conclusive, it goes a long way in establishing his connection with Buddy's abduction. We all knew you had nothing to do with harming Buddy or any of the other boys, Miss Addy, and the evidence backs that up."

"I am strongly convinced the deaths of your in laws are linked to the deaths of your husband and the Carr brothers." Kraemer added. "They were all involved in the illegal distribution of alcohol and most likely they were taken out by some of their Chicago associates after the discovery of the abductions. You and the other ladies had nothing to do with any of those activities, so there isn't any reason to suspect they will return for you."

"We will make sure Nurse Fielding is taken to a safe house in another city even though she doesn't have a direct connection to them. I am on my way upstairs to explain all of this to her. It is because of her and Miss Ruthie that we found the Lecher boy still alive." Kraemer rose from his chair and exited the room towards the spiral stairs leading to the bedrooms above them.

"Imagine that. Nurse Fielding and I saved a boy's life together. Miracles do happen." Ruthie's dry statement made John smile. "Will we be able to reunite with Georgie and the others soon? Can we return to our cottage together? "

"I am willing to take you to meet Georgie and bring everyone back here together." John nodded as he spoke. "The cottage was badly damaged by the Carr brothers and Lucian before they fled, but with enough work, I am sure it could be put back to rights. All of those choices will be yours." John smiled at Ruthie's gasp of joy at the news they would all be reunited again soon.

"Who will own the cottage now? With Lucian gone, what happens to it?" Addy suddenly realized Lucian held many of the cards even in his death.

"I'm not sure you understood what Officer Maloney meant when he said you were the sole survivor of the St. John family, Miss Addy." Detective Zellmer sat at the table quietly until that moment. "The police and solicitor have already found the documents and wills left in the safe at Stone Place. Your in laws left everything to Lucian after their deaths while Lucian left everything in your name. You own all of it, Miss Addy. The money, the businesses, and all the properties including the one in Scotland. Miss Swenson was left as your guardian in the event of Lucian's death. I am sure she can assist you with all of the financial dealings and legal processes."

"You are the one who gets to decide, Miss Addy." The words felt like the first taste of freedom both Addy and Ruthie had longed for forever.

CHAPTER 37

SEPTEMBER 30, 1925 – SUNNYHILL HOME

The dark stillness of predawn lay over the small bedroom like a heavy cloak as Nurse Fielding sat in the rocking chair next to the bed. A breeze stirred the branches of the tree positioned outside her window, casting faint shapes onto the opposite wall and a scraping noise against the glass pane.

She had been advised by Detective Kraemer to prepare to leave Wauwatosa in the wee hours of the morning when he came to tell her the news of Lucian St. John's passing. She had put her few possessions back in the valise she had brought to the police station, readying herself for departure at any time.

Detective Kraemer had been very solicitous, offering to send an officer to bring any other items from her former office to her. She had scribbled a note of instruction to her assistant head nurse, Eva, asking for a list of items to be sent to her. The detective was as good as his word; two small boxes had been delivered last night.

Nurse Fielding sorted through the items in the boxes, using her usual practical efficiency to guide her actions. One box sat beside the valise and the other sat on the bed that had gone unused over the night hours as she sat in the rocking chair deep in thought.

Normally Nurse Fielding immersed herself in a high level of activity to keep the darker images of her memory at bay. She had come to Wauwatosa as a young woman, employed as a kitchen worker at the asylum, and slowly worked her way up through the ranks to the nurses corp. Ida Fielding was well known for her industriousness and no-nonsense practicality.

She had taken the more difficult patients into her care, gaining recognition with the board of administrators and the Director. When, at the young age of twenty-seven, she had been promoted to an assistant head nurse, it was well known in the asylum and in the community that Ida had a particular talent for keeping the worst of the violent lunatics in calm submission.

It was at about that time a young physician named Dr. Thomas Howard came to the asylum with a degree fresh from Harvard. He was the dashing young physician who had changed Ida's future with his passion for the study of Eugenics.

The thought process of selective breeding had been popular among the more elite social circles, but it had not interested Ida until Dr. Howard had shared his vision for conducting sterilizations on the most severe patients at the asylum, removing the genes of the imbeciles and the criminally insane from reentering the collective gene pool.

She worked alongside Dr. Howard for months before realizing that not only did her intellectual interests align with the handsome physician, but her romantic interests did as well. Ida immersed herself in the studies. She understood the groups that proposed all social ills could be removed through the sterilization, segregation, and social exclusion of anyone who did not possess "pure" Nordic white bloodlines.

Once she was involved with Dr. Howard and his experiments on the asylum patients it gradually became easier to accept the harsh standards set forth against anyone deemed feeble. It also became easier to accept the practices that allowed them to subdue asylum patients, the beatings, the immersion in cold water baths for hours, the shock therapies, and even intentionally infecting the patients with malaria to cure different forms of insanity caused by syphilis.

It was a gradual progression that led her to becoming the head nurse who gave the orders for all these tortures to be doled out on the vulnerable patients of the institution. Ida continued to rationalize her actions as part of a greater good and with each step she took, she saw the patients before her as less human. If the lunatics were not human, one could condone any number of atrocities being done to them for the betterment of the good people of society.

Ida's world came to a crashing halt, when, after ten years of work in close proximity to Dr. Howard, he suddenly introduced his new fiancée, a young woman of impeccable breeding and social standing, to the Wauwatosa community. Ida's crushed romantic hopes only fueled her ambitions to prove herself as the foremost authority in the asylum, giving her the final push into almost complete antipathy for the patients under her care.

Her methods became stricter, and the experiments became harsher as she resolved to never give herself over to feelings and emotion again. The choices had been completely her own, no one had forced her to become the pariah and recluse who sat here in the dark alone.

Ida had guarded her heart so well over the following years, no one had been able to gain access again. She was resolute in remaining the unwed spinster who ruled the entire asylum with an iron fist and caused fear in the hearts of the staff and the inmates. She had not anticipated her dam of emotions breaking over the small eight-year-old boy who had been abducted and murdered under the guise of the bootlegging operation hidden underneath the asylum.

The overwhelming crushing tide that had flooded into her entire being, brought down the carefully constructed barriers set over so many years. This child had been an innocent, a smiling freckle-faced little boy with a sunny smile and a cheery wave to everyone, including the cantankerous matron of the asylum. She had sometimes waited near a window or door for a glimpse of him skipping along with his fishing pole towards Sanctuary Woods. He had become the tiny pinpoint of light in her dark world of her own creation.

Now he was gone. All his future, his birthdays, his games, his future marriage and even possible children had been robbed from him by an uncaring assailant who thought they had the right to do as they pleased which superseded his right to the rest of his days.

It was at that moment of revelation that the most tragic divulgence became transparent to her. She had done the exact thing to the host of patients she had deemed as unfit over all those years. She did not have the ultimate right to inflict harm on other people and treat them as nonentities. She had robbed so many of their futures just as Buddy had been robbed of his. The weight of her actions lay on her like a blanket of lead.

A small, short rap on the door startled her. She had not heard the doors being opened below to admit Officer Wrasse who was to be her armed escort on the train. She stood and made her way to the door, turning the doorknob quietly.

Ida pulled the door open, allowing a small crack to look at who stood waiting in the hallway. A small sigh of air escaped her lungs involuntarily, but she pulled the door open to admit the visitors.

Ruthie entered the room, her slight limp dragging her foot across the wood floor producing an eerie sound in the darkness. She carried a small lamp but held no other weapon that Ida could see. Addy followed Ruthie into the room. The usually bold young woman seemed hesitant to cross the threshold. It was as if she expected Nurse Fielding's former minions at the asylum to jump out at her at any moment.

They stood side by side in the center of the room, their faces illuminated by the small lamp that cast even more shadows upon the wall. Ida closed the door behind them and came to stand in front of them, steeling herself for an altercation. She did not know what Ruthie intended to do to her, but she did understand what she deserved. A piercing pain of recognition and guilt surrounded her heart.

"Detective Kraemer said he came to tell you about what has transpired. He said you would have to leave soon to an undisclosed location in protective custody. I was more than ready to let you leave, hoping it would be the last time I saw your face on this earth." Ruthie set the lamp on a small table near the rocking chair and turned back to face Ida directly.

"I wanted you to go, I wanted those criminals to find you and inflict the pain on you that you have inflicted on so many of us. I have even thought of inflicting pain upon you myself." Ruthie's voice was little more than a whisper, but it was strong and passionate in its intensity.

Ida closed her eyes momentarily and nodded her head in agreement. She deserved this woman's wrath and vengeance, a retribution for herself and all the others including little Cora who was no more than a child herself. The pain in her heart sent out impulses throughout her limbs like sparks. Her throat felt clogged as though an invisible hand was squeezing it, choking the life from her body. Ida opened her eyes and braced herself for a possible strike against her.

"You caused the death of our innocent friend by allowing that doctor to hack her womb apart," continued Ruthie. "She posed no threat to anyone, and you took her and destroyed her. Then you took me and used your torture devices on me because I stood up to you. You had them put me in those ice baths all day long and then put my cold wet body on a metal slab while they applied electrical shock."

"When I tried to brace my foot against the tub you had them break my ankle so I could not resist drowning. By the end I was begging for death to come and yet you still withheld even that measure of comfort from me. Until that point, I had no comprehension of the unlimited capacity of cruelty by those who claim to do noble work to better humanity." Ruthie spoke without wavering while Addy stood beside her in silence, tears streaming down her face.

"I needed to be able to tell you to your face what you have done to me in the name of your causes." Ruthie looked at Ida directly. "I also needed to tell you that you have not broken me though you despised me and wished me dead. You and all of those like you will face a final judgment for all you have done. The blood of many is on your hands and it will not go without retribution on that last day."

"It is not mine to avenge because it would only make me your equal in injustice. I was ready to let you go away hoping for your judgment upon your demise and holding those things against you as I deemed it my right." Ruthie paused, her hands trembling slightly. She grasped the arm of the rocking chair and seated herself quietly.

"It was late last night I found a passage in the worn bible that has always remained hidden under my pillow no matter where I am," Ruthie declared. "My bible followed me through your dungeons of hell. I did not want to read it, in fact, I put it aside several times in anger. I presumed I had the right to hold all you have committed against you, but according to that good book I don't have that privilege. I read all night trying to justify my unforgiveness, but it is equal to whatever arguments you used to justify your sins against me."

"That is what brought me here before you leave. I must choose to forgive you for your actions against Cora, against me, against all of us. It is not an emotional response; it is a choice of my will. I will probably have to remember that I choose to forgive you every second of every day, so I won't hold any of it against you. It is the only way to truly be rid of it forever. Understand, I don't do this for you. I do this for me." Ruthie was spent after relinquishing her burden; she put her head in her hands.

Ida Fielding stood mute in disbelief. She had anticipated hateful threats and physical beatings; she almost welcomed them to move the mountain of guilt that rested on her chest. Instead, one of her victims stood before her proclaiming forgiveness for the many years of abuse she had inflicted.

She was unprepared for the force in Ruthie's proclamation; it drove her to her knees in front of the rocking chair where Ruthie sat. Ida knew there was nothing she could say that could match what had just been said to her. She only knew the necessary few words.

"I'm sorry. Thank you for your forgiveness. It is undeserved."

The faint light of dawn touched the windowpane when Officer Wrasse knocked on the door. Ida rose from her knees slowly and crossed to the bed. She picked up the box she had placed there along with the note she had written and brought it to Addy. She handed the box to the young woman and turned to pick up her hat and coat from the end of the bed.

Once she had put them on, she picked up the valise and the small box beside it. She paused beside Ruthie in the rocking chair, then crossed to the door and opened it for the police officer. She quietly left the room.

Addy waited for Ruthie to stand before she crossed to leave the room and travel back down the hallway to the large corner room they shared. Addy placed the box on a table and helped Ruthie to the chair nearest the table. She paused before the box, waiting for a response from Ruthie before opening it. Ruthie's whisper was faint.

"Open it, Addy."

Addy opened the box, removing a sheet of stationery that had a hand-written note. Addy cleared her throat before reading it aloud.

"I write this after realizing the irreparable damage I have inflicted on your lives. There is nothing I can do to give back what I have taken from you but there is something that can affect your future. Please find all the patient files for each woman in your cottage. I have taken them and marked them 'released' so you will no longer be committed to the asylum and can go wherever you wish to go without interference. Your future is yours to decide." Addy picked up the paper files and placed them on the table.

A small photograph with an additional note remained in the bottom of the box. Addy picked up the old photograph of a young Ruthie and three little boys. She handed the picture to Ruthie and waited to see her friend clasp the frame to her chest before continuing to read.

"To Ruthie, you were told your boys were missing after your youngest boy died of diphtheria. I searched recently and found this to be untrue. They are alive and well and do not know you survived as their father told them you had died. I leave their current addresses here with you and leave it to you to decide what you will do. My sincere hope is it will bring a measure of hope and happiness to your life. Ida Fielding."

CHAPTER 38

OCTOBER 5, 1925 – PRAIRIE DU CHIEN, WISCONSIN

Brilliant colors blazed in the trees lining the Mississippi River as Addy and Ruthie sat on a bench outside the Rolette House Hotel near Prairie du Chien. Bright gold interspersed with crimson reds and rich oranges reflected from the leaves to the churning river below.

The waters of the Mississippi spanned between the shores of two states at this site, Wisconsin and Iowa, and the confluence with the tumultuous Wisconsin river sat a mile downriver. Addy watched as the ferry, the Rob Roy, made its slow return journey from Marquette, Iowa, towards the shoreline where they waited.

The four days since Nurse Ida Fielding had revealed Ruthie's two sons were still living had been full of planning and purchasing of train tickets and accommodations. It struck Addy as no small coincidence that Ruthie's sons, now grown men, had left the Milwaukee area after their father died and had moved to the farmlands of Viroqua, Wisconsin.

Both sons, Elias and Emil, were hard working tobacco farmers. They ran the Viroqua Leaf Tobacco Company, a large warehouse on the edge of the picturesque town in Vernon County. The coincidental portion was that Addy and Ruthie had planned to travel as far as Prairie du Chien to reunite with Georgie and the others who would join them from Dresbach, Minnesota. Prairie du Chien was the county seat of Crawford County; Viroqua was located only forty-five miles to the north of where they currently sat.

Ruthie had experienced a mixture of emotions, overjoyed at the good news of her sons and yet fearful they might not choose to see her after almost twenty years of separation.

Addy had offered to enlist her solicitor to send an immediate telegram on Ruthie's behalf, informing the boys of the misinformation that had been propagated by their father concerning Ruthie's demise and allowing them to decide whether they chose to contact their mother for a conversation.

Ruthie prepared herself for a negative answer. They had lives of their own and had been led to believe she had deserted them and then died. She wondered if relationships could be repaired after so many years of detachment.

Ruthie was not prepared for the prompt response she received by telephone on the same day the telegram was sent. Both Elias and Emil were ecstatic at hearing the news. Both boys begged Ruthie to allow them to come and get her to bring her home with them to live.

The tears of many years wasted had poured down Ruthie's face as she held the receiver. She heard the love in Emil's voice as he proclaimed, "Mama, please come home."

Ruthie had agreed to travel to them after accompanying Addy as far as Prairie du Chien. She wanted to stay until Georgie, Freda, Ingrid, Mary, and Ella had all arrived so they could be together for a short time before she left to reunite with her sons.

The second greatest revelation was that both young men were married and had children of their own. Ruthie was a grandmother to five grandchildren, the youngest being still a babe in arms. She could hear the excited squeals of her daughters-in-law and her grandchildren as Elias announced that "Grandma Crane" was coming to see them soon.

It felt as though her entire life had changed in a matter of moments. The good lord had given back to her the years eaten by the locusts and more. The smile that played often on her lips since their conversation spoke of the grace she had found in letting go of her old wounds.

Addy's next venture was to purchase train tickets for Ruthie and herself. She had asked Officer Maloney if he would be willing to accompany them as an escort, and he had willingly agreed. Detective Zellmer had also volunteered to travel with them. He had offered to take Ruthie to her destination. Several of his siblings resided in La Crosse so he would drive to Viroqua and on to La Crosse for an extended visit.

Ruthie was amazed at how all the events seemed to line up in a straight row, she had lived a crooked path not of her own making for so long she didn't realize that at times life was meant to be good.

They had arrived at the train depot in Prairie du Chien late yesterday. John had opted to travel on to Dresbach right away so he could escort the others back before Ruthie left. Addy noticed how excited the young officer appeared at the thought of seeing Georgie again. She was certain Georgie would be equally excited to see him. She hoped the two would see a bright future together. It made her happy when good things happened to good people.

Addy had asked Detective Zellmer if he would be willing to drive her and Ruthie to Iowa via the car ferry. Detective Zellmer had agreed and had borrowed a car from Georgie's brother who resided in Prairie du Chien.

Detective Zellmer stopped the car down the street from where the two women sat. He hopped out to open the doors for Addy and Ruthie as the ferry made its final approach to the dock on their side of the river. The car made its way to the queue waiting to drive aboard the Rob Roy. Soon they were aboard the ferry, chugging its way across the Mississippi.

Addy glanced down at the brown water churning from underneath the ferry. She glanced at the pontoon bridge built for the railroad in the distance. It was one of the first of its kind to span the huge river and allow for the trains to cross the Old Miss.

"It's a beautiful day to be on the river." Detective Zellmer adjusted his fedora. He wore wire rimmed sunglasses to keep the harshest of the sun's glare from his eyes. "I don't wonder that you asked to cross the river, but I am curious about what you would like to do on the other side. Do you have a particular destination in mind, Miss Addy?" He glanced at Addy who sat quietly in the front seat next to him. He noted that she twisted the handkerchief she held in her hands.

"I have a very specific destination in mind, Detective Zellmer. I wish to go to McGregor, which is just a few miles down the road from the dock in Marquette. An old friend of mine moved to McGregor a few years back, and I wanted to see her since we were so close by. Miss Louise worked as the head housekeeper for the Seipp family home in Lake Geneva. I met her when I lived at Stone Place and would visit the Seipp family often in the summer. She decided to retire and move back to her hometown of McGregor. She now owns a beautiful bookshop in the town; I have always wished to see it and visit with her again. Miss Louise was one of very few people who showed kindness to me when I arrived in America." Addy kept her head turned away from Zellmer as she stared at the river around them.

"That is very specific. I am glad I could facilitate your visit with an old friend. I hope I won't be in your way during your visit. I could find a park while you visit if that would make you more comfortable, Miss Addy." Zellmer glanced at her again. She had turned her head slowly to look at him, a determined look on her face.

"No, thank you. I asked you to accompany me today because I know that of all the people involved in the past few months you have had the most questions about my past. You have been very polite about it, but I can tell it is there just below the surface. I think perhaps I can answer a few of those questions with our visit today. I don't trust people easily, Detective Zellmer. Most of the people in my life have proven very untrustworthy, but you are one of the rare few I know I can trust with my story. Ruthie is, of course, one of the others. She knew my whole story long ago when I first came to the asylum." Addy turned to smile at Ruthie in the back seat before facing out towards the river again.

"I am honored by your trust, Miss Addy. I will do anything in my power to make you not regret it. I admit I did have a few questions, but I knew that if they did not relate to our investigation, they were not my questions to ask of you. Did you realize at some point that Lucian was trying to drug you? I have noticed how perceptive you are and thought you might have." Zellmer asked the question politely. It was only the tip of a huge iceberg of questions he had for this mysterious young woman, but it was a start.

"I didn't realize it right away but yes; I knew after a while the tea he was giving me was causing me to lose some of my sensibilities. I often discarded the tea after that and only pretended to consume it.

I knew I would have to imitate some of the aftereffects of the drug so he would not become suspicious and try to drug me using a different method. I didn't know his goal was to have me committed to an insane asylum, but I knew he wanted my fortune. I made certain that much of it was secured away in trusts before we were married so he had no knowledge of how much I was worth."

"Everyone thought I married him for his money when it was actually the other way around." Addy continued. "His family's businesses were failing after the war with the decrease in the need for steel manufacturing, and he needed my fortune to rebuild his. Fortunately, my father's dearest friend in Edinburgh was also my attorney. He placed the trusts in his own name so there would be no record of them in my name. Lucian received a huge amount, but he did not even come close to getting all of it. Honestly, he was arrogant enough to assume I would never outthink him in anything, and that worked to my advantage." Addy adjusted her handbag in her lap, a small smile touching her lips.

"I think that answers my next question." Zellmer replied. "Nurse Fielding admitted she did not give you the intended drug once you reached the asylum. You were diagnosed with insanity by the physician upon admittance. But as I have often observed, it is common for them to get the diagnosis wrong because they are looking for insanity. If all you have is a hammer, everything looks like a nail, so to speak." Zellmer appreciated the small chuckle that emanated from both Addy and Ruthie before he continued.

"I take it from your information thus far that you were far from insane when you entered the asylum. You allowed them to commit you to remove you from Lucian's family and their possible plot against you, just as you came to confess at the police station to escape being taken away by Lucian." Certain parts became very clear suddenly. Zellmer's curiosity increased as the ferry pulled into the Iowa dock.

"I was sure you had already figured that out, Detective Zellmer." Addy admitted. "I was just as sure it only caused more questions to surface as it does for anyone as truly inquisitive as both of us are. Please understand it was never meant to make light of those who suffer from mental illnesses. It was the only way as a woman in this country to be removed from the direct authority of my own husband. I had no rights of my own that he did not afford me."

"He could commit me or do just about anything else and be supported by the rule of law. I have seen the desperate need of those with mental illnesses to have advocates who will speak the truth on their behalf. I desire to be one of those advocates in the future." Addy looked forward as the vehicles ahead of them began to disembark.

They waited their turn to leave the ferry and turned the car south towards the little town of McGregor, Iowa. The road followed the path of the river as it bent around the bluffs that towered overhead. The trees that dotted the steep bluffs were brilliant in their full autumn colors; it was a feast for the eyes to behold as Zellmer drove the winding road to the main street of McGregor. He was sure that in all his travels around the world he had never seen a town quite as beautiful. The hamlet was hemmed in with the mighty river on one side and the majestic bluffs on the other.

"I can see why Miss Louise would choose to return here. I am not sure why anyone would ever leave it." Zellmer's admiration for the haven made Addy smile in agreement. She pointed to the slight angle turn onto A Street and the quaint brick building with the large front window.

Zellmer parked the car along the street and helped Addy and Ruthie with the passenger side door. They climbed the steep steps to the sidewalk and entered the door. A melodic bell jangled merrily upon their entrance, bringing an older woman with graying hair and a friendly face from a storeroom in the back. She stood staring at Addy, transfixed as though she had seen a ghost.

"Upon my soul, I never thought I might see you again, Addy, but how good it is to clap my eyes on you." Miss Louise stepped forward to embrace Addy before stepping back to appraise the other two visitors. "I see you brought company, and this one looks like a flat foot. Have you brought me good tidings or bad?" Miss Louise examined Zellmer carefully through her eyeglasses, which she had remembered were perched upon the top of her head before pulling them down to her nose. "We are a good honest business here, Sir. You can ask the local sheriff when he returns from his fishing trip."

"Detective Zellmer isn't here to arrest anyone, Miss Louise. He came to escort my friend Ruthie and me. I came for a quick visit and possibly a cup of your tea." Addy's eyes held tears of happiness as she hugged her friend. "Please show me your beautiful bookstore, it was your dream to own one."

Addy followed her friend towards the stairs at the front and up to the second floor. It was fashioned as a long balcony running the length of the first floor. A short set of stairs led to the third floor and Miss Louise's private quarters. Shelves of books were tucked everywhere, in each nook and cranny. Addy's heart soared at the sight of so many books.

Miss Louise seated them at her little parlor table and left for the small kitchen where she put a kettle on the stove. She brought back fresh cookies and biscuits on a porcelain platter and placed them in the center. The smell of warm oatmeal and raisins assailed Zellmer's senses and awakened a hunger that he had not realized was there.

He politely took the warm cookie Miss Louise offered and quickly ate it. She smiled as she shoved the platter towards him encouraging him to take another. Soon he had eaten three cookies before the tea had been served. At the whistle of the kettle, Miss Louise exited the room and brought back a tea pot with cups and saucers on a tray.

"I have a specialty about my tea, Detective, but I don't wish to offend you. I assure you that even the minister takes a small bit in his tea when he visits." Miss Louise took a flask from her apron pocket and handed it to Zellmer for inspection. "I don't sell it or distribute it you understand." She winked as she poured the whiskey into the tea, placing the flask back in her pocket.

She poured the steaming amber liquid into the teacups and handed one to Zellmer. The heady fragrance of the tea swirled around his nostrils, inviting the first sip. Zellmer took a small sip. The tea was pure heaven on earth.

"So, you haven't told me how you came to be here, Addy," Miss Louis inquired. "My heart ached when I received the note that your friend, Mr. Eddy, brought. I was certain that Lucian had won and was going to take you so far away this time that we would never find you again."

"However, I think this other friend of yours would have done anything to prevent that from happening. Mr. Eddy told me all about you, Miss Ruthie. You are the truest friend to my dear girl here, and I owe you all my thanks for it." Miss Louise took a handkerchief from her apron pocket and wiped her eyes. "All these years you couldn't send me a letter, and I couldn't send one to you because it was just too dangerous. I am so thankful to see you again."

"I was rescued by some of the police officers in Wauwatosa. They wouldn't allow Lucian to take me. He was killed later, so I am sure they saved my life in more ways than one. I have been released from the asylum, so I am able to begin a new life on my own. We came to reunite with other dear friends in Prairie du Chien, so I sensed that it was finally time to come and visit you. I owe you so much." Addy had sipped her tea and put it aside. Her hands trembled slightly in her lap.

"Well, that says a lot right there. There is no need to thank me for anything, Addy. You have always been the brave one." Miss Louise collected the teacups and took them to her sink to soak in the sudsy water there. She returned with her hat and put her hand on Addy's shoulder.

"Would you be wanting to take a quick walk before you have to leave again?" Addy nodded and rose, and the others followed her and Miss Louise back down to the first floor and out the front door. Miss Louise hung a sign on the door that simply said, "Be back in ten minutes"

Miss Louise led the group down to the corner of A Street and Main Street. She took a right turn and walked towards the public park, a triangular piece of land in the center of the town. The buildings along the way held various people who waved to Miss Louise as she traveled along. She paused at the far corner of the park and turned to look at Addy who stared at the park grounds ahead of her.

A large group of children played noisily as young women sat on benches watching them. It was the ideal setting of a small town and its citizens. Addy smiled broadly as tears escaped her eyes and streamed down her cheeks. Ruthie held one of her hands while Miss Louise grasped the other. The three women stood in silence listening to the laughing children.

Zellmer stood behind them waiting quietly. He observed a small boy running along the path chasing a ball. The child looked robust and laughed heartily as he trotted along. Zellmer regarded his distinct auburn curls and green eyes that resembled a stormy sea. He was the miniature replica of his mother, who stood watching him with tears flowing freely down her cheeks. The child caught the ball and turned to a beautiful dark-haired woman standing nearby.

"Mama! I caught it! See, Mama?" The child held the treasured toy up for his mother to inspect as she hugged him close, planting a kiss on the mountain of auburn curls.

"What a good job, Charlie. We will have to tell Papa all about it." The woman hugged the child again and turned him away to walk back towards the group of children at play. Addy turned and slowly walked past Zellmer on the sidewalk.

"I think that answers your other questions, Detective Zellmer. I had to do all of it to protect him from harm. I knew Lucian would eventually send me away somewhere, and I could not leave my baby boy there to fend for himself with those evil people. I posed as an unwed mother, and Miss Louise helped me put him up for adoption. She found a wonderful family who would love him and raise him as their own. I had to remain in an asylum to protect him from being taken away from all that was good. Everyone had to think that I killed my own baby so that I could rescue him. Now that you know, I trust you to guard his identity and my story for all of your days."

At first Zellmer thought he had consumed too much whiskey in Miss Louise's tea. He surely hadn't heard that Miss Addy had taken her son from her husband and his parents and had given him away, taking credit for his demise so that he would be given a chance to live a life free of the burdens that came from being a St. John. Zellmer knew that if Addy hadn't broken a few laws, she had at least severely bent them.

He knew that as a lawman he had pledged to uphold the laws of the land. He knew that Addy had proven to him that not everyone was protected equally under those laws. Finally, he knew that he would protect Charlie's identity and Addy's story for the rest of his life.

CHAPTER 39

NOVEMBER 5, 1925 – SUNNYHILL HOME

Addy sat in a wicker rocker on the large side porch trying to soak in the faint rays of November sun. She watched the wind blow through the barren trees scattering the leaves that lay in heaps at their bases. A crisp rustling sound was the harbinger that autumn was leaving and making way for winter to appear.

Addy pulled her crocheted sweater tighter around her middle and tucked it around the sleeping Little Buddy in her lap. She relived all the events that had taken place since she had returned with Georgie from Prairie du Chien.

The first order of business had been to arrange a small private service for Lucian. His remains had been kept for the investigation initially and had been released after the coroner had ruled an accidental death. They had concocted an outlandish story about Lucian and both Carr brothers accidentally setting off the Tommy guns that had never been recovered.

It was the officials' way of saying that they did not wish to pursue any other suspects. It also left a modicum of dignity intact for the benevolent Mr. St. John who had been so beloved by the community. While the bold face lies grated on Addy's nerves, she found that she did not really care one way or another about what had happened.

She felt no great amount of grief at Lucian's passing, only a brief sadness about his choices that led him to his end. She was more aggravated that the community expected a large show for Lucian's wake and funeral. She shocked everyone by insisting that it be kept completely private with only herself, Georgie and John attending a small graveside service in a remote cemetery near Lake Geneva.

She had also purchased burial plots for Lucian's parents next to him but insisted that there not be a service for them. She would not pretend to grieve their passing and didn't expect anyone else to either.

The second order of business had been to determine where she and the other ladies would live. After seeing the havoc created in Cottage 5, Addy decided that she would hire someone to fix the cottage but that she would not return to live there. She found that too many shadows of dark memories lingered there, and she wished for a new beginning for all of them. With that in mind, Addy made a generous offer to the current owner of Sunnyhill, and a deal to purchase the huge home was soon struck.

She would not run a boarding house, but she would have ample room for Georgie, Freda, Ingrid, Mary, and Ella if they chose to stay in Wauwatosa. Ruthie, after visiting her sons, had decided that she wanted to cherish every minute she had left with them and their families. Though she would miss her dearest friend very much, Addy had encouraged Ruthie to stay in Viroqua and come back to visit her at any time.

Addy had sold the steel company to a cooperative of the long-time workers; they deserved the dividends from their years of laboring for Oscar and Lucian with very low pay. She had her lawyer set up a trust fund that Miss Louise could draw from for her own living expenses and to help Charlie's family with theirs. A college fund was also established for Charlie, and Addy insisted that Miss Louise take all the credit for generosity towards him.

She never wanted Charlie to be confused about who his real mother was, the wonderful woman who now raised him. She was still deciding what to do with Stone Place and the house in Chicago. She had several ideas that would benefit others who might be in need. It pleased her to give much of the St. John fortune to the disadvantaged. Addy continued the benevolence towards the asylum, insisting on many improvements that made the lives of those who resided there better.

Addy looked up to see Detective Murphy and John approaching her on the sidewalk. Officer Maloney had quickly transitioned to John in her mind due to the amount of his free time spent at her home in the company of Georgie. The two were obviously head over heels for each other and Addy couldn't be happier about the prospect of upcoming nuptials in the spring of next year. John had waited until he had been promoted to Detective a few weeks ago to ask Georgie for her hand.

Addy hoped that they would take her up on her offer of creating an addition to Sunnyhill for them to call their own home. She waited for the two men to ascend the steps. Addy was reminded of how both had come to the cottage porch to visit when they were searching for Buddy. A pang of sorrow for the Schumacher family pierced her heart.

"Hello, Miss Addy. Is my girl inside?" John grinned as he walked past Addy on the porch and opened the side door. "Georgie! Sweetheart! The love of your life is here!" he chuckled as he entered the house while Murphy sat down in a chair next to Addy. She noticed that he was carrying a small bag which he placed at his feet.

Little Buddy, who had been awakened by John's shouts, stretched and stood. He jumped from Addy's lap into the waiting arms of Murphy, one of his favorite people. Loud purring replaced the sound of rustling leaves as the cat made himself comfortable on Murphy's lap. Addy watched the quiet undemonstrative man scratch the cat's ears gently as Little Buddy settled himself for sleep once again.

"I suppose I should be jealous that he likes you as much as he likes me, but I'm not. Little Buddy is an excellent judge of character. He never liked Lucian; I think that says something doesn't it? Too bad the rest of the city officials and much of the community do not have the good sense of this cat."

"Detective Kraemer stopped by before he left on his next assignment," Addy continued. "He was very disgusted that the DA would not recognize the Carr brothers as suspects in the abductions and murders of all these little boys. The DA claimed that there wasn't sufficient evidence against them or against Lucian for bootlegging either. I suspect he was more concerned that he had spent so much time licking Lucian's boots that he couldn't allow Lucian to appear to be involved in criminal activities when both he and the Chief of Police had no clue." Addy thumped her foot repeatedly against the porch floor. It was a sign of her frustration which she knew the quiet detective seated next to her shared even if he wouldn't own it.

"I realized once we had received word from the Minneapolis police that they had apprehended a man named William Brandt who claimed he had abducted and murdered the Schumacher boy, that Chief Baltes would turn to that as the answer to the crimes." Murphy shook his head. "Brandt murdered another little boy near the twin cities. He began claiming all kinds of crimes because the sheriff there offered him special allowances in the jail to come clean about his murder spree. Detectives Kraemer and Zellmer both went to interview him. It had been reported by several eyewitnesses that Brandt had been on one of the trains that passed through Wauwatosa around the time Buddy disappeared."

"Zellmer in particular refused to believe the confession," Murphy continued. "The supposed murderer got so many of the details surrounding the case wrong, things the murderer would know and often only he would know. Obviously, Brandt was guessing at details to garner more special treatment because he knew he was going away forever already. He claimed he had also abducted the Tolzmann boy and little Mike Lecher as well. Imagine Zellmer's surprise when Brandt said that Mike was dead and buried in an alley as he survived this ordeal and is very much alive."

"I am upset for all of those families, especially the Schumacher family," said Addy. "They deserve the truth of what happened and who did it rather than a concocted version that makes sense to the Chief of Police and the District Attorney. I was relieved to find out that Lucian was not the killer, but if he had been, I would still want them to know it. My reputation or Lucian's or those of the city officials is not the primary issue in the matter. It is removing murderers from our streets so they will never harm another child."

"You may be shocked that I am relieved that the Carr brothers are dead because I believe many more little boys will be spared. It's odd that we may be beholden to a criminal element that felt the same way and decided to remove the threat themselves." Addy rocked her chair as she spoke, watching the leaves blow about in the wind.

"It is an odd circumstance to be sure, but I will say that I agree wholeheartedly with your assertions, Miss Addy." Murphy admitted. "I believe our city is much safer now that Adam and Nicholas Carr are no longer alive. The District Attorney appeared before the city council this week and requested new city ordinances that prohibit the men who live in the reeds down by the river from being anywhere near the city and township. I am sure that he feels very satisfied with himself in his endeavor. He increased the difficulties for men who were already disadvantaged, but I believe he has worsened the situation for everyone."

"If society cannot help those who need assistance, however will we progress as human beings? It was obvious in this investigation that it was not the vagrants or the asylum patients that were the danger to our community, it was a man with great power and those who answered to him who did the harm to the most vulnerable, the children." Murphy reached for the bag at his feet slowly so as not to disturb the sleeping cat on his lap.

"I was sorting through the evidence in the Schumacher case," continued Murphy, "and came across something that I believe belongs to you. It had been found early on and kept in case it came to light that you were involved in some way. I wanted you to have it back and to know that both John and I never suspected you of doing any harm to anyone."

"There are few kind souls on this earth, Miss Addy, but I want to say that you are one of them." Murphy opened the bag and removed Cora's chipped and cracked porcelain doll. He handed the doll to Addy and watched as she ran her hands over the dirty cracked face and smoothed the silk scrap of a dress.

"It's my guess that Adam Carr removed the doll from the bent oak and threw it in the river in order to implicate you in Buddy's abduction," Murphy surmised. "We brought it to Lucian the night we found it. Even though he knew you had not taken the boy, he did not defend you but allowed us to think it was a possibility."

"I hope that you will forgive me for making a personal observation, Miss Addy. Your husband did not deserve you; he tried to obtain you like one of his many possessions, but he could not corrupt your character as he had so easily done to others around him. You are priceless to your friends, those who know you best. I hope that I can count myself among that number." Murphy's quiet words, spoken from a genuine sense of friendship for Addy, were the balm she needed for her confidence that had been shattered by her narcissistic husband.

"Thank you, Detective Murphy. I needed to hear that from a friend. I am learning that I should have my own voice, but it is a slow process. All this time I was told to speak less and now I find that I cannot be heard unless I make myself heard." Addy held Laura close to herself as she continued," It is why Cora's doll means so much to me. She reminds me that while some see the scars and ugly parts of what has brought us to where we are, our truest friends will only see the beauty that is a result."

The screen door opened as John and Georgie joined them on the porch. Georgie held a tray with hot tea and cocoa in steaming cups. Her face was flushed as though she had stood over the stove, but Addy knew that wonderful look of stolen passionate kisses when she saw it. Her smile and wink at Georgie did not go unnoticed by John, who seemed to be a little out of breath himself. He chuckled as he plopped down beside Murphy and pulled Georgie to perch upon his knee.

"Murphy, did you tell Miss Addy about the extraordinary story from the Lecher boy yet?" John continued at Murphy's slight shake of his head. "We brought the Lecher boy in with his parents last week to see if there was anything he could remember about his abductors. The poor boy had been through such a terrible time that most of his memories have been hidden away in a corner of his brain where he cannot retrieve them."

"Detective Zellmer was talking with him," John continued, "and suddenly little Mike asked if we had rescued the other little boy who had been with him. Of course, we were shocked because there wasn't anyone else on the train except him. Detective Kraemer asked if it could have been Roy Tolzmann who had been abducted at about the same time, so we showed him a picture of the Tolzmann boy. Mike insisted that he had never seen Roy and insisted even more that another boy was there trying to help him. He said the boy kept telling him to hold on because the police would come and find him, he was going to make certain of it." John paused briefly to take a sip of the cocoa Georgie was holding in her hands before resuming his story.

"We were all pretty sure that the poor kid had some hallucinations in his torment and decided to just leave him be about it. Zellmer thanked him when Mike reached in his pocket and pulled something out, putting it right in Zellmer's hand. He said the boy had given them to him to hold." John looked at Murphy, who had also been present and waited for Murphy to finish the story for him. The seasoned lawman cleared his throat.

"Zellmer opened his hand to find three small smooth stones," Murphy's voice trembled slightly as he spoke. "The same kind of stones you and Buddy placed on Cora's grave. The same kind of stones we found in various locations as we searched for Buddy Schumacher. Zellmer took them and placed them on Buddy's grave before he left."

CHAPTER 40

JULY 23, 1947 –
SUNNYHILL HOUSE, WAUWATOSA

The warm breeze rustled the trees as Addy bent over the flowers in her garden. It was early morning; the plants were still wet with the previous evening's dew. Addy could hear the faint buzz of the bees in the hives she had cultivated at the far end of the property. She loved the bird song of the robins and the mourning doves in the large trees overhead.

She loved the noise and bustle of Georgie and John's large family, but she also relished the quiet mornings in the garden. She came here to think and sometimes relive parts of the past while keeping her hands busy pulling weeds. There was a gardener who had been hired for all the heavier labor in the yard. Addy still loved the feel of the fresh dirt in her hands and underneath her fingernails.

Many changes had been wrought in the world since Addy had come back to live in the huge home that she shared with Georgie and John and their brood of seven children. There had been the stock market crash in 1929 and the resulting Great Depression. Addy had secured enough of her funds in various places that she was able to remain solvent, but millions of others lost everything.

The years that followed were filled with bank robbers like Bonnie and Clyde and Pretty Boy Floyd who were often notorious for stealing money from the banks and giving parts of it to the poorer farmers who had lost their farms to the banks.

John Dillinger and Al Capone both roamed the Midwest including the state of Wisconsin. It was not until J. Edgar Hoover and Melvin Purvis created the modern Federal Bureau of Investigation that the bootleggers and the bank robbers were taken out of commission one by one. Addy would watch the newsreels after each local picture show about Public Enemy Number One and their captures. She couldn't help but wonder if Lucian would have ended up on the Public Enemies list had he survived.

The early 1940s brought the atrocities of war back to the country as the United States entered World War II after the Japanese attack on Pearl Harbor in 1941. Adolf Hitler, who had begun a reign of terror in Germany, attacked Poland in 1939.

The Allied forces of Great Britain and France began the campaign to stop the Nazi regime from taking over the entire world. Before the completion of the war in Europe, known as VE Day, millions of people would die including the innocent people murdered in Nazi concentration camps by Hitler and his minions.

Addy still shuddered at the ultimate power handed to one man and his political party because they had caused fear and hatred to fester against the Jewish people. She hoped the world had learned an eternal lesson at the Allied liberation of Dachau, Auschwitz, and Bergen- Belsen among over a thousand others; man's inhumanity to other people, especially the vulnerable, must never go unchecked and unchallenged.

Addy's own little world had endured a few changes throughout the passage of two decades. Freda and Ingrid had graduated together from a school for the deaf and the blind in Mankato, Minnesota. Both women were so inspired to help others who, like Freda, had been misunderstood, that they started a school of their own. Addy instantly knew a perfect location for the school, Stone Place, on Geneva Lake. She donated the house and the grounds and began a foundation to help sustain the school for years to come.

Mary and Ella had returned to work with the kitchen staff at the asylum while living with Addy. They eventually decided to relocate to Lake Geneva with Ingrid and Freda. They became the new heads of the kitchen staff for the school, combining their love of cooking with their need to feel useful.

Addy smiled wistfully as she recalled that none of these women were deemed "fit" to be part of society when they first entered the asylum. All the women worked together to improve the lives of the asylum patients in Wauwatosa and throughout the state.

Addy worked around the huge mound of forget me nots; the tiny blue flowers with their yellow centers always reminded her of Ruthie. Her dear friend had spent her final years as a beloved matriarch in the center of her family. It had been five years ago since Georgie received the call from Emil to come and visit his mother in her last days after a major stroke had left her bedridden.

Addy and Georgie had left for Viroqua on the next train and made it in time to spend precious moments, holding Ruthie's hands as she made her journey homeward. The look of peace and bliss on Ruthie's face spoke volumes to Addy about the ultimate power of forgiveness. She would never forget Ruthie's last words to them as Ruthie pointed towards the ceiling above her head with a beautiful smile on her face.

"Cora is here for me now. She says it's time to go."

Addy had grieved Ruthie's passing with her whole heart and yet she knew that both Ruthie and Cora waited for her to join them one day. While many of the policemen had discounted young Mike Lecher's story about seeing Buddy so many years before, Addy believed it in her heart to be true. There had been so many times that she knew she too had entertained angels unaware.

A sudden rustling of the tall grass beside her had Buddy Jr. pouncing upon her lap. He was the spitting image of his grandsire, the original gray kitten who had rescued her from her hour of despair. The kitten batted the strings of Addy's garden apron, his unique black and gray swirls gleaming in the morning light. Addy dangled the apron string in front of him allowing him to swat it until he scampered away to chase a gopher at the edge of the lawn.

"Aunt Addy, you have visitors at the front door. I invited them in and seated them in the parlor. I will ask Mrs. Vatch to make some tea." Coralee, Georgie's first born, stood next to the garden where Addy sat. The twenty-one-year-old beauty was the spitting image of her mother, dark hair and large brown eyes with perfect skin.

It was Coralee's sweet personality that went straight to Addy's heart. Her compassion for others and her courage to speak out against wrong made the girl one of Addy's favorites though she never admitted it out loud. She had accompanied Addy, Georgie, and John on their trip to Edinburgh the year before, and Addy had relished seeing the beauty of Scotland through the young woman's eyes.

"You had better ask Mrs. Vatch to make coffee as well as they are probably Americans." Addy smiled at Coralee's giggle. "Did they say what they wanted or am I to be surprised when I arrive in the parlor?" Addy was accustomed to visitors of all kinds coming to ask for her financial assistance for a hardship they had endured.

She wouldn't have it any other way. Occasionally there was a charlatan who sought money, but most were people who needed someone to care about them just as she had so many years ago. She was often more than pleased to give away part of the vast St. John fortune to anyone who sought her help.

"They didn't say in particular, so I tried not to be nosy. The young man is very good looking." Coralee's laughter drifted as she followed the path back to the house.

Addy put her cut flowers in the garden basket, stood, and brushed the dirt from her knees. She supposed she should take the time to go to her bedroom and change her dress, but she really didn't care about all the fussiness of societal propriety. She enjoyed just being herself and allowing others to be themselves without pretense.

Addy made her way up the garden pathway, calling for Buddy Jr. as she went. She knew if she left the scamp outdoors by himself, he would be meowing piteously by the door in a matter of minutes. The kitten left his revels to join her at the back door.

Addy entered the house and noticed Mrs. Vatch and two of Georgie's youngest children gathered outside the parlor door. Eight-year-old Willie was down on his hands and knees while six-year-old Ruthie stood on his back to gain a vantage point into the room. Mrs. Vatch caught Ruthie as she toppled after Willie became startled upon hearing Addy enter the hallway. Both children and the head cook looked sheepish as they stood in a row with their heads down after being caught spying on the guests in the parlor. Addy fought the spurt of laughter that threatened to bubble forth. She placed the garden basket of flowers on a small side table and turned her attention to the threesome.

"Did we see anything good while we were not spying?" Addy kept her voice low and firm to maintain her composure. She knew she would have been inclined to do the same if she were in their position, but she also knew that Georgie and John worked hard to teach the children good manners and she would not undermine them in any way. On the other hand, young Willie was already showing the amazing investigative skills of his namesake, Detective Murphy. Ruthie was Willie's willing cohort in any adventure, her sharp analytical skills complementing the skills of her older brother.

"Please don't tell Mama, Aunt Addy. We just couldn't resist a peek. The young man is wearing a military uniform, and we are sure that he is probably a hero." Willie's pleading voice went straight to Addy's heart while his sense of the dramatic tickled her fancy. Perhaps young Willie would be treading the boards of a stage instead of following his father into a career in law enforcement.

"First of all, I don't lie to your mother, and neither should you. Not saying something is just as big a lie as saying something false. I will defend your cause to her, however, if you go and tell her yourselves. I will say that you were helping me instead of being nosy, which I am sure is the case with all three of you." Addy lifted an eyebrow at Mrs. Vatch who blushed beet red.

"I was just setting a table for the coffee and tea you requested, Mum. When I came from the parlor, I found these two hooligans out there and thought I should stay to keep them out of trouble.

Mr. Willie is right about the young man, though. He is in a military uniform, and he is very good looking." Mrs. Vatch bobbed her head for emphasis as she spoke.

This was the second person who had mentioned that the young man was good looking. Addy decided to just nod back and release them while she walked to the parlor door. As Addy was about to push the door fully open, she discovered a silent figure seated on the curved front staircase to her side.

"Were you curious about the visitors too, Adelyn?" Addy's heart skipped a beat at the sight of the pretty twelve-year-old girl seated quietly on the stairs watching her like an angel from above. Adelyn was the quiet child compared to the rest of her siblings, she preferred reading to conversations and solitude to companionship.

Addy felt a deep kinship with this young soul; she remembered Adelyn's delight when she had taken her to the old bent oak in Sanctuary Woods and proclaimed it as part of Adelyn's inheritance. A place of refuge all her own.

"No. I wanted the morning paper right after Papa was finished. I hate it when everyone starts to tear it apart in sections. Did you want it first, Aunt Addy?" the young girl held out a newspaper in her hand.

"You read it first, Sweetie, and then save it for me next." Addy's wink sent Adelyn up the stairs to carry the coveted newspaper off to one of her favorite reading nooks in the cupola. Addy turned back to the parlor door while simultaneously smoothing her hair slightly. She didn't want pretentiousness, but she also didn't want to be considered one of the hooligans in the house.

Addy entered the parlor, noticing the morning sun that streamed in the curved windows. A beautiful, dark haired, middle-aged woman sat on the sofa while a young man stood admiring the piano with his back to her. He stood straight and tall in an air force officer's uniform, his hair trimmed short in a military style.

He had removed his hat and placed it upon the piano along with the family pictures scattered across the top. He turned at the sound of the door opening and Addy's heart went to her throat. There was no mistaking his auburn hair and the green eyes that resembled a sea in a storm.

"May I help you?" Addy's voice trembled slightly. She fought to control it, the sweat already gathering at the back of her neck as she managed a serene smile in his direction. "I was told that you arrived in search of me." Addy moved to her favorite chair and sat facing her son and his adoptive mother in front of her.

She could feel her heart hammering in her chest; there was great joy in seeing Charlie again but also great trepidation. She needed to treat them like any other petitioners who came to her door, offering her assistance and then allowing him to leave her life all over again.

"Yes, thank you for seeing us. My name is Lieutenant Charles Anderson, and this is my mother, Rebecca. This might sound odd, but are you acquainted with a woman named Louise Parr? She lived for many years in McGregor, Iowa, and ran a much-loved bookshop there. She was a wonderful part of the community and an even greater friend to our family." Charlie's eyes were kind; it made tears form in Addy's eyes. How she had prayed that he would be spared any of the malevolence from his biological father by way of genetics.

"I did know Miss Louise. She was a good soul." Addy answered his question honestly without offering additional details of her association. "I was sorry when I heard that she had passed away last year." Addy had kept in contact with Louise but had not returned to McGregor.

She was concerned that with each return she made, the longing to know Charlie would grow until she ruined the secret the two had kept all the years together. Now her only child stood a few feet from her, and she still needed to behave as though it did not affect her in the least.

"Her passing was a great loss to many but especially to my son and myself." Rebecca Anderson spoke from where she sat on the couch. Time had added only a few wrinkles and some gray hairs at her temples; she was a gentle beauty.

"My husband and I were unable to have children of our own and Miss Louise brought Charlie to us from a young woman in a hard situation." Rebecca continued. "Miss Louise said the woman was an unwed mother and did not wish for anyone to know her identity. I always longed to thank that wonderful woman for giving us the most precious gift she had. I wanted her to know that we would never stand in judgment of her. Hard times fall on all of us, and it is up to each of us to help others when those hard times come. I wished to know her, but I also wanted to respect her wishes at the same time."

"We have always let Charlie know that he was adopted, not so that he would feel that he did not belong to us, but so he would know that he was especially chosen by us. To keep his adoption from him would have been a lie told out of my insecurity that he would love his birth mother more than he loved me. I reasoned that if two mothers could love one son so much, then that son could also have the capacity to love two mothers. I knew there might be a time when he had questions about his 'other mother' as I have always called her. I embraced the opportunity for us to learn the information together." Rebecca paused to sip the cup of tea she held in her hands.

"My husband died in an accident ten years ago and Charlie and I were devastated at his loss. He loved both of us so much. Miss Louise was always there with the right word, the necessary hug, and anything else that we needed. She made sure that Charlie had the college education he desired and encouraged his love of reading and books. It was part of what caused Charlie to decide that he wished to be a professor of literature." Rebecca's eyes glowed with pride as she glanced at her son before continuing." He graduated with high honors from Marquette University and then left for the Airforce to serve his country."

"Please excuse my mother. She gets carried away when she speaks of me." Charlie smiled at his mother. "I did the same duty to my country that thousands of other men did and was lucky enough to return home. I was sorry to hear that Miss Louise had passed in my absence, she was a genuinely good person. The only additional thing I could have asked of her was to tell me more about my birth mother, but I understood her need for silence on the matter. She had made a promise, and she was good to her word." Charlie came to sit beside Rebecca on the couch and picked up a cup of tea from the table in front of them. Addy drank in each movement, every word of her son.

"I am not sure how I can help you. I'm happy to offer assistance if I can." Addy felt the stale words in her mouth. She had just told Georgie's children that not telling something was as big a lie as telling a falsehood. She didn't want to lie to them, but she wanted to protect Charlie from anything that might cause him harm, including her own past. Still, her heart cried out for her to blurt out the truth and face the results as her consequences. If he turned his heel and left, he would be as lost to her as he had always been.

"Well, we wondered if you might be able to help us with a letter I found in one of Miss Louise's books. It was an old, tattered copy of *The Phantom of the Opera by Gaston Leroux*. I was intrigued because it has always been a favorite of mine and obviously this copy had been a favorite of someone else. The inscription inside mentioned a man named Mr. Eddy but it was the note tucked away in the pages that was even more intriguing than the novel. I brought the book with me to see if you knew of Mr. Eddy and how I might locate him. Several local people told us you were the best source for historical bits of information. You will understand when I read it to you." Charlie took the old book from his coat pocket and opened it gently to reveal a yellowed slip of paper. He began to read the words that Addy already knew by heart.

"Miss Louise, my friend Mr. Eddy, brings this letter to you. He has been much abused by the powers that be in Wauwatosa, they have accused him of harming missing boys when he is a kind and gentle man. Please take him into your confidence as the only other person besides Ruthie who will truly know my story. I want him to understand my attempt to locate Buddy and all the lost boys. As we both know, my heart breaks for lost little boys as, I too, lost my little boy. At least I know Charlie is well and dearly loved and I only wish that the parents of all lost boys would have the same assurances. I would hope that Charlie knows that I love him. In fact, so much to allow him to be taken forever to prevent the harm that I saw coming. I will leave Wauwatosa soon and it may be the end of me, but I will live on through him. If we do not speak again, Miss Louise, please continue to love my Charlie for me. As the Siren would serenade, I sing each night to him from far away, the Siren's song that would guard him and protect him and someday bring him home."

The only true response Addy could give was to rise from her chair and walk to the piano bench. She sat and paused for a moment, bidding Charlie and Rebecca to join her on either side. The notes of the piano were rich and deep, and Addy's voice was clear and sweet as she began to sing.

    'Hie thee home, bonny boy. Hie thee home.
    The day grows long waiting for thy return.
    Hie thee home.'
    'Hie thee home bonny boy. Hie thee home.
    Answer the call of the Siren's song.
    Hie thee home.'

Addy's lost boy had returned home, because not all that is lost remains unfound. Addy knew that from the depth of her heart she would always continue her daily prayer,

"Lord, let all the lost boys come home."

ACKNOWLEDGEMENTS

To the many readers of my novels, Face Down In Rising Sun and Borgia Rose; your support and encouragement is beyond compare. Thank you for your patience in waiting for Serenade of Sirens to come to life.

Thank you to the many indie bookstore owners who took a chance on an unknown author and featured my novels in your store. Ocooch Books and Libations, Driftless Book Warehouse, Arcadia Books, and Paper Moon, (along with their shop cat, Pearl) were among the very first. I encourage everyone to support local indie bookstores. Thanks also to the retailers including Oakwood Fruit Farm Retail Store for including my novels in your beautiful shop.

Thank you to my beta readers, Lorrie, Michelle, and Alyssa for reading Serenade of Sirens and giving your valuable input. Thank you to my outstanding copy editor, Marilyn, who gives so much of her time and energy for the good of others. All of you deserve so much more than my thanks.

Thank you to Charlie, who gave me her honest input about dealing with mental illness and the reality of the disparities against those who struggle daily. Keep writing, Charlie!

To Ghislain of Creative Publishing Design, thank you for your artistry in creating the book cover and interior formatting and your patience in listening to my suggestions.

To my daughters, Michelle, and Alyssa. Thank you for always lending your support in my book endeavors. You are both my greatest masterpieces. I am proud to be your mother.

To my husband, John, thank you for listening to every chapter as I wrote it and for attending so many book signings, author talks, and public markets to sell books with me. Your never-ending love and support keep me going!